Juggler

John Beresford

Copyright © 2021 John C. Beresford

The moral right of the author has been asserted

All rights reserved.
No part of this book may be reproduced in any form or by any electronic or mechanical means, including information storage and retrieval systems, without the express written consent of the author, except in the case of brief quotations embodied in critical articles or reviews, and certain other non-commercial uses permitted by copyright law. For permission requests, please contact the author as detailed on the inside back cover.

All characters in this publication are fictitious and any resemblance to real persons, living or dead, is purely coincidental.

ISBN: 9798527608892

For Blythe

CONTENTS

Acknowledgments	i
The Story So Far	iii
Chapter 1	1
Chapter 2	10
Chapter 3	26
Chapter 4	41
Chapter 5	62
Chapter 6	79
Chapter 7	95
Chapter 8	107
Chapter 9	122
Chapter 10	139
Chapter 11	159
Chapter 12	171
Chapter 13	185
Chapter 14	200
Chapter 15	216
Chapter 16	232
Chapter 17	250
Chapter 18	262
Chapter 19	282
Chapter 20	303
Chapter 21	317
Chapter 22	340
Chapter 23	354
Chapter 24	374
Chapter 25	400

Acknowledgments

As always, thanks are due to my friend Mik Peach (500px.com/mikpeach) for the cover artwork.

Jen from Olde Tinkerer Studio came to my rescue for a second time with her simple GIMP tutorial on how to generate a "black glass" effect on lettering, which I used here to represent the dark power of the Juggler.

Tiffany Munro (https://feedthemultiverse.com/) provided the long overdue, and wonderful, new map of Berikatanya. Thanks Ti!

My small group of beta-readers for this work is reduced to its core: Natalie & Blythe Beresford. They may be small, but they're perfectly formed and their input has, as always, been invaluable. The story is so much stronger as a result of their comments.

And finally thanks to you, dear reader. I hope you enjoy Juggler. If you do, and you'd like to take a few minutes to leave a review on its Amazon page, I would be extremely grateful.

John Beresford
August, 2021

Also by John Beresford:
The Berikatanyan Chronicles Series
Gatekeeper
Water Wizard
Juggler

Other Work
War of Nutrition
Well of Love
Valentine Wine

Map of Berikatanya

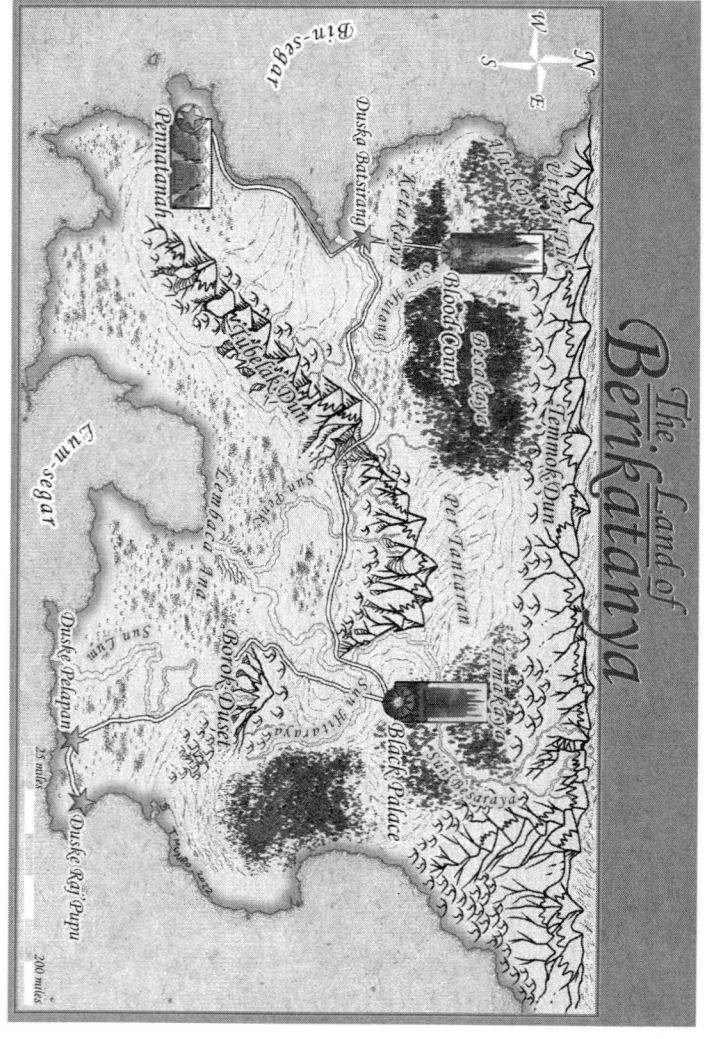

The Story So Far

Book 1 – Gatekeeper

Some years before the story begins, on the earth-like planet Berikatanya, a colourful gathering assembles in the valley between rolling green hills. The hillsides are dotted with observers from two realms but the main throng has assembled in the valley, where four impressive figures stand at the corners of a granite quadrangle. A choir chants—three separate and distinct melodies that join and swell as one—and a lone man takes up a central position on one side of the square. Musicians play, a peal of three bells rings in a hillside tower, and a sparkling mist begins to gather in the valley. Sucked inward it rotates slowly as it accretes, until it disappears into a small, black, star-filled void, dragging three of the four figures, the man and a few of the closer observers with it. The crowd gasps, but the void is gone and nothing remains of those who have been taken except a single yellow ribbon. The bells give a last ear-splitting peal before the tower cracks along its entire height, sending them to shatter on the rocks below.

Years later the monarchs of the two realms gather again in a memorial ceremony for the lost. The King has attempted to re-forge the shattered bells, hoping the replay will be as close a likeness to the original as possible. But the forging is unsuccessful. One bell is damaged, one cracked, and the third so badly made its tone is painful to hear. The ceremony is a fiasco, and is never repeated.

*

Elaine Chandler is a fire poi artiste in the Metropolitan Extended Toronto Area. The urban conurbation of the MeTa has grown to absorb 12 million residences. It stretches from Cambridge along the entire northern coast of Lake Ontario as far as Kingston. To the north it reaches up to Orillia and includes the whole of Lake Simcoe. She has spent four years with a travelling circus company, though she hates large crowds and despises the ringmaster. Her life before that is a bit hazy. When the cracked brass bell rings, she awakes from a recurrent dream featuring the off-world colony of "Perse." Without understanding how, she knows it holds the answer to the missing part of her memories.

Patrick Glass is a graphic artist whose choice of career is driven by a subconscious desire for control. It's the best match he can find for his needs and abilities but it's not perfect. He has never felt entirely settled. Continually passed over for promotion, he can't hold down a relationship and, as an orphan, has no family ties either. Deciding he must have one last roll of the dice, he too signs up for Perse.

Terry Spate is a gardener. As far as he can remember it's all he ever wanted to be, and he's been doing it a long time. A lifetime. At least 30 years. Most of his customers think he's a bit slow—mentally and physically. He talks slowly. He moves slowly. He takes his time. But his few friends know he's a warm-hearted man who would do anything for anybody. It's never occurred to them to wonder why such a gentle, unselfish man never found himself a wife, but Terry doesn't stay in one place long enough for anyone to start wondering. He gets on with his job, plants up the gardens of his customers, and moves on. Over the years the gardens he's left behind have become beautiful oases of tranquillity and colour. Some are famous. When visitors ask: "what a wonderful garden. Who designed it? Who planted it?" the owners can only recall a quiet unassuming man who didn't appear to be anything special. And no, they don't know where he is now. They lost touch with him years ago. One day Terry is in the middle of planting an avenue of leylandii at a country mansion. He steps back to line up the next sapling and tramples on a flower in the border of the driveway. His clumsiness in destroying the beauty he tried to create opens a long-forgotten window in his mind. He rests his spade against the trunk of the last tree he planted, takes his jacket, and leaves.

Fifteen-year-old Claire Yamani maintains an outwardly airy mien, despite losing her father at the age of eleven in a street crime incident. Since then Claire and her mother have been evicted from one slum dwelling after another in the poorest areas of the MeTa, where sunlight barely grazes the tops of the building and the incessant rain spreads oily puddles on every road and sidewalk. After five years of struggling to find a way out of the grinding, dangerous existence, her mother wins a Lottery place for them on the Valiant. The prospect of a new life in the clean fresh air of Perse fills her with hope and excited expectation.

All convicts are wrongfully imprisoned. Jann Argent is no different. Except for him it's true. He could never remember how he came to be in the room with the dead body, but that didn't stop them convicting him. After eight years on the prison moon Phobos, and three attempts at the Tournament, he wins. Since the authorities cannot allow convicted murderers true freedom, his "prize" is enforced transportation to the new colony world of Perse.

At the spaceport he meets several other characters, each with their own reasons for exile. A young girl and her mother, hoping to start a new life after the death of her father. A gifted graphic artist looking for adventure. A skilled agriculturalist searching for a fresh challenge. And a mysterious, statuesque and quick-tempered woman whose reasons for travelling she keeps to herself.

The Prism ship dominates the spaceport. A massive gleaming tube reflecting the sunlight not from its polished hull but off the low frequency forcefield that surrounds it. Following centuries of tradition the ship is named with hopeful and confident intent: Valiant. Its sister ships Endeavour and Intrepid already left for the new world nine years before. A catastrophic failure of the third launch with enormous loss of life prevented the remaining two ships from departing at the same time. That third ship—Endurance—was almost totally destroyed, causing the colonisation program to be halted until a thorough investigation had been completed. A replacement ship to be named Dauntless has been commissioned and is nearing completion in the adjacent space dock, but the death of so many colonists rocked the popularity of the program. The Valiant has only recently been filled, partially as a result of opening the opportunity to the public through the Lottery. Valiant stands ready to use its graphene prisms to focus gravitational energy and leap away from the solar system at near-light speed. It waits only for its human cargo and their limited possessions.

Even for planet hoppers, Jann Argent travels light. Other colonists have several uniform aluminium flight cases stacked neatly on maglev harnesses. As the only person with a single scruffy backpack, he stands out. Having awoken at a crime scene and spent the intervening years in prison, he has had no opportunity to amass similar crate-loads of belongings.

The travellers watch a public information film about cryosleep, journey times and waking procedures, accompanied by artists' impressions of life on the new world of Perse. There is no way of returning real images from the colony, but even if there was, at the time of Valiant's departure the first two ships have not even completed ten percent of the ninety-seven light year trip.

On Perse, ex-cop Felice Waters investigates strange occurrences, reported as crimes, in the Earther community. People have gone missing, met with freak accidents, been injured or killed. As the Earthers begin to mix more with the indigenous population, reports become more widespread.

With five years of her spaceflight remaining, Claire Yamani wakes due to a cryopod malfunction. Her mother, and the other seven people in her capsule, are dead. The ship's systems react to her presence to provide food, water, and entertainment, but with no spare cryopods she's forced to travel alone and keep herself occupied for those five years. The rest of the crew and passengers wake a few days before arrival at Perse. When the ship enters the atmosphere an unusually fierce storm is raging on the planet's surface. Claire watches from a viewport, loving the elemental power, but the hurricane-force winds send the ship crashing into the docking infrastructure. It is forced to ditch in the sea. Many of the travellers, still groggy from the effects of cryosleep, don't make it out before the huge craft sinks. Jann Argent plays a pivotal role in saving many lives, positioning himself in a doorway to help those trapped inside as well as those in the water.

The survivors take stock as they are processed through planetary immigration. They learn that "Perse" was already populated before the Earth ships' arrival. The native people call their planet Berikatanya. Life there is nothing like the public service videos. The newly-arrived Earthers spend a few days "acclimatising" before choosing to join one of the local monarchs—the Black Queen or the Blood King—or electing to remain with the small group of non-aligned Earthers on one of the few projects that are in progress.

Claire and Terry take a forest clearance detail. He is naturally drawn to the opportunity to work with the soil and wants to make sure the land is cleared in a sympathetic way. After all spaces at the Black Palace—her preference—are taken, Claire decides to accompany him and spend some time in the fresh air after five years of solitude and recycled life support. In the forest, they work to clear land for the cultivation of crops transported from Earth. The weather is still unpredictable, high winds blowing in a strange synchronicity with Claire's mood. When she's happy and airy the gusts are breezy and gentle. When she's mad or frightened it's more stormy and wild. The native workers are in awe of Claire, believing she is causing the storms. Word of this reaches the Black Queen.

She invites Claire to the Palace, where she discovers the previous Air Mage was her father. Claire learns how to control her power and takes up her father's position.

Having read his prison record and seen his heroic rescue efforts, Felice asks Jann to tag along with her investigation into the latest report of an inexplicable event at the Blood King's court. Patrick Glass joins them. Elaine Chandler has already demanded assignment to the Court, seeming to know her own mind better than any of the others. During the journey to Court, Felice explains that the two realms are engaged in a generations-long feud that waxes and wanes between periods of uneasy peace and all-out war. To maintain balance the Elementals divided themselves between the two houses. The Air Mage and Water Wizard align with the Black Queen while the Fire Witch and the Earth Elemental (known colloquially as the Gardener) hook up with the Blood King. Alone of the Elementals left on Berikatanya since the vortex was created in the valley of Lembaca Ana, the Water Wizard has not been seen since for almost a century and is believed dead.

At the time of Valiant's arrival, tensions are escalating again and a few skirmishes have broken out. The travellers are attacked by a raiding party, during which Elaine reveals her powers—she is the Fire Witch. Along with the original Air Mage and the Earth Elemental she fell to Earth through the portal created by an Elemental rite many years before, arriving at different times. As a side-effect of traversing the portal their memories, along with knowledge of their powers and how to use them, was stripped from them. Following their return to Berikatanya, those memories begin to return at a rate inversely proportional to their portal time displacement.

On arrival at Court, Jann is mistaken for the Earth Elemental. He is given a position in the Court guard so the King and his cohort the Jester can keep an eye on him while his memory recovers. That process is helped along when Jann, on guard duty in the Court archives, discovers an account of the original portal ceremony. The Fire Witch confronts the King, who attempts to persuade her to rejoin his side. The revelation of her return, and that of the Air Mage, along with the supposition of the Gardener's return, leads the King and the Jester to plot a repeat of the portal ceremony, intending to rid Berikatanya of Elementals and their powers once and for all.

In the meantime, still hoping to exploit those powers to secure victory, the King mobilises forces against the Queen. During the ensuing battle Elaine uses her powers even though they are not fully recovered. Claire, on the opposing side, attempts to counter this but only succeeds in making Elaine's Fire even more powerful. The battle appears to be won by the Blood King when Felice arrives on the battle plain in a flyer, which immediately quenches all Elemental powers. The Blood King is defeated, though no-one really understands why.

After the debacle of the battle, Jann is keen to ingratiate himself with the King. He and Patrick journey to the Valley to recover material the King needs for his new ceremony. There, they meet the Pilgrim, who has lived in the Valley since the first portal incident. He recognises Jann as the Gatekeeper—the one who controlled the vortex and who also fell through in the company of the Elementals. They also discover the Valley is enveloped in an after-effect of the portal: a time-dilation field that slows time down in the area local to the Valley.

Jann and Patrick relay the Pilgrim's message to Elaine. Realising that most of the original participants in the portal ceremony are coming together again, Elaine travels to the coast in an attempt to summon the Water Wizard. Jann and Patrick pay a visit to the Court archivist, who recognises Patrick's favourite doodle as the symbol of the Pattern Juggler—the final piece of the jigsaw, as the Juggler was a key member of the group and the last to be accounted for.

The King and his entourage journey to the Valley, where he intends to reopen the portal having invited the Queen, with her Air Mage, to attend and play their parts. Lautan arrives in response to his summons, intercepting Elaine on her return from the coast. He carries her warning of the King's intent to Jann and Patrick, and all the players converge on the Valley independently, arriving in the nick of time to stop the ceremony. Thwarted, the King turns instead to the power of his forefathers, which he has resurrected through the ancient blood rituals. He creates clones of the Elementals with the Bloodpower, and begins to open a vortex in the face of their opposition.

In a grisly mirror of the original portal, the final battle plays out in the Valley. Terry, who has belatedly awoken to his power as the Earth Elemental, arrives last, and the Elementals join forces, deploying their powers in combination for the first time to prevent the portal opening and defeat the King and his Blood clones.

Book 2 – Water Wizard

The Blood King does not survive the injuries he sustained during the battle in the Valley. He leaves no heir, or any known family member in a direct line of descent. The great house of Istania is thrown into disarray and the knock-on effects of the uncertainty are felt in Kertonia. There is general unrest.

As the senior ranking court member, King's confidante and the only one present at his death, everyone looks to the Jester to decide how to proceed. The only precedent for selection of a Blood King is combat, although this has not happened for centuries. The Jester opens nominations for a contest but no-one comes forward. Several of the Puppeteers urge him to stand, but he refuses on the grounds that he could never win a physical contest, having no battle skills. He believes he can achieve their aims more easily by influencing any new King.

In the months following the battle at Lembaca Ana, the

Fire Witch once more takes her place as head of the Fire Guild, forcing the previous leader—fire mage Kepul Seri—to seek another leadership opportunity. With little hope of winning, he approaches the Jester, who is initially thrown by the prospect of having to invent contests at which a mage would be equally matched against a warrior. He invites Seri to his chambers to discuss the quandary and poisons him there. With no other candidates forthcoming, the Jester establishes the Darmajelis (Blood Council) as an interim measure, leaving the Blood Throne vacant. He populates the Council with a number of Puppeteers. They determine to seize the Valley. Now that it has been stripped of its time displacement, they want to establish coastal rights and begin to explore the oceans.

Through the Puppeteers, the Piper finds out about these plans and informs the Queen. Dismayed by the lack of progress with peace talks, and disgusted by the Jester's double-dealing, she sends a small force to protect Kertonian interests in the Valley, intending that a larger army should follow. She discusses the situation with the Elementals, but they opt out of the conflict. Since Lautan is missing and there are no longer any Elements on the Istanian side there would be no balance. The Queen resigns herself to deploying only traditional forces.

With opposing armies massing in the Valley and both sides once again on the verge of outright war, the confrontation is disrupted by a massive and unheard of daytime rainstorm which causes both sides to believe at least one Elemental has broken their promise to remain neutral.

A few days later the twins Douglas and Kyle Muir arrive on the Dauntless, the final Prism ship from Earth. The ship is overdue by several months compared with the expectations of the Valiant crew, and once again no preparations have been made. On this occasion the intense rains do not disrupt the landing, although the pilot has trouble with the gravnull field and has to bring the ship in using the Prism drive, whose latest modifications allow its use near-planet in extremis. The mooring mast has been repaired and disembarkation follows the previous procedure, with colonists dividing up between the two houses and the Earther projects. In view of the ongoing and escalating conflict, fewer elect to join the houses, and a sizable number remain at the landing point while they decide what to do. These campers argue that the site is an ideal colony position. Close to sea, forest and lake but well removed from Court and Palace. It should be developed as a permanent community, and the last ship should not be broken up for materials as the first two were.

At Court, the warrior Sepuke Maliktakta—distant cousin to the King—arrives to stake his claim. The Jester tricks him into a test of Bloodpower to prove his heritage, drowning him.

Lautan appears in response to the disturbance of Water lore, which created the malamajan centuries ago. He seeks out Elaine, who calls a meeting of Elementals so they can all share what has been happening to each of them. Their conversation is interrupted by the arrival of Jann Argent, returning from his quest with news of the Northern people—the Beragan. He found a "Shangri-la" style warm spot between high peaks and spent several days there recovering his strength. Continuing his journey over the higher northernmost peak he almost died of exposure, but was found by a young woman who had been undergoing a rite of passage - a test of worth among her people. She brought him back to her village at the foot of the mountain and nursed him back to health, when the village elders were keen to hear his story. He learned that the mountains were raised long ago by a powerful Banshirin (Stone Mage) - or group of them - to separate the "civilised" folk from the ones they refer to as the Keti Caraga ("warring tribes") - the antecedents of the Blood King and Black Queen.

The elders of the Beragan knew that, although the

mountains would protect north from south, they would not protect the Keti Caraga from each other. They agreed to divide the minor elements between the two houses; the balance of forces intended to keep the two sides in check. But still there were worries that their enmity would undo them. One each of the senior Banshiru and Kayshiru (Stone and Wood mages) agreed to exile in the south so that they may watch over the tribes. Realising this was a permanent exile, and wishing to prevent any future use of their power, they fashioned artefacts that would suppress its use. In the case of the Kayshirin, these are the obsidian artefacts worn by the Queen - the descendant of the original Kayshirin. Claire believes her experience of a rush of power when in the forest clearing may have been due in part to Wood magic, which may also explain her affinity with the Queen. She also relates that she's seen some hints of power in the Queen when they are away from the Palace. But the Blood King had no known corresponding wooden artefact, and was not adept in any form of magic other than Bloodpower, so the fate of the original Stone Mage remains a mystery. Jann suspects the power may still be present, as he remembers Felice telling him the tale of an Earther whose hand became embedded in a rock.

Jann's story and the Elementals' discussion last well into the night until a rider brings news of the Dauntless. Claire immediately sees the parallel between her arrival and its attendant storms, and the new ship. She tries to persuade Jann to travel with her to the landing point to investigate but he's exhausted, so Lautan volunteers. Elaine and Terry decide to seek out the Earther in Jann's story to find out whether he is a true Stone mage.

Word of the possibility of powerful Water mages having landed reaches the Puppeteers, who see another chance of ascendancy. They dispatch an emissary to pay them special attention, play up to the twins' vanity, and bribe them to Court with lavish clothes and chattels. Douglas' head is turned with the promise of an easy life at

Court, but his sister Kyle is suspicious and tries to convince him to return to the Earth colony. Their arguments flare up. The rains worsen, lakes overflow, and the landscape is devastated by floods.

Lautan and Elaine work together to redirect the waters and in doing so discover the power of Combinations. Jann helps, revealing his new-found control of gates. Opening a gate to divert a flood from an engorged river, he saves his fellow Elementals' lives.

Delayed by the dreadful storms, Claire is too late to prevent the Muir twins being taken to Court. Undaunted she follows them, arriving in time to witness their worst fight. The corresponding storm is longer and louder than anything that has gone before. Claire's assumptions about the parallels with her own arrival are confirmed. She tries to explain it to the twins, and calm them down with an offer to teach them how to better control their power. Douglas refuses, believing he already has all the control he needs. His reaction to Claire, and to the devastation he is causing, convinces Kyle she should leave him and rejoin the Earther colony. Claire is able to work with her to bring her mastery almost up to her brother's level. Once back at Pennatanah, Claire discusses the anomalies with Felice and begins to conceive of the connection between magic and technology based on the evidence of the two Prism ships and the flyers at her first battle. When magic is attempted in the vicinity of a gravnull field, but outside the field, it is nullified. If the mage is inside the field, it is the field which is nullified.

Claire returns to the Palace. After Jann's revelations she persuades the Queen to lay aside the obsidian crown and bracelets, after which the Queen begins to draw on her wood power. Wood magic is a natural, lambent energy that can be called from most woods. Different species evoke different kinds of magic. The blackwood that is so prevalent around the Palace has a protective force, like a warding or a Word of Forbidding. Other woods offer healing, renewal. Wood embodies the elements of Water and Air, its magic can be used to lift and carry, to attack or defend, but also has a profound effect on growing things - even more so than Terry's Earth power. Gradually the Queen learns to draw light and warmth from certain woods, but it is the healing side of Wood magic that she proves strongest in - something that aligns with her established desire for peace and prosperity for all the peoples of Berikatanya.

Elaine and Lautan are also too late to find the stone mage. The whispering walls of Court have passed on this knowledge and the Jester is salivating at the thought of coercing a mage with even greater power than Douglas Muir. Believing he can spin the man a tale of heritage and entitlement to the throne, based on the Queen being some kind of Elemental counterpart, he first offers him a seat on the Blood Council and later suggests his candidacy for the throne. Stone embodies the elements of Earth and Fire, so its magic always has an orange colour, it can be used to destroy or stop things, to attack or defend, but also has a profound effect on static, inanimate objects. An adept can use the power to transform rocks, earth, soil, and even buildings into crystalline structures of immense strength or extremely fine detail, or construct urban infrastructure from raw materials, if their lore is strong enough. Piers Tremaine - the Earther in question - has been aware of his power for some time, and practising in secret. He is far more adept than anyone realises. He plays along with the Jester's scheme at first, After learning it was the Jester who killed the King's only legitimate heir, he destroys the Blood Throne.

Douglas Muir is incensed when he sees the Jester's attentions are focused on someone else. He was never offered the throne! His anger and jealousy fire him up to even greater feats of Water power, threatening to overwhelm both Court and Palace. Thwarted in his use of fresh water, especially by the increasing powers of his sister, he turns his attention to the ocean. He raises a tsunami that threatens to overwhelm the Court. Its height and force are reduced by Kyle's influence and by Elaine, Claire and Lautan working in harmony. In a final battle at the coast, the Elementals defeat Douglas, and an enormous stone sea wall raised by Piers deflects the tsunami at the last moment.

The Puppeteers, once again thwarted in their exploitation of both Douglas and Piers, retire to lick their wounds, while Kyle, who blames the Jester's influence for encouraging the damaging use of her brother's power, decides to remain with the other Elementals at the Palace.

Chapter 1

pennatanah
6th day of sen'sanamasa, 966

A final thin, silvery finger of moonlight stretched across the dark rolling waves of Pennatanah Bay. In a few moments the larger of the twin moons would slip below the horizon, leaving Patrick Glass alone with his thoughts in the dark. He shivered, and pulled his jantah tighter around his shoulders against the chill of late Sanamasa. The first hints of dawn were yet to suggest themselves over the distant tops of Tubelak'Dun behind him. The day would be a great deal older before the newly-arrived sun could lend it any warmth.

The night-time malamajan had ended long before Patrick began his vigil, now that Elemental normality had been restored. News reached the Earther camp some days before, of the success of his fellow Elementals at Utperi'Tuk. The defeat of the mad man Muir, and the cost of that success. He tried to imagine how the loss of Lautan would affect each of his friends, but the fall-out from that frightful confrontation was immeasurable. A small part of him regretted staying away from the fight, but he kept it locked in a corner of his mind. The power at his command still frightened him. Even a threat such as that offered by Douglas Muir had not been enough to persuade him to wield it. No, he would stay here, among his fellow Earthers. Away from temptation and risk. At least until he felt more certain of his mastery of Pattern Juggler lore.

The long days he spent in isolation, poring over his father's book, delivered ever-decreasing insights into those aspects of the wisdom that eluded him. Yet what else could he do? It was his heritage, and his alone. Who knew when the Elementals may face an even greater threat than Muir? Since arriving on this world, and the unexpected discovery that it had been the home of his family for untold generations, his companions had faced two supranatural threats. Those battles had been won, but the uneasy peace between the houses of Kertonia and Istania remained fragile. In his heart, Patrick knew another conflict or confrontation would not be long in coming. Would it reach this small enclave of Earthers? Would it bind them into its fight? Or would the increasingly militant occupants of Pennatanah insist on their independence, cut any last remaining ties to the indigent people, and strike out on their own? Whatever lay in store, he would be better prepared for it with a full understanding of his abilities. Something that still lay far in his future, if recent progress was any guide.

While lost in his thoughts, the rising sun had painted the sky with a pale cerise. Patrick gazed over the ocean, his eye caught by a flock of seabirds, circling and diving to catch the first, tastiest fish of the morning. Behind them an unusual cloud formation rose from the unquiet sea, an empurpled, mushroom-shaped pillar that reminded him of atomic bomb pictures he had seen as a boy. At the base of the strange apparition, a spiralling wisp of black smoke hovered above the waves. As he watched, fascinated, the smoke spun into a vortex. A pair of birds from the flock flew into the small eddy and disappeared, leaving only a single feather that floated down to rest on the heaving waters.

Patrick stood, squinting to see more clearly, but the smoke was gone along with the birds; the scene restored to a banal normality of surging surf and wheeling wings.

darmajelis chamber, court of the blood king
6th day of sen'sanamasa, 966

'So, you have yet to decide?'

The air in the chamber crackled with the tension between the two men. Dry to begin with, at this time of year, and prone to the strange discharges of Elemental-like energy that none of their best minds could explain, it was further overburdened with the echoes of Sebaklan Pwalek's frank assessment of their situation only nine days earlier.

Nine days which had dragged on until they felt like a full season. Jeruk Nipis was a hard man, given to extraordinary explosions of temper. He could be cruel, too. Seb had personal — and practical — experience of that. But they had been friends for a long time. And compatriots, working towards a single goal. Surely an argument, even one with such a keen edge as this, could not stand between them for much longer?

'On what?'

Nipis sat at the table, staring disconsolately through the open door at the ruin of the Blood Throne. The misshapen puddle of red rock was all that remained of the impressive seat of power since the departure of the Stone Mage Piers Tremaine.

Seb sighed. Though Nipis believed he had left his "Jester" persona behind, he could still play the fool. He took a seat opposite his leader. 'On how we move forward from here. How we bring this Darmajelis back to full strength. How we keep the peace. The time for sitting with your head in your hands is past, Jeruk. The people need leadership. Direction. And in the absence of a lead from you — from us — they will follow whoever is in front.'

'Do they even know which is "front" now? Not sure I do.'

'Front is whichever side you choose. But choose you must, or we are done.'

'Oh. You're leaving?'

'For Sana's sake! No, I'm not leaving. I mean, our dreams of ruling, of leading Istania into a bright new future, will be gone. These are dangerous days. We have all seen what happens when an Elemental is left unchecked. No-one wants to return to that, and...' he shrugged, a small smile playing across his lips, '...we have little choice in the matter.'

Nipis snorted.

'But it is also an opportunity,' Seb continued, ignoring the reaction. 'These early uprisings and spats are small. Their leaders uncertain and untried. Squashing them will be as easy as treading a bug underfoot. If we act, and act now.'

'It can't be any easier for the damned Blacks.'

'Really? Is that at the front of your mind right now? What the Blacks are doing? The short answer is, we don't know. But what we do know is they have the combined strength of the Elementals on their side. Those few who remain. And they still have a ruler. You may not agree with her or what she stands for, but the Black Queen is a proven leader. Strong and sure. You can bet their people are not rising up as ours are.'

'Lucky them.'

Seb held his tongue. Even after knowing the diminutive man for as long as he had, he could not tell whether he was being baited, or if his old friend really was so far along the path of despair that he could not find a way back. Angering him would achieve nothing.

'Perhaps that is a start we can make, then?'

'What?'

'We don't know what the Blacks are doing. We must find out. We've lost the Piper, but he wasn't our only option. Just need to work out how we can move our man into a more influential position.'

Nipis lifted his head from his hands and rubbed his long nose. He regarded Seb without comment before steepling his fingers in front of his face. 'I suppose we have nothing to lose. Any intelligence is good intelligence, though we are not in the best place to act on any of it.'

Silence fell again between the two men. Seb screwed up his eyes against the bright, pale morning sunlight streaming through the high windows of the chamber. The few remaining Darmajelis members would soon be arriving to commence the day's work. 'What of Pennatanah?' he asked.

'What of it? Why should we concern ourselves with a handful of Earthers?'

'Their numbers will have swelled to considerably more than a handful by now.'

'Oh?'

'We lost dozens of Earthers during the rains,' Seb said, 'even those who had been with us since the time of the first ship. We can't be alone in that. They will have abandoned the Palace too.'

'So?'

'One more source of unrest, that's all. And if it makes sense to know what the Queen is doing, then the same must be true of whoever is leading the Batu'n.'

'Do we have anyone there?'

'Not yet.'

Nipis shook his head. 'I'm not convinced it's worth it, but do what you will. If it were me, I'd think it smelled like a month-old barawa fish, a stranger turning up from Court?'

'Maybe if he was alone, but we're still shedding people. Only one of them needs to be ours.'

pennatanah
6th day of sen'sanamasa, 966

Felice Waters stood watching the lone figure sitting on the cliff-top above Pennatanah Bay. She knew little about him, beyond the fact that he had returned to the base shortly before the rains stopped. Patrick Glass was the very definition of an enigma. He had abandoned the Istanian life he chose on arrival, but spent no time with Earthers either. He climbed to his perch each morning and sat for hours staring out at the water. Felice had no idea what he expected to see, if anything. Beyond the subtle changes brought by the season, the scene remained the same every day: sky, sea, the glistening hull of the downed Valiant. As the Berikatanyan winter took hold, he wore an extra layer or two, but the cold weather had not dissuaded him.

As she watched, he took to his feet and picked his way carefully across the uneven rocky surface back towards the squat, utilitarian buildings of the base.

'Morning!' she called. 'Cold one.'

He stopped, staring at her for a moment before replying. 'Did you see that?'

'What?'

'Just now. Out there.' He pointed out into the bay.

'Nothing but the usual. What did you see?'

He glanced back over his shoulder, a haunted look on his face. 'Never mind. Alvarez's first meeting later today, isn't it?'

Silvia Alvarez, co-pilot of the second ship, Intrepid, had been elected leader of the base following the recent loss of Commodore Oduya. Captain of the first Prism ship to arrive, Oduya had been a constant point of reference for the colonists for ten years. His sudden death hit the community hard, at a time when they faced their biggest challenge in all of those years. Increasingly, people were reaching the same conclusion as Glass. Seeking refuge in the only other familiar place on the planet. With their population already swollen by the Dauntless passengers who never left, the prefabricated buildings of the base were almost at capacity, yet each new day brought another influx of returnees.

'Yeah. Some big decisions to make.'

As the only other Earther who had remained at Pennatanah for the duration of their stay, some had regarded Felice as the most logical candidate to step up and take Oduya's place. She had always been happier in a supporting role, and for the time being had accepted an appointment as Alvarez' deputy.

'Will you be joining us?' she asked.

'If you think it will help.'

'I think you should have your say. You were one of the first to come back to the base. The rest of the team respect your opinion. We all remember the part you played in the Valiant rescue.'

'No other reason?'

The slight smile on his face gave no clue to his meaning. Felice had never liked mind games, and certainly had no time for them today. She shrugged. 'It's a good chance to get to know everyone. Come along, share your wisdom, and we'll see how the runes fall.'

'You're an enigma, Ms. Waters. I'll see you later then.'

Felice's spine tingled at the comment and its strange congruence with her earlier thought about this tall, mysterious man who observed much and said little. She watched him amble towards the canteen, and decided she was ready for a bite of breakfast herself.

pennatanah
6th day of sen'sanamasa, 966

Felice pushed her empty plate away and folded her arms on the edge of the table. They had eaten late, and taken their time, so they could make a start with the meeting as soon as the breakfast service was done. The last few tables were emptying rapidly. On her left, Jo had finished eating some time ago. She sat back, stretching languidly in her tight jumpsuit and bringing a hot melting feeling to Felice's stomach. Sitting opposite Jo, Cary Cabrera still chewed noisily, but as always his plate had been piled higher than anyone else's.

Silvia Alvarez approached their table after dropping off her empty plate at the counter.

'Is it too early to start?' she asked, staring pointedly at Cabrera. He held up his hands, and chewed faster.

'If folk keep arriving at the same rate we've seen for the last few days, we have something like three days' space left.

After that we'll be putting people up in corridors and offices.'

'Dauntless?' Felice offered.

'Has been mothballed since arrival. Air won't be very fresh, plus you know how small those cots are. Not a long-term solution, and it would take work to make it even a short-term one. Effort I'd rather spend on the real answer.'

'Which is?' Jo asked.

'Pennatanah was never designed for permanent occupation, certainly not for so many people. We can build one or two more pre-fabs to cover the immediate problem, but...' Alvarez fetched a chair from the nearest table. 'I don't know about you, but I don't want to live in modular housing. That phrase still makes me feel sick. I spent my childhood on a modular estate. I want something more real for our home here. Anyone who returns has had anything up to ten years to work out whether they want medieval, and they've decided no.'

'What kind of numbers are we talking about?' Felice asked. 'We're not short of land, but building materials are another matter.'

'They're not all going to come back, but even if they did that's still, what? Fifteen hundred from each of the first three ships plus a couple thousand on Dauntless. Assume any offspring are offset by deaths.'

'Less than that,' Felice said. 'We lost most of the Valiant inventory to the sea in Pennatanah Bay.'

'Of course. Let's plan on five thousand max then. And we've got a couple thousand here already?'

'Must be close to that. How many have we checked in since folk started coming back, Cary?'

'Two hundred and thirty-four. And I reckon fully three-quarters of the Dauntless people never left.'

'So my guess was pretty much on the money. Means we're gonna need at least twice the accommodation we have now.'

'And if you don't want it to be prefab, then it all needs

building from the ground up,' Cabrera grinned. 'Pun half intended.'

'People aren't coming here for the comedy, are they?' Alvarez said, rolling her eyes.

'What are you going to call yourself,' Jo asked, 'now you're in charge? Your title, I mean. You're not a Commodore are you? That's a military rank. So... what? President? Minister?'

'Head Girl?' Felice said, winking.

Alvarez laughed. 'Well I prefer Head Girl to President. That's far too grand!'

'How about CEO?' Cabrera suggested.

Alvarez tapped her chin. 'We're not a company, but I might take the "Executive" part and use that. Exec was an old term for the second in command on a ship, or submarine, and I feel like I can never entirely replace Brian. I'd be comfortable being the Exec though.'

'Our first decision,' Felice smiled.

'First of many.'

'And I missed it,' Patrick Glass said, taking a seat at the next table. 'Sorry I'm late.'

Chapter 2

the palace of the black queen
6th day of sen'sanamasa, 966

Piers Tremaine sat in the deserted Palace refectory, sharing a last, late-evening glass of buwangah with Petani. The Queen approached. Having stayed as a guest in her Palace for only seven days, Piers was still a little awe-struck in her presence. Embarrassingly tongue-tied, like a schoolboy standing before a teacher he had a youthful crush on. She was so completely different from the so-called leader of the Blood Court. That diminutive fool — ex-fool, he corrected himself — had no air of authority. No gravitas. He was given to unpredictable explosions of temper and the exercise of his wickedly sharp tongue. In contrast, in his short acquaintance, he found the Queen measured, calm, almost friendly. True, she was a fellow Elemental — his counterpart indeed, being the only other second-level Elemental so far discovered. That, at least, they had in common. A shared significance that gave them a frame of reference in which to relate. And yet... she was still the Queen.

Soft moonlight trembled over her plain black dress as she walked towards them, limning her long dark hair with ghostly silver and lending her an air of even greater mystery.

'Forgive our interruption, gentlemen,' she said, taking a seat at the long table. 'Petani, it was principally you with whom we wished to speak.'

Piers made to leave.

'No, stay,' the Queen said, laying a gentle hand on his arm. 'This may involve you too Stone Mage.'

'I think I can guess what you want to talk about,' Petani said, a haunted look flitting swiftly across his face.

'No need to guess, my dear Gardener,' the Queen said, 'it is the Landing that has been much on our mind since the defeat of the troubled young Muir boy. We believe everyone should be sufficiently rested now for work to recommence.'

Petani collapsed down into his seat. A smaller version of himself, almost as defeated as Muir. 'My guess was right.' He regarded the Queen with an expression of distilled despair. 'As your Majesty wishes. I can leave first thing tomorrow.'

'That pleases us immensely,' she said.

'I'll come with you,' Piers said, the words out before he had chance to consider their implications.

Petani straightened in his seat, his eyes flashing. 'I am perfectly capable of completing the work, thank you young man.' He paused, scratching his chin. 'Though the season will by now have made the seas quite... challenging.'

'Well within your prodigious powers, we are sure,' the Queen said, standing. 'Now if you will excuse us.'

She swept away in a sparkle of silvery moonlight.

'You can tell when she's in Queen mode,' Piers said, watching her leave.

'Queen mode?'

'Yes. When she's thinking like the Kayshirin, she drops into normal language. When she's acting as the Queen, making the royal wishes known, she uses "the royal We." A lot.'

He turned his attention back to his friend. 'Are you sure I can't help?'

'I'm sure you can,' Petani smiled, 'but I'm also sure you have better things to do than trailing all the way down to Lembaca Ana to pick up after an old man who should be able to look after himself.'

the palace of the black queen
7th day of sen'sanamasa, 966

Dawn at the Black Palace was Kyle Muir's favourite time of day. She stood at her window, gazing out over the still, dark, Besakaya forest. Watching the sky turn from inky black to rosy pink, and marvelling at each change in hue. As the sun crested the horizon, throwing a golden outline around the low clouds, her door opened.

'Look at this, Duggie!' she cried, before recognising the face of her friend and fellow Elemental Claire Yamani, and remembering her loss all over again. She burst into tears.

Claire crossed the room quickly, taking her in a tight embrace.

'I still can't believe he's gone,' Kyle sobbed into the Air Mage's shoulder.

'I know. It's too soon. Give yourself time.'

'It's been eight days! I should at least remember he's not here anymore, even if I can't get used to not having him around. I was there. I bloody saw him die!'

She broke into a fresh wave of sobbing. Claire led her gently away from the window and sat her down on her bed.

'I know' she repeated. 'Don't expect it to be logical. You're grieving.'

Kyle dashed away tears with the back of her hand. 'He doesn't deserve my grief, the little shit! What he put me through. What he put all of us through. How many people did he kill? And yet every time I see something lovely, something that takes my breath away or makes me warm inside, I still want to share it with him.'

'It's what you've been doing your whole life,' Claire said, holding her hand. 'You can't expect to change that in a few days. You're too hard on yourself.'

'The bloody Water Wizard,' Kyle snorted. 'Can't even stop her own tears. A lot of use I'm going to be! And they expect me to stand up in front of everybody next month and accept the title.'

'It's yours already. You don't need the ceremony to truly be the Water Wizard of Berikatanya. You're the only candidate.'

'I'm a fucking fraud!' Kyle wailed, burying her face in a

pillow.

Claire walked over and closed the window against the chill of the Sanamasan morning. 'You're not a fraud,' she said, turning back to face Kyle. 'Lautan believed in you.'

'Lautan!' Kyle said, her voice quavering. 'Another one gone! He taught me so much, but it was still only a tiny part of what he knew. I can't replace him!'

'No-one expects you to. You're Kyle, not "pretend Lautan". We're all different, all unique. There's no rush. No timescale. Remember what Felice Waters' gene map showed. You're at least as powerful as your brother was, or you will be, once you start to believe in yourself.'

Fresh tears started in Kyle's eyes at her friend's kind words. She meant well, but Kyle did not — could not! — believe it. She would never enjoy the level of control Douglas had so easily commanded. 'Can we go for breakfast?' she asked, laughing through her tears to break the tension of the moment.

'I ate earlier, but I'll keep you company.'

'Good. I can eat for both of us. I'm bloody starving.'

the palace of the black queen
8th day of sen'sanamasa, 966

The door to the Queen's chambers exploded into a myriad blackwood shards, flying into the room in all directions. A tall, dark figure stepped into the room, its footfalls resounding with heavy vibrations that shook her bed on its carved pillars. The golem was made entirely of stone; black and cold. It lumbered towards her, heavy-lidded eyes glowing with malevolent crystalline intent.

Before the Queen could cry out, or call for her guards, the creature closed its frigid hands around her throat, squeezing. There was no pain, but she could not breathe. She squirmed under the dead weight of the intruder, to no effect. Blackness encroached on the edges of her sight, panic making the bile rise behind the monster's grip. In the kernel of her mind, a small voice reminded her she was more than the Queen of Kertonia. She was Kayshirin. She had nothing to fear from this leviathan of rock.

The room, and everything in it, became suffused with the light of her Wood power. Not only the familiar cold blue of her staff. Each of the wooden artefacts in her chambers added its own colour, a rainbow of Elemental energy coruscating through the air towards her. The Queen stretched out an arm, reaching to grasp the staff which stood beside her bed. She felt its healing strength flow into her. Her other hand found a fragment of blackwood from the door, and closed tightly around it. She opened her eyes and met the creature's opalescent gaze. Its hands loosened. She took her chance.

'Begone,' she cried, twisting her body and sending an ebony pulse of repelling power from her clenched fist. The golem tumbled crashing to the floor, its arms and legs flailing for balance. One arm caught the Queen's bed, pitching it sideways and tipping the Queen out. She rose in a sickening arc, her mind reeling with combined relief and fear. She had exchanged one peril for another! Before she crashed into the intricately tooled ceiling, the room dissolved. She flew out into the night, the lamplit windows of the Palace receding below her. A nascent glow of pre-dawn light traced the horizon, bright against the darkness of the moonless sky. She felt free, for the first time since finding her staff in the storm-scarred forest. Free and powerful. Energy from the woods below her, and the staff in her hand, flowed through her in waves as she dived and swooped around the black edifice of the Palace.

With the joy scarcely born in her mind, a second chill of terror ran down her spine. Silhouetted against the incipient line of dawn, a vast swirling black cloud flew towards her. A twisting, violent vortex of unimaginable power, it ripped up the ancient trees as it passed, leaving a torn and empty path through the forest. The agony of the trees, transmitted through her Wood sense, stabbed into her mind like a thousand splinters. The whirlwind caught her, throwing her down again toward the shadowed Palace roofs.

Panic returned at the realisation that she could not control this flight. The dark walls of her quarters came flying up to meet her. The Queen closed her eyes in anticipation of a painful impact. None came. When she opened them again she was lying in her bed, which had righted itself. Her staff stood propped once again beside her pillow, quiescent. Of the golem, there was no sign. She stared at the door to her chamber. The kaytam panels stood undamaged, unmarked. Through an open window, the call of a lone ghantu echoed from nearby Timakaya.

the palace of the black queen
8th day of sen'sanamasa, 966

'And when I opened my eyes, everything had returned to normal.'

The Queen took a mouthful of breakfast. Her Air Mage had joined her for their regular morning ritual, and listened politely to the tale of her dream without interrupting.

'You already know what this means Ru'ita,' Claire Yamani said, setting down her empty plate. 'It is not the first time your power has revealed itself in your dreams.'

'But flying, Claire! I have never dreamt of flying before.'

'I'm not the one to advise you on the limits or abilities of Wood power. No-one can. Will it allow you to fly? Who knows. I believe it's more likely to be allegorical.'

'I'm sorry my dear, I am quite proud of my English, but... allegorical?'

'Forgive me. Symbolic. Flying as a way to show freedom, or release. A representation, rather than any suggestion you really will be able to fly.'

The Queen fell silent, thinking about the dream and its

different elements. 'So the vortex? What did that mean? And the golem... made of black stone?'

Claire wiped her hands on a napkin. 'I'm not certain about the winds. Some connection with Air is the most obvious possibility but I can't explain why it would appear out of control. The golem, though—'

The Queen clapped her hands, smiling broadly at Claire. 'Of course! It's the Palace!'

'Yes. Just like your early dreams before anyone realised you had this power, before you took off your bangles. The stone of the Palace is suppressing your power.'

'Strangling me.'

'Yes. Symbolically. It's holding you back. Who knows what you can achieve with the power of wood, but if you remain in the Palace you may never find out. You have lived here a long time—'

'All my life.'

'Exactly. But I think your dream is telling you that the time has come to leave. Permanently.'

'Who will run the Palace if I'm gone?'

'It runs itself more or less. And your Elementals will still be here to keep an eye on things. You don't have to live in a Palace to be Queen, Ru'ita. But you can only be the Wood mage — truly come into your power — away from here.'

'But where will I go?'

'If you want my advice, I'd say removing yourself from the Palace is only half the answer. Instead of surrounding yourself with stone, I believe your true power won't reveal itself until you are surrounded by wood.'

'Live in the forest? Like a hermit?'

Claire laughed.

'It's not funny, Claire! I'm serious. I've slept in a warm, comfortable bed for years. Waited on from dawn 'til dusk. I can't live outdoors.'

'Didn't you tell me the night you spent in the forest was the best night's sleep you'd ever had? And you were lying on nothing but a pile of leaves. I'm sure the Palace artisans can construct something more in keeping with your station, your Majesty.'

The Queen walked over to the window overlooking the forest. 'When we're in private you only call me "your Majesty" to make a point. Don't think I haven't noticed.'

Claire joined her at the window. 'It's not like there's a shortage of building material,' she said, grinning. 'And yes, I was making a point. I'm your friend and your Air Mage. If I can't make a point, who can? In any case, if my guess is right, once you are in the forest, an answer will present itself.'

'I will go then,' said the Queen, 'though this is hardly the best season to begin living outdoors. I do hope you are right Claire, or I may never be warm again.'

court of the blood king
8th day of sen'sanamasa, 966

'We have restored order, for now Jeruk,' Tepak Alempin said, standing and straightening his tunic with a tug, 'but it can only be a matter of time before another outbreak.'

'Thank you Alempin. Post extra guards at the gate, and double the patrols. I want any trouble closed down as soon as it starts.'

'With respect, we do not have enough men for double patrols. Guards, yes. But in the last month I've lost more than half the Batu'n who had joined our forces since their arrival. Gone back to Pennatanah muttering about being led by donkeys — whatever that means.'

'I never knew we had such a large proportion of Batu'n,' Sebaklan Pwalek said, stroking his chin. 'Perhaps not the wisest move. Are there no young men of our own, keen for the honour of serving in the Blood Watch?'

Alempin sighed. 'These are strange times,' he said with a shake of his head. 'When I was a boy—'

'Yes, thank you Alempin,' Jeruk interrupted with a wave of his hand. 'I think we understand the problem. Do what you can. We shall have to think of a way to recruit more eager young warriors to our banner, but for now, we are where we are.'

The door opened to admit a serving boy, carrying a tray upon which two steaming bowls sat. The smell from the bowls filled the room as he set them on the table.

'Your lunch, sire.'

'What in Sana's name is it?' Jeruk asked, wrinkling his nose. 'Smells like it's been scraped from the stable floor!'

The boy reddened. 'Very sorry sire, it's all we could manage. Cook left us this morning an' we don't have anyone who can follow his recipes. My mam made this from what we had left in the kitchen.'

'Don't tell me. Cook was a Batu'n and he's gone back to Pennatanah.'

'That's right sire! Who told you?'

Jeruk ignored the shaking of Pwalek's shoulders. This was not in the least amusing. 'One of my many spies in the kitchen, boy, so mind what you say back there. And bring some tepsak, will you? Surely we have someone left who knows how to make that?'

The boy turned a deeper shade of red and backed out of the room, bowing. Whether tepsak would be forthcoming was anyone's guess.

'Well, I shall leave you to your meal Jeruk,' Alempin said, holding a hand to his mouth and looking decidedly queasy. 'See if I can rustle up some extra guards, as you suggest.'

'Try the kitchen,' Jeruk said. 'There must be someone there who can fight. They certainly can't cook!

'You want to try this?' he asked as the door closed behind the Tepak.

'No thank you!' Seb replied. 'I'm just about holding on to my breakfast as it is.'

'This is ridiculous. We cooked decent meals and kept

order at Court long before the Batu'n came! How can we have become so dependent on them in such a short time?'

'They were always very keen to do the jobs many of our people didn't want to do,' Seb said with a shrug. 'Seemed ideal. We never expected them to leave. But it's all part of the same problem Jeruk. I've tried to tell you—'

'Yes, yes, I know. Leadership. Security. Integrity. Whatever. You do know this is why I gave the Muir boy and the Stone Mage seats at our highest table? Both Batu'n, both powerful. Thought they would set an example, both for their people and ours. How was I to know one was mad, and the other a turncoat?'

'To my mind, the problem is not so much what they did, as how their story has grown. We made the mistake of not being open about what happened. In the absence of the truth, the rumour-mongers have filled in the details for themselves. I'm afraid they haven't painted us in a very good light.'

'Us? Me, you mean?'

Pwalek stared at him.

'Your silence speaks louder than your words,' Jeruk sighed.

Neither man spoke for some time. Jeruk watched their lunch bowls until the steam stopped rising from them. He did not want to look too closely at their congealing contents.

'So where do we go from here?' he asked at length.

'I have someone in mind for the... position at Pennatanah,' Pwalek said. 'He has agreed to go, but we need to work on the timing. Make sure he travels as part of a group.'

'Excellent. Some good news at last. And the Palace?'

'We have someone there already, but not in the best position. That needs more careful playing if we're not to arouse suspicions. Since we lost the Piper, getting word to the Blacks is considerably more difficult. I should work on the problem, Jeruk, if you'll excuse me?'

'Certainly. And send the kitchen boy back will you? I don't want these bowls stinking up the chamber for the rest of the day!'

timakaya
8th day of sen'sanamasa, 966

The Queen walked a woodland path, enjoying the crystal blue sky and bright sunlight of the late Sanamasan day. Timakaya stretched north of the Black Palace, straddling the Sun Besaraya and reaching almost to the foothills of Temmok'Dun. She did not know its full extent. This was only the second time in her life she had ventured past the treeline. Yet she knew she was heading in the right direction. Though only a few paces from the Palace walls, she already felt as if a huge weight had been taken off her shoulders. Yes, and her mind too. Her thoughts flew free in the chill air. She stretched, and carried on walking.

Unsure what exactly she sought, she was content in the belief she would know it when she saw it. The living wood around her sang its muted song, something she had never heard inside the black walls of what had been her home. Not surprising, since all the wood used in its construction was dead. Some of it — such as the heavy kaytam doors of her chambers — still offered an almost imperceptible hint of its power, but for the most part she could glean nothing from any of it. So perhaps not dead, but certainly dormant. Claire had used a Batu'n word for it. Comatose.

The thought of the Air Mage brought back memories of their conversation. How strange it seemed, to be considering a life outdoors. She had not even camped out as a girl and now, as Queen, any nights away from the Palace were spent under the heavy burlap of her royal ramek. With a brazier against such cold as there was at this time of year. A glowing brazier and heavy fur blankets! Still, it had not been all that much earlier in the season when she slept in the forest. Her arm crooked around the staff she now carried. Its wood always felt warm to the touch. Perhaps that was how she could be comfortable? The idea that wood could provide heat seemed illogical. Any flame would consume it, so surely the wood itself could have no affinity with Fire?

The lore Claire had passed on, which the Gatekeeper had gained from his time with the Northern peoples, made it clear that Wood derived its power as an extension of Air and Water. Fire was not involved. Indeed it could be considered diametrically opposite. But both Air and Water could carry heat. It was so confusing! She was used to being in control; giving orders. Finding herself at the mercy of the elements, even those aligned with her own power, was new and — she admitted privately — frightening.

A glade opened up in front of her. A scene of some devastation, with several felled trunks criss-crossing the clearing. Two large kaytams lent each other unlikely support, appearing to be in imminent danger of collapse. New growth had begun to spring from the decaying wood. Clumps of bright blue flowers decorated the forest floor where the sunlight could now reach. To her left, a large durmak tree bore a pale scar where a branch had split away. At the sight, her staff thrummed in her hand. A tingle of recognition ran down her spine too. Of course. Even without the numinous blue light that had traced the outline of every tree and the veins of every leaf on her first visit, this place was still recognisable.

She glanced around the clearing, half expecting to see what she sought, but there was no hint that this was the right place. It was a special place, certainly. But it was not *the* special place. She walked on, lost in thoughts of the different kinds of tree which populated Timakaya and the powers they might confer. Timakaya was home to many species, most of them hard to differentiate at this time of year. One bare branch looked much like any other, although there were subtle patterns to the bark if she looked closely enough. The deeper into the forest she journeyed, the more convinced she became that the trees were offering hints to their strengths, if only she could still her mind to hear them.

She tried to recall if Claire had offered any insights in the past that may help her quest, rerunning conversations on Elemental topics she had had over the months with her Air Mage, and occasionally with the Fire Witch. That woman was not easy to befriend, but she was civil enough. They had grown closer in the short time Bakara had been staying at the Palace, but the Queen would still not call her a friend. She laughed aloud, the sound echoing through the stillness of Timakaya and disturbing a nesting ghantu which screeched and flew off towards the Palace. She had thought, only moments before, of the Elemental antipathy between Wood and Fire, so it should be no surprise there was some tension between the two women. Perhaps the presence of the new Water Wizard, still yet to be inaugurated, was helping to alleviate the tension?

The Queen rounded a curve in the path and let out an involuntary gasp. Before her, an enormous ancient kayketral rose from a thick bed of bracken and fern, towering above her to overtop all the other trees of Timakaya. Despite the season its twigs and branches were laden with glossy, dark-green leaves the size of a person's hand. A few small purple flowers still clung to the magnificent tree, all that remained of a last, late blooming of Tanamasa. A hint of their subtle rich perfume hung in the air.

A low humming noise filled her mind; the song of the tree. It had no words, no discernible tune, and yet it spoke to her. It said, 'home.'

valley of lembaca ana
8th day of sen'sanamasa, 966

The ahmeks of the Valley landing project glowed fiery

orange in the slanting late evening sun as Piers Tremaine rode carefully down the rocky hillside path. He had pushed his kudo, Jiwambu, hard at the start of his journey in an attempt to catch up with Petani. Having reached the coast before nightfall he was content to let the animal pick its own way down the trail, rather than risk an unfortunate slip.

'Are you sure you don't want me to come?' he had asked that morning, while Petani checked the tightness of the saddle on his own mount.

'I'm sure you have better things to do,' the old Earth Elemental had replied, echoing his sentiments of the previous evening. 'I have some ideas I should like to try before I'm ready to admit defeat.'

In Piers' opinion, accepting an offer of help from a friend was not the same as an admission of defeat. Before he could voice it, Petani had swung up into his saddle. He rode out without another word. Piers returned to the refectory. Jann Argent waved to him as he crossed on the side of the courtyard but he neither stopped nor spoke.

He had eaten a lonely breakfast before spending the rest of the day moaching around the Palace, wondering what to do and trying to keep warm. Of the Queen, and the other Elementals, there was no sign. Finally, he decided he should follow his instincts and ride out after Petani. Though the old man had denied it, Piers knew he would fare no better with his latest attempts than he had with his previous ones. Not without the help of Stone. He arrived at his decision too late to start out. The Valley was a full two days ride away at the speed Petani travelled, so he would by now have camped for the night. But the path was treacherous in the dark at this time of year, and it would be well after midnight when he reached the old man's camp, if he could even find it.

He had set out that morning certain he could make the trip in one day, at a gallop, and so it had proved. The crackling of a well-fed fire and the heady smells of

Umtanesh's famous rebusang told Piers he had arrived in time for dinner. Petani sat beside the blaze, stirring the pot while Nembaka peeled a few extra vegetables.

'Enough in there for another hungry friend?' Piers asked as he tied up his kudo.

Petani smiled. 'My grumpiness didn't put you off then? Yes, I'm sure we can stretch to a fourth. Um always makes a pot big enough for an army.'

'Army?' Nembaka asked, pausing with his peeling blade halfway along a purple vegetable Piers did not recognise.

'Pashbala,' Piers said. 'But I didn't bring one along. It's just me.'

'You must have travelled fast,' Petani said. 'I've not been here long enough to start work myself. Unless you count starting the fire under this pot.'

'Jiwambu is a strong beast,' Piers said, 'and I enjoy a good gallop when the need arises. And you weren't bad tempered. Just... assertive.'

Petani laughed. 'I've only been here for a couple of seasons. Back on Earth I worked alone for many years. It's a hard habit to break, but these guys have helped me learn the value of teamwork. And since you're here...'

Piers sat down on the heavy blackwood log, deliberately taking a position at Petani's side, rather than opposite him. 'Smells good,' he said.

Umtanesh smiled. 'Be ready soon.'

'So, you've not started?' Piers asked.

'Dusk was almost upon us by the time I arrived,' Petani said, sampling the stew with the end of his stirring stick. 'Too dark to see what state the works are in, or how rough the seas are. Tomorrow will be soon enough. I'm sure it will be short work with your help.'

'No pressure then.'

'Only on me. The Queen made it quite clear this is all my responsibility. I'll be glad to get it done and return to my gardens.'

'With a belly full of this excellent rebusang to keep us

warm on this cold night, I'm sure tomorrow will look a whole lot brighter my friend.'

Petani's face, heavily lined in the flickering camp fire, suggested he was not convinced.

Chapter 3

the palace of the black queen
9th day of sen'sanamasa, 966

'Begging your pardon, ma'am, I'm not sure I understand your meaning. Tree house?'

Having found the ideal spot, the Queen had returned to the Palace to seek the help of her artisans in the realisation of her vision. A dwelling place befitting her station — both as monarch and Wood Mage — in the heart of Timakaya. Even though Pandenok, her master woodsmith, had been working timber for as long as she could remember, he seemed unusually slow in comprehending her intent. Five of his contemporaries stood with him, sharing similar puzzled expressions.

'Yes, man. Surely this is not the first time you have been asked to construct an elevated dwelling? We have a variety of trees in the Palace grounds and nearby villages, and an even greater variety of children. Have none of them ever asked for a tree house?'

Pandenok scratched his head. 'Most certainly they have, your Majesty. But not in the middle of Sanamasa.'

'Or the middle of Timakaya, for that matter,' another interjected.

'Or in a kayketral either,' added a third.

'Does any of that make a difference?' she asked.

The others shuffled their feet, avoiding eye contact. Only Pandenok held her gaze. 'Of course it's entirely a decision for yourself ma'am,' he said, 'whether you live out of doors, or in the forest, or anywhere else for that matter. But on mastersmith Maliok's last point, well, that does pose a problem. Does it have to be a kayketral?'

She turned to Maliok. 'Why is that an issue?'

The man shrank from her stare. 'Difficult wood to work, your Majesty,' he said, holding up his hands. 'Doubtful whether we could fashion a dwelling place light enough for the tree to bear.'

'And there's the bark, too,' he added.

'Bark?'

'It's poisonous, ma'am,' Pandenok said. 'Well known for it. Brings on a rash when you touch it. We'd have to wear gloves—'

'Thank you, gentlemen,' she said, cutting the man short with a dismissive wave. It was no use. Their concerns may have been valid, but her choice was not a matter for debate. In truth, it was not even her choice. The kayketral had chosen her. She would not be able to explain it in a way these men could understand. The image of what she had conceived was clear in her mind, but did not lend itself to description in any language. A flash of blue light along the length of her staff signalled her frustration. As if the spark of Wood power triggered a memory, she realised the answer lay in her own hands. She had fashioned the staff itself without recourse to traditional skills; she could do the same this time.

'I won't keep you any longer. I'm sure you have plenty of work around the Palace to keep you busy.'

The artisans bowed as one and backed nervously out of the room. The Queen collected her heaviest cloak and a warmer pair of leggings, and strode out of the Palace into the chill Sanamasan day. The pale lemon orb of the noon sun, though shining brightly, offered no warmth.

Returning to the tree — her tree, as she had already begun to think of it — she paused to catch her breath. The silence of Timakaya was unbroken by animal, bird, or wind. In the stillness, the Queen became aware once again of the tree's song. As she stood before it, the ancient sentinel filled her thoughts, hinting at changes and enhancements to her idea of a dwelling in ways she would never have considered. Once they had been revealed to her, the improvements seemed as natural as breathing. She sat on a grassy mound, letting the message percolate through her mind. Her connection with the tree warmed her. It felt like she had been wrapped in a blanket of insulating leaves and bark. Here was the answer to how she could live outside in the harshest season of the year. The trees had their own protections against the icy blasts of Sanamasa, and they were happy to share them with her.

The new image fixed clearly in her head, the Queen stood, tightened her grip on her staff, and made a start.

valley of lembaca ana
9th day of sen'sanamasa, 966

Petani stood watching the young Stone mage, his eyes closed in concentration. For the sixth time since they began work, a smooth pillar of rock rose above the choppy sea. It came to a halt at exactly the same height as the previous five. Flecks of spray, whipped from the muddy, foaming peaks of the Lum-Segar by the blustery wind, stung his cheeks like knives.

Piers opened his eyes and smiled. 'Two more?' he said.

Petani wiped the icy seawater from his face. 'Remarkable,' he replied. 'Such extraordinary precision. The men will be able to lay a platform on those foundations without need of shim or chock. Yes, I believe two more will be sufficient, if you are up to it. Though I have to say it appears to cost you no exertion at all!'

Piers gazed out across the bay. 'The stone here feels energised,' he said. 'It almost lifts itself.' He nodded in the direction of Pun'Akarnya, standing a few metres inland behind them and observing their works in enigmatic silence. 'You're no slouch yourself when it comes to raising a mountain.'

Petani shook his head. 'That was mostly earth when I summoned it. Without the influence of the Witch and the Air Mage, it would have collapsed long since. It is they who transformed it into rock. But yes, now that you mention it, the summoning was not hard. I didn't think much of it at the time, with the excitement of the conflict and feeling split in half by those fearsome Rohantu.'

'I don't pretend to understand it, and I've only heard third-hand accounts, but I guess it's possible some vestige of power remains here. Something that might explain the way the stone feels almost willing to be controlled.'

'The Battle of the Blood Clones was only the most recent event to bring power to this place,' Petani said. 'It's been the focus of Elemental magic on many occasions. The most obvious being the day we were cast back to Earth through the vortex. The aftermath of that dreadful day remained here for decades.'

'It's a shame Claire isn't with us. I've seen how often she's glued to the archives. She may have come across something that would explain it. For now though,' he said, turning back to face the churning waters, 'let's crack on with our work. If I can raise these last two columns we can both have the afternoon off!'

Petani snorted. 'Our work! Like I am playing any part in this outstanding effort.'

He rested against an outcrop of rock while Piers closed his eyes once more, bringing his full concentration to the task. To Petani's astonishment, two stone columns thrust from the water in unison. Seawater fell from them in a silvery cascade as they shot skyward, coming to rest at the same height as the others.

'Now you're just showing off!'

Piers clapped a hand on his shoulder. 'I wasn't sure I could pull that off, but I had to try. I really wish I could buy you a beer — it feels like we should celebrate.'

'We'll have to make do with a pitcher of Umtanesh's juice. At least it doesn't need to sit in the river to keep cold at this time of year!'

The two men made their way back up the path towards camp, passing into the foreshortened midday shadow of Pun'Akarnya. As they neared the rocky edifice, a strange shimmering of the air to one side of the mountain caught Petani's eye.

'What's that?' he said, pointing.

The thin, stooped figure of a man resolved itself in the centre of the strange light. Dressed all in rags, he staggered forwards, putting out a hand to the face of Pun'Akarnya to save himself from falling. His cry echoed across the empty space between them.

'Nerka jugu!'

valley of lembaca ana
9th day of sen'sanamasa, 966

The terrifying wave of power swept towards him, destroying everything in its path. Trees, grass, flowers, all turned to dust as the ripple approached. Animals, running before it in terror, were caught and dissolved instantly where they fell, even their bones crumbling to powder. Whatever this nameless terror was, he would never outrun it. All his long years in this forsaken place had come to this. Everything he had learned would be lost. Everything he had built, demolished. He closed his eyes against his certain doom.

A strange feeling passed through him, making the hairs on his arms stand up such as sometimes happened during a violent storm in the heat of the year. From a distance, he heard a voice speaking in an unfamiliar tongue. He opened his eyes. The air in front of him twisted and turned. He could not make out where the words came from. As quickly as it had come, the strange churning of the air ceased. He staggered forward, putting out a hand to stop himself collapsing. Two figures approached. Beyond them the familiar sight of the Lum-Segar rolled and splashed. The chill in the air made him shiver. What sorcery was this? It had been Bakamasa and now it felt more like Sanamasa.

The older of the two men spoke again. Unintelligible gibberish. 'I am sorry,' he replied, 'I don't understand you.'

'You speak it Istanian,' the man said, his words heavily

accented.

'Yes of course, what else would I speak? I am Istanian.'

The older man said something in the strange tongue to the younger, whose eyes widened.

'Who you? Where come you from?' he asked.

'I am from here. At least, this is where I have lived for many years. My home is up there,' he pointed towards his hut. 'On the hillside overlooking the Valley.'

The older man peered at him more closely, a look of astonishment decorating his face. 'No. Cannot be. You the Pilgrim?'

The Pilgrim smiled. 'Some do call me that, yes.'

valley of lembaca ana
9th day of sen'sanamasa, 966

Piers poured a cup of sabah for the Pilgrim before filling two more for himself and Petani. Umtanesh had left the camp to check his traps and hunt out vegetables for the evening. With luck there would be a rabbit or two for the night's pot.

'I still don't understand,' Piers said as they took seats beside the campfire. 'Who is the Pilgrim?'

'I don't know much about him or his story,' Petani said, throwing another log onto the fire. 'Only the few bits Patrick and Jann told me about their first visit to the Valley. He lived here while it was still affected by the curtain of time displacement.'

'You've lost me again.'

'Sabah yanak', said the Pilgrim.

'Sen ku myanya' Petani replied.

'Something about the juice?' Piers said.

'He likes it. Can't believe you lived in Duska Batsirang for ten years without learning some Istanian.'

'I know enough to get by. I can't call myself fluent though. I recognised "juice" didn't I? Don't judge!'

Petani briefly recapped what he knew of the Pilgrim's

story. Umtanesh returned with a double brace of rabbits and a bird that neither of them recognised. It would be a rich stew tonight, with more than enough for their new guest.

'That's weird,' Piers observed once Petani's short tale was done, 'after what we were saying earlier about the power in this place.'

'It is. We assumed the Pilgrim had died along with all the other living things behind the Valley curtain. I suppose something must have protected him.'

'Ask him. And tell him to use simple language, so I can follow. I don't want you to have to translate everything. Unless I'm stuck.'

Petani relayed that to the Pilgrim before switching to what sounded to Piers like pidgin Istanian. 'How you survive end of curtain?'

The Pilgrim stared into the flames for some time, before holding up his hands.

'I not know for sure. But I spend years hunt for metal. For brass. When I not find brass, I keep.' He reached into the folds of his filthy rags and brought out a handful of metal fragments. 'These King not need,' he said. 'Metal have power, so I keep.'

'What kind of power?' Piers asked.

'Not like usual Elemental power,' the old man said. 'Stronger. More like Stone power. What we not have now, in my time.'

'You'd be surprised,' Piers said, stretching out his hand. A boulder flew from beside the fire, landing in his palm with a loud slap. He opened his fingers and held the rock out. It glowed, twisting as if molten until it had taken on the shape of the mystery bird which Umtanesh was even now plucking for their meal.

The Pilgrim dropped his cup and leapt to his feet. 'You Stone Mage?' he asked, astonished. 'Banshirin?'

'I am.'

'That was pretty impressive, Piers, even for you,' Petani

said. 'I didn't know you had that kind of control.'

'What say, Earth man?' the Pilgrim said, frowning.

Petani repeated what he had said in rapid Istanian which Piers could not follow.

'It true,' the Pilgrim said, bowing to Piers before retaking his seat. 'Stone magic talked of many years, but never see. Forgotten. Until now. Thank for showing.'

The old man bowed his head again, his eyes glowing with firelight and emotion.

'But then you must know metal power,' he continued, leaning forward. 'They almost same.'

'I never heard of metal power,' Piers said. 'I only know Stone.'

'Metal purer form,' the old man said. 'All metal come from rock and stone. Heat that make the stone will bring metal out.'

'He means ore,' Petani said. 'Mineral deposits and smelting. Arbelan,' he said to the old man.

'Yes! Arbelan! That what I said. It start as stone and end as metal, so metal have pejakus Stone power.'

'Sorry — pejakus?' Piers said.

'Enhanced,' Petani said. 'Or focused. Concentrated.'

'Wouldn't I have felt this?' Piers said. He picked up the cooking pot. 'This is metal. I get no hint of power from it. I can feel the Stone all around me, waiting only on my call. But this...' He hung the small vessel from its frame ready for Umtanesh, and ran a hand around its rim. 'This doesn't give me anything at all.'

The Pilgrim nudged Petani, who repeated what Piers had said. The older man stroked his chin, his gaze jumping from Piers to the cauldron and back. He shrugged. 'I not know why,' he said. 'But I know metal have power. Man with metal weapon stronger than man without.'

Piers stifled a laugh. There was nothing magical about a sharp sword, especially when wielded against an opponent without one. Was there? But then, swords had been held in awe in mythology for centuries. Given meaningful names

— names of power — and imbued with supposed magical properties. Excalibur the most obvious example, but there were many others.

'You not believe?' the Pilgrim asked.

'I don't know,' Piers replied. 'I guess it's possible.'

They fell silent, the import of the Pilgrim's words and the effort of communicating complex concepts in simple language defeating them all for a time. Umtanesh added each of his ingredients to the pot, which was soon bubbling fiercely and emitting rich smells that tugged at Piers' gut. The day had flown by, and the sudden appearance of their new companion had displaced lunch. None of the men had eaten since breakfast.

Once they had full bowls in front of them, and were forced to wait for the contents to cool before eating, Piers returned to the subject of metal and its power.

'Not all metal needs arbelan,' he said, pleased to have the opportunity to use the new word he had learnt earlier. 'Precious metals, for instance. Silver. Gold.'

'What?' said the Pilgrim, blowing on a spoonful of stew and picking out a chunk of rabbit to chew on.

'Repgola,' said Petani, 'and amegola. They don't need arbelan.'

'No they not need,' agreed the Pilgrim, 'so that why they have magic all their own. Great power. Great wealth they bring. Men fight and die for amegola.'

'I guess some things never change no matter what civilisation you live in,' Piers said.

Their meal done, they sat in the glow of the fire for a short time before the Pilgrim began to nod.

'You should sleep,' Petani said.

'Yes. My hut over there.'

'Ah,' Piers said, 'yes. I slept there last night. I didn't bring an ahmek.'

The Pilgrim favoured Piers with a hard stare. He stood, brushing floating fire ash from his rags, which smudged to join the many other dirt stains patterning the cloth. 'I happy to share with Banshirin,' he said, and walked off into the night without another word.

valley of lembaca ana
9th day of sen'sanamasa, 966

Piers watched the old man disappear into the darkness. Their fire had subsided to a pile of glowing embers, occasionally giving a subdued crack from a last pocket of sap, and emitting a bright spark.

'What are you going to do with him? When you finish here?'

Petani warmed his hands. The stocky Gardener thought at the speed his plants grew, or tectonic plates moved. Piers never expected a quick reply. Although their Elements were aligned, Piers was like flint. Strong, sharp, and brittle. Petani was more like... mud.

'He can come with us,' he replied. 'We have three days work left, maybe four. Time for him to decide. Forest clearance may not be his first choice, but he has no reason to stay in this lonely place now.'

'We never did celebrate finishing the pylons,' Piers said. 'What I wouldn't give for a cold beer.'

'Been a long time since you had one of those. I'd bet the best any ale house in Duska Batsirang could do was river water temperature. Unless there'd been a snowfall.'

'Aye,' Piers nodded. 'And Sanamasa isn't really the time of year to appreciate a cold one. Even so, I'd sink it in one go tonight.' He turned to Umtanesh, who sat a little removed from the Elementals, not wanting to intrude. 'That was another wonderful meal, Umtanesh. Thank you.'

'Welcome.'

'What are your plans now?' Petani asked. 'You finished the Stone work in double-quick time. The rest of this project is an easy job for us. Nothing to keep you here is there?'

'I guess not. I enjoy the company though. Never

thought I'd say that. Always been a bit of a loner.'

Petani chuckled deep in his throat. If his voice had a colour, it would be the same as his Element: brown. 'No more than me! I hadn't worked in a team until I met these guys. Always my own master, and my own slave.'

'I never felt grounded at the Palace,' Piers admitted. 'Everyone there is busy with something. Claire has her Guild, and her research; Jann and Elaine are always wrapped up in themselves; the new Water girl busy with preparations for her ceremony.'

'Can't be long now, surely? The ceremony?'

'To be honest I have no idea. I don't mix with them much. I've been wondering about visiting Patrick.'

'At Pennatanah? Careful, there.'

'What do you mean?'

'We hear all sorts. Rumours of a Batu'n rebellion. Quite a bit of resentment building up if you ask me. Most of those Dauntless people haven't joined in the way the earlier colonists did. Like you did! Decided where you wanted to go, made a life for yourself for all those years.'

'Yeah, don't run away with the idea of a rural idyll,' Piers said, poking the fire with a long stick. 'It's a bit of a backwater, is Batsirang. With a backwater mentality. Soon as they began to suspect I had "strange" powers, they didn't react too well. Just confirmed my view of myself as a loner, really. I've felt different all my life. Never one of the cool kids, or part of their crowd. Thought I could leave it behind coming here, but it hasn't turned out like that.'

'So you plan on running away again to Pennatanah?'

'Maybe. Didn't spend much time with Patrick, but he seemed a regular kind of guy. I'd like to catch up, get the inside track on what life is like there. At least it would give me something to compare with.'

'It doesn't compare though, does it? It's not a backwater, like Batsirang and it's not a Palace. It's another completely different way of living.'

'Might be exactly what I need.'

'True. It also might not.'

'Well I won't know unless I go, will I?' Piers said, beginning to lose patience with the old man. 'What are you going to do anyway? Earth work is finished here too, as well as Stone. Creating a landing stage is all woodwork. Where are you going? Don't you have a Guild, like Claire?'

Petani's cheeks took on a ruddy hue beyond a simple reflection of the fire's dying glow.

'I do. Or at least, a few of us decided to resurrect it a little while ago. I can't pretend we've done much about it. Things move slowly with Earth. They happen at their own pace. Like plants growing.'

Or tectonic plates.

'But to answer your question,' Petani continued, 'I hadn't really thought about it. I didn't expect us to be finished so soon. But you sound like you've already decided.'

'Yes and no,' Piers said, stretching his legs and standing. 'I'm going to sleep on it. Decide in the morning.'

valley of lembaca ana
9th day of sen'sanamasa, 966

Petani remained sitting by the dying fire, alone again now that the Pilgrim, Piers, and the other members of the squad had retired for the night. The twin moons had risen; it would not be long before the nightly malamajan began. For now he was dry, still warm considering the lateness of the day, and content to watch the flickering of the last flames.

A part of him empathised with the young Stone mage. He was no stranger to that feeling of isolation. As he had often observed, he was not a joiner. And yet on the other side of the argument, he had always hated fragmentation. In the same way his beloved plants grew more vigorously when bunched together, people worked better in a group. More could be achieved with harmony than with antagonism, although there was no doubt that having a rival could spur you on to greater achievements.

When rivalry escalated to the point where society started to fracture, a path had been laid from which it was difficult to turn. Petani worried that this was the path they were now beginning to tread. Earther discontent was growing. The latest arrivals were clearly unimpressed with what Berikatanya had to offer, and preferred to dig in to an exclusive encampment. One that was now proving quite compelling to the earlier arrivees too, including Piers. Having put Petani firmly in his place that very day, the younger man was now intent on sampling the Pennatanah life. No doubt he would be tempted.

For Petani though, even having spent several decades living and working on Earth, his heart and soul remained Berikatanyan. While intellectually he could see the appeal of the Batu'n base, emotionally he believed Piers was taking a wrong turn. As an Elemental — especially a second-level one — the young man's loyalties should lie with the place that had blessed him with its powers. He sighed. Perhaps it was different for him, having been born here. Returning to this place, his home, after many years in his forgetful wilderness, had been like putting on a familiar pair of comfortable slippers. Piers had no such connection. For the younger man, this was only the most recent in a long line of places he had run to, in his ongoing quest to find somewhere he could belong. And if Pennatanah should fall short of his expectations, where was there left for the Stone Mage to run?

A first fat spot of rain fell hissing into the firepit. If he had been waiting for a reason to take to his ahmek, this was it. An eventful day, to be sure, and it looked as though the next one would be no different.

valley of lembaca ana
10th day of sen'sanamasa, 966

Having been lulled into a deep sleep by the sound of the malamajan falling on the soft canvas of his ahmek, Petani woke refreshed. Peering out through the flaps he saw the morning shrouded by a seasonal mist. A faint echo of the now-famous time curtain, though an entirely natural one, unlike its arcane counterpart. From across the camp, the snort of a kudo could be heard through the blanket of fog.

He dressed swiftly and made his way past the ash-filled firepit to the simple roped corral where the kudai were kept. Piers was there, preparing his mount for a journey.

'Early start?' Petani said, stating the obvious.

'Soonest begun is half done,' Piers replied.

'Your night's rest has made up your mind then.'

'If I'm honest I had decided last night, my friend. Perhaps I didn't want to admit it, even to myself.'

'I hope you find what you're looking for.'

Piers paused in the act of lifting his saddle onto the animal. 'Whatever that is.' He smiled ruefully. 'Should I pass your greetings on to Patrick?'

'Please do. Tell him I hope he is faring well. Ask him if he's finished his book yet.'

Piers laughed. 'I'll ask him. What about you, Petani? Have you decided your next move?'

Petani scratched the kudo's ear, murmuring nonsense to the beast. It lifted its head, leaning into the scratch and blowing a steamy breath into the cold morning air.

'No. There's time.'

'All the time in the world,' Piers said, cinching the girth and checking his stirrups were secure.

It seemed there was little more to say. At least, nothing he could think of. Something would no doubt sprout like a stalagmite from the basement of his mind as soon as Piers was gone. When it was too late.

'Go carefully in this fog,' he said. 'These paths can be tricky.'

'I will. Don't worry. I'll see you soon, I hope, one way or another. Perhaps at the Water Wizard's inauguration? The invites should be arriving soon.'

'Perhaps,' Petani nodded, giving the kudo a gentle slap. 'Goodbye Piers.'

'Au revoir, Petani!' the young man said, swinging into his saddle and urging his mount onto the stone-strewn path.

Chapter 4

the court of the blood king
10th day of sen'sanamasa, 966

'Has there been any word yet from the Black Palace? Or the Batu'n base?'

'It is not yet three days since I set our plans in motion, Jeruk,' Sebaklan Pwalek replied. 'Calm yourself. Our man will only now be arriving at the coast. I have given him clear instructions on how he should approach the Batu'n leadership. They are distrustful people to begin with, and even more on edge in these times. He will need to be subtle.'

'Subtle be damned!' Jeruk said, banging his fist on the desk in front of him. 'We need action, man! We need results.'

'And we will get them, but not immediately.'

'Surely the Palace then?'

'The contact we have there was already established, but again care is needed. In the end the Piper's duplicity was revealed—'

'He always was a worthless fool!'

'—which makes it even more important that we make no obvious moves. A one-for-one replacement of the Queen's steward with an unknown is bound to arouse suspicion. We must bide our time—'

'How much damned time do you think we have, for Baka's sake? We are as good as blind here!'

'We are no worse off than they! Better, if anything. Everyone in a position of influence at Court is known to us. They have all worked with us for years — Puppeteers or not. If the Blacks do have spies here, they are lowly placed. Easy to exclude from meetings and discussions. As long as we are circumspect in the presence of serving staff, stable hands, and the like, we will retain the advantage.'

'But—'

'I know it's frustrating, Jeruk,' Seb ignored the flash of anger in the small man's eyes at his interruption. If allowed to run unchecked, his impatience would undo any slim edge Seb had managed to carve. 'You must exercise some restraint. These things will unfold at their own pace. It is beyond our influence now.'

'Do they at least know what they are supposed to be doing? Whenever it is they manoeuvre themselves into a position to actually do it?'

'Of course — do you take me for a fool? You have discarded that role, do not assume I have adopted it! Both of them are skilled at stirring up dissent. The Batu'n are already divided. They are taking back their people from both realms, discontented and looking for something "better." Those that never left were disaffected from the beginning by what our world has to offer. Ripe for unrest. They have limited housing space, limited resources of *any* kind, and their leader has recently suffered an unfortunate and untimely death.'

'Some progress, at least!'

'So now, in that melting pot of discontent, it will not take more than a few well-placed arguments and barbed comments to have them at each others' throats.'

'I notice you're dodging the question of the Blacks.'

Seb sat down opposite his hook-nosed chief. Some days it felt like he was more the leader. Today was one of those days. All the diminutive man ever did recently was moan, demand, and throw fits when things did not happen according to his idea of a schedule.

'The Black Palace is more of a problem, to be sure,' he said with a shrug. 'But we may have a trump card to play there. They are about to crown a new Water Wizard.'

'How does that help us?'

'It's Muir's sister. The Batu'n girl. I don't suppose there are many Kertonians who are happy at having an Elemental — *another* Elemental — from the Earther ranks. The Air Mage was bad enough, but at least she is a direct descendant of the previous one. These Muirs have no connection whatever with Berikatanya.'

'And her brother!' Jeruk said, leaning forward and smiling for the first time. 'Not the most popular Batu'n on the planet!'

'Indeed. Allied himself to us and then proceeded to try and drown the entire population. I'm sure the antipathy towards the Muir family did not die with him, or if it did, we can soon resurrect it!'

the palace of the black queen
11th day of sen'sanamasa, 966

Jann Argent stuck his notepad under his arm and rubbed his hands together to loosen his fingers, encourage circulation, and make it easier to hold a yumbal. Given the choice he would still be in bed at this time, snuggled up next to the Fire Witch and warm enough without the need of her Elemental power. But his task was easier at this time of day, so he here stood instead.

He was mapping gates.

An early morning breeze rustled through the bare branches of Timakaya, the cold sound making him shiver. Though dressed warmly, the sun had not yet risen above the treeline and the day was still icy. He felt chilled to the bone.

As the old Water Wizard Lautan had assured him they would, Jann's memories had now fully returned, and with them the knowledge of his Gatekeeper powers. He missed Lautan. The wise man's absence was keenly felt by everyone. His long experience and ready command of his Water power had served as an instructive example to Jann. The new Water Wizard suffered Lautan's loss more than Jann, he knew, but the two men had been close companions. Partners in adversity and during the few short days of peace they had enjoyed together.

His thoughts turned to his other principal teacher,

Dipeka Kekusaman. An elder of the village he had journeyed to on his Northern quest, Kekusaman was conversant with the ways of the Gatekeeper. Sensitive to the power in others though she did not share it. She had told him he would eventually be able to find gates almost anywhere, of one kind or another.

"Gates exist everywhere, Gatekeeper. The more practised you become, the easier you will find it to discover them."

She had been right, and Jann had made a project of uncovering the locations of all the local gates. At present, he had no urgent need of them. But if his experiences since returning to this world were any indicator, he soon might. His work had two benefits: he was learning where they were; and he was becoming more adept at finding them.

Since starting his mapping project shortly after the Battle of Utperi'Tuk, he had noticed an inexplicable increase in the number of gates he was locating. In the beginning, in the immediate vicinity of the Palace, there had been few. Those early days had seen him travelling ever further afield before encountering a new one. More recently, they were popping up even in places he had thought his map complete. Were the deeper gates somehow moving closer to the boundary between their mysterious dimension and his? Or he was finding altogether new ones? Impossible to tell, but he was recording an almost fourfold rise in the count.

As he pondered this, a small one opened up directly in front of him, startling his kudo Perak and almost unseating him. The gate had a dark aspect, unfamiliar to him. As he stared at it, stroking Perak's neck to settle the animal, it began to rotate slowly. He dismounted, tied his ride to a nearby tree, and walked over to examine it more closely. About the size of the one he opened in Tenfir Abarad to trap the kuclar, this gate leant at perhaps fifteen degrees from the vertical. It was the first he had seen to do this. Normally they were perfectly vertical or horizontal. He had always assumed some natural phenomenon, such as lines of gravitational force, governed the orientation of openings at ground level. The only horizontal ones he knew of were opened much higher, like the famous vortex at Lembaca Ana which had drawn him and the others to Earth. Perhaps centripetal force was more of a factor at altitude, but it was all supposition on his part. Despite her familiarity with the lore, such as it was, Kekusaman had never mentioned this aspect of gates.

This was also the first gate he had seen, since his encounter with the kuclar, that he had not consciously opened. He had never been surprised by one popping up unbidden. Moreover, it was not passive. The closer he looked, the more he realised it resembled a vortex more than a regular gate. Its angle, its gentle rotation, and the way it pulled a fine jumble of material towards itself. Roadway dust, dried leaves, small twigs, and fibres of vegetation from abandoned nests, all flew toward the gate in dreamlike slow motion, defying gravity and normal physics. Jann felt the pull on his tunic, though it was slight and easy to resist.

Even so, he did not risk moving any nearer.

'There you are!' came a voice from behind him.

It was Elaine. At her words, the vortex-gate disappeared with a soft snap, leaving the slightest trace of strange, dense black fog in the air where it had stood. He whipped around, holding up both arms. 'Don't come any closer!'

'What is it? What's wrong?' Sudden flame licked from her hands, an unconscious reaction to imminent danger.

'I'm not sure. It's gone now, but—'

'What's gone? I can't see anything.'

He grinned, rubbing his aching shoulders as the tension of the moment passed. 'Well, no. It's gone. There's nothing to see. You didn't have to come looking for me out here in the cold. I was almost done anyway.'

'The Queen has called a meeting of her council. A

breakfast meeting. Didn't want you to miss it.'

'Not like her to make such an early start,' Jann said, remounting his kudo. 'What's it about?'

'Beats me,' Elaine replied, 'but at least we get one of her big spreads out of it. She's holding the meeting in her chambers.'

Jann's eyes widened. 'Something secret, then.'

the palace of the black queen
11th day of sen'sanamasa, 966

A gentle knock came on Claire Yamani's door, waking her. Pale light, filtering past the edges of her curtains, told her the day was only recently dawned.

'It's open.'

Kyle Muir put her head tentatively through the smallest gap. Her red-rimmed, puffy eyes gave testament to another night spent crying over her lost brother. 'Sorry. I know it's early, but—'

'It's fine. I was awake. Almost. Come in.'

She sat up in bed and reached for a robe. Kyle closed the door quietly behind her and crossed the room to sit on the edge of Claire's bed.

'I've been thinking about Pennatanah,' she said.

'Really? I'd have thought you would be completely occupied with your ceremony.'

Kyle grimaced. 'Don't! I'm not ready for that. I don't think I'll ever be ready.'

'Of course you are! I know it's not even been a half-month since we lost Lautan, but you and I are most definitely not "master" and "apprentice" any longer. You must be sure of your powers by now!'

'Water power doesn't bother me,' Kyle said. 'I can't claim to be at the height of my powers — I hate that term by the way! — but being Water Wizard doesn't faze me as much as it did at first. No, it's more... well... the politics.'

'Not sure I know what you mean.'

'All that stuff about loyalty. Te'Banga, is it? How the Queen might expect us to fight on her side, or whatever. It was bad enough being responsible for the death—'

She paused, clutching the bedcovers with white knuckled hands. '—for Douglas. And Lautan, my mentor—'

'It wasn't just you.'

'Partly responsible, then. Anyway I don't want to do any more of that. And besides, I know I have these powers, and it's all very exciting and magical and everything, but I'm from Earth.'

'So?'

'Well, there's talk about people going back to Pennatanah. Colonists, I mean. Building a proper Earther colony there, instead of forcing ourselves to be part of the two realms.'

'Ah. Yes. So that's why it's on your mind, right?'

'Yes. I'm surprised it's not been on yours too, to be honest.'

'It's different for me. I was born to Berikatanyans. I didn't know that's what they were for the first fifteen years, but still. It makes me feel more of an affinity with them, you know? The Queen has been so good to me—'

'She doesn't do it out of the goodness of her heart! She's a monarch. There's always a quid-pro-quo.'

'I know, but... well, she could demand her pound of flesh without being so nice about it, if she wanted to. Like you said, she's the ruler. She could be all, "off with her head!"'

They laughed. Kyle lay back along the bottom of Claire's bed, staring at the ceiling. 'She is very nice. Almost friendly. But even so, I've been wondering if I wouldn't feel more at home among... Oh God, this sounds terrible, but... among my own kind.'

'Well, that's something you have to decide for yourself,' Claire said, throwing back the covers. 'We all do.'

'So you have thought about it!'

'I suppose, a little. I guess I feel torn. I'm a lot more important here than I would ever have been back home. I have the ear of the Queen, she calls herself my friend. I'm at the head of the Guild, I've learned the lore — a lot of it — and used it in new ways. I kind of feel settled.'

'There's something you're not saying.'

Another knock came at the door.

'Come in,' Claire said.

An elderly man in the livery of the household stepped into the room and bowed to the two women. 'If it please, Kema'satun, the Queen has requested your presence for a working breakfast. In her chambers.'

'It's a little early for breakfast, surely?' Claire said.

'Oh not immediately, Sakti,' the man said, colouring slightly. 'She has said mid-morning, to allow everyone time to assemble.'

timakaya
11th day of sen'sanamasa, 966

The Queen surveyed her handiwork, and smiled. She sent out a silent word of thanks to the kayketral. The majestic tree had had a hand in the work too, impelling rapid growth in some areas, hinting at possible improvements to her design concept in others. The result, she decided, without even a trace of embarrassment at the slight conceit, was a tree house of surpassing beauty.

A work of this magnificence, one essentially Elemental nature, demanded a name. Summoned by her thought, it came to her. Huramapon. The leaves of the kayketral shivered in a light breeze, as if pleased with the christening.

Kayketral was an evergreen species, and provided a roof canopy of interlocking leaves more waterproof than any traditional tile. The thickened leaves of such trees were naturally waxy, and shed water easily. When overlapped as they were, not a single drip could penetrate. She had bent branches and trunks to her will to create surfaces for walking and standing, and support structures. Within these, using only fallen timbers, she had made floors, walls, windows and verandahs. The wood, both dead and living, was hers to command. She found kaytam — the forbidding wood, so often used in doors made with more prosaic methods and skills — and used it for her own doorway. Should she request it, the barrier would prevent anything from entering. Come what may, this was somewhere she would always feel completely safe.

One of the biggest changes the tree itself had suggested, allowed her to construct the dwelling at a far greater height than she originally intended. One of the lower branches had been in imminent danger of collapse. Through means the Queen could perceive but not yet explain, the tree had released its hold on the branch. It had fallen to the ground, but retained a sinewy connection with the main trunk. Thus, a stairway had been created. A wide, sloping walkway leading to the first level of the house.

Slanting rays of early morning sun reflected off the foliage in all directions, giving the structure an appearance of shimmering silver. She walked the length of her staircase and turned, gazing back towards the Palace and breathing in the scent of old wood, leaf litter, and freedom. She could feel her power swelling. Taking new paths, offering renewed health and a burgeoning sense of other possibilities that until now had been closed to her.

Claire had been right. Her young Air Mage offered so much. Wisdom, counsel, friendship. She must think of a way to express her gratitude. The sight of the Palace and the thought of Elementals reminded the Queen of the meeting she had arranged. She glanced at the sun. It must almost be time. One last gathering in the dark stone tomb of a place she had once called home. Reluctantly, she retraced her steps down the gently sloping branch, bid a mental farewell to Huramapon, and set off toward the Palace.

the palace of the black queen
11th day of sen'sanamasa, 966

By the time the Queen entered her chambers, most of the expected attendees were present. A selection of breakfast foodstuffs had been arranged on her long table, as she had instructed, and those who were here had helped themselves. Good. They all knew by now she was not one to stand on ceremony. Her predecessor would have insisted everyone wait until she had filled her own plate. In contrast, while the Queen was happy to wield her status when it was necessary, she was equally happy to avoid it when it was not.

Her Air Mage and the Muir girl sat together in a pair of easy chairs beside the fire. Although it appeared to have been burning for some time, the room had not lost its chill.

'Throw another log on, would you Claire? Since you're closest.'

The Gatekeeper and the Fire Witch occupied the window seat, sharing from a single plate. She was glad they had abandoned any pretence of not being a couple.

'Where is the Stone Mage?' she asked.

'He had a change of heart ma'am,' the Witch replied. 'He has followed Petani to the Valley in the hope he can be of some assistance with the Landing.'

The Queen beamed. 'Splendid. A shame they could not travel together, but as long as they *come* together in the end it is of little import. I see you all have something to eat. If we need not await Tremaine, let us begin.'

'Will you not take a bite, your Majesty?' the Muir girl asked.

'Thank you dear, but no. At least not for the moment. After being outdoors for so long we find the Palace a deal more oppressive than we expected. If we may conclude our business as swiftly as possible, we shall be happy to make our return to the forest.

'And since we have mentioned it,' she continued, taking a seat on the settle opposite the two girls, 'perhaps that should be our first agenda item.'

The others bowed their assent.

'As Claire knows, the environment of the Palace, the seat of power in Kertonia for almost as long as the realm has existed, is not conducive to expressions of Wood power, let alone explorations of its possibilities. We have therefore concluded we must leave this place.'

'How long for, your Majesty?' asked the Gatekeeper.

'Forever, young man,' she replied. 'We will make — have made — our home in Timakaya.'

Claire clapped her hands together and let out a small squeal of excitement. 'So you found somewhere!'

'Yes. In a way. Let us just say we have found a place where we can be comfortable. It is, though we say it ourselves, perfect.'

'So what will happen to the Palace?' Argent said. 'May we remain here? Who will run it?'

The Queen laughed. 'We did not involve ourselves in the running of this place when we lived here Jann Argent! Our absence will make little difference to the smooth operation of Palace business. We have been seeking a replacement steward for some time — someone to step into the big boots of our esteemed Piper, who is much missed. For the time being we have offered the role to Gadys Kepatakan. She has many years' experience, and is ably assisted by several deputies. You may rest assured there will be no interruption to Palace activity.

'Though we will no longer attend, we hope you, as both Elementals and senior members of the Palace, will continue to hold these meetings and keep a watch on political matters—'

'It would be an honour, your Majesty,' the young Water Wizard said.

'Really, young lady?' the Queen raised an eyebrow. 'We would think all of your thoughts and time would be devoted to your preparations for inauguration. It cannot be many days away now?'

Muir blushed, but said no more.

'And on the subject of political matters, the most pressing of those must surely be the rising influence of the colony of Pennatanah on the people of Kertonia.'

The Queen would not have sworn to it, but her new Water Wizard appeared to colour even more deeply at these words. So much so that some of the girl's redness seeped over to her Air Mage.

'Do either of you two young ladies have an opinion on this you would like to share with us?'

Claire looked momentarily flustered. 'I... that is we... were only discussing that earlier this morning your Majesty.'

The Queen adjusted her position on the settle. 'And what was your conclusion?'

'I'm not sure we reached one ma'am. Merely that we hear rumours of its increasing popularity. We have seen several riders leaving in recent days.'

'They don't know when they're well off!' the Fire Witch said. 'What does that dull backwater offer that they do not already have in abundance here at the Palace? Nothing!'

'It cannot be "nothing", Bakara,' the Queen said, 'or they would not go. We may not understand it or agree with it, but... Anyway, that was our primary concern in the political arena. Please keep abreast of how the situation progresses. Perhaps put some effort into finding out, from our remaining Batu'n, what the attraction is? There may be some steps we can take to tip the balance back in favour of Kertonia?'

One of the household staff arrived to clear the plates. Claire poked the fire back into life.

'And what of our other activities,' the Queen continued. 'How goes your mapping, Gatekeeper?'

'Yes, I was going to bring that up your majesty,' Argent said. 'It has been quite successful, although not without its surprises, especially earlier today.'

'How so?'

'At first my only surprise has been an increase in the number I have managed to find. I am at a loss to explain it, but there are many more gates surrounding the Palace now than were apparent when I started. But the real shock came this morning when one of them opened by itself.'

'How is that possible?'

'It is another thing I cannot explain, ma'am, I am embarrassed to admit.'

'I can confirm it was not his imagination,' the Witch added. 'I saw it for myself. Or at least, Jann's reaction to it.'

'We did not doubt the Gatekeeper's words Bakara,' the Queen said, drawing herself upright on her seat. 'We were merely commenting on the unusual nature of the occurrence.'

'What did it look like?' Claire asked. 'Was it like a normal gate?'

'That was the thing,' Argent said. 'It wasn't. It turned like a slow vortex and—'

'Like a tornado?'

'A small one, maybe yes. Small and slow. And it left a strange trail of dark fog in the air when it snapped shut.'

Claire leapt to her feet, her eyes wide. 'Like a black smoke, you mean?'

'Yes! Why? Have you seen it before?'

'Once only. But it doesn't make sense. He's not here.'

'Who?'

'Patrick. The last time I saw it, he was using his power to calm the kudai. When we crossed the Sun Hutang in full spate. Are you sure it was a real gate? You said it wasn't normal. What else was strange about it?'

Argent described the phenomenon. To the Queen, he looked more than puzzled. By the time he concluded his brief tale he looked decidedly unsettled. She might even have said frightened.

'What does it mean?' she asked. 'Is there danger here at the Palace?' Her blood ran cold 'In the forest?'

'I have not checked Timakaya for gates. I couldn't say for certain whether any danger lurks there. But we should all keep watch for anything like this happening again. It had a definite pull. This one was small, but a larger one may prove more perilous.'

'This is perhaps not the best time for a move to the outdoors, ma'am,' the Fire Witch said.

The Queen stood and reached for her staff. The wood felt warm to her touch. 'Thank you for your concern, Bakara. We believe we are safe enough in our new home. Whatever power this is, it will need to be stronger than we have yet seen before it can stand against Wood.'

the palace of the black queen
11th day of sen'sanamasa, 966

'Turn round. I'll do your back.'

Jann slid around in their shared tub, his muscled shoulders slipping deliciously across Elaine's nipples. She gasped, and reached for the soap.

'That feels good,' he said, as she massaged peaks of white, fragrant foam over his knotted sinews. 'A bit of boost for this water wouldn't hurt.'

'Never satisfied,' she replied, summoning her power with practised ease. The water temperature rose rapidly.

'Mmmmm,' Jann murmured. 'Perfect.'

Her soaping hands completed their task and Jann lay back against her breasts. 'I didn't see any strange looks or hear any snide comments this morning. How about you?'

'Me neither. Not even any surprise. Maybe we'd given them enough clues.'

'I guess. It was a weird meeting though.'

'What was weird about it?'

'Kidding, right? Queen leaves Palace she's lived in all her life. Air Mage admits to discussing the Pennatanah

Problem, but won't admit what that discussion was really about.'

'Young Claire is turning into quite the politician,' Elaine said, another involuntary wave of Fire power rippling through the water at the thought. The girl clearly could not decide where her loyalties lay. 'And if anyone showed any sign of an adverse reaction to us being together — openly together I mean — it was her.'

Jann sat up with a start, sending water splashing onto the floor of their chamber. 'What? Why?'

'Oh come on!' Elaine laughed. 'She's had a thing for you for — oh, I don't know — forever!'

'A thing? You mean a crush?'

'Yes!'

'You're not serious? Since when?'

'When was the first time I saw you both? Armstrong spaceport! She was mooning after you there.'

'We'd only just met for Baka's sake!'

'Don't bring my God into this!' Elaine said, feeling the blood rise in her cheeks. Their bathwater temperature rose another couple of degrees. 'Anyway her feelings for you — whatever they may or may not be — are beside the point. I'm far more interested in her thoughts on the Batu'n rebellion.'

Jann levered himself upright and stepped out of the bath. 'I think you might be overstating it a bit,' he said. 'It's hardly a rebellion.'

'You think? This is exactly how these things start. Claire Yamani is an Elemental. Her loyalty should be with us. With Berikatanya. Her parents were Berikatanyan; her powers are Berikatanyan; and her heritage is Berikatanyan. I may not agree with everything the Queen does, but her treatment of Claire has been exemplary.'

'She likes having an Air Mage back.'

'It's more than that! She knows where her duty lies. Claire could do worse than follow her example.'

'Are you going to dry me off, or do I need to fetch a

towel?'

'I can dry us both,' she said, standing and allowing her power to flow again. 'That Muir girl is no better, although I suppose she has the excuse of not being born to Berikatanyan parents. And Water was always...' she stared down into the bath '... hard to pin down.'

She stepped out into her lover's dry arms.

'You're going to tell me there's a long-standing feud between Fire and Water?'

Elaine smiled. 'Not a feud exactly but, well... they are opposites.' She pulled on a plain white robe, for once feeling strangely reluctant to remain naked. 'You sounded jokey when you called it the Pennatanah Problem. You still don't take it seriously, do you? Even with hordes of people leaving Court.'

'Hordes? I've seen maybe a dozen. You really think it'll turn nasty?'

'I saw a dozen *today*. It wouldn't surprise me if it's already nasty. All we see is the exodus. We don't have a clue what's happening over there.'

timakaya
11th day of sen'sanamasa, 966

Returning to Timakaya felt like plunging into a cool mountain pool after a long, hot, arduous trek through dense jungle. The Queen could feel the stone-induced fog clearing from her mind, freeing her senses once again to perceive the woody sights and scents of the ancient forest. The chill of Sanamasa stung her nostrils when it brought the fresh smell of earth, the pungent aroma of old leaves, and the faint sweetness of a last bud, left to decay on the branch. The animals living here were busy foraging their final meal of the day, their scratchings and chitterings resounding in the still air.

Though she had not admitted it in the Elementals' company, Argent's tale of the new vortex had unnerved her. If it was indeed some sign of fell power at work, she would have to master all other aspects of Wood if she were to assist in defeating the mysterious force. Her thoughts dwelt for a moment on the assumption that it would come to a conflict. If history was any indicator, it was a valid worry.

Her path took her beside a tall kaytam tree. Its black wood was commonly used throughout Kertonia, for both construction and furnishings. Her new Wood sense had perceived its protective, or warding, properties even inside the Palace. She held out her staff, appreciating its limitations for the first time. It had been a happy chance, finding the shattered durmak branch that made it. She had exercised its health-giving nature on several occasions but only now, when the need for other Wood powers was clear, did she realise its restrictions. Those other powers would doubtless be imbued in other species and varieties. Kaytam was but the closest example of many.

The Queen approached her new home. The lowered branch of the entrance walkway stretched up into the main area of Huramapon. The kayketral had offered her this branch as the solution to the problem of access. Of course! What one tree did, others could repeat! She had no need to wait for lightning strikes or old age before she could collect the forest's bounty. She had only to ask. She turned, excitement hurrying her steps as she retraced her path to the kaytam she had passed moments earlier. Standing before the venerable native of Timakaya she sent out a silent mental request. *I have need of your protective force. Help me.*

Nothing happened.

Was the tree too old to hear her? Or too young to shed a branch in the way Huramapon had? But no. As her doubts crept up on her, the tree creaked as if bent by a fierce wind. On the opposite side from the path, a small branch fell. Knocking off the few remaining brown shreds of leaves as it descended, it whispered to the forest floor, landing with a dull thump in a deep pile of leaf litter. The Queen walked over to the spot. The branch was a little longer than her staff, but narrower. About the thickness of her wrist. She hefted it. It felt heavy, but not enough to prevent her carrying it. Returning to the path, she made her way back to Huramapon.

White durmak for health, and kaytam — blackwood — for protection. What else? There had been a hint of something on her return to Huramapon. Another quiet voice from the forest that wanted to help her with her task. Was that the general search for wood powers, or the particular work of carrying her latest acquisition? A chime, clear as a bell, sounded in her head at the thought of carrying. For the second time, she retraced her steps, the knell in her mind growing more distinct with each one. At the foot of a young memhomak tree, another branch lay waiting for her. She sent out her gratitude to the memhomak. When mature, it had the thickest trunk in the forest and easily bore the burden of its own heavy branches. Beneath silver-grey bark, its wood had a russet shade, almost orange.

With no more signals making themselves known in this part of Timakaya, the Queen set off in the opposite direction. Without a clear idea of how many different Wood powers there were to discover, she had to keep going. Trusting that Timakaya would let her know when the quest was done. Each tree she passed had something to impart. She felt the warmth of familiar healing. She sensed protection, now apparent in other species related to the kaytam, although that was still by far the strongest. The whole forest was connected in some way, each tree aware of the others; each playing its part in this vast organism. Did the forests communicate too, between themselves, or was it only possible within a single extent of woodland? The answer came immediately and unbidden, as she sensed a message relayed from ancient Besakaya — the largest forest in the land.

Did the trees all communicate equally? Or, in the same way kaytam was the principle protector but was supported by lesser species, was there a King of Communication? *Over here!* came the reply. A willowy ponektu made itself known to her, the clarity of its woody message slicing through her mind with frightening precision. As if embarrassed at its success, where before it had always had to shout to make itself noticed, the ponektu reduced the stridence of its call. A slim, elegant branch bent towards the Queen. With an almost imperceptible snap, it fell into her outstretched hand, still warm, and still echoing the message of its parent. Its creamy-yellow wood was the lightest she had so far encountered. The ponektu quieted itself to allow her Wood sense to catch other messages.

She walked on, the late evening sun dropping towards night. Pera-bul and Kedu-bul were already riding the horizon, shining bright silver in the pale pink sky. She began to wonder if she had unknowingly reached the end of her quest, when she received a hint of another kind of power. Almost lost in the plethora of other growths, this was a pure message of growth itself. A tree that embodied the lifeforce of wood, and other growing things. She did not recognise it, but recognition was unnecessary — the tree knew who it was: a kaykaste. The Queen smiled at the thought that Petani would have some competition if she were able to master this aspect of Wood lore. She was not at all surprised to see that its wood had a distinct green tinge.

At the instant she collected the kaykaste's offered branch, a darker power made itself known. Now matched by the darkness of the forest, as the sun finally slipped from sight, this was a kayati. Where kaytam provided woody defence, this mighty kayati embodied the forces of attack. She laughed, the sudden sound unnaturally loud in the quietening gloaming of the forest. It should have been so obvious. For it was this wood her Palace artisans used in the shafts of spears and arrows, and in the sharpened pilings that protected against attacking forces on kudo-back. The young wood was favoured by her fletchers. While still bright red in colour it was easier to work into perfectly straight flights. With age, it faded to a more muted crimson. She took a step back, half expecting the tree to launch its branch at her like a weapon. The familiar blue glow of the night-time forest transmitted amusement at her thought as the heavy kayati branch landed at her feet, before dipping almost to blackness. A silent but unmistakable signal that her search had come to an end.

The Queen made her way back to Huramapon. Although burdened with her collection of branches, the walk seemed to pass more quickly. When Huramapon came into view, she saw that ukba beetles had lined its walkway and the railings of her verandah. Their chitinous chirruping echoed around Huramapon but their glowing bodies provided ample light for her to pick her way along the walkway. She had not wanted to bring fire into the forest, but had been concerned she would be unable to move around safely after nightfall. Silly. She should have known Timakaya would provide. She set the branches down and took a seat on a bench beside them. Now what? If she were to have ready access to the six powers, she would need to fashion a staff from the wood of her original combined with the five new samples here on the floor. In comparison, sealing the shattered ends of her lightning-struck durmak shaft seemed child's play.

She focused her mind on the task. The forest — her new home — would not have provided this bounty if there was no way for her to use it. She closed her eyes in concentration, visualising the colours of the six woods intertwined intricately along the length of a new shaft. Holding this image in her mind, she took up her staff, planted its heel on the deck and held it upright. She reached for the first new wood, but a sudden shock of movement almost made her drop the staff again. The sinewy branch of the ponektu wrapped itself around the rod in a helical shape, seeming to embed itself in the surface. The wood warmed under her grip. The Queen adjusted her hold to avoid trapping her hand beneath the snaking ponektu.

Taking their lead from the first, the remaining branches moved as one, twisting up the length of her white staff like a plait in the hair of an old woman. Within moments, the process was complete. She passed the rod from one hand to the other, examining it closely. She could not tell where one wood began and another ended, save for the striations of different colours that decorated the surface. She hefted it. Incredibly it did not feel any heavier. Then she remembered that one of its parts came from the memhomak tree, most skilled in bearing its own weight. Its carrying power must make the shaft lighter than it would naturally be.

The Queen levered herself to her feet, the sudden movement causing the ukba to fly from the railings in a blaze of incandescence before settling back into their places. Despite being now fashioned from six different woods — some commonplace and others hitherto unknown — the staff felt familiar. It belonged in her hand. She remembered once again the folklore of her childhood. She had named her new home, now this magical artefact demanded a name too. She opened her mind to the muted song of all the strands that comprised her staff. Of course! The name came to her with such a rush of recognition it made tears spring in her eyes. Enkaysak.

Chapter 5

the palace of the black queen
12th day of sen'sanamasa, 966

Elaine stretched her arms around her lover and snuggled closer against his back.

'Ow.'

'Sorry, is that still sore?' she said, sliding away and sitting up in bed.

Their fire was out and the room had reverted to the damp chill of a Sanamasan night. She pulled the covers up around her neck.

'Yes.'

'I could fetch some salve from the Keeper? He's bound to have something.'

He sat up beside her. 'Don't bother.'

She held up her hands, pulled back the covers and stepped out of bed.

'Sorry,' he said. 'What I meant was, it's not all that bad. Not like you to lose control though. Scared me.'

Elaine felt the colour rising in her cheeks, their heat more noticeable in the cold air. The political debate of the previous evening had quickly escalated into a full-blown argument. Their first.

'I brought us a snack,' Jann had said, returning to their chambers with a tray. 'Looks like cook and the rest of the refectory staff haven't adjusted yet to having fewer people here. There was loads left!'

'I saw another dozen setting off this afternoon,' Elaine had replied. 'Madness.'

Jann set the tray down on a small table. 'Is it? Up to them where they live, surely?'

'They live here. They chose to live here. And before that, they chose to *come* here — to find a new life.'

'Maybe it hasn't worked out the way they hoped?'

'Didn't give it much of a chance to "work out" did

they? Some of those who left earlier today were on our ship. We haven't even been here a year yet.'

'You want any of this?' Jann asked, holding up an empty plate.

'I don't feel much like eating right now.'

'Suit yourself. I can eat for both of us.'

A wisp of smoke curled from Elaine's palm at the memory — an echo of her reaction to his comment. His sense of humour was one of the things she loved most about him, but sometimes his misplaced flippancy was more annoying that amusing.

'Don't you care?' she had asked, her voice cracking with a sudden blaze of emotion. 'Our society is fracturing in front of your face and all you can think about is filling your belly?'

'Starving myself isn't going to help the politics,' he said with a shrug.

Tiny flames licked across her smoking palms. 'Damn it! You told me your memory is back to normal now! But even if it wasn't, you've been here long enough to see how finely balanced things are. Istania and Kertonia have been at loggerheads for as long as anyone can remember. Beyond living memory, actually. For as long as records have been kept! More than three hundred years.'

'I know,' he replied, taking a bite from his loaded plate and chewing with an open mouth while he spoke. 'Longer than that, even. It was me who brought back the story from Tenfir Abarad, in case you've forgotten? The original leaders of these realms had been fighting long before they travelled south.'

'Well then! You think throwing a Batu'n "separatist state" into that volatile mix is a good idea?'

'Doesn't really matter what I think though, does it? It'll happen anyway.'

'We're Elementals!' The flames in her hands burned brightly now, sparking reflections from her topaz-studded bracelets. 'We're supposed to lead — not shrug our shoulders and let things go their own sweet way!'

Jann looked guilty. She could have sworn he had been on the verge of a second shrug but stopped himself in response to her words. 'Earth people are not as argumentative as Berikatanyans,' he said. 'I'm sure you're overthinking it. It'll sort itself out in the end.'

'For Baka's sake!' She had thrown up her hands in an explosion of temper at that moment, forgetting her power was already at flashpoint. The Fire flared across the room and caught Jann full on the chest.

An uneasy peace had descended and they spent an uncomfortable night in silence. Now that angry, red burn stared her in the face, giving mute testimony to her loss of control.

He caught her gaze and shivered, pulling the covers gingerly over his muscled, reddened pectorals. 'Cold in here! Can't you do something about it?'

He was grinning but she had the distinct impression he had not yet entirely forgiven her. 'You're over your fear of my Elemental power then? Baka's Fire is about more than making your life more comfortable Jann Argent. Heating your bath water; warming your bedchamber. You'll be asking me to take the chill off your slippers next.'

'Well, since you mention it...'

She punched his shoulder, but quickly relented and sent a wave of power into the room, dispelling the chill instantly.

'That's better. I don't know how the Queen will survive in the forest. It's bad enough in here. Must be ten degrees colder out there.'

'She'll manage. I'm glad she's gone.'

'You never really got on with her, did you?'

'She made me uneasy. So cold and aloof. I could never explain it until we found out she is Kayshirin.'

'What difference does that make?'

'Think about it.' She stared at him, but he remained clueless. 'Fire and Wood? A literally combustible combination.'

'Seriously? You were worried about setting her alight? Mind you,' he mused, rubbing his sore skin, 'this is bad enough, and I'm not even made of wood!'

'Part of you is,' she observed with a smile. 'Sometimes.'

the palace of the black queen
12th day of sen'sanamasa, 966

'The Palace feels different without the Queen.'

Claire Yamani slid along the refectory settle to make room for Kyle. The soon-to-be-Water Wizard put down her overflowing plate and took the offered seat. 'You think so?' she said, taking her first bite. 'I hadn't really noticed. It's not been much more than a day.'

'I'm going to pay her a visit tomorrow. See how she's getting on.'

'In the Forest?'

'Well, yes. She said she wouldn't be coming back to the Palace. I guess if there was an emergency or something, but now that her Wood powers are on the up, she hates being here. You coming with?'

Kyle stopped with a sunyok-full of vegetables halfway to her mouth. 'No. I don't think so. Not unless you need the company. I have a meeting with Gadys Kepatakan. More inauguration arrangements. I'll be glad when it's all over!'

Claire knew this was only a convenient excuse. 'You're avoiding her really aren't you?'

Kyle shrugged. 'I guess. I've never been very good at hiding my true feelings. She's made no secret of her views on Pennatanah. To be honest, for me, it's a good thing she's moved out.'

'You've made up your mind then? You're leaving?'

'Just as soon as I'm properly Water Wizard, yes. Don't tell her!'

'Of course I won't.'

'Are you staying here? I thought you said it would make things easier for you to be that much closer to Court?'

'It would certainly shorten my trips to see the Keeper, but I'm pretty sure I've exhausted the lore in his records now. Any new ways of using Air will have to come from me. Returning to the catacombs would be more of a social visit. I like the old man.'

'Me too. So what's stopping you?'

Claire switched her dinner plate for a bowl of dessert. The pale blue sweetsauce covering the buwan dumpling had cooled and congealed into a thin skin. Her favourite part. The noise of the dinner service waned as Palace people finished their meals and left for their evening activities.

'Loyalty, I suppose, like I said yesterday. Ru'ita has been good to me.'

'Up to you. You've spent more time with her than I have. I don't feel any tie to this place. But I do feel a kind of pull to Pennatanah.'

'The Pennatanah Pull?' Claire grinned.

They both laughed.

'Beats the "Pennatanah Problem",' Kyle said, 'which is what it's usually called. Aren't we supposed to be meeting about that tomorrow?'

'Yes. Elaine and Jann arranged it. I don't know what there is to say. We don't know any more about it now than we did the last time we discussed it. But I guess it can't hurt. Especially if you're serious about moving there.'

'You might learn something that helps you make up your mind, too.'

'Maybe.'

'Come on! Come with me!'

Her enthusiasm was infectious, and Claire enjoyed her company, but the Palace had always felt like home. Maybe it was something as simple as having the portrait of her father hanging in the main hall. A small but significant reminder of her family history here.

'It'll be fun!' the young Water Wizard went on. 'All those younger Earthers. No language problems. Proper heating. Or stay here with the old, and the cold.'

'I'll sleep on it,' Claire agreed. 'You said you weren't going until after your ceremony anyway. There's no rush for me to decide.'

'They might run out of space!'

Claire stood, stacking her bowl atop her plate. 'You joke, but the number of people I see heading out — they must have run out of space already!'

the palace of the black queen
13th day of sen'sanamasa, 966

The next morning Claire had to scratch the ice off her window before she could see out over the expanse of Timakaya. The quiet forest shone and sparkled under heavy white blanket of frost. She hoped the Queen had found a way to stay warm in her new home. She watched, hoping for sight of a majestic ghantu setting off for a last hunt before settling in for a long day's nap. A flurry of ice crystals exploded from the left of the forest. She shielded her eyes against the early morning sun and peered at the site of the disturbance. A gap had appeared in the treeline, as if one or two of the uppermost branches had been ripped out. Around the edges of the hole, the ice had settled back into a perfect spiral pattern.

She breakfasted alone, wrapped in a heavy woollen jacket and wearing a pair of fingerless gloves against the cold. The gloves had been a gift from the Queen, knitted by the Palace seamstresses from a rare wool. Claire could not even remember the unfamiliar animal's name. The toasty warmth of her hands as she ate was a poignant reminder of her relationship with the monarch-turned-Wood mage. She could not rid herself of the feelings of regret and guilt that plagued her whenever she thought of joining Kyle at the Earther base.

She met up with the Water Wizard on her way to the morning's meeting.

'Made your decision yet?'

'Don't!' Claire said, holding a finger to her lips. 'Let's not talk about it now. Not until we know how the others feel.'

'We know that already,' Kyle said with a shrug. 'At least, where the Fire Witch is concerned. She will toast you alive as soon as she finds out you're coming with me.'

'I never said—'

'You didn't need to. It's written all over your face. Soon as I asked, you looked guilty enough to have murdered someone.'

The others were waiting for them. Jann and Elaine were now sharing sumptuous quarters in the same wing of the Palace, and always arrived together. A fifth attendee sat with them at the Queen's council table.

'Good morning,' Claire said, as Kyle closed the door behind them. 'Who—?'

The man stood and walked over to shake her hand. Whoever he was, he had spent enough time among Earthers to be familiar with that gesture, at least.

'Good day to you Kema'satu,' he said with a slight bow. 'My name is Seteh Seruganteh. Gadys Kepatakan sends her apologies.' He nodded towards Kyle. 'She is busy with preparations for your inauguration, Kema'satu, and has asked me to attend in her stead.'

Claire glanced at the Fire Witch, who gave a slight shrug. 'It is commendable that we are able to maintain a Palace presence at these meetings,' Elaine said, 'now that the Queen is no longer attending.'

A shadow passed across Seruganteh's face at mention of the Queen. It was gone so quickly she could not be sure it had been there at all. She pulled out chairs for herself and Kyle, and took a seat at the table.

'Have you seen any more of those unusual vortices?' she asked, turning to Jann. 'I may have caught sight of one this morning, over the forest.'

She described the gap in the trees and the strange scarring of the frost covering.

'One must trust her Majesty has found a place of safety out there beyond the security of the Palace,' Seruganteh observed. 'We do not have sufficient forces to mount a guard around her, wherever she is.'

'I'm sure the last thing she needs is a Palace guard,' the Fire Witch replied. 'She is more than capable of looking after herself, believe me.'

Again a brief but distinct reaction flitted across the deputy steward's face at her words. A quick glance around the table suggested Claire was the only one to have noticed. She could not tell if the strange expression was connected with the Queen, or a dislike of the Witch. Either way, if the man could not control himself more readily than this, they were in for interesting times at these council meetings.

'Anyway,' Claire said, anxious to get the meeting over with and return to more interesting pursuits, 'you called this meeting. What are we talking about?'

'News from Pennatanah is that they have a new leader,' said Elaine, after favouring Claire with a hard stare.

'Good for them,' Kyle said. 'Anyone we know?'

'Silvia Alvarez? I don't know the name,' Elaine replied.

'I only remember Waters,' said Jann.

'Yeah, I remember her too,' Kyle agreed. 'Never heard of Alvarez. Why did they need a new leader?'

'Oduya died.'

'He was quite young, wasn't he? I thought?' Claire said.

'Supposed to be a heart-attack,' Elaine said, 'but it sounds fishy to me.'

'Fishy?' Seruganteh asked.

Elaine explained the term. 'He had no history of heart disease, as far as we know.'

'So what are you saying?' Kyle asked. 'That there's some suspicion of murder? That implicates Alvarez? Some

Court connection?'

'Hard to be sure,' Elaine said. 'Let's just say I wouldn't be sharing any state secrets with her. At least, not until we're certain where her loyalties lie.'

'Well they won't lie with the Black Palace, will they?' Kyle replied. 'Whether or not she's in the Jester's pocket. She's more likely to favour the idea of Earther separatism. Why put herself forward as leader, otherwise?'

'And if that's true, she may be just as much of a threat to the peace as if she were a Court spy!' Elaine smacked both hands on the table, her sudden anger making small wisps of woodsmoke curl up between her fingers.

pennatanah
13th day of sen'sanamasa, 966

Patrick sat on his rock, a glass of fruit juice in one hand. He watched the sun falling inexorably towards the sea and wished his glass was filled with beer. Almost a month had passed since his decision to remain with the other colonists at Pennatanah. The days had flown by. During the hours of daylight he occupied himself with whatever tasks the leadership group threw his way, happy for the excuse to keep his mind off his nemesis for a while. After sundown, and in the privacy of his own quarters, he summoned what remained of his courage and returned to it. To The Book. It had, eventually, revealed its name: The Tang Jikos. Reading, and rereading the glyphs, confirming his interpretations of the patterns, and chancing the occasional practice when he thought it was safe, Patrick grew more certain of his command of the Pattern Juggler's power. And more certain of its potential to wreak utter havoc.

As that month had worn on, their early discussions about a proper separate state, independent of Queen or absent King, crystallised into a coherent and recognisable form. They had a plan. Still a young and perhaps only half-grown plan, but a plan nevertheless.

A movement on the edge of the small base caught his attention. Though it was late evening, and almost dark, another contingent of refugees had arrived seeking what Pennatanah offered. Word had spread quickly. Remarkable, in a world where communication over any distance was uncertain, sporadic, and slow. He took a mouthful of his juice, savouring the sour taste.

'Don't jump!'

The man's voice echoed around the clifftops before being drowned by the crashing of a wave below. Piers Tremaine picked his way across the rocks in his direction.

Patrick laughed. 'Always the joker,' he said.

'But never the Jester,' Piers replied.

'I should hope not. That's one refugee we would not accept! Is this a visit, or have you come to join us?'

'If there's still room, I've come to stay.'

'I'm sure we can find space for the Stone Mage. Or if not, a man of your abilities should be able to make somewhere for himself.'

'It's not just me! I struck up a conversation with a couple on the journey. Turns out they have low-level powers too.'

'Not Stone?'

'Well, no. I'm still the only Stone Mage as far as I know. He's an Earth adept though, and she's Fire, so between them...' he grinned, his teeth flashing pale in the late evening light. 'Are you coming in? Sun's almost down. This time of year, it won't be long before it's too cold to be outside anyway.'

'I normally stay out until the malamajan starts. Or come out early, before dawn. But you must be hungry after your trip.' He stood, brushing rock dust from his leggings. 'We should share a meal and catch up. Where have you travelled from, the Palace?'

Piers recapped his recent travels as they crossed the clifftops and headed in to the canteen. The large space doing double duty as an induction centre, this time for travellers in the opposite direction.

pennatanah
13th day of sen'sanamasa, 966

Piers took a moment to drink in the atmosphere. The canteen was full, and not only with the evening meal service. A queue of new arrivals lined one wall, waiting patiently to be allocated accommodation. He smiled. He had not expected it to affect him like this, but it already felt as though he had come home.

'I should probably join that queue,' he said.

'Nah,' Patrick took his arm and steered him towards the servery, 'there's time enough for that tomorrow. Stay with me for tonight. We can have a proper catch up.'

They filled plates and found seats. One or two familiar faces, fellow passengers on the Intrepid, waved or shouted a cheery hello.

Piers poured a glass of water and took a deep draught. 'There isn't much I like about this time of year,' he said, holding up the half-empty glass, 'but at least the water is cold. Probably the only thing I miss from Earth.' He looked around the canteen, searching for anyone else he recognised. There was hardly a spare seat in the place. 'I can't believe there are so many people here.'

'I think we struck a chord with the idea of a proper Earther settlement,' Patrick nodded. 'Or a nerve. It looks like there was always a low-key dissatisfaction with local life. It never had an outlet until now.'

They fell silent for a time, enjoying their meal and the buzz in the hall.

'Any idea what you're going to do, now that you're here?' Patrick asked.

'Not really. More of the same seems to be the obvious choice.'

'The same?'

'I did some building when I lived in Duska Batsirang. I was an architect back on Earth, did I mention that? Can't remember. Quite a good one, though I say it myself. It was a while ago now, but I still have the tools.' He tapped his head with one finger, grinning. 'And these bring a few new tricks to the party too,' he added, waving his hands. 'You think they'll come in handy?'

Patrick laughed. 'I think Alvarez will bite them off. She's desperate for new housing.' He waved his hand around the room. 'As you may have noticed.'

'So where is everyone living right now?'

'We've been lucky so far. We haven't yet reached the numbers that arrived on the Dauntless. Of course a lot of them never left, but a few hundred did. So we have all the bunks and settles from their original induction days. After that we'll be filling spare rooms, spare beds and couches in existing homes. You staying with me might be more than temporary, if I'm honest.'

'There's an incentive to get building if ever there was one!'

'Always the joker!'

A dark-haired woman stopped as she passed the table. 'Hello Patrick. Who's your new friend?' She held out her hand. 'I'm Silvia Alvarez,' she said, smiling down at him. 'Colony Exec. As of seven days ago, that is. So you might say I'm "new" too, in a way.'

He stood, and took her hand. 'Piers Tremaine. Pleased to meet you.'

Alvarez frowned. An expression that strangely made her look even more attractive. 'I'm sure I know that name,' she said, squeezing his hand.

Piers hesitated. What the hell? It was no secret. 'I arrived today from Kertonia,' he said. 'I've been staying there since we defeated Douglas Muir. I'm the Stone Mage.'

Alvarez' eyes almost popped out of her head. 'Of course! Wow — doubly welcome then!' She gripped his hand tighter, shook again, and released her hold on him. 'We can really use your help.'

Patrick laughed. 'We were just talking about that.'

'Have you sorted yourself somewhere to stay?'

'Done,' Patrick said. 'He's staying with me for now.'

'Excellent! Well, rest up tonight. Come and find me tomorrow. We can talk about setting you to work. If you've no other plans?'

Piers smiled. 'I'll find you first thing.'

the palace of the black queen
13th day of sen'sanamasa, 966

The charred handprints, grey against the black of the table top, kept attracting Jann's eye. He rubbed absently at his sore chest, which itched in sympathy with the wood. He must learn to think before opening his mouth in future! The Fire Witch had a legendary temper, matched only by the fierceness of her Elemental power. When the two combined — a grin stole across his face at the irony — there were bound to be fireworks.

The argument that had instigated those marks waxed and waned for the rest of the morning and on past noon. They were no further forward, and now his stomach was contributing to the debate. Its gurgling must surely be audible to the others. Perhaps he could find a small gate in the room and slip silently away for a bite of lunch?

'Are we getting anywhere with this?' Claire was saying. 'I had hoped it would be a short meeting and I could get back to—'

'Oh! So sorry to have kept you!' Elaine interrupted, her eyes flashing.

Jann glanced at her hands, expecting to see more telltale expressions of Fire power mirroring her ire. There were none. So far.

'What important business are we interrupting, Claire? Please tell.'

The young Air Mage coloured under the Witch's trademark stare. 'I—'

'Stop this,' Jann said, almost surprised to hear his own voice. 'It serves no purpose to argue amongst ourselves. It's bad enough to be debating divisions among the people. At least let's be united in here. We're all on the same side for Baka's sake.'

His choice of the Fire God was deliberate, though he knew Elaine did not like him using the God's name "in vain." But this was neither accidental nor Elemental blasphemy. If you believed in the Elemental Gods, then you must also believe they would not appreciate their mortals being at each other's throats.

At his words, the anger left Elaine's eyes, and the colour subsided in Claire's cheeks. 'It's not so long ago I was a prisoner,' he said, reminding them of his time on Phobos. 'It was like a crucible, that place. The divisions and conflicts of the outside world distilled into a smaller space. Almost like a law of physics that arguments would burn hotter, and have much greater effect on the people concerned.' He looked each of them in the eye. 'And that is exactly how it played out.'

'What does that have to do with now?' Kyle asked. 'Genuine question. I'm not trying to be argumentative.'

'Some people don't have to try,' Claire said with a wink.

'We're seeing this society fracture — even further than it was before. Divisions only lead to conflict. We need to come together. Joint ventures lead to healthier, happier communities. With the King dead, we should be healing wounds, not sticking the knife in deeper.'

'Fine words, Gatekeeper,' Seruganteh said, 'but how do you propose to make them real?'

The enigmatic man had been silent for most of the meeting, apparently content only to observe. Perhaps since their discussion centred on Pennatanah and the Batu'n, he had no interest in the topic. Jann could imagine him saying *"Palace stewards concern themselves with Palace matters. All else is for others."*

'Like I said, it would be a start if we could stop bickering. And for myself, I should like to visit Pennatanah. Try to begin the process of building bridges.'

Elaine regarded him for a moment, eyes moist and a small smile lifting the corners of her mouth. 'You want to see Patrick.'

Jann nodded. 'His decision to stay at the base was very sudden. I never had chance to speak with him about it. I'd at least like to understand his motivation.'

'Fear,' Elaine said. 'I can tell you now, without any doubt. Fear is his motivation. He has never come to terms with his power.'

'Well, you might think there is no doubt, but I should like to hear it from him. He may have an entirely different reason.'

Elaine's eyes began to smoulder once more. 'Whatever his "reasons," he is an Elemental, that is the beginning and end of it. Not just an Elemental, but a third level Elemental. The *only* one. You may wish for peace, Jann, and I cannot argue with that. It is a laudable aim. But at the same time we should prepare for war. And in the event it cannot be avoided, we must at least be certain the fearful power of the Juggler will not be wielded against us.'

pennatanah
13th day of sen'sanamasa, 966

'Plenty of room here,' Piers said, shielding his eyes against the low sun, 'and a sea view!'

The two men had left the canteen soon after lunch. The hall had become stifling with the body heat of a couple of hundred diners, queuing refugees, and a larger than usual contingent of tabbuki. The narcotic users spread themselves across half a dozen tables in one corner to while away the rest of their day in a drug-fuelled stupor. In contrast, the chill air of a Sanamasan afternoon, laden with salt spray from the ocean, had soon revived their senses. The walk to the cliff top made the blood pump in Piers' ears. He was already in love with this place.

'Look at all this land,' he continued, with an expansive wave of his hand. 'And it's all rock too. Perfect for building. I don't need to fetch any material. It's all right here, under our feet.'

Out in the bay, the late sun glinted off the hull of the downed Valiant, flashing and sparkling like a strange petrified sea creature.

'Alvarez will love you,' Patrick said, but Piers hardly heard him. His attention was fixed on the sea below.

'You know, we could build a harbour here too.'

'Eh? No-one's ever mentioned that before.'

'I'd have to check what the seabed is like, but if it's similar to what Petani and I worked with at the Valley—'

'Different coast,' Patrick said. 'What do we need a harbour for, anyway? We don't have any ships.'

'Neither does the Queen, yet. Didn't stop her wanting a harbour. Who knows what's out there?' He stared once again across the frigid ocean. Rolling waves crashed against the Valiant and sent gouts of spray into the air. 'No-one has ever suggested leaving this place?'

'Not that I know of. But you're right, there's nothing special about it. It's where we landed, but I don't suppose anyone has a sentimental attachment to it.'

'Think longer term,' Piers said, turning his back on the water. 'What happens if our plans for a permanent home don't go down too well with the locals?'

'Funny you should mention that. There's already been some unrest. Just minor skirmishes really — people have reported arguments breaking out in villages they passed through; the odd raid on overnight camps. Maybe it's a sign of things to come, who knows?'

'See? That's how it starts. Fast forward a few months. We know what these Berikatanyans are like. They've been warring between themselves for centuries. Now here we come, giving them a new target. They're just as likely to join forces against us as they are to carry on fighting each other. More likely, if anything.'

'So how does a harbour help?'

'It doesn't. Not on its own. But if we have ships, we have an escape route, if it comes to that.'

'You think it will?'

'Listen, I barely got away from the Jester and mad Muir with my life. And before that I was nearly beaten to death by my own village. Nothing about this place surprises me anymore.'

'But houses first, right?'

'Well, yes. Otherwise we'll have riots with our own people to contend with, let alone war with the Berikatanyans!'

Chapter 6

**pennatanah
13th day of sen'sanamasa, 966**

Felice Waters watched Tremaine and Glass crossing the rocky cliff top. They ambled towards her, talking animatedly. Their faces reflected the deep red of the late afternoon sun, bouncing off the squat, white buildings of Pennatanah base.

'Alvarez is looking for you, Tremaine,' she called.

'You should mention that harbour idea,' Glass said. 'See what she thinks.'

'Come with me. We can go straight on to dinner after.'

'Harbour?' said Felice. 'We're getting a harbour?'

'Just an idea,' Tremaine grinned. 'Might be useful if we need to make a hasty retreat.'

Felice looked at him. She remembered his records. Berkeley graduate. Award winner. Hand-picked for the colony program. Presumably there was some intelligence in there somewhere. She moved her gaze pointedly from him to the Dauntless. The ship hovered at the mooring post surrounded by the electric blue glow of its gravnull field.

'I think that will go faster than any seafaring vessel,' she said.

'Oh,' Tremaine said, colouring slightly. 'Does it still work?'

Felice laughed. 'It's still in the air, isn't it?'

She led them through the canteen hall to Alvarez' office. 'I guess there would be some prep work to do if we intended to fly her again, but yeah, she still works. Good enough to get across the planet anyway.'

'Still gonna mention it,' Tremaine said, sticking out his jaw. 'Always good to have options.'

The line of refugees awaiting allocation of living quarters had not shortened during the morning. Felice scratched her head. 'I have no idea where we're gonna put the rest of these.'

'I guess that's what Alvarez wants to talk about,' Glass said.

Felice knocked on the Exec's door and entered without waiting for permission. Oduya had commanded deference from everyone without breaking sweat. In her opinion, Alvarez had yet to earn that level of respect. Especially since she spent most of her time behind her desk when there was work to be done. Work she seemed only too happy to leave to others.

'I found them,' she said.

'Ah, good. Come in, come in,' Alvarez said. 'How's the queue?'

'No shorter. And Cabrera is due a break.'

'Could you—'

'I just got done with my own queue. I haven't eaten since breakfast. If I don't shower soon people gonna start keeling over when I walk past.'

'I guess that leaves me, then.'

'Guess it does.'

'Have you given any further thought to—?'

'The answer's still no.'

Alvarez had approached her earlier in the day with a proposal. The work load was overwhelming, she said, and she needed a more permanent deputy. Was Felice interested? Felice most definitely was not. Who would be? Do her own work, and the Exec's work — most of it — while said Exec sat with her feet up? No thanks.

'Do we at least have some good news on the building front?' Alvarez asked, turning to Tremaine.

'I haven't started yet, if that's what you mean,' Tremaine grinned.

'This isn't a joke!' Alvarez said, moving round from behind her desk.

Felice knew the explosion of attitude came from being forced to do some work, rather than anything Tremaine had said. In her place, Felice would not have risked upsetting the one man who could magically — literally! — solve their housing crisis in a few days. If the tales were to be believed.

'Sorry,' Tremaine's grin faded. 'Yes, there is some good news. There's plenty of space, and material, between here and the cliffs. I can start tomorrow. First thing.'

'Fine.' She regarded him thoughtfully. 'Know anyone who would be interested in a deputy leader's badge?'

Tremaine hesitated. He glanced at Glass, Felice, and back to Alvarez. 'Me, you mean?'

'Why not?'

'Er...no. Thanks, but no. Not leadership material, me. I'm enough of a target as it is. A lot of Earthers are still... sceptical... when it comes to Elemental magic.'

'Fair enough. Worth a try. If you think of anyone...'

'Cabrera's break?' Felice said.

Alvarez scowled. 'OK, OK, I'm coming.'

Glass gave Tremaine a nudge.

'Oh, yes,' Tremaine said with a start, 'I'll tag along with you for a while if I may? I have another idea.'

pennatanah
14th day of sen'sanamasa, 966

Silvia Alvarez dawdled over her breakfast. Another long day stretched ahead, and she was in no rush for it to start.

Repeated conversations with Waters echoed around her mind on a loop. She had some sympathy for the ex-cop. Silvia had always seen herself as a second-in-command too. Happier being one step behind someone else. Yet here she was, taking on the leader's job. What had she been thinking? The question answered itself: Oduya had trusted her. She would have done anything for the charismatic commodore, including stepping into his shoes.

If she could not persuade Waters to carry on as her

deputy, she would need to be careful choosing an alternative. Oduya always suspected the base had been infiltrated by one or other of the royal houses. Probably both. If anyone displayed the kind of candlepower necessary for high level subterfuge, it would take time for her to develop the level of trust she had enjoyed with her much-missed colleague.

Tremaine's idea of a harbour intrigued her though. On one hand it was a bit of a distraction. There were more important — more *urgent* — things to think about. But it had merit. Or at least, it could do no harm. The man had some recent experience in the art of harbour-making — a strange skill to boast about to be sure — and it would keep him occupied. If his estimate of the building time for a hundred new apartment blocks was accurate, he would soon need something else to do. It sounded too good to be true, but she had no experience of working with magic. She had to take him at his word.

Waters took the seat opposite, her breakfast plate hardly holding enough to feed a small girl.

'You'll need more than that to get you through the day.'

'I used to think so. Back when I was a cop I was fuelled almost exclusively by donuts. I kinda miss them. But my waistline doesn't.'

'Keeping yourself trim for lover-girl, huh?'

'Don't knock it.'

'Oh, I wasn't. I should be jealous really, but I don't ride your flyer, and the choices here are...' She rolled her eyes.

Waters laughed.

Alvarez decided it was worth one more shot. 'Look, I don't want this to be a thing between us...'

Waters paused with a piece of sosij halfway to her mouth. The aroma of the local delicacy made Alvarez salivate despite having eaten. 'Then don't let it.'

'Can't I persuade you to hold on to the deputy's job for a little longer? I promise to keep looking for someone permanent, but I really need the help right now.'

The other woman examined her breakfast morsel closely. 'How much longer?'

'How quickly can I find a replacement? End of the month? If the influx stays at the current rate there should be someone suitable by then.'

Waters sighed. 'I guess it's worth sixteen days extra hassle if it makes you shut up about it.'

Alvarez rubbed her hands together, smiling broadly. 'Excellent. In that case, you can take over the building supervision. Tremaine said he would start first thing.'

They both glanced around the hall, at each other, and burst out laughing.

'Maybe his idea of "first thing" is different,' Waters said.

the palace of the black queen
14th day of sen'sanamasa, 966

'All I said was, I can understand how they feel.'

Kyle stood against the window, hardly daring to breathe. The tensions between the other two women had begun over lunch, simmered for most of the afternoon, and were now boiling over. Claire had become a close friend in the short time Kyle had known her, but she was doing herself no favours. Her attempts to justify the Pennatanah Problem faced mounting hostility from the Fire Witch. All her learning, and her position at the head of the Air Guild, had not improved her diplomacy skills. If anything they made her more opinionated and argumentative.

'And agree with those feelings, no doubt,' the Witch retorted. 'You should remember who your father was, and where your service now is, young lady.'

'How dare you! I've not forgotten my father or what he stood for. I've done my best with his legacy. You can't deny I've taken Air lore to new levels! I know he would be proud of me.'

'Pah!' the Fire Witch spat, her eyes blazing, 'Proud? Of a daughter who stands on the side of the Batu'n against her own people!'

'I said I *understand* them, not that I'm on their side!'

'I know what you said. And I know what you meant.'

Claire picked up the costume design she had been working on. 'I hadn't realised Fire power included mind reading!' she said, spinning on her heel. 'We can talk about this later Kyle,' she said, brandishing the parchment, 'I have to leave before I say something we'll all regret.'

'That's it, run away,' the Witch shouted after her. 'Blow hot, blow cold, wind girl!'

'I suppose that's what they call a *prevailing* wind,' she said, turning to face Kyle with a frown, 'blowing in the direction of greatest convenience.'

An awkward pause descended. Kyle could not think of a suitable reply, or indeed if she should reply at all. The Witch stalked around the room. She ran her finger idly over surfaces, and looked askance at ornaments and artefacts, before picking one up and examining it closely. The frown never left her face.

'What a grim place this is,' she said at length. 'The Black Palace! It is well named. Black by name and black by nature. All is dark, gloomy, cold. There is no life here!' She paused, a small, sad look replacing the frown. 'No home,' she added.

'It's the closest thing to home I've had since I arrived,' Kyle said, swallowing past the lump in her throat.

The Witch regarded her for a moment. 'You were not at Court for very long,' she said, 'and not in the best of circumstances. In good times, there was life there. Music, and laughter, and good food. All gone. Only that evil gnome left to pull his political strings.'

'Maybe we should carry on with the planning?' Kyle said. 'Unless you have something better to do? I imagine you have a lot on your plate, but now the Queen is off in the forest, and Claire has... left, I have no-one else to help with the ceremony. Though the gods surely know I would just as soon not have one at all.'

'Nonsense girl! It's not every day a new Elemental is anointed. There has to be some kind of celebration! Some pomp! Even in a place as bleak as this.'

She retook her seat at the table, and pulled over the parchment on which they had started trying to draw up a seating plan. 'You know,' the Witch said, all trace of her frown smoothed from her face, 'it's really a myth that Fire and Water don't get along all that well together. I always enjoyed dear Lautan's company, and I was very impressed how you coped with your brother's misdemeanours.'

Mention of her predecessor brought another muted pang of grief to Kyle's stomach. She turned away to hide the tears that started once more in her eyes. Damn it! Would she ever be rid of these feelings?

'You didn't shrink from the task, as a lesser person would,' the Witch continued. If she noticed Kyle's discomfort she gave no sign. 'I admire that. And you haven't spent the time since bemoaning his loss, or feeling sorry for yourself. I'm happy to help you prepare for your ceremony.'

'Thank you,' Kyle said, blotting her face on her sleeve and taking a seat to the Witch's left. She glanced at the seating plan. 'I must admit to a slight worry about holding it outdoors at this time of year.'

Elaine smiled for the first time since their meeting started. 'Don't concern yourself about that. I'm sure I'll be able to warm things up.'

pennatanah
14th day of sen'sanamasa, 966

'I've never shared my vigil until now,' Patrick said. 'Not sure how I feel about it, if I'm honest.'

'I can go, if you'd rather be alone?'

Piers made to stand but Patrick laid a restraining hand

on his arm. 'No, stay. Rest. You look exhausted. I just want to sit here for a while before we go for dinner. If that's OK?'

'If you're sure I'm not disturbing your... whatever it is you do out here.'

They sat together on a rock at the edge of the cliff overlooking Pennatanah Bay. The view thoroughly familiar to Patrick in one way, and yet not. The ocean, constantly in motion, never looked the same twice. The cloud cover waxed and waned. The seabirds flew in new patterns, caught fish in different places, shouted their haunting cries at each other at varying volumes. What did he do out here, exactly?

Patrick laughed. 'I can't even explain it to myself.'

The men fell silent. They had made incredible progress. They? Piers had done all the work, which explained his drained appearance. Slumped on the rock as though he had become part of it. A heavy irony, since he was the Stone Mage. And how he had wielded that power today.

'I've never seen houses like these before,' Patrick had observed, when Piers took a brief break for a cup of hot panklat and to recover his Elemental strength.

'They're based on the design I used back in Batsirang,' Piers said, 'with a minor variation to accommodate more dwellings per block. The villagers all thought it was pretty special too, until they decided it was the devil's work. Or whatever the local equivalent of the devil is.'

'I've switched the design up another way too,' he added, 'so I can make them from the materials to hand. The original required a lot more construction.'

'Pun not intended.'

'Yeah. No. I didn't have this level of control over the power then. And even if I had, I couldn't have used it like this. Not unless I worked under cover of darkness.'

'How do you mean?'

'Well here you are, watching me work. Watching buildings apparently form themselves from fluid rock and set into place as soon as they've taken shape. Can you imagine the reaction if the locals had seen anything like that? They took against me for something as simple as moving the chimney to a wall instead of having a central vent! Nothing magical about that, it's just common sense to you and me. If they'd seen what I'm doing here today they would all have had fits!'

After a day's work, Piers had created fifty of the one hundred houses Alvarez requested.

'I thought one more day would see it done,' Patrick said, breaking the silence. 'But looking at you now, I don't know whether you'd survive another day like this!'

Piers rubbed his eyes. 'Yeah. No. Takes it out of me. So much all at once.' He squinted at Patrick. 'I've been meaning to ask. You have some kind of power, don't you? Could you maybe help out a bit? Sorry, no offence. I don't know anything about it. Just wondered.'

Patrick's blood ran cold at the question. How could he explain? He gazed out into the bay. The drowned Valiant, washed by the freezing waters of Sanamasa, still stood as a memorial to his and Jann Argent's rescue of the few passengers they managed to pull from the submerged cabins and corridors. Until that moment, he had not appreciated how much he missed his friend, and all they had shared. That terrifying arrival had been only the first of their adventures together. He thought of their journeys to the Valley. Meeting the Pilgrim, and later for the Battle of the Blood Clones. Jann had helped him access his power for the first time, when he brought down the fey curtain of time. If the Gatekeeper had been sat here in place of the Stone Mage, there would be no need of explanation.

But Jann was not here. And that was his own doing. He should have more in common with Tremaine, anyway. Both Earther-born, both with higher Elemental powers. Both natural loners. Or as near as made no difference. Perhaps he could trust this young man after all.

'It's not... that is, yes. I do have power. Not sure I can explain it, or at least, why I'm reluctant to use it. It would help, for sure. But it can destroy just as easily as it can build.'

Piers regarded him with a thoughtful expression. 'Well, sure. I can tear stone down quicker than I can throw it up. But I'd have to want to pull it down. I don't think I could do it by accident.'

Patrick's gaze was drawn back to the glistening hull of the Valiant. The setting sun struck sparks of red and gold from its surface, almost blinding in their intensity.

'Lucky you,' he said.

huramapon
14th day of sen'sanamasa, 966

Blow hot, blow cold? The damned Witch had a nerve, accusing her of that. Bakara was the most volatile of all the Elementals. If anyone could blow hot it was the Fire Witch. Yet when she wanted to, she could flip to an attitude that would freeze the sun in the sky.

Claire stomped through the Palace corridors and out into the icy day. She glanced at the reddening clouds. Scant daylight remained, but enough for her to reach the Queen's new forest home. She drew her cloak more tightly around her chest and set off, her pace and her continued anger at the Fire Witch's words helping to keep her warm in the Sanamasan evening.

She passed beyond the treeline. The low sun threw long shadows onto the pathway, striking through the trees and highlighting dancing motes of dust in the crisp air. Claire shivered, increasing her pace even further, trying to generate more body heat. She reached the fork in the path which the Queen had mentioned, and took the left track, narrower and more overgrown than the alternative. The shadows in the forest deepened with each step, each passing moment. Ahead of her through the gloom, she saw an opening. Approaching the gap she stopped dead and let out a gasp. Utterly awestruck by the unexpected sight in front of her, breath clouding the frigid evening air, she stared at the Queen's new home.

A mighty tree of incredible age stretched skyward, overtopping its nearest neighbours by several metres. An evergreen, its uppermost branches appeared to be folded together, forming a perfect watertight shroud for everything below. A fallen branch — no, Claire looked more closely — not fallen. Still attached to the main trunk. The end nearest her lay beside the path, forming a natural stairway that led up into the main body of the tree. Branches there grew in unnaturally perfect horizontal lines. Evidence of the Queen's handiwork, no doubt. They had been set with boards and railings at their outermost parts. Closer to the central trunk a network of smaller, intertwined branches made walls that hid the inner areas of the home. The levels spiralled upward gently, revealing further rooms, walkways, and rails. Incredible to think only three days had passed since the Queen's last meeting in the Palace. All this had been achieved in that short time.

As daylight faded, small beads of bright white light began to dot the structure. They settled along the horizontal surfaces of rail and branch, illuminating the whole like the Christmas trees of her childhood. The glowing light gave the whole scene a magical, ethereal quality. With another gasp, she realised she had been holding her breath since the moment the tree house came into view.

'Hello Claire,' came the Queen's voice, echoing through the rapidly darkening forest. She stood at an opening in the second tier, looking down.

Claire waved. 'Hi! This is beautiful! How...?'

'Thank you. Welcome to Huramapon. That's not my name. The tree itself told me. And all this,' she waved a hand, 'the tree did most of the work. All I had to do was ask.'

'Remarkable. You look... radiant.'

'I can't tell you how much better I feel Claire,' the Queen said. 'I was never sick, exactly, while I lived in the Palace, but I have never felt this good in my whole life. It's like being young again.'

'Yes! Young! That's precisely it. Like a younger version of the Queen I knew before.'

She laughed, the soft, joyful sound bouncing off branch and trunk all around the now black forest floor.

'Come up,' the Queen called. 'I will meet you. The walkway is perfectly safe.'

Claire set foot gingerly on the enormous branch. Though the stairway had no guard rails at this level, she felt perfectly safe. The wood was wide enough for four people to walk abreast, and ukba beetles lined the edges, providing ample illumination. As she approached the first landing, Claire noticed the air becoming warmer. She stepped off the branch into an unexpected embrace from the Queen.

'I'm so glad you're here Claire,' she said. 'To be honest, I've been hoping for a chance to show the place off!'

'I'm not surprised. It's wonderful! And... warm!'

'I know! It's partly the tree, helped by a touch of Wood power.'

The Queen was not carrying her staff. The first time Claire had seen her without it since she first brought it back to the Palace.

'Where is your staff, Ru'ita?'

The Queen waved a hand dismissively. 'Oh, I don't need it for simple tasks like taking the chill out of the air,' she said with a smile. 'But that too is different now my dear. Wait 'til you see what I've done with it!'

She disappeared into another room and returned holding... was that it? What she held in her hand bore only a passing resemblance to the staff Claire remembered. Multiple coloured striations of different woods snaked along its length, each seeming to be one with the rest, and yet distinctive in its hue and grain. Even to Claire's eye, the staff glowed with power.

'What...? How...?'

The Queen laughed again. 'I'm not sure I understand it myself, if I'm honest. Timakaya offered me her riches and I imagined them all as one. This was the result.'

She held the staff out. Claire shrank back. 'No! I dare not! It is yours Ru'ita. The power is not mine to command.'

'You can do no harm Claire. I am offering it to you. Feel its energy.'

Tentatively, Claire reached out a hand and laid it on the smooth surface of the staff. It thrummed beneath her fingers. The feeling was similar to the shock she had experienced when working at the Forest Clearance Project in Besakaya, but also different. More subtle, more complex, and way, way more powerful.

She stared at the Queen, her eyes wide. 'Wow!'

'Yes! Even if Huramapon were not keeping me warm, the power of Enkaysak would be enough to sustain me. I sometimes wonder if I shall ever need to eat again!'

'Enkaysak?'

'That is how it wants to be known,' the Queen said. 'A name of power, similar to the appellations fighting men give to their blades. But in this case my weapon lives. It is quietly sentient. And it knows its own name. It means "the harmony of six".'

Claire leaned against the railing, disturbing two ukba. 'This is remarkable Ru'ita. Everything you have achieved in such a short time. A new home; a new staff. Truly remarkable.'

'I can take almost no credit,' the Queen replied. 'It's almost like the forest itself wants to teach me. To give its powers freely and readily. I feel so blessed.'

'You called Enkaysak your weapon. I've only ever seen you use it to heal — never to attack.'

The Queen stroked the length of the shaft. 'Each wood

brings its own particular power,' she said. 'It was pure chance that I found durmak first. It is that which gave me such immediate access to healing power. Now that all the woods of power are amalgamated into Enkaysak, I can call on any of them.'

'We may have need of your attacking strength sooner than you expected,' Claire said, staring out into the blackness of the forest. The tops of the bare branches shone silver in the light of Pera-Bul.

'How so? No, wait. Even with Huramapon's protection you must be feeling the cold out here. Come inside. Sit with me.'

They walked through to the inner rooms. The air was indeed warmer, but more than that, the woody smells and creamy surfaces made it feel cosier. In the corner of the room, a bunk had been fashioned from planks, strewn with springy moss and dry leaves. Not long ago Claire would not have believed the Black Queen of Kertonia would ever consider sleeping on so crude a bed. Now, it seemed perfectly fitting and nothing out of the ordinary.

They sat on a log which had been sculpted into the shape of a chaise longue. It had been the Queen's favourite perch back at the Palace. Claire recapped recent events at the Palace, and the news from Pennatanah, finishing with the tale of her earlier argument with the Fire Witch.

'Bakara was always hot-headed,' the Queen said with a smile. 'But where do you stand on this so-called "Pennatanah Problem", Claire?'

She hesitated. Since first arriving at the Palace the Queen had shown her nothing but open friendship. She did not want to hide the truth from her, and yet... She was pretty sure it would be an unpalatable truth at best. She swallowed nervously.

'I...' she began, 'I was born on Earth. For the first fifteen years of my life — twenty if you count the long lonely years I spent awake on the Valiant — I had no notion of my heritage. You only know me as my father's daughter and your new Air Mage, but for all of my formative years I was simply an Earther. A Batu'n.'

'So your sympathies lie with them?' the Queen asked, her face clouded.

'Well, no, not exactly. It's more complicated than that. I feel torn. I can understand them wanting their own place. Their own rules. But on the other hand I — of all people — know what Kertonia can offer. I don't really know much about politics, although I'm exposed to it every day. Expected to have an opinion on each tiny detail of statecraft. Deep down I'm just an Earth girl who usually feels a little out of her depth.'

The Queen turned away. Claire could not see her face, or read anything from her body language. A chill draft blew through the room from the open doorway. She shivered.

'I'm sorry if that disappoints you, Ru'ita,' she said quietly, 'but it is the truth.'

The Queen stood, pulling the wrinkles out of her black tunic with a tug. 'Thank you for that, at least,' she said. 'Though I cannot pretend it is other than a distasteful truth, it is better than a lie.'

She fell silent for a moment before continuing. 'I find I can understand Bakara's anger,' she said. 'You have been honest with me and deserve nothing less in return. You say you're "just an Earth girl" but that's not really true, is it? You are an Elemental. One of the most powerful people in this world. A leader in effect, if not in title. I understand the mantle may feel uncomfortable. It's still early days. But it is your birthright. You are Berikatanyan by nature, though clearly not by nurture. It is that which gives you the power you enjoy. Surely you cannot turn your back on it?'

This could quickly turn into an argument she did not want. A repeat of what had happened with the Witch. Only now, she could not walk out. Without light to see by, in the middle of the unfamiliar forest, she would soon be lost amid the winding paths of Timakaya. As if in response to her thoughts, the Queen moved to a second internal doorway.

'It is late,' she said. 'Perhaps it would be sensible to sleep on it. You must stay here tonight my dear — it is far too late, and too dark, to venture back to the Palace now. Sleep here. I have a bed in another part of Huramapon that will serve me very well for tonight. It may not look much, but believe me the cot is comfortable.'

'Thank you,' Claire said, not trusting herself with anything more.

'Then I shall see you in the morning,' the Queen said, turning without a further word and walking from the room.

Chapter 7

huramapon
15th day of sen'sanamasa, 966

When the early morning sun began to filter into Claire's room, she sat up. Though the cot was as comfortable as promised, she had not slept. Her arguments with the Queen, and earlier with Elaine, replayed in her mind over and over as the night wore on. She was glad of the excuse to leave both the bed and the magnificent tree house. The good manners instilled in her by her parents, not to mention the huge debt she owed the Queen, prevented her from stealing away without saying goodbye. Even so, on this occasion, she would gladly have made a surreptitious exit and avoided further confrontation.

'Ah Claire, there you are,' said her host as she emerged into the main chamber of the tree house. 'An early riser too, I see. Will you take some breakfast with me?'

A low table had been set with a variety of nuts and berries, and — unexpectedly given the season — a little fruit. Claire's stomach rumbled.

'Thank you, Ru'ita, no. I should—'

'Nonsense!' the Queen said, steering her to a seat. 'Your belly has given you away! Please, try the butam at least. It is the last of the year, slightly frozen on the branch and extremely sweet. I'm sure you will enjoy it.'

What could she do? Though the Queen's manner was outwardly friendly and calm, Claire had not missed the sideways glance and the hard set of the older woman's mouth. She had not yet been forgiven.

'It does look good,' she admitted. 'If you're sure.'

'Of course! I can't send you out into this frosty morning with no food inside you.'

For the first time, Claire noticed the Queen had abandoned use of "the royal we" in her speech. She smiled. It was a clear sign that Ru'ita had accepted the mantle of Kayshirin, and abandoned royal privileges. This simple, though impressive dwelling had nothing regal about it.

'Have I said something to amuse?' the Queen asked, pressing her lips together in an even harder line.

'Oh, no,' Claire replied, 'it pleases me how swiftly you have taken to the Elemental life here in the forest, that's all. Breakfast does look very nourishing.' She reached for one of the butam and bit into it gingerly. Blue juice spurted onto her chin as she sucked in the sweet, tangy flavour.

'Delicious!' she said, wiping away a drip with the back of her hand.

The Queen nodded, and took a handful of nuts for herself. 'I don't want to rake over old embers, my dear,' she said, 'but nor do I want our conversation of last night to stand between us.'

'I don't want that either.'

The Queen's eyes reddened, but she did not look away. 'Good,' she said. 'I have always said I would only ever use the Kayshiru for the benefit of all. I never to exclude the Batu'n. Obviously my sympathies are, and will always be, with the locals.'

'Different powers for different hours,' Claire said.

'I don't understand.'

'I'm sorry. Meaning no offence, but it was easier to say "for the benefit of all" when you thought healing was the limit of your power. And before the Kertonians and Batu'n had started facing off against each other. Now, they are. And you have a new attack component in your Elemental arsenal.'

The Queen moved out of the room onto the outside walkway and dropped a handful of broken shells over the edge. She remained there at the rail, looking out over the forest. An early ghantu screeched a warning cry which met with a loud fluttering of several pairs of wings.

'I do,' the Queen said at length. 'I'm surprised you have not mentioned Te'Banga. As Wood Mage I should bind myself with its precepts too. Do we know whose side the Stone Mage stands on?'

'We have had word that he has travelled to Pennatanah.'

'So, as a Batu'n, living among the Batu'n, we can surmise his loyalties are to the Batu'n.'

Claire shrugged.

'Then we have a balance between the higher powers,' the Queen declared. 'And I am free to defend Kertonian interests in whatever way I see fit.'

pennatanah
16th day of sen'sanamasa, 966

Patrick had never heard noise like it. He could almost see the walls of the canteen vibrating. Newly arrived "refugees" stood on one side of the hall, each jostling for position in the queue to be inducted. Pennatanah residents filled the remaining space, lining up for the lunch service or carrying a full plate in the search for a seat. The queue spilled out of the building, blocking the doorway.

'You know how you thought you'd finished raising houses?' he said.

Piers favoured him with a resigned look. Before he could speak, Alvarez pushed through the crowd in front of them.

'I think we're going to need—' she began.

'I'm way ahead of you,' Piers said, raising his voice to be heard over the din. 'I'll make a start as soon as I've eaten something.'

Two of the queuing newcomers caught Patrick's attention. One nursed a large red blister across his chest around which his shirt had been burned away. The other, supporting him, added to the noise in the hall with loud curses at the slow queue, the crowd, and the poor organisation. He noticed Patrick looking his way.

'We only just got away with our lives!' the man said. 'If

we'd known we were coming to *this*, we wouldn't have bothered.'

'How did your friend come by his injury?' Patrick asked.

'It's mostly my own fault,' the injured man replied, reddening. 'I'm not used to using Fire in anger, but we were set upon. It all happened so suddenly.'

'You're a mage?' Piers said.

His colour deepened. 'I wouldn't go that far. I have some limited ability, but not much control.' He gave them a sheepish grin. 'As you can see,' he added.

Patrick turned to Alvarez. 'We should have someone look at that,' he said, 'before it becomes infected. We can't leave him standing in line like this. What's your name, friend?'

'Jared,' the man replied, wincing as the queue inched forward and his clothing rubbed against his wound as he moved. 'Jared deLange. And this is Wendell Hopwood. We've come from the Blood Court. Things have turned right nasty there, since the rains.'

'I'll find Viswanathan,' Alvarez said. 'There may be other medics returning now, but he never left. We've been calling him the Dauntless Doctor. Looks like you have your first customer for today's housing Piers!'

'You're Piers Tremaine!' deLange said, watching Alvarez' retreat closely. 'I thought I recognised you. No offence, mate, but you were part of the problem. You got out just in time.'

'I don't understand,' Piers said. He grabbed a couple of recently vacated chairs. 'Here, sit. Tell me why I'm the problem.'

DeLange and Hopwood took the seats with grateful smiles. 'Thanks. I guess it was more that Muir kid, really. But with you both being Earthers, well, it wasn't long before the locals started causing trouble for all of us. It might not have been so bad if the Jester hadn't put you both on his Darmajelis but that just added insult to injury.

Folk complaining about Batu'n lording it over them, taking their places and jobs. It was worse for the few of us that were known to have powers.'

'There are more of you?'

'Well yes, you're not the only one you know. Though you're probably the most powerful and the most well-known. That's why I said it was your fault. Sorry, I guess I'm just feeling sore. In more ways than one.'

'What did you do at Court then, before the trouble started? I don't remember seeing you there.'

'You could say I was part of the problem too, thinking about it,' deLange replied. 'I worked with the Jester, and the King before him. General Court duties, fetching and carrying. I was a logistics guy back on Earth, so it's second nature to me. They're not very well organised, the Istanians.'

He glanced around the hall. 'Although...'

Patrick laughed. 'Yeah. I know. These are strange times. We could probably use a man like you to knock this place into shape. Once you've recovered.'

DeLange brightened. 'Oh this? It's not that bad. I wouldn't even call it first-degree. Soon as I realised what was happening I shut it off. We made our escape using more traditional skills.'

'He means we ran away,' Hopwood said. 'Us and a few more.'

'Mages?' Patrick asked.

'One of 'em did a bit with Earth,' Hopwood said, 'but mostly regular friends. We weren't gonna throw Jared to the wolves even if he is a bit... different. Besides, now they've got started, they've taken against all Earthers, not just those with power.'

'And the Earthers didn't help,' deLange added. 'It's like they couldn't read the political landscape at all. Maybe I was closer to it, working in the Court. When they began demanding separate rights, and ignoring the Guild rules, that turned the wick up under the whole thing. Was never gonna be long before it exploded in their faces.'

Alvarez returned with Doctor Dauntless. While he attended to deLange's burn, Patrick took her on one side.

'You were looking for a deputy, weren't you?'

'Waters is doing the job temporarily, but yes, I'll need someone to take over pretty soon. She's made it clear she's not interested, and this latest influx will only make things worse. Why do you ask?'

'I think we've lucked out — this guy deLange was effectively "operations" at Court.'

'I didn't recognise him,' Piers said, 'but I wasn't there long. He knew about me.'

'You'd better get working on a home for him then. Can't have him camping on someone's floor now, can I? Tell him to come find me once he's settled in.'

pennatanah
16th day of sen'sanamasa, 966

The queue did not look any shorter when Jared deLange returned to the canteen. His chest had been expertly strapped by Doctor Dauntless and a new home erected for him in moments by the Stone Mage Tremaine. Altogether happier with his lot than he had been on arrival, his only remaining problem was to find the colony Exec. Someone else had taken over at the front of the queue, processing the arrivals.

'I was looking for Ms. Alvarez,' he said, putting his Court manners into action.

'I'm her deputy, Felice Waters,' the black-haired woman said. 'Can I help?'

This could be embarrassing. 'To be honest, it was her looking for me,' he said. 'I was told to come and find her. So yes, you might be able to help, but since I don't know what it's about...' He shrugged.

A loud voice from further down the queue attracted his attention.

'Never had to wait this long for anything in the Black Palace,' the owner of the voice said. His angry, beet-red face almost matched the colour of his hair. 'You'd've thought they'd be able to look after their own better.'

Murmurs of assent passed along the line, along with a few shouts of encouragement.

'Specially us with them fancy powers,' the man continued, his soul patch bobbing up and down with each angry word. 'We deserve better than this!'

'And you'll get it,' Jared called back to the man, 'if you'll just have a bit of patience.'

'Patience is it? Alright for you who've been here for months.'

Jared walked back to stand in front of the agitator. 'I just got here today, as it happens,' he said, raising his voice to make sure everyone in the room could hear him. 'I've been properly looked after since the moment I stepped through that door.' He pulled up his shirt. 'Bandaged my wounds — self-inflicted, I might add, on account of my *Fire* power...'

He accented the word "Fire" heavily, to make certain no-one doubted that he was as much of a mage as any of them.

'...and built me a brand new house too,' he continued, 'so don't you go stirring it up against the people here. They're doing their best to cope with you all — escaping just like me from angry Istanians—'

'I came from Kertonia,' the man said.

'Well I'm sure it's every bit as dangerous there as it was for me at Court,' Jared said, laying a hand on the man's shoulder. 'But you're safe here. You're among your own people. Calm down and give them chance to find you somewhere to live and something to eat, and tomorrow things will look a whole lot brighter. Or even today! Trust me; they can work pretty quick when they want to.'

'Thank you,' Waters said, smiling. 'That was well done. If you'll come with me, I'll take you to Alvarez. I'm not abandoning you,' she said, addressing the line-up. 'Cary Cabrera will look after you, and I'll be back momentarily.'

She led the way through the hall and down a short corridor. They came to a door bearing a simple, handwritten sign that read "Silvia Alvarez - Pennatanah Colony Exec". Waters knocked.

'Come.'

'You wanted to see Jared deLange,' Waters said as she opened the door. 'He's here.'

'Ah good. Come in deLange. Take a seat.'

'Thanks. Call me Jared.'

'I'll get back,' Waters said. 'I've left Cabrera on his own.'

Alvarez' office was small, but tidy. Considering the pressure the woman must be under, he had expected there to be tell-tale signs of time poverty. Surprisingly, there were no piles of paper, discarded coffee cups, or scribbled notes.

'So what can I do for you, Ms. Alvarez?'

She smiled. 'Call me Silvia. Seems only fair to return the favour, especially if you're to be my new deputy.'

'Woah! That came out of left field! Top-class medical treatment, new house, new job. I could start to like this place. But before we get carried away, what does being your deputy mean, exactly?'

'From what I've heard, pretty much the same as you were used to at Court. Only without the drama.'

'Be careful with those promises. We had some drama in the canteen a moment ago.'

He filled her in with an outline of the incident while she poured coffee for the two of them.

'Sounds like you handled it with skill and diplomacy,' she said, handing over his cup. 'Two key parts of the deputy's role.'

'You're making this up as you go along.'

'Maybe a little. I was deputy to the previous leader — Brian Oduya — but to be honest there wasn't a lot to do.

We only had a skeleton staff back then. We were on the verge of deciding to close the place down altogether when this all kicked off. And Brian died,' she added, taking a sip.

Jared savoured the aroma. Coffee was an increasingly rare luxury. There had been none at Court and he suspected there could not be much left here either. The agronomists had so far failed to grow any in the heavy clay soils of this planet.

'So yeah,' Alvarez continued, 'I guess you called it. The demands of increased population are starting to tell on our supplies. We do most of our trading with the Court. So far that hasn't dropped off, but if this trouble gets any worse we may need alternative sources. The villages between here and there aren't usually militant, but they don't have the same capacity either, so it's a worry.'

She took another sip from her mug.

'And I wouldn't want you to be under any illusions. It's not just "us" and "them." We have our own factions here too.'

'Factions?'

'Sure. There are those who want to stay here at Pennatanah. A separate but growing group would prefer to set up a base somewhere else. Pretty much anywhere else as far as I can tell. And then we have our mages — no offence — most of whom don't seem to be comfortable with any of the options. Keeping them happy will be a real test.'

'Anything else I should be worrying about?'

Alvarez laughed. 'OK, if that's not enough to be going on with, assuming we stay here, there's a bit of "town planning" in the mix too. Although you'll probably be able to leave that to Tremaine. Waters tells me he was an award-winning architect back on Earth.'

'Well, like I told him and the other guy earlier, I'm pretty handy with logistics. I guess I do have some low-key diplomacy skills too. I had no idea what I was gonna do once I got here, so I'm happy to be your stand-in.'

'Shall we say a month's trial then? See how you get on. Bit of a baptism of fire, if the current trends continue, but that will just make it a realistic test of your mettle. Maybe start by shadowing Waters? She's only officially been my deputy for two days, but she's been here at the base forever. She can show you the ropes.'

'Fine with me.'

They finished up their coffees, and returned to the hall. There was still no noticeable let-up in the number of new arrivals waiting in line. Waters and the other man — Cabresi? No, Cabrera — worked side-by-side interviewing people, asking about family groups, expectations, skills. The usual stuff. As they approached, Tremaine returned. He looked ready to fall asleep where he stood.

'I've done another fifty,' he said to Alvarez. 'Gotta stop for today. I'm done in.'

The troublemaker Jared had confronted earlier sat against the wall. Part of the group who had been processed and were waiting for accommodation. He grinned at Jared.

'Not bad, young 'un, not bad. Good as your word. I guess one of them houses is mine.'

Jared bowed. 'Welcome to Pennatanah, where good things come to those who wait.'

The man's face clouded. 'What's that all about, anyway?' he said loudly. Something in his voice or his manner always attracted attention. The noise in the main hall abated as his words carried across the room. 'Pennatanah? What does it even mean? Is it Kertonian? Istanian? Who knows? This is an Earther base, for Earther people. Can't we come up with a better name than "Pennatanah" for Chrissake?'

The crowd picked up on the idea instantly.

'Yeah!'

'Well said.'

'Quite right.'

'Give that man a medal.'

'What are we gonna call it?'

That last question kicked off another wave of clamour as suggestions were shouted out and minor arguments started up among dissidents. If Jared had thought his new position would be an easy ride, he was rapidly learning better. He walked into the centre of the hall and held up his hands.

'Order!' he said, deliberately not shouting. 'One at a time.' The noise subsided, his psychology sound. 'All suggestions have merit. Bear in mind this is effectively our capital. Our seat of power. Names with some history and gravitas would be good.'

One of the tabbuki sat upright, his drug-induced torpor evaporating. 'You mean, like, our Washington?' he said.

'New Washington!' shouted the original troublemaker.

'Yes!'

'That's it!'

'That's the one!'

'I love it!'

The consensus roared around the room. There were no dissenting voices.

'All agreed?' Jared asked, to be greeted with a resounding 'Yes!'

Tremaine stood, shadows of fatigue smudging his eyes. 'I think I can manage one last job today,' he said, walking from the hall.

Jared, Alvarez, and a small group of others who were not waiting to be processed followed him out into the chill of early evening. At the edge of the settlement, just beyond the line of new houses he had created earlier that day, Tremaine came to a halt. Stress lines on his face stood out in the half-light as he closed his eyes in concentration. A moment later a slab of rock rose from the mud. Roughly five metres wide and half a metre thick, the block slid out of the earth, rising silently to the height of a man before coming to a stop. As smooth as ground marble, the grass and soil fell away to leave a plain matte surface. Tremaine remained motionless. Shadowy at first, so that Jared wondered whether he was actually seeing it, but with depth and size increasing with each passing moment, the words NEW WASHINGTON etched themselves into the slab, creating a signpost that would be visible from a kilometre or more away.

Chapter 8

new washington
16th day of sen'sanamasa, 966

The sun had not quite set on the new sign before Patrick concluded it may not have been the best move. Soon after they returned to the hall, a late group of arrivees joined them in a state of agitation. They reported being set upon by locals, intent on scavenging what they could from the travellers' meagre supplies. Seeing the New Washington marker, the raiders became angered. They abandoned their thieving in favour of simple assault. One of the Earthers suffered a broken leg and had to be carried the last few hundred metres to safety. Many of the others had nasty cuts or large bruises from rocks and other missiles. The new arrivals were united in one demand.

'We need a wall!'

'Can't believe this place is so badly protected.'

'Anyone could walk in at dead of night. Look at this! Lucky they didn't have my eye out!'

The troublemaker who had instigated the change of name, who Patrick had later learned was called Morain, added his voice to the clamour.

'If you're serious about this being a "new state", gonna need some border controls,' he said, standing with his hands on his hips and watching Doctor Dauntless attend the various wounds. 'Things'll only get worse once the word spreads.'

'He's not wrong,' Patrick said to Alvarez.

DeLange walked over to engage Morain in a muted conversation. Good to see the new deputy taking charge to calm things down. 'He's a find, isn't he?' he added.

'He's made a good start, I'll give him that,' she said. 'How about this wall, Piers?'

The Stone Mage sat to one side, his head in his hands. 'Isn't anything built in the regular way around here anymore?' he mumbled. 'I can't be everywhere. Do everything.'

'We could do it the traditional way, if the materials were to hand and the need not as urgent,' Alvarez said. 'But you can see how these people were treated. We can't risk the same happening overnight to people in their homes. In their beds.'

'Gonna have to be an awfully big wall to keep people out altogether,' Piers said, lifting his head. 'I can start tomorrow, I guess. I need to sleep on it. Get my strength back.'

'If we had a working ship, we wouldn't need a wall,' Morain said.

'That's right,' another man added. 'Why do we have to stay here? Just because this is where our Prism ships landed. It's just a pile of rocks. We have no idea what's on the other side of this ocean. Could be perfect. At least we'd be away from these damned Court raiders!'

Patrick glared at the man. Apparently deLange had not done a very good job of calming these people down after all.

'Have you never heard the expression "out of the frying pan, into the fire"?' he asked. 'You admitted we don't know what's over there. Yes, it might be a glorious land of plenty, but it could just as easily be filled with people-eaters.'

'Dauntless is moth-balled anyway,' Alvarez said. 'It would take some work to make her flight-ready again. And then there's the docking issue.'

'Docking issue?'

Waters looked up from her table, having completed processing the last arrival for the day. 'Prism ships can't land,' she said. 'Not without a cradle. They were designed to float at a docking gantry, like Dauntless is now.'

'They told us about this on the Intrepid,' Piers said. 'Seems like another life now. While we were approaching the planet they explained how the first ship sent flyers to the surface to scout a suitable site. This was the first place they found. They built the gantry so the rest of the passengers on the Endeavour, and all the later ships, could disembark.'

'Thanks for the history lesson,' Morain said, 'but how does it help us now? Are you saying we're stuck here? Waiting to be invaded by hordes of rampaging Istanians and their spooky magic?'

'Wait,' Patrick said. 'What spooky magic?'

'Took Anders from right in front of me,' Morain said, a horrified look crossing his face at the memory. 'There was this swirling black cloud and then he was gone. Blink of an eye. Ain't never seen nothing like it.'

Patrick felt the blood drain from his face at the man's words.

'I mean we all know about Air and Fire and all them,' Morain went on, 'but this? I've heard 'em talking about "The Vortex" at the Palace. Never thought I'd see one, but that must've been what it was. And then I got a rock in the face and I was running just to keep from getting killed!'

'Calm down,' Alvarez said, 'we agreed to build your wall. We'll post guards on all the roads and entrances tonight, to be safe. That do you?'

The man harrumphed, but said no more. Patrick closed his mind to the apparition his words had conjured, concentrating instead on the issue at hand. 'Might be an idea to extend the wall though,' he said.

'Extend it where?' Waters asked.

'Out into the bay, I mean. From the headland. The cliff shelves away steeply there, but further round it would be possible to make a landing. Mount an attack. If we're seriously talking about invasion. Sounds a bit paranoid to me, but I'm not sporting bruises like these guys.'

'Damn right,' Morain said, rubbing the purple welt on his brow.

'How far out are you suggesting?' Piers asked.

'At least a couple hundred metres.' Patrick said. 'Far

enough to deter any water-borne attacks, or at least give us some warning.'

Piers scratched his head. 'I dunno. I can tell you the seabed here isn't the same as I worked with at the Valley. I can maybe raise a wall in the shallows, but further than twenty metres out, it's too deep.'

'Could you do it if there was no water?'

'It's the sea,' Piers said, frowning. 'You just gonna lift it to one side?'

'Not me,' Patrick said, grinning. 'Didn't you say we had a new Water Wizard now? We could ask her to help.'

'Who's this?' Alvarez asked.

'Kyle Muir,' Piers said. 'Last I knew she was still at the Black Palace.'

'That's a good three days' ride from here,' Waters said. 'If you're planning on asking for her help we'd better send someone right away.'

'I can make a start without her,' Piers said. 'But yeah, for the deep water, we could use her for sure.'

new washington
17th day of sen'sanamasa, 966

Whether dissuaded by the lack of travelling Earthers, or exhausted from the previous day's attacks, their wall building activities progressed without disturbance from irate locals. Patrick stood in awe again, watching his friend deploy his remarkable power. He marvelled at the speed of construction and Piers' seemingly limitless reservoirs of Elemental energy.

As the New Washington signpost had done the evening before, the wall slid from the ground in sections. In contrast, this rock continued rising past the two metre mark, stopping only when it had attained more than twice that height. It towered over them; a smooth, sheer face, impossible to scale without ladders or climbing frames. Any marauders would find scant material from which to build such siege engines, the supply of timber in the area being almost non-existent.

'Take a break,' Patrick said, 'you probably need it even though you don't look tired.'

Piers grinned, but said nothing until the latest section of wall had grown to match the height of the others.

'It's funny,' he said, sitting on one of the two outcrops of rock he created earlier for them to rest on, 'the more I use this power, the easier it gets. I don't feel drained like I did yesterday, building houses.'

'Not as complicated though, is it?'

'True.'

'What kind of stone is this? I've never seen it before.'

'No-one has. I just invented it.' He was grinning again. 'I mean, it starts off as the base rock, down there, but I've been experimenting with some changes to it when I draw it upwards. It should be even more difficult to climb than it looks. I've made it slippery.'

Patrick reached out a hand to touch the wall. Sure enough, it had a greasy feel.

'Is it oil-bearing? You could almost squeeze oil out of it.'

'Not as far as I know. I guess there may be oil somewhere on this planet. The rest of the ecosystem is similar to Earth, so it would make sense. Not around here though. At least, not this close to the surface.'

'What's he doing here?' Patrick said. Some distance away, Jared deLange stood watching them.

Piers shrugged. 'No idea. Maybe Alvarez told him to keep an eye on progress? The duties of a deputy, eh?'

'Kinda creepy.'

'He's just doing his job. Speaking of which, I should get back to mine. This wall won't build itself.'

'All evidence to the contrary,' Patrick laughed. 'From where deLange is standing I bet that's exactly how it looks.'

With a short stop for a midday meal, Piers continued

building for the rest of the day. As the afternoon wore on, he took more frequent breaks. Constant use of his Elemental power had a penalty, visible in the deepening lines and grey pallor of his face. By the time the sun began to turn red over the sea, he had extended the wall almost fifty metres out into the bay.

He wiped a bead of sweat from his brow. 'Gonna have to stop there,' he said. 'Did better than I thought, but I can't reach out any further.'

'Incredible. I wish I could've helped.'

'Not a problem. It'll be at least four days before Kyle will be here. I should be recovered enough to help her by then. Unless Alvarez demands any more housing.'

the palace of the black queen
19th day of sen'sanamasa, 966

Of all the displaced Elementals, Elaine Chandler had held on to her "Earther" persona the longest. She turned away from the Water Wizard to hide a smile. It would only spark questions she had no wish to answer. Truth was, even in her most private moments, she still thought of herself as Elaine. Especially now, in Kyle Muir's company.

As Bakara, she could project the well known and frightfully intimidating demeanour of the Fire Witch. Useful when it was necessary to command, cajole, or coerce. But there was a quieter, gentler side of her nature. She had only begun to admit its existence since spending time with Jann Argent. It still required some cultivation before it would sit easily in her mind. Bakara was always there, ready with a quick retort or a fiery outburst — sometimes literally. The Water Wizard was not a natural companion for her. When Fire and Water mixed, there was likely to be an explosive outgassing of steam. Nevertheless the girl needed her help, and providing it came much more naturally to Elaine that it could ever have done to Bakara.

She snorted involuntarily at the thought. Not so long

ago, the Fire Witch would not be seen dead discussing costumes or planning table decorations.

'What?' Kyle asked, looking up from the outline drawing of a design for drapes around the ceremonial dais.

'Oh, I... was only thinking it would be nice to have Claire's help with this.'

The Air Mage had returned from Timakaya in a foul temper four days before. She had squirreled herself away in her room ever since, refusing to come out.

'I had not expected her mood to last this long,' Elaine continued.

'Me neither,' Kyle said. 'Has she said anything about it at all?'

'Not to me. As far as I know she hasn't spoken to anyone.'

'It's not like her. I'm quite worried. It must be something to do with the Queen but I can't imagine they would fall out as badly as this. They were always very close.'

'No point worrying about it,' Elaine said. 'You have enough to occupy your mind with all this.' She waved a hand over the drawings, swatches, and samples. 'If we don't make a decision soon there won't be enough time for the Palace artisans to pull it together before your big day.'

A knock came at the door.

'Come in,' Kyle called.

A houseman in Palace livery entered with another man. 'Messenger for Miss Muir,' the houseman said, 'just arrived from Pennatanah.'

'Actually we're calling it New Washington now,' the man said. 'Forgive the intrusion ladies, my name is Stuart Smallman. Our new Exec there, Silvia Alvarez, has asked if you would accompany me back to the coast as soon as you can. We have a project in hand that is in desperate need of your help.'

'New Washington!' Elaine said, feeling her Earther

sensibilities slipping away, and Bakara reasserting herself. 'What was wrong with the old name? It has served perfectly well for more than ten years. The Water Wizard is busy with matters of public duty. What possible need can the Batu'n have of her?'

'The Stone Mage has said the coastal waters are too deep to complete the works he is engaged in alone. He asks that you bring your Water powers to bear on the problem, hold back the ocean so he may work unhindered.'

Kyle's eyes were aglow with excitement. 'Fantastic!' she cried, jumping to her feet. 'I can come right away!'

Elaine stood too, laying a restraining hand on Kyle's arm. 'Hold on! What about the ceremony? We haven't finished.'

'Oh never mind that!' Kyle said, shrugging her off. 'Plenty of time for that when I come back. The ceremony can't go ahead without me, can it? And we haven't set a firm date yet. This is far too exciting to miss.' She turned to the houseman. 'Have the head ostler saddle my kudo right away. It sounds like there's not a moment to lose.'

'Begging your pardon miss,' Smallman said, 'but I've been riding hard for three days without much sleep or a proper meal. I was hoping—'

'It'll be dark soon anyway, Kyle,' Elaine said. 'It's too late to start back tonight. Wait until tomorrow.'

Kyle stuck out her bottom lip in a pitiful pout. 'Oh. Yes, I suppose you're right. Forgive me, Stuart, I was caught up with the idea of it. I never thought you must be worn out. Tomorrow morning will be soon enough, but early! Straight after breakfast, yes?'

'Of course, miss, thank you. I'll be ready first thing.'

new washington
22nd day of sen'sanamasa, 966

Kyle Muir barrelled across the frozen ground on her

kudo Pembariru, the messenger Smallman close behind. Ahead of her the late evening sun approached the horizon, painting the whitecaps rosy pink. Pembariru's breath steamed in the cold air but the strong animal kept up the pace she demanded even after three days' hard riding. The familiar squat buildings of the settlement came into view, now almost hidden by a neat row of unfamiliar structures. The whole area had been surrounded with a high redstone wall, reminiscent of the hated Blood Court.

'You've been busy,' she called back to the messenger.

'Not me miss,' he replied. 'That's Tremaine's work.'

'That too, I guess,' she said, waving at the New Washington sign as they passed through a gateway. A small group of guards recognised Smallman in time to move out of the path of the galloping kudai.

Approaching the main buildings, Kyle caught sight of a recognisable shape on the clifftop. Piers Tremaine and another man sat together, deep in conversation. She reined Pembariru to a halt, dismounted and handed the trembling animal's traces to Smallman.

'Take her for me,' she said. 'Make sure she's properly rubbed down and dried off. And fed. I can walk back from here.'

'Mind how you go on the rocks. They can be slippery this time of year.'

'Thank you.'

Kyle rubbed her sore arse. Not only would it have been quicker if she had "flowed" here, it would have involved considerably less pain. She really must find time to practice the technique! Shading her eyes against the rapidly-setting sun, she approached the two men. 'I guess I'm too late to do anything today?' she called.

'You've made good time,' said Piers, standing and giving her a bone-crushing hug. 'I wasn't expecting you until tomorrow.'

'I'm Patrick Glass,' the other man said, 'and you're right. We don't have much light left.'

'You're probably too tired from your trip to move oceans anyway,' Piers grinned.

Kyle punched him on the shoulder. 'Where to?'

'Seriously?' He pointed at the wall. The red stone continued down the sloping cliff side, snaking out into the water and coming to an end about fifty metres from the shore. 'We need to build out about four times further,' he said, 'but I can't... what did old Petani used to call it? — summon the stone from water that deep. I—'

He fell silent, an astonished look on his face. From the visible end of the wall, the waves drew back on both sides, roiling and foaming in a straight line towards the setting sun. Within moments two glassy walls of water stood apart three times the width of the stone, exposing the sandy seabed.

'That do you?' Kyle smiled.

'I... yes. Yes, that's perfect,' Piers said.

'Most impressive,' Patrick agreed. 'How long can you keep it up?'

'How long do you need?' Kyle asked.

Both men laughed.

'Maybe I can achieve something tonight after all,' Piers said, focusing his attention on the nearest stretch of exposed sand.

*

By the time the blazing arc of the sun dipped below the line of the horizon, and the two Elementals could look on their work without squinting, the sea-washed wall extended forty more metres.

'Almost double what we started with,' Patrick said.

Piers rubbed a hand over his eyes. 'If we can do another ten-metre stretch it will be. You OK with that, Kyle?'

'Sure.' She stared once more at the line of red stone. Walls of water rose again on either side beyond it, their foaming tops now stark white in the fading light. The image tugged at Kyle's mind. 'Make it quick,' she said, 'Not sure I can hold it for long this time. I'm scunnered.'

Patrick frowned. 'Eh?'

'Sorry. Tired. Beat. Knackered.'

'Oh, right. Amazing you've done this much, after all that riding. There's no doubt you're more powerful than your brother, as old Lautan predicted.'

Kyle's heart skipped a beat. Mention of Douglas ripped away the sticking plaster over her memories of that final, fateful battle. Standing again at the coast, with darkness approaching and walls of water out in the bay, echoes from the other scene lent the memory even more power. She felt her Elemental energy failing as the tears sprang again from her eyes. With a soft whoosh, her walls collapsed, crashing down over the stump of red rock Piers had begun to build.

'What...?' he said.

Kyle touched her temple with trembling fingers. 'Sorry. I...'

'It's OK,' Patrick said, laying his hand over hers. 'You're exhausted. Tomorrow?'

She smiled and wiped a tear from her cheek. 'Thanks.' She stared out at the rolling ocean. 'I'll be fine by then. With some daylight.'

'We may not have any beer,' Piers said, 'but I'm pretty sure one of Alvarez's people still has a little wine. We've done well — I think we have an excuse for a small celebration?'

'Twist my arm,' Kyle said. 'I'm glad I came!'

Once she held the wine in her hand, Kyle began to wonder whether she was glad after all. They had left the gathering gloom and entered the main hall back at base. She remembered it vividly, of course, but it had never been this busy during her brief stay after disembarking the Dauntless. The enormous Prism ship still hovered at the docking mast, its sleek silver hull outlined by the electric blue glow of its gravnull field. New Washington now provided refuge for many more than had arrived on that last trip.

'I see why you built so many new homes,' she said.

They carried their dinner plates to a table on the opposite wall to the tabukki group.

'I haven't finished yet,' Piers said, 'but I have slowed down a lot since the first sixty or so went up. I don't have to tell you how much it takes out of you, using the power.'

'All evidence to the contrary,' Patrick said, 'at least today. It hardly seemed to touch you, Kyle, holding up several thousand tons of seawater. Until that last one,' he added, watching her closely.

Kyle hesitated, unsure of her voice. 'Piers is right,' she said after a moment, 'I couldn't have done any more today.' She took a forkful of the famous Pennatanah — New Washington — bloostoo. Her brother's name for it popped unbidden into her mind. She swallowed down another brief pang of loss, along with the food. The second time her dead brother had forced himself back into her thoughts that day. 'You must know anyway,' she added, waving her empty fork in Patrick's direction. 'Didn't I hear something about you having powers of your own?'

Patrick shifted in his seat but said nothing. Mention of his power was clearly an uncomfortable subject.

'Patrick doesn't—' Piers began.

'—like to talk about it,' Patrick finished for him, favouring the Stone mage with a glare.

'Oh.' Kyle said. 'OK. Sorry.'

They fell silent, enjoying their meal. The question of Patrick's power hung in the air, like the fine mist of sea-spray that Kyle's work had whipped up earlier in the day. When their plates were almost empty, a disturbance at another table attracted her attention. In the space between them and the tabbuki group, two men faced each other, arguing.

'I'm telling you we'll need more!' a short ginger-haired

man with a tiny soul patch said, his beet-red face betraying his anger. 'Four guards just won't be enough to hold the gate!'

His opponent in the shouting match was of average height and build, with brown hair and eyes. Mister Mundane. Norm Normal. 'And I'm telling you, you're being paranoid,' he growled. 'Go on, show me your scars, or your bandages, or whatever. Tell me they'll be back every night until they've killed us all in our beds.'

'Make a joke of it all you like,' beet red man said, 'you'll be laughing on the other side of your face when you're dead.'

'That's Morain,' Patrick said. 'The wall was his idea.'

'And the other one is Jared deLange,' Piers added. 'Alvarez's new deputy. Funny, I would have expected him to be on Morain's side.'

'If you're so keen on guarding,' a third man said, walking over from another table, 'why not do some of it yourself? Instead of sitting here in the warm and dry yapping about it? Malamajan will be up soon. Guarding's a cold, wet business at this time of night.'

As he spoke, the malamajan began, icy raindrops rattling against the roof and resounding through the hall. Kyle sensed the old jamtera, marvelling anew, as she did most nights, at the simple elegance of it. Even now, with a growing degree of control over her power, she would be unable to create a jamtera even half as strong as the malamajan. Her Water sense gave her an appreciation of how it worked and an even deeper respect for the ancient Elementals who created it.

The noise of the rain, and the reality of being out in it, suppressed any further argument from Morain. Before long the hall began to empty as people took to their beds.

*

The next day, work progressed apace. With the morning half done, and the northern stretch of wall complete, they agreed to take a short break. Long enough to walk around the headland to the southern end of the boundary which Piers had built some days earlier.

Kyle noticed Patrick nudging Piers. 'What?' she said. 'Something wrong?'

Patrick pointed along the path. She recognised Jared deLange from the night before. Norm Normal. He stood beside the wall, watching them. 'Our supervisor is here again.'

'Supervisor?'

'He must think he is. He's been watching us every day. First with the landward wall, and now the wetwork.'

Kyle laughed. Back home "wetwork" meant something completely different, as Patrick must know. Perhaps embarrassed by their stares, deLange walked over.

'Morning!' he called cheerily.

'Seen enough?' Patrick said, adopting a confrontational stance.

DeLange's face turned a little pink. His fixed smile did not reach his eyes. 'Merely checking on progress,' he said airily, 'so I can give Alvarez an up-to-date report.'

'You can tell her we'll be done today,' Piers said. 'Now that we have Kyle's help, the job's as good as finished.'

'Most impressive, young lady,' deLange said with a supercilious bow. 'I had not realised quite how far you've come into your power. Last I heard it was your brother who was the more powerful.'

Patrick stepped in front of the man again. 'Less of the patronising tone, deLange. This is the Water Wizard of Berikatanya. Show some respect.'

DeLange raised his eyebrows into a cartoon expression of surprise. 'Forgive me,' he said, 'I was unaware she had thrown her lot in so wholeheartedly with the locals.'

'What do you mean?' said Piers, moving to stand next to Patrick.

'It's simple enough,' the brown man said. 'I assumed Ms Muir might join us, since she is Earth-born and bred.

We have others here who exhibit powers — I need not tell you gentlemen that — whose loyalties remain with the people of their birth—'

'Don't be so quick to judge, Mister deLange,' Kyle said. The man's voice had begun to irritate her, even before he had summoned the distressing spectre of her brother. She was keen to return to their work. 'But it's a subject that will keep. Right now, we're busy.'

She pushed past him and continued down the path, with the tiniest of tiny winks at Patrick.

'Well, deLange, that's you put in your place,' he said. 'Trot on now and make your report to the boss. We've got work to do.'

Chapter 9

new washington
23rd day of sen'sanamasa, 966

Cresting a gentle rise above New Washington, Kyle brought her kudo to a halt, turned, and gazed back at the settlement. The thin red lines of Piers' wall snaked around the outlying buildings and out into the ice-blue sea from both north and south, each reaching out to the other but stopping short of meeting. As she hoped, the bright sunlight had burned away the memory of Douglas and his grisly demise. She had completed the work without a repeat of her earlier failure.

Beyond the opening, well out into deeper water, sat the shining hull of the Valiant. It rode above the waves like a strange metallic sea creature, basking in the early evening sun. Towards the end of the afternoon they had debated whether to close the gap, but decided it was wiser to leave open — literally! — the option to build a harbour.

'OK then,' Kyle had said, once the decision was made. She dropped her power. The vertical sea walls collapsed with a deafening crash. A plume of spray rose fully fifty metres before falling back to soak the stone, leaving it glistening in dark, ruddy rivulets.

'Oh! I hadn't finished!' Piers cried, breaking into a grin as Kyle spun round with a horrified look on her face.

'You joker!' she laughed, punching him on the shoulder.

'But never jester!' he replied.

'What are your plans now, Kyle?' Patrick asked. 'Will you stay? I mean, I don't want to make deLange's argument for him, but you'd be welcome here.'

'I know. And thanks. But no, I have to go back. The Queen has done so much for me. And Claire. I have to see this damned ceremony through.' She screwed her face into a grimace. 'Not looking forward to it, if I'm honest.'

'Why go then?' Piers asked. 'You don't actually owe them anything. The Queen was really only looking after her own interests. She loves having a gaggle of Elementals at the Palace.'

'Is that the collective noun for Elementals?' Kyle laughed.

'It'll do for now. She does though! She enjoys the cachet. And getting one over on the Jester. Doesn't mean you have to dance to her tune.'

'I know,' she said again, taking a deep breath of salty sea air to dispel the mood brought on by thoughts of the Black Palace. 'But still. We're not sure how this will play out, are we? How successful New Washington will be.'

'It has a better chance with the Water Wizard onside,' Patrick said.

'Don't.'

'So when are you gonna leave?' Piers asked.

She checked the sun, still riding high in the early afternoon sky. 'Plenty of daylight left. I could make Besakaya before midnight at a gallop.'

'Oh?'

'No reason. It's a convenient place to spend the night, and it's almost half the journey done. One less night on the road, not to mention a decent meal.'

'Rebusang!' the two men shouted in unison.

They had all laughed, the sound of fun and friendship still fresh in her mind. Patrick had tried to persuade her to take a bite before setting out, but she declined. With a full belly, and in the warmth of the New Washington canteen, she was certain to delay leaving for another day. Although dreading the ceremony, she knew herself well enough. It was better to face it. Get it over with. She had half a mind to try the journey in fluid form, but that still felt like a step too far. Inauguration first. As the official Water Wizard, there would be one less psychological barrier to entering the realm of water.

So she had saddled Pembariru and set off, before she

could change her mind. Now the path to Besakaya lay in front of her. The huge mass of Tubelak'Dun rose to her right, its tops shining white with snow in the dazzling sun. Fortunately she need not travel higher than the foothills. The evening was already cold enough without having to contend with altitude.

She patted Pembariru's neck fondly. 'Come on girl,' she said softly, 'let's see if we can make it before nightfall.'

besakaya
25th day of sen'sanamasa, 966

Petani stirred the embers of the Project camp fire with a long stick. The fire glowed in response, redly illuminating twin tracks of tears on his cheeks like miniature lava streams. He let the tears fall. No-one else shared his late vigil, but even if they had he would not have cared whether or not they noticed his distress.

He had maintained a cheery demeanour when bidding farewell to the young Muir girl the day before, but even then he had been feeling sorry for himself. Hearing of her success with the sea wall at Pennatanah, or New Washington as it was now apparently called, had only served to undermine his confidence in his own project.

Naturally, he had not revealed his feelings. The girl was understandably elated at her achievement. "Yaldi," as she had put it. He would never have dreamt of putting a dampener on her happiness. But the Landing project would have been equally successful, and perhaps saved him some embarrassment, had she been invited to help as she had at Pen— New Washington.

It was his own fault. As usual. He watched the colours flux through the fire as a breeze caught them and fanned the ash. If Piers' had not followed him to the Landing, and persuaded him to accept help, he would still have been struggling alone with the work. Alone! The word defined him, and had done all his life. He lived alone, worked alone, and here he sat now, alone.

He shook his head. Stop feeling sorry for yourself old man! Most people could only dream of power like his. But — and there always was a but — he could not shake the feeling that he should be doing more with it. More than flowers and vegetables. Look at Claire Yamani. Young, bright, reading every last scroll of Air lore, inventing new ways to apply it. Kyle too — on the verge of being installed as Water Wizard, already comfortable enough with her power to hold back the seas! Still a little nervous of taking water form though. A trick which had unnerved Petani more than a little whenever old Lautan used it. No matter how often he saw it done, it always seemed a bit... unnatural. Watching a column of foaming water resolve itself into the shape of a man — or woman — and walk from a river or stream. Often talking in that weird bubbly voice that never properly solidified until the body had. He shuddered, and sent a silent prayer of thanks to the Gods that none of the other Elementals, himself included, could perform a similar feat.

'What you doing sat out here this time of night?'

Nembaka approached, resolving out of the gloom in a strange parallel with Petani's earlier thoughts of the lost Water Wizard.

'It too cold for your lonely vigil, Petani,' the small man said. 'Malamajan start soon, and fire be gone. Come inside. Some rebusang left, if you hungry?'

Petani threw his stick into the fire and wiped his face hurriedly. Perhaps he was a little embarrassed after all. 'Thank you, Nem. You're a good friend.'

Nembaka held out a hand to help him up from his log. The two men walked through the night towards the soft glow of the largest Project hut. David Garcia stood in the doorway, a glass of buwangah in each hand.

'A little wine to wash that rebusang down, Petani?' he said with a smile.

the palace of the black queen
26th day of sen'sanamasa, 966

The sight of the Black Palace, nestling in the shadows of Timakaya, sent a shiver through Kyle Muir. How excited she had been the day of her first arrival here. The thought of meeting a real Queen, living in a palace, and mixing with the other Elementals while learning her lore, had filled her with eager anticipation. None of that buzz remained. Worn down by the interminable council meetings, endless antagonism between Earthers and locals, and long days spent planning her forthcoming ceremony. Now, the dark towers stood like a mirror of the darkness in her soul. She just wanted it over with. Fulfil her duty to the Queen, as she saw it, and leave. These were not her people, and this was not her battle. She spurred Pembariru on, across the bridge spanning the Sun Besaraya, and through the Palace gates.

The basilica glowed with lampfires, lit early against the encroaching night, and Palace staff were busy with the evening business. The entrance hall resounded with loud conversations echoing from the refectory, where she found Claire Yamani finishing her meal.

'You're back!' the Air Mage exclaimed, laying down her sunyok. 'Are you eating? I can stay, if you want the company? How was Pennatanah?'

'Interesting,' Kyle said. 'And it's not Pennatanah anymore. They're calling it New Washington now.'

She filled a plate, and brought Claire up to speed with the events of the last few days while she ate.

'Your friend Petani was in a dark place,' she said, on reaching the last part of her tale. 'I don't know why, but nothing I said cheered him up at all. Not even my profuse compliments on the state of his garden.'

'Is it recovered from the rains?'

'The bit I saw is. I arrived in darkness, and it wasn't much lighter when I left yesterday, so I can't speak for most of it. But never mind the Forest project, we have something much more important to talk about.' Kyle stacked their plates. 'Not here though.'

The two women returned to Claire's chambers. A fire had been set, and lit. It roared merrily in the grate. Claire poured them each a glass of buwangah. 'I'm guessing this is about Earther politics?' she said.

'I suppose that's as good a headline as any. I'm not going to waste time explaining. We've talked it to death before now. When my ceremony is over, I'm leaving. Or joining, whichever way you want to look at it. Moving. To New Washington. Will you come with me?'

Claire stared into the fire. A frisson of doubt shivered through Kyle. Had she spoken out of turn? Until this moment she had assumed her friend thought the same way. That they would leave together. Weren't they both Earthers, really? Or was Claire more the haughty Air Mage now, after all? Kyle moved closer to the fire and bit down on her need to ask again.

When Claire still did not reply, she could hold herself back no longer. 'I mean, I feel guilty, you know? Of course I do. After all the Queen has done. But she's not here anymore is she? Is she even Queen at all, really? Living in the forest. She's more Wood Mage now, than Queen. And in the end, what do we owe her? Piers said she'd only been looking after her own interests. If you think of it that way, then there's nothing wrong with us doing the same, is there? I don't want to be caught up with... Sorry. I'm gabbling.'

Claire laughed. 'Just a bit. But you're not gabbling anything I haven't thought myself. I've not stopped thinking about it, to be honest, since you've been gone. I've fallen out with Elaine. Even had a bit of a falling out with the Queen.'

Claire refilled their glasses and recounted the tale of her arguments with the Fire Witch, and her visit to the tree house. Kyle felt a surprising disappointment that she would not have chance to see the Wood Mage's new home. It sounded, well, magical.

'And I left her there,' Claire said, reaching the end of her story. 'By that time I'd pretty much made up my mind. I don't know why I don't just come out and say it. Except the words will make it real. Yes. Yes, I'll come with you Kyle. Whenever you go, I'll go too.'

the palace of the black queen
27th day of sen'sanamasa, 966

Kyle had hoped they could breakfast together the next day, but there was no answer at Claire's door and no sign of her in the refectory. She had not taken the first bite from her overloaded plate when the Air Mage appeared in the doorway, her face drained of all blood. She trembled violently.

'Whatever is the matter?' Kyle cried, leaving her meal forgotten on the table and hurrying over to her friend. She reached Claire's side in time to catch her as her legs gave way and she sagged to the floor.

'I... attacked,' she murmured.

With the help of two others, Kyle carried her to a seat. One of the housemen brought a glass of water.

'What happened?' Kyle asked, once Claire had recovered enough to speak.

'I went out early,' she said, 'to send the inauguration invites by Air Mail. It's easier in the early morning before the sun is warm enough to set off the convection currents...'

*

Early morning, right after daybreak, is one of my favourite times of day. The air is like fine wine, crystal clear and fresh. I carry a small pack of invites and find a spot by the moat where I can set them down in the dry. I conjure the Air jamtera I use for the Mail, and the first two fly off without any problem. As the third one starts to rise, one of those weird vortices appears and snatches it from existence. I hardly have time to react before a small group from the nearest village approach, all shouting at once.

'So it is you, Air Mage!'

'Told you it was her!'

'Those cursed twisters took my best baleng, damn you and your Elemental tricks!'

They run toward me. Some of them are armed with farm tools. One of them throws a rock which whizzes past, narrowly missing my face.

'It wasn't me!' I shout, but it's no use. They are convinced the vortex was a manifestation of Air power, and clearly not in a mood to listen to sense.

'We had enough of you damned Elementals with that dreadful rain!' the nearest shouts. 'We're damned well not going to put up with having your Air power wrecking our homes and lives now too!'

'Damn right, Mulkas,' says another. 'Come on, don't let her get away!'

It's worse than I thought. It's not only that they won't listen. The angry, murderous looks on their faces make me fear for my life.

'Don't come any closer,' I shout, 'or I'll show you what real Air power looks like!'

One or two of them hesitate, but only for a moment. They are caught up in the madness as the rest of them push past, still running towards me and coming nearer all the time. Too near. I can't run. There are too many. A few have circled round behind me, cutting off my escape back to the safety of the Palace.

There's nothing for it. I send my thoughts to my core of power, summoning a whirlwind. It crosses my mind that this form of Air may only strengthen their conviction that the vortex was my fault, but I can't help it. It's the most effective weapon I can think of. I set my arms into the gesture. For once, I use the word. It has to work first time. I can't risk a misfire.

The crystal clean air I drank in when I first stepped out of the Palace only moments before now begins to turn, twisting itself into a maelstrom that circles the group with me at its centre.

'See?' the nearest man yells. 'I knew it was her!'

His eyes pop as the wind intensifies, sucking his feet out from under him and sending him sprawling. The next man shouts a warning when his feet lift from the ground and he flies, spinning, into the water, landing with a loud splash. The spray he throws up is whipped by the tornado and flung into the faces of three others, blinding them. The roar of the wind grows louder, until their shouts are lost in its deafening crescendo. Those behind me stagger back, offering a clear path away from the moatside.

*

Claire fell silent, dashing angry tears from her eyes.

'Were any of them hurt?' Kyle asked.

'I didn't stick around to see,' Claire replied. 'As soon as I saw a gap, I ran for it. I was terrified Kyle! They would've killed me! If any of them were injured or killed, it's no worse than what would have happened to me if I hadn't done anything.'

She took another sip of water, the glass shaking. 'I think I could manage a bit of breakfast now.' She ran a hand through her hair, her eyes flashing. 'Those fuckers,' she said, her face twisting into an angry scowl. 'I haven't been that scared since I was mugged on the stairs back home.'

'At least you had your powers this time.'

Claire rolled her eyes. 'Damn right. I guess I should thank Sana for that!'

'Well, if we hadn't already decided to leave, this would have made the decision for us!' Kyle said. 'It proves we are still outsiders. And always will be, no matter what the Queen says. We'll only really be safe at New Washington, behind the wall.'

'There's a wall here. Battlements too. No, safety comes from being among friends. Friends who can fight.' She gazed around the room, and out into the basilica. 'Not from buildings, no matter how safe they look.'

new washington
27th day of sen'sanamasa, 966

It did not feel like a day off for Patrick. He had done nothing — physical or elemental — since helping clear up after the rains. But it was a day off for Piers, after four continuous days of construction, so he was happy for his friend at least. His lonely cliff-top vigils were no longer so lonely, and their conversations kept his thoughts from dwelling on Juggler powers.

His stomach had begun to suggest it might be lunchtime, when a strange white bird caught his attention. It crabbed through the air towards them. Having seen similar creatures before, he recognised it right away.

'Looks like a note from Claire,' he said.

Piers looked up from his close examination of a rock formation that stood guard at the edge of the cliff. His gaze followed Patrick's pointing finger. The Air Mail covered the remaining distance to the two men, and came to rest hovering in the space between them.

'Must be for both of us,' Piers said, 'or it would have picked one to land on.'

Patrick reached for the note, unfolded it, and read the contents aloud.

'Her Gracious Majesty Queen Ru'ita of Kertonia gives notice of the inauguration of Kyle Muir as Water Wizard of Berikatanya. You are cordially invited to attend the ceremony on the first day of Far'Utamasa, in the New Year 967. Celebrations will take place in the basilica of the Black Palace, commencing immediately after noon.'

'Very auspicious,' Piers said, 'holding it on the local

equivalent of New Year's Day. A new year, and a new start for Kyle. Will you go?'

'Good question. Will you?'

'I kinda feel like I have to. After she came over to help with the wall, you know?'

'I guess.'

'You're not convinced, obviously.'

'I came here for a reason. It's still a valid reason.'

'Not gonna relent? Even for a special occasion?'

Patrick picked up a small rock, turning it over in his hand. The mineral crystals flashed and sparkled as the sun caught them in turn. 'She doesn't need me there.'

'Not sure it's a question of "need". She's a friend, as well as a fellow Elemental.'

He pitched the rock off the cliff, watched it arc down into the water. The ocean swallowed it. Within moments, there was no sign it had ever existed.

'Then as a friend,' he said, 'she would allow me to make my own decision.'

Piers frowned. 'I'm not trying to persuade you. Just understand. You never did explain why you didn't help with the building. And now you're being all mysterious about why you don't want to come to the Palace.'

'Not sure I can explain,' Patrick said, scouting around for another rock, 'but I'm happy for you to represent both of us.' He handed the note to Piers. 'Represent the whole of New Washington for all I care.'

'The Queen will invite the leaders here too, surely?'

Patrick shrugged. 'Maybe. Even less reason for me to go in that case. You'll hardly miss me.'

'You're sure?'

'I could ask you the same. You sure you want to go?'

'I owe her.'

'Yeah, you said. And I don't.'

the palace of the black queen
27th day of sen'sanamasa, 966

Pakcil still loved farming in the fields around the Black Palace. This time of year, life was hard. A constant battle to stay warm, keep his animals fed, and protect them from scavengers, both animals and people, who were also finding it hard to feed themselves. But he loved it, even so. The fresh, crisp air, the steaming breath of his herd, and their blembil of greeting each morning when he brought whatever feedstuff he had scraped together.

True, there had been a lot of weirdness recently. Stretching back ten years, since the strangers from another planet arrived here. Pakcil had never agreed with their attempts at integration, and as far as he was concerned he'd been proved right. Lucky, really, that few of them wanted to be farmers. It was an Earther who brought the rains, and even now his sister was living in the Palace. The towers stood hazily in the distance, sucking the shine out of the midday Sanamasan sun. No pennants flew — the Queen was no longer in residence. And there was another chunk of weird. Once, he had drawn comfort from his proximity to the Palace. It was unchanging, stolid, a close source of security and certainty. Now, the Queen was off in the woods by all accounts, turning herself into another of those Elementals. No good would come of it. And if she joined forces with mad Muir's sister? What then? More horrors, no doubt.

'Daddy!'

The call of his daughter, Orbara, cut through his troubled reverie. She ran across the field toward him, carrying a bepermak in each hand. A farmer's travelling lunch. He always enjoyed sharing it with his youngest. She had not covered half the distance between them when a dark shadow appeared in front of her. Black smoke twisted and roiled into a strange inverted cone shape, hovering above the grassy surface, and spinning silently.

Running too fast to avoid it, Orbara hit the twister at full pelt. Her mouth opened in a surprised O, but she had no time to shout. With a soundless pop, the black phantom, and his daughter, winked out of existence.

'Orbara!' he cried, running towards the spot. But it was too late. She had gone. The only evidence she had ever been there was a single bepermak, lying open on the grass where it had fallen.

*

The ancient woodland of Timakaya spanned the Sun Besaraya as if holding it in dark, clenched fist. The river provided a constant supply of fresh water, running down from its source in Temmok'Dun. It brought minerals and nutrients to constantly replenish the supplies the forest needed to survive. In this ideal location, it thrived. Every species of Berikatanyan tree was represented in the forest, but in common with all mature woodlands, the older parts were populated mainly with the most long-lived trees — kaytam, kayati, and the mighty kayketral.

Far to the north of the Black Palace, on the opposite side of the forest from where the Queen had built her new home, the treeline stretched up into the low rises at the edge of Temmok'Dun before curving back into the natural depression carved by the river over the centuries. This was the oldest part of Timakaya, almost exclusively kaytam. The tall blackwoods grew closely together, creating their own microclimate and providing a home for countless birds, rodents, and small mammals. Though many of them were bare, owing to the season, the densely packed trunks and branches still cast deep shadows, becoming impenetrably dark within scant metres of the treeline. This sepulchral section of woodland echoed to the calls of the animals, and the gurgling of the Besaraya, running swift and clear over the sandy river bed.

No Kertonian had ever visited this part of the forest. No hand had touched trunk, no axe had felled tree. And so no eye was present to witness the death of the grandfather of the forest; the most ancient of all the original kaytam. All trees have a finite life, most measured in decades, some in centuries. This one had stood since before Temmok'Dun was raised. It had been passed by the warring tribes as they made their way through the burgeoning mountain range and even then was already several hundred years old.

The venerable behemoth could easily have stood for several hundred more, but as the sun fell towards the mountains, a strange swirling cloud of black smoke curled out of the air above the surface of the river. Growing in size with every passing moment, its speed of rotation increased. Soon it spanned the water, creating a whirlpool in the fast-flowing current that foamed and bounced, soaking the trunks standing on the riverbank and revealing the riverbed beneath. The tornado leaned, unhindered by natural law, until it spun at an angle. Sliding sideways into the forest, it encountered the oldest tree. The lines of smoke, darker black against the already black woodland, wrapped themselves around the trunk, centring the wood in its vortex. Branches groaned under the extreme forces, twigs snapped and flew off deeper into the forest.

For a short time, the tree stood against the pull of the frightful phenomenon, but its strength was inexorable. With a deafening crash the mighty kaytam was sucked into the maelstrom, branch, trunk and root disappearing in an eyeblink. The blackness collapsed in on itself, dragging earth, water, and riverbed sand with it before winking out of existence as mysteriously as it had appeared.

*

'It's happening all over,' Claire said. 'Mine wasn't even the latest.'

'And more frequently too,' Elaine added. 'At this rate we may not even be able to hold a ceremony.'

'Oh please. Don't say that,' Kyle said. 'I've only just got

my head around it at all. And everything's ready. Nearly.'

'Yes, but if it's not safe?'

The four sat alone in the Palace refectory. They had not intended this to be an Elemental conclave. Elaine had observed that it was perhaps not the most private space for such a conversation. But the lunchtime rush was over and the last member of the Palace staff had left after completing his duties. None of them were keen to move. Though large, the hall was warm, and they each nursed their drink of choice.

'Are we sure it's not the Istanians?' Jann asked. 'I wouldn't put it past the damned Jester to be behind it.'

'He doesn't have this kind of power,' Elaine said with a dismissive wave of her hand. 'Or any power come to that.'

'He might have tapped into Bloodpower?'

Claire shook her head. 'No. I've checked the accounts for that. You have to be of the blood line. A direct descendant of the original King. Even if he knew how to do it — which he almost certainly doesn't — it simply wouldn't work for him.'

'What about Patrick?' Jann continued. 'I'd hate to think it's him, but you said it reminded you of his energy Claire?'

'Well that's true,' the Air Mage said, 'although I only saw him use it once, and briefly.'

'Surely he would've said something when I was there?' Kyle said. 'I know I didn't stay long, but he had plenty of chances. Never even mentioned any reports, or gave me any sign he knew of any disturbances in the area.'

'Call them vortices,' Claire said with a tut. 'That's what they are. No need to beat about the bush. We might not know who or what is causing them, but we know what they are.'

'And we know what they're not,' Elaine said. 'They're not Fire, and they're not Air.'

'And they're obviously not Water,' Kyle added, 'though there have been several seen over or around water.'

'Coincidence, I'm sure,' Claire said. 'Don't worry Kyle.

No-one's blaming you.'

'Could it be the Queen?' Elaine asked.

They all fell silent. Claire had had a similar thought, that very morning. Soon after escaping with her life from the angry mob of Kertonians. Maybe she was being paranoid, but her first thought had been that the Queen was still mad at her. She had discovered a frightening new dimension of Wood power.

'I don't know,' she said at length, 'not for certain. But I'd doubt it. She may be angry — at me more than anyone — but she's not vindictive, or cruel. And the vortex I saw was every bit as dangerous to her own people as to me. One of the locals said a vortex had snatched one of his animals. Why would she do that?'

'You say "snatched" like it was a deliberate act,' Kyle said. 'Far as I can tell from the reports we've had, they're more random. Things fall into them, like—' she glanced nervously at Jann. 'Like a gate.'

Jann held up his hands. 'Believe me,' he said, 'I've wondered. But it's nothing I'm doing, at least consciously. And remember, gates don't spin. All of these vortices behave the same. Like miniature versions of the one that sent us falling to Earth.'

Claire frowned. 'Surely it can't be the same thing? That famous vortex took the combined powers of all the first-level Elements to create it, and you and Patrick's father to control it! These are cropping up anywhere, even in places where *none* of us are present.'

'I know,' Jann shook his head, 'I can't explain it. None of us can. But we need an answer, somehow.'

'What about the ceremony?' Kyle asked. 'I wasn't keen, I hardly need to say, but it's all organised now. Invites have gone out and everything. Some people will be travelling by now.'

'You're right,' Claire said. 'It's too late to call it off. All we can do is stay alert. Keep a look out.'

'And do what?' Elaine said. 'If we see one? None of us

know how to shut one of these things down. They do that on their own.'

'None of them last very long,' Jann said. 'Maybe the best we can do is get people out of the way. Post guards at strategic view points, give us the best coverage. The best chance of spotting one.'

Claire caught Kyle looking at her. It was clear what she was thinking. But the two of them would not be any safer behind the New Washington wall than they were here.

Chapter 10

the court of the blood king
27th day of sen'sanamasa, 966

The Palace message arrived while Sebaklan Pwalek was eating his lunch. He had been looking for Jeruk ever since. He thought he understood how this "Air Mail" worked, but if his understanding was right, the message should have found his leader by itself. Instead it had fallen to the ground inside the Court gates, and been brought to him by one of the Blood Watch. Maybe the sender, being uncertain who was in charge at Court, simply directed it to the building itself?

Annoyed at this waste of time, Seb finally spotted the familiar, diminutive figure sitting beside the moat, feeding the pipit.

'What in Baka's name are you doing out here?'

Jeruk looked up. 'I felt stifled in there,' he replied, throwing another handful of grain into the water. The pipit scrabbled and squabbled over the food, shouting their distinctive cries at each other and eliciting a strange smile from their benefactor. 'Needed some air.'

'You'll freeze your nuts off if you sit there much longer. Here. This came.'

He handed over the small piece of parchment.

'What does it say?' Jeruk asked.

'I haven't read it. Figured it was official.'

'You're my deputy. You're allowed to read official.'

'Too late now. You read it.'

Jeruk unfolded the message, glanced at the first line, and snorted. 'Gracious Majesty! Pompous bitch, more like.'

'What does she want?'

Jeruk scanned the rest of the text, refolded it, and tucked it away inside his jerkin.

'Water Wizard inauguration,' he said. 'At the Palace.'

'When?'

'Four days from now. After noon.'

'The first of the new year? Very auspicious.'

'I'm sure that's what they're hoping for, yes.'

'Will you go?'

Jeruk snorted again, but made no reply.

'You should. Help reduce the tensions between the Houses. Rub some salve onto the wounds?'

'I'd rather rub salt into them.'

'And what good will that do?'

'It's just as likely to be a trap as a real celebration.'

'Take some Blood Watch with you then, if you're worried. I'm sure they won't want any trouble. Not inside the Palace.'

'Easier to not go in the first place.'

'And risk a diplomatic incident?'

'Better than having my throat cut.'

'Aren't you being a bit paranoid?'

'Look, I've said I'm not going. That's an end to it. You go, if you think it's that important.'

'OK, I will.'

Jeruk stared at him, a mixture of surprise, anger, and resentment flitting across his face in waves.

'Don't get mad. If nothing else it'll give me chance to check in with our local... information source.'

'Always a silver lining, I suppose. I'd still be taking some guards with me.'

'I can take care of myself,' Seb said, placing a hand on his pilattik. 'If it comes to that.'

'You'll be leaving first thing then? Three days' ride if you don't rush.'

'Thanks, I remember how far it is. If I leave tomorrow I'll have an evening to spare before the ceremony.'

'I'm sure the Queen will look after you. And like you said, chance to catch up with old friends. Hurry back.'

Jeruk threw the rest of his grain at the squawking birds and strode into the Court without another word.

new washington
27th day of sen'sanamasa, 966

Jared deLange snatched the floating parchment out of the air as it drifted past. He knew what it was, of course, and could guess where it was heading, but he had never really trusted Elemental magic. His own was wayward enough. Good for party tricks and to persuade others he was someone worth having on-side, or, occasionally, someone to be feared. He had never mastered it sufficiently well to use it for anything meaningful.

He had heard of this "Air Mail" trick the Yamani girl had invented. He could not imagine how she could control the power at such long distances, or ensure the messages reached their intended destinations. He would not have trusted it. He smiled. There might always be someone in the way, ready to intercept the dispatch, whether for legitimate reasons or otherwise.

He read the text scrawled in a feminine hand on the parchment. So it had come from the Air Mage herself, but sent on behalf of the Queen. Interesting. The long-heralded "inauguration" of the new Water Wizard was finally going to happen. And on the first of the year, too. The locals would treat that as a "sign", no doubt. He snorted. So much superstition and magic. Still, at least it made things easier to turn to his advantage.

He entered the main building. The surge of new arrivals at New Washington had slowed to a trickle. There was no queue waiting to be attended. The whole canteen was strangely deserted, given that evening meal preparations were underway. He hurried to Alvarez' office, knocked, and entered without waiting for a response. The small space was empty. Damn the woman! No wonder she had been so keen to appoint a deputy. She had not done a stroke of work since he took the role on.

Returning to the main hall, he encountered Tremaine and Glass. They were like Tweedledee and Tweedledum.

He rarely saw one without the other.

'Have you seen Alvarez?' he asked, waving the parchment. 'This arrived for her.'

Tremaine took an identical paper from his pocket. 'We had one too.'

Glass frowned. 'If it had been for her, it should have found her for itself. What are you doing with it?'

'It flew past me. Thought I'd better make sure it reached her.'

'Not doing a very good job then, are you?' Tremaine said.

'You'd be better off letting it go,' Glass added. 'It will find her quicker than you can.'

Alvarez walked in. 'What will find her?' she asked, as the message tore loose from deLange's grasp and flew towards her.

'That will,' Piers said, laughing.

'I was bringing it to you,' Jared said, moving to Alvarez' side. He paused while she read the script, then added 'We should decide who to send, I suppose?'

Alvarez folded the note. 'And decide quickly. Whoever is going will need to leave tomorrow if they're to arrive in time. I can't believe they left it this late to send invites.' She stared at Jared. 'How long have you had this?'

'It arrived a moment ago,' he said. 'I've been trying to find you.'

'He's right,' Tremaine said, patting his pocket. 'Ours came today too. Not long ago.'

'So you two are going,' Alvarez said, 'who else?'

'Not him,' Tremaine said, nodding at Glass. 'Just me.'

Alvarez favoured Glass with a quizzical expression, but made no comment.

'You should go Silvia,' Jared said. 'The Queen and the rest of them will probably expect senior representation from here. Anything else may be thought a snub.'

'Yes, thank you Jared,' Alvarez said, 'for the lesson in diplomacy. I will go, naturally. The question is, who shall I take with me, other than Piers?'

'I feel I should remain behind,' Jared said hurriedly. 'As your deputy. Someone needs to keep things running smoothly?'

'So you don't count yourself as a "senior representative" then?' she said.

The half-smile on the leader's face gave him no clue whether she was serious or only mocking him. Before he could reply, she let him off the hook.

'It's fine. I'll take Waters. We don't need a huge delegation, and she's spent the last ten years travelling all over. Taking colonists to their new homes and following up on her pet projects. She knows the road better than any of us.'

*

True to form, Alvarez had left him to make all the arrangements. In the end she decided to take one of the Dauntless lot. Smith, was it? He could not remember. Waters, of course, and the woman who he assumed was her partner, Jo something. The two of them were still coy about declaring their relationship, but he'd seen the signs.

That made five kudai to prepare for the journey, along with sufficient supplies for three overnight stops. Alvarez had confirmed they would not be breaking their trip at the Forest Clearance Project. She preferred the more southerly route, through the pass between the two peaks of Tubelak'Dun. It would save them a full day's travel or more.

Even so, they would arrive at the Palace late on the morning of the ceremony itself, so there was little scope for delay. Alvarez quizzed him several times about the lateness of the invite, despite Tremaine's insistence theirs had arrived at almost the same time. Was it his fault if the Palace could not get their act together?

Tweedledee and Tweedledum walked out of the building, shielding their eyes from the low sun.

'Give everyone my regards,' Glass said, 'and tell Kyle congratulations again. I'm sorry to miss her big day.'

'It's not too late to change your mind,' Tremaine said. 'I'm sure deLange can rustle up another kudo.'

'I'll see you when you get back,' Glass said. 'I'm not big on goodbyes.'

He slapped Tremaine on the shoulder and murmured a word of greeting to Alvarez and Waters as he headed inside. The two women approached them with another man.

'This is kind of exciting,' said the man, fumbling with stiff fingers to button up his coat.

Jared cinched the last of the girths and gave each animal one last check over. 'Who's this?' he asked. 'I thought Smith was going?'

'Late change of personnel,' Alvarez said. 'Turns out Smith has never ridden anywhere. We don't have time to spare making allowances for a new rider. Aftab volunteered.'

'Any excuse to see the Palace,' Aftab said, 'I almost chose it when we landed here, but the weather put me off. And then we got talking about New Washington and all that. Seemed sensible to stick around and see how it panned out. But I couldn't pass this up. I rode bareback in my spare time back home,' he added. 'These beasts are a piece of cake.'

He patted the nearest kudo on the neck. The animal tossed its head and snickered, pulling on the traces Jared held in his hands.

'Steady on, boy,' he said. 'They might be placid, but they're not stupid. Have a care, eh?'

'OK, OK, boss man,' Aftab said laughing. 'Take it easy, I know what I'm doing.'

He swung into the saddle and snatched the reins from Jared's hand. 'We making a start, or what?' he shouted, turning the kudo in a full circle and kicking up flurries from the thin covering of snow that had fallen overnight.

Waters' partner came running out of the building. 'Sorry, sorry, I'm here.'

The others mounted up and the travelling party rode out without another word. He watched them go before turning on his heel and heading back in, to the warmth of Alvarez' office.

besakaya
29th day of sen'sanamasa, 966

Petani sat alone in the main project hut. He would have preferred to be outdoors but the malamajan had started some time before, forcing him to take refuge. The weather had been unseasonably warm. For the first time in many days the night rain fell as rain. Whatever arcane mechanism drove the ancient jamtera was beyond his understanding, but the rainfall was continuing for far longer tonight than usual. His project fellows had long since retired, and still the drumming of drops on the roof resounded through the room.

He threw another log into the fire pit, and picked up the scrap of parchment that lay beside him. If words could be worn away by reading, the message would long since have been abraded to nothing. It was a brief, formal message, but he had read it so often he could recite it word for word.

Knowing what it said, and acting on that knowledge, were two different things.

'I not know why it hard decision, Petani,' Umtanesh said earlier. The Air Mail had arrived and he read its contents to his friends. 'Queen do you great honour.'

'And other Elementals will be there too,' Tanaratana added. 'You not want to see everyone again? Catch on?'

'Catch up,' he gently corrected, something he needed to do far less frequently these days. 'And yes, that's partly why it *is* a hard decision. I would have loved to spend time with them all, hear the news, and tell them what's been happening here.'

'So? What stopping you?'

A question he could not answer for himself, let alone put into words for others to understand. No, that was not entirely true. Be honest with yourself, Petani, even if you can't be honest with them. It's the catching up that puts you off. It was bad enough with young Kyle. Tales of her success contrasted starkly with knowledge of your mundane achievements. Let's not go down that rabbit hole again. Let's sit at its entrance and ponder how many other rabbit holes there are in this hillside. How much more embarrassing and galling it would be to listen to Claire, and Piers, and Bakara, and probably even Jann and Patrick, relating at length and in great detail all their many accomplishments.

'And what about you Petani? What have you been doing since the events of Utperi'Tuk?'

'Well, I've grown some flowers. Planted some winter veg.'

He stared at the parchment, as he had countless times since it arrived the day before yesterday. "Celebrations will commence immediately after noon." If he was going, he was in danger of leaving it too late. He repeated the mental calculation he had performed several times over the last two days. The answer did not change. At the speed he could ride, given the time of year, the journey to the Palace would take a full two days. He would have to leave at daybreak, and it was already past midnight.

He read the message for the fiftieth time. "Cordially invited." During Kyle's brief visit, it had become obvious she had developed a close friendship with Claire. The Air Mage, before there was any inkling she had that phenomenal power, had been his closest companion since his return to Berikatanya. Was that reason enough to go? The new log popped in the fire pit, a pocket of sap exploding and flaring briefly. As if a switch had been flipped, the rain stopped its beating against the roof; the malamajan done for the night. Petani screwed up the parchment and cast it into the fire, where it caught and flamed into ash.

new washington
30th day of sen'sanamasa, 966

Not for the first time, Patrick wished he had stayed in his father's house. It had taken months of effort, not to mention many days of help from the villagers, to rebuild the place. If he was going to be alone, he would rather be alone there than stuck in a bare cell at New Washington. The new dwelling places Piers had created in moments from the raw rock of the Pennatanah Peninsula were comfortable enough, but spartan. The settlement did not have the resources for luxury. The thought of the rich, plush furnishings and rugs in the place he briefly called home brought a rueful smile. He had been forced to leave all that behind. The only item he took from his family seat was the one thing he would never abandon: the Tang Jikos. The treasured lore book of his father.

Would he ever think of the tome as his, rather than his father's? In truth, it belonged to all his ancestors; distant and recent. Whichever Pattern Juggler had committed the early lore to paper had long since been lost to history. More than one author, that much was certain. Some glyphs and graphics were older than others, many clearly drawn in different hands, though his father's idiosyncratic style was recognisable on many pages.

Outside, the ocean pounded against the nearby cliffs. At least he still had that. He had always loved the sea. This, the Jin-segar, visibly different in colour and movement from the coastal waters below his father's village, where the shallow draft permanently stirred the ocean floor into the muddy brown for which that sea had been named: Cok-segar. But no matter the colour, every sea had the attributes that fascinated and moved him. Its changing motion, swelling reflections, and the salty tang the booming, breaking waves lent to the air. The day had worn too late for his cliff-top vigil. Having grown used to Piers' company on those watches, Patrick was less inclined to while away his time at the rocky vantage point.

After the Stone Mage's departure, he returned his attention to the book. It lay open on the table in front of him. The sum total of Void lore, the only record in existence. He had learned to call it Void power. There was no more accurate translation of the ancient word for it. He had discussed this with Claire in the past. The Air Mage had remarkable retention of everything she had read during her long days in the Keeper's crypt. Even before her arrival, she had been well-read on a huge variety of subjects after exhausting the library aboard Valiant. She revealed that ancient mythologies from various Earth cultures called the highest Element "Aether." But Void was an alternative term that sat more easily with him. He liked to think this was because he had some innate, familial connection with the lore. Maybe it had spoken its name to some deep recess of his mind. Or perhaps he was kidding himself.

He had examined the codex from cover to cover several times since discovering its hiding place, but still two sections remained a mystery to him. The arcane scratchings refused to reveal their meaning, no matter how he viewed them or how many guesses he attempted. Days he had spent wracking his brains to interpret them, without success.

Recently, he had felt on the verge of a breakthrough with one of the two. It referred obliquely to a strangely different aspect of Void power, unconnected with anything he was familiar with. His feeling of imminent triumph had eventually come to nothing, though the practises it had caused him to perform made some of the simpler Void-enabled tasks easier.

That final section, though. Nothing he tried was any use in deciphering it. Its pages stood alone, removed from the rest into a kind of addendum to the main work. All he could glean was that it appeared to describe an invasion. Exactly who or what was invading, where they would invade, or when, remained hidden. The more he tried to understand it, the more confused he became, as though the pages themselves tried to obfuscate their meaning. With a sigh, he admitted he would have to abandon the attempt for yet another day.

He crossed the concourse to the canteen, filled a plate, and took a seat with a man and a woman he recognised from Waters' crew of engineers. The chance to talk about mundane matters and leave all thought of Void behind for a time was a welcome respite.

'You look like death,' came a voice from behind him. 'Mind if I join you?'

Jared deLange pulled out the last chair at the table and sat without waiting for an answer.

'Thanks.' Patrick replied.

'I'm serious,' deLange said, 'you should see the doctor.'

'It's nothing. I've not been sleeping.'

'Missing your little friend?'

Waters' people made their excuses and left, taking half-filled plates back to the servery. They said nothing, but their expressions spoke volumes. Patrick wished he could join them, but deLange must have seen him arrive.

'Of course. I'm not losing any sleep about it though.'

'What's worrying you then? Must be something?'

'Must it? I mean, it's not like there's a long list of stuff to worry about, is it? Overcrowding, local raiders, disruption of trade, lack of good conversation. I'm amazed anyone can sleep.'

'You missed vortices.'

Patrick felt the blood drain from his face. 'And vortices. Although there's no definite evidence they're a threat.'

DeLange laughed, but there was no mirth in it. 'No? I've heard they can snatch grown men away in the blink of an eye. If that's not threatening I don't know what is.'

the palace of the black queen
1st day of far'utamasa, 967

Kyle Muir gazed out into the Palace basilica, watching an army of housemen hurry from one side to the other, busying themselves with the final preparations. She could not guess what remained to be done: the whole area looked beautiful. A dais had been built against the southernmost wall, large enough to hold perhaps six people. The running order for the ceremony did not require speeches from the other Elements. Protocol demanded their presence though, and a seat at the "top table."

'You've done a superb job,' Kyle said, as the Fire Witch joined her.

'You did most of it,' Elaine said, 'and Claire helped.'

Kyle laughed. 'I sketched out maybe one idea. I was away at the coast during a lot of the planning, and Claire took off to the woods. Don't be so modest. If anyone did this, it was you.'

Drapes hung from every window, relieving the dour, uniform blackness of the Palace walls all around the courtyard. Predominantly a deep blue in honour of her Element, they looped across the granite surfaces in huge swathes. Occasional splashes of red, white, and black accented the blue, an homage to the other Elements which would be represented. The question of a colour for Wood and Stone had exercised the minds of Palace staff. Since these second-level Elements had only recently been revealed, they did not have traditional colours. In the end it was decided that balance would be maintained by not using a special colour for either.

Strategically placed braziers dotted the perimeter. Their dancing flames provided no practical help against the chill of the first day of the new year, but the Witch had a solution for that. Her Guild members stood beside each, and would maintain a gentle flow of Fire power throughout the ceremony. Attendees would need no seasonal clothing to be comfortable during the proceedings.

Decorations were not restricted to drapes. Local village schools had engaged in a competition for the most original representations of Water, and these dotted the basilica. Paintings, sculptures and even some outlandish costumes — many intended to mimic the water form so beloved of the old Water Wizard Lautan, and which Kyle had yet to attempt — were on display. Pride of place on the presentation dais was reserved for the winner: a stunning sculpted waterfall made from rare birbab, a mineral found only in a few isolated parts of Kertonia. Palace gardeners had installed a line of ceramic troughs in front of the dais, planted with a selection of Sanamasan-flowering specimens. Similar, smaller tubs stood against the walls and on either side of the gate. Beyond the Palace walls, they also lined the moatside, providing colourful relief of the otherwise barren countryside.

'Petani would be delighted. He has many of those in his own gardens.'

'Is he coming?' Elaine asked.

'The invites didn't require an RSVP, so I can't be certain. But I'd expect him to come. I'd expect everyone who was invited to come.'

'I hope you're not disappointed. I'd better check the Fire mages are all present and correct. Don't want anyone to catch a chill!'

They laughed, and the Witch walked off. Below her the basilica was filling. Visitors who had arrived the day before had breakfasted, and were emerging to check out the decorations and absorb the atmosphere of the day. A sense of excitement was building. There was still no sign of the Queen, but Kyle expected her to leave it late, knowing of her mounting antipathy towards the Palace buildings. She recognised Sebaklan Pwalek, dressed in the uniform of a Blood Watch captain, standing by the dais. He appeared to be the only delegate from Court, and was engaging Seteh Seruganteh in animated conversation.

As she watched the two gesticulating, a group of five kudai rode in through the gate, with Piers Tremaine in the lead. She checked the faces of the other riders, but of Patrick there was no sign. She hurried down to greet the Stone Mage.

'Cutting it fine!' she called, waving.

'It's a long trip,' Piers replied, 'and some people who claimed to be seasoned riders, apparently don't know one end of a kudo from the other.' He grinned at the man riding behind him, who scowled back without a word.

Piers dismounted and handed his reins over to the head ostler, who was looking decidedly frayed. 'Do you think I have time for a bite? We set off early this morning. I've had nothing but a bepermak all day.'

'You have time,' Kyle said, 'but if you can hold off until after the ceremony, you'll be glad you did. The Queen — or rather her new steward Seteh — has laid on an enormous spread.'

'I don't know whether I can sit through an interminable set of speeches without drowning out the speakers with my stomach rumblings. How is the old Queen anyway?'

'She's not here yet. Claire tells me she's been a little out of sorts lately, but that may just be with her.'

'Only out of sorts when she has to return to this dark, dismal place,' the Queen's voice said.

Kyle jumped, spinning around. The monarch-turned-Wood-mage had appeared from behind them, hidden by the last three kudai waiting to be stabled. 'Oh, I'm sorry your Majesty,' she began, 'I didn't mean—'

The Queen gave a wicked smile. 'I'm only teasing my dear. I feel so much more an Elemental now, and less a Queen. I think we can dispense with royal protocols from today. Feel free to pass that message on to the others, whenever they arrive.'

She swept away in a rustle of black cloth, towards Seteh, who was still stood by the dais talking with Pwalek. Jann and Elaine approached from the main door.

'Piers! Welcome back,' Jann said, smiling and moving to embrace the Stone Mage. He glanced around the basilica. 'No Patrick?'

'He... couldn't make it.'

Jann frowned. 'That's a shame. Don't feel you have to make excuses for him. He's been even more of a loner since he took off for the coast. New Washington, you're calling it now, I hear?'

'As of fifteen days ago,' Piers said. 'News travels fast, even without the benefit of Air Mail. Speaking of which, where is Claire?'

'Here!' Claire called, rushing over to greet them. She waved at Felice Waters, who introduced her to Silvia Alvarez. There were a few more expressions of regret at Patrick's absence, and one or two more introductions. An awkward silence fell over the group, no-one knowing what to do next. At length, Elaine broke the deadlock. 'Shouldn't you be getting ready, Kyle?'

A shiver ran through her at the Fire Witch's words. The time had come.

'I suppose so.'

'Need any help?'

'I know I don't wear a dress very often,' Kyle said, feeling her cheeks grow hot, 'but I think I can remember how to put one on, thank you. Why don't you all find your seats and I'll see you momentarily.'

She would never have admitted it, but Kyle came close to wishing she had not been so quick to dismiss the offer of assistance. Her ceremonial dress, probably the most beautiful item of clothing she had seen since arriving on this planet, was not the easiest thing to get into. Fortunately Sangella, whose services she shared with Claire, had seen her return to her chambers. She had sufficient wit to realise Kyle could not manage it alone.

'Thank you, Sangella,' Kyle said, as the girl tied the last of the ribbons at the back of her neck.

'You look fabulous miss,' the girl replied, blushing. 'I'd love to be there to see you being honoured as our new Water Wizard.'

'Oh! I...' Kyle hesitated, unsure of the protocol. 'Yes. Yes, why not? It's my day. If you want to be there, come as my guest,' she said.

Sangella clapped her hands and squealed. 'Oh, thank you miss! Thank you so much!' A look of panic flashed across her face. 'Should I get changed? I can't go like this!'

She wore a plain white shift, the usual garb for a Palace maid, but it looked fresh on that day. 'Don't worry,' Kyle said, 'you're fine. Come as you are.'

The orchestra, under the leadership of Mimempus, struck up the Inauguration March. A new piece written for the occasion by the Palace composer Lemgaran. 'Come on!' Kyle said, 'They've started!'

The two women raced down the main stairs and out into the midday sun. The air, while not exactly balmy, had lost its chill; the Fire mages appointed by the Witch doing their job to great effect. Kyle led Sangella to a seat next to Alvarez.

'Look after her,' she said, 'she's my special guest.'

She mounted the dais and took her place beside the Queen, who waited patiently for the Inauguration March to finish. The music suited the occasion perfectly, being at the same time rousing and gentle. Reminiscent of water running clear over a rocky river bed, but also stirring, and powerful, like a cataract roaring from a subterranean mountain chamber. The final passage opened out in a perfect musical representation of a river delta flowing slowly and majestically into the ocean.

'Thank you, Mimempus, and your players. A lovely rendition. And thanks also to its writer, Lemgaran. I'm sure I speak for all of us when I say that is your finest work to date.'

She turned to face the centre of the courtyard. 'Welcome, everyone, on this auspicious occasion. I have accepted the honour of inducting our new Water Wizard. In the absence of a Guild leader, and, sadly, the outgoing incumbent, the Elementals agreed that I should lead the ceremony. I do not believe—'

A hoarse cry from the main gateway interrupted the Queen's address. A young man, his clothes tattered and his face bruised and swollen, staggered through the open gate.

'Wasdah!' he cried, his voice echoing around the basilica. 'Wasdah, malpatak imperita!'

The audience gasped as one and leapt to their feet as the man collapsed in a heap on the cold, hard ground.

south of the mountain
date unknown

He knew what he was doing, of course. Had practised the move many times. It was not enough. Totally unprepared for the effect of such enormous distance, he fell forward, his head splitting with the most fearsome headache he had ever endured. Pain fogged his eyes. Blades of agony from his knees, as they hit the stony path, joined the pounding from between his ears.

'Aaaaach!' he cried, hands flying to his face, squirming to escape the torment. He keeled over and lay on the frozen earth, panting. Waiting for the recovery he knew would come. He had no notion how much time passed. Eventually the pain subsided. He sat up, rubbing his bruises and hugging himself against the cold. Whatever forces had caused his injuries had also affected his clothing. It hung from him in tatters. This was like nothing he had experienced in previous attempts, but it brought him no benefit to dwell on the why of it. The fact of it was enough for now.

He looked around, recognising none of his

surroundings at first, until his gaze fell on the enormous mountain range behind him. The distant white peaks had a familiar shape, even if his perspective had shifted. So his destination had to lie in front of him, though he knew not how far. He would not reach it by sitting here, contemplating the task. He struggled to his feet, wincing at a stab of pain from his left ankle. He leaned his weight onto it gingerly. A sprain only. Thank the Gods not a break! He set off, limping at first, judging his direction to be south from the position of the sun. The exercise loosened his injured tendons. Within a few dozen paces, he was walking almost normally.

The morning passed swiftly. He covered ground at a good pace, stopping once to harvest the unexpected bounty of a handful of berries which clung to a roadside bush. He skirted an enormous forest to his left, and as the sun approached its zenith, so he approached his destination. The black towers crouched beside the dark of the forest, separated from him by a mighty river. Spanning the waters, an impressive stone bridge had been erected. Its ornate pillars were carved from the same black stone as the Palace.

As he neared the gate, a woman's voice rang out in an unfamiliar tongue, though he could recognise some of the words. She addressed a crowd of people, all dressed in finery and sitting in neat, serried ranks. The air in the courtyard had a surprising warmth for the time of year. He welcomed the small relief from the cold, which had seeped right into his core during the journey. He stood for a moment by the gate, taking in the scene and gathering his last vestige of strength.

'Beware!' he shouted, though his voice sounded hoarse and weak to his ears. 'Beware, for your doom is almost upon you!'

The blackness of utter exhaustion closed in on him. He fell to the ground once more, this time senseless to the impact.

the palace of the black queen
1st day of far'utamasa, 967

Jann reached the fallen man before the others. Up close his face was even more badly bruised than had been apparent at first. He cradled the man's head, shouting for a houseman to fetch a blanket. Elaine was not far behind him.

'What did he say?' she asked. 'I couldn't make it out.'

'Something about doom, I think,' Jann said. 'I only caught a bit of it.'

'We should take him inside. Out of the cold. The mages are helping, but a decent fire and a warm bed would be even better.'

'Take him to my chambers,' the Queen said, approaching with Kyle in tow. 'I'm sorry my dear I'm afraid we shall have to curtail the ceremony for now. Whoever this is, he's in desperate need of help.'

'You take his legs,' Piers said to Jann, 'I'll grab his shoulders. He doesn't look heavy enough to need more than two of us.'

'I could probably manage him on my own,' Jann said, 'but you're right. Safer with two. He looks like he could use some of your healing energies, Ru'ita.'

'Of course,' the Queen replied, colouring slightly. 'That should have been my first thought. Thank you, Gatekeeper. I shall fetch my staff and meet you upstairs.'

The rest of the audience milled aimlessly around the courtyard. The Queen remounted the dais. As Jann entered the building he heard her voice ring out across the space, telling everyone the celebrations were on hold for the time being but refreshments would be served right away. Seruganteh hurried past him to make sure they would.

In the Queen's chambers a fire roared in the grate. No more than a word from even an absentee Queen could apparently still work wonders in this place, the machinery of the Palace clicking smoothly into action.

'Wasdah...' the man murmured, as Jann and Piers laid him on the bed.

'Don't try to speak,' Jann said. 'The Queen will be here soon. You'll feel better then, believe me.'

The man's eyes fluttered open. 'I seek... Argent,' he managed.

Elaine's eyes popped. 'What's that?' she said. 'Does he really mean you?'

Jann stared at the stranger. He did not recognise the man, and yet the cadence of the few words he had uttered struck a chord deep within him. 'How can it be anyone else?' he said. 'I'm the only one here called Argent.'

'Do you know him?'

Jann hesitated. Now that he looked closer, perhaps he did look familiar after all. 'No,' he said at length. 'I don't know him. But he does remind me of someone.'

Chapter 11

the palace of the black queen
1st day of far'utamasa, 967

He woke. A feeling of utter calm suffused him. His head no longer ached; his ankle did not twinge; he was warm! He opened his eyes, surprised to discover he was lying in a bed. A small group of strangers stood around him. One — a tall, dark-haired woman with an air of authority, held a large, striated wooden staff. The source of the energy he could feel. Wood power! Long rumoured in conversations with the village Elders that lay scattered throughout his past. The Wood mage had her eyes closed in concentration. The others all watched him. A man and a woman stood together, both with strikingly unusual hair. His short and brilliant white without a trace of colour; hers long and thick, a vibrant red. Their soft expressions showed only kindness and concern. To one side, two other, younger women shared worried glances. At the window, his face shadowed by the brilliant sunlight washing into the room, a short, stocky man with brown hair faced him with his hands on his hips. A slight smile played over his lips.

He moved to sit up. The woman with the staff opened her eyes.

'Remain,' she said. 'It be not sense to motion.'

Though her intent was clear, the words were strangely arranged. Archaic terms in an unusual order. The Elders had warned him there would be differences in language. From their experience with the Visitor, they expected he would at least be able to understand, and make himself understood.

'Please,' he said, feeling the flow of health diminish as the woman's focus moved away from him. His tongue rolled around his dry mouth. 'Could I have water?'

'I will fetch,' said the woman with light coloured hair.

'And I will bring eatings,' said the other, leaving the room behind her.

'I must not stay here,' he said. 'I have to find Jann Argent and speak with him.'

At the mention of the name the silver-haired man stepped forward, a look of surprise on his face.

'I be Jann Argent,' he said, 'though I not recognition you. You say my name two time. We meet ever in past?'

'You have been spoken of long in my village,' the man said. 'Men call you the Visitor. You it was who told us of the sky people, and the metal magics they have. A way that can warn you. We know this. Oh! Your doom is upon you soon, if it is not already too late. Search the skies! You must hurry!'

'You say "doom" before you falling down,' Argent said. 'What is the doom you speak of? It sound fearsome.'

'The doom is coming!' he said, feeling his strength fading. 'The rock that flies from the darkness. You must use your metal magics. Protect yourselves. Or all will die.'

the palace of the black queen
1st day of far'utamasa, 967

Elaine moved closer to Jann. After fighting to speak, the stranger had fallen back in the bed, exhausted by his efforts.

'What did he say? Flying rock?'

'Yes,' Jann said. 'Flying rock out of the darkness.'

'What does it mean?'

Claire and Kyle returned carrying a jug of water and a plate of food for the man. They helped him sit up and take a drink, and a bite.

'I don't know. Neither of the Houses has a siege engine. Like a catapult or a trebuchet.'

'And even if they did,' Piers added, 'they never attack at night. Whatever rocks they throw at us would never come "out of the darkness".'

'We're missing something,' Elaine said, trying to focus on the stranger's words. His eyes distracted her. The shock when he woke, and looked at her, had hit her like a physical force. Pale blue irises, but with deep iridescent cobalt-coloured rims. She had only ever seen eyes like that once before. She gazed into them every night and every morning. They belonged to her lover. She put a hand on his shoulder, more to gain reassurance than give it. 'Something about metal magic. And you mentioning it to his people.'

'It's obvious he's Beragan,' Piers said. 'I remember your tale well, Jann. Of your visit to the northern people. How their language was different in some ways, and for some words, but still intelligible. That's exactly how he sounds. And who else would refer to you as "the Visitor"?'

'Piers is right,' Elaine said. 'What did you tell them about the Earthers?'

'He's coming round again,' Claire said. 'Are you feeling better now?' she asked the man. 'Well enough to sit up? Can you tell us your name?'

She turned to the Queen. 'Perhaps another injection of health, Ru'ita? If you're able?'

'Of course,' the Queen replied, taking up her staff again. 'But our visitor is not the only one who will require sustenance. None of you have eaten since first light. Claire, ring for Seteh. He can have some of the celebration food brought up.'

She moved back to the man's bedside and recommenced the flow of healing power.

'Ahh, my thank-yous,' he said. 'I feeling abashed being lie down. I health enough to sit inside chair.'

He swung his legs out of the Queen's large, soft bed and moved to a seat beside the window. 'My name Ahnakpenyabangung,' he said, 'but if it fills your mouth too much, you will call me Ahnak in its place.'

No-one else spoke. Elaine caught the expression on Jann's face. He gave the man a strange look. Half shocked and half of... almost recognition. 'Ahnak,' she said, breaking the silence. 'Welcome to Kertonia, and to the Black Palace.'

'Thank,' said Ahnak.

She walked around the room, introducing the others, returning to Jann's side. 'And Jann Argent you already know,' she said curtly, wondering what memories the Beragan's words had stirred in her partner's mind.

The door opened to admit the steward. 'You rang, ma'am?'

The Queen opened her eyes. 'Ah, Seruganteh,' she said, 'fetch up some of the inauguration meal for our guest and our Kema'satun, will you?'

'At once,' the man said, bowing and hurrying away.

Elaine's attention returned to Ahnak. He stared out over the forest beyond the window. In spite of his earlier urgency and insistence on delivering his message of doom to Jann, he said no more.

'Ahnak,' she said, 'you say our doom is almost upon us. What did you mean? What darkness does this doom come from? What form will it take? And how do you even know it will happen?'

'My people know,' he said. 'We have seen.'

Piers stood behind the man's chair. Unseen by Ahnak, he shrugged. If not for the topic, Elaine would have thought it a comic gesture.

'You said it came from the sky. What was it — "flying rock from the darkness"? Did you mean night-time?'

'Darkness beyond night,' Ahnak replied. 'Darkness beyond even darkness.'

'Can he mean space?' Kyle asked.

A look of horror creased Claire's face. 'Oh my God! "Flying rock"? Does he mean an asteroid?'

'You never mentioned the Beragan having telescopes, Jann,' Piers said.

'They don't. At least, I never saw any evidence. Our discussions didn't include much science, they focused on their history, political and Elemental. They appeared to be a simple, rural people, with little understanding of technology, and certainly no astronomy.'

'And yet here we are with a Beragan who has clearly endured a difficult journey to warn us of a threat from space.'

'Speak slow please,' Ahnak said. 'I not follow.'

Piers walked around from behind the man. 'If there's any truth to his story — and I'm not saying I believe him — Alvarez should be included in this conversation. New Washington is the only place with enough tech to work the problem.'

'I believe him,' Jann said. 'Don't ask me why. I can't explain it. But I don't think he's lying.'

Piers left to find the Earth leader.

'Should we move to the council chamber Ru'ita?' Claire asked. 'It feels strange holding a meeting like this in your chambers. Almost like an invasion of your privacy. And there's more room there.'

The Queen smiled. 'Thank you for your concern, my dear, but these are no longer my rooms. In fact I surprise myself how little it troubles me to have this meeting here. But look, the fire is set, the food will soon arrive. Unless this Alvarez is bringing an army with her, I am sure we can accommodate them.'

the palace of the black queen
1st day of far'utamasa, 967

'We should eat.'

The sound of Waters' voice broke her train of thought. Silvia Alvarez had been wondering about the disruption to the ceremony. Who was the strange man? What was wrong with him? What did he say before collapsing? Would the inauguration restart? Where had all the Elementals gone? So many questions rattling around in her mind, and no answers. It did not sit well with her.

'What?'

'There's food. In the refectory. We haven't eaten all day.'

'How can you think of eating at a time like this?' she asked. 'Don't you want to know what's going on? Where is everyone? I thought you were a detective?'

'I was, but I'm done with all that. Come on, Jo. Our dear leader may have a stomach of iron, but mine is made of flesh and it needs filling.'

Tremaine hurried towards them from the main building. 'Wait,' he said, as the two women moved off. 'I think you'll want to hear this.'

'Hear what?' Granger said. 'It better be good. Nothing comes between Felice and food!'

'I don't know about good, but it might be serious. There's food up there anyway. Kill two birds. Come on. All of you.' He turned on his heel and strode back inside.

'Up where?' Silvia asked, hurrying to match the Stone Mage's pace. 'We don't know where everyone went.'

'Royal chambers,' he said. 'Or used to be.'

Tremaine led the way into the Palace. The enormous hall was hung with portraits of luminaries from time gone by, set with blazing bowls providing both light and heat. Even so, the air indoors was noticeably colder that it had been in the quadrangle.

'Cold in here,' she observed as they climbed the impressive main staircase.

'The Fire Witch had some of the Guild members warming things up out there,' Tremaine replied. 'It's plenty warm enough in the Queen's rooms.'

He was not wrong. The heat hit her as they entered the capacious chambers through a pair of heavy blackwood doors. A fire blazed in an enormous grate set in the middle of the wall facing the ornately carved bed, its covers thrown back in disarray. Everyone she had missed from the ceremony was here, all wearing the same clouded look of concern. The Queen stood beside the stranger, a staff made from a complex and intricate weave of various woods held in one hand. The man sat in an overstuffed armchair, looking a little recovered after his collapse. He watched them enter, but said nothing.

Waters and Granger made a beeline for the long table that had been filled with morsels from the ceremony spread.

'What's this about?' she asked, glancing from face to face. 'Looks like whatever it is has scared you all half to death!'

'Who this?' asked the stranger.

'You should introduce yourselves,' Tremaine said, 'if your Kertonian is up to it. Speak slowly. His own command of the language isn't all that good.'

'Allow me,' said the blonde-haired woman standing next to Muir. 'We don't want anything lost in translation. Things are — might be — bad enough as it is.'

From her looks and assertive manner, this must be the Air Mage, Claire Yamani. Waters had often spoken of her. The stranger, whose name apparently was Ahnak, adopted a puzzled expression which cleared as Yamani concluded her introductions.

'So you sky people?' Ahnak asked. 'You must hurry! Flying rock upon us!'

'We figured he means an asteroid,' Tremaine said. 'He thinks it's going to hit us.'

Waters and Granger stopped filling their plates.

'What?' said Waters.

'That can't be right!' said Granger.

'When?' asked Silvia.

'He's a bit vague on the timing,' Yamani said. 'But he seems pretty certain it's going to happen.'

'And I believe him,' Argent added. 'You can see it in his eyes.'

'Oh, so you noticed his eyes too?' the Fire Witch said, a strange expression on her face. A wisp of smoke curled up between the fingers of her clenched fist. She turned away without further comment.

'No, sorry,' Granger went on, 'you must have misunderstood. Even if he's telling the truth he can't be talking about an asteroid impact. We would know.'

'Jo's right,' Waters said. 'We have a long range scanner on Dauntless. The ship is mothballed, but the warning systems are still operational. We would have had an alarm if it detected anything on an impact trajectory.'

'What saying?' Ahnak said. 'I not hearing. But I tell truth. Flying rock come. It vast. It spoil all earth, all land below mountain.'

'When?' the Queen asked, 'can you tell us when the flying rock will come, Ahnak?'

'What date now?'

'Today is the first of the new year,' the Queen replied. 'The first day of Far'Utamasa in the year nine sixty seven.'

'Surely he knows what year it is!' the Fire Witch said.

'I not hearing your days,' the man said.

'I think he means he doesn't understand the calendar,' Yamani said.

'Yes,' Ahnak nodded, 'that. But flying rock come long before snow melts to water. Cannot say exact day number.'

'Before Spring, he means,' Yamani said, her condescending manner beginning to irritate Silvia. 'Utamasa, I should say.'

'That doesn't give us long,' Silvia said. 'If he's right, the best we can do is try to prepare for impact.'

'But he said it's gonna "spoil all earth",' Muir said. 'How can we prepare for that?'

'The first thing to do is find out if he *is* right,' she replied. 'We need to get back to New Washington as soon as we can. Find out if there really is an asteroid on a collision course with this planet. And,' she added, 'why we didn't have any warning of it besides a half-crazed refugee from the other side of the mountain.'

'It won't take you long to work out he's telling the truth,' Argent said. 'We should come with you. We're going to need everyone to pull together to handle this. And that includes Patrick Glass. He might take a bit of persuading.' He turned to Ahnak. 'Sorry, brother, I know you're exhausted but we will need you to come with us. You're the only one with any knowledge of this thing. I'll need your help getting Patrick on-side.'

'On-side?' Ahnak said, scratching his head. 'No explain. I come with.'

the palace of the black queen
1st day of far'utamasa, 967

They left for New Washington that same afternoon.

Jann Argent checked his own kudo, Perak. The sturdy animal preferred its girth cinched tighter than the Palace ostler thought good for it, but Jann knew his mount. He felt safer in the saddle knowing the beast was happy. It was going to be a fast ride.

There had been some debate about whether to wait until the next day, and who should go. An early morning start was the usual rule for long journeys, but Ahnak was still vague on the exact timing of the asteroid impact, if that was indeed what he meant by "flying rock". They had agreed in the end it was better to find out sooner than later.

'If this threat is real,' the Queen had said, 'it poses the greatest danger to our civilisation we have ever encountered. Greater than the social unrest that created our two societies in the first place, or the threat of the vile Bloodpower, or — forgive me my dear — mad Muir's monsoon. Those recent challenges required all the Elementals to pull together to defeat the evils. If it's true, then this is no different. We cannot leave it to the Batu'n to handle alone. We must all travel to New Washington, and we must face the threat as one.'

An air of excitement hung over the quadrangle. The housemen and women had been busy since the interruption to the ceremony. No sign of festivities remained. All drapes and decorations were gone, chairs stacked, even the dais had been dismantled and stored away.

'Are you actually the Water Wizard now,' he asked Kyle with a grin, 'even though you've not been formally inaugurated?'

'Kyle was the Water Wizard from the moment we lost dear Lautan,' the Queen replied. 'The ceremony was a nicety, only. There is no doubting her ability, or her position.'

'That's me told then,' Jann said, swinging into his saddle.

He completed his preparations ahead of the others, with the exception of the Queen. She maintained an air of calm and quiet despite having already dressed for the journey, organised the preparation and delivery of travelling victuals, instructed the ostlers on the number of riders, and given clear commands to her deputy steward for the running of the Palace. The head steward Seteh Seruganteh was nowhere to be found.

Claire stood with Kyle, checking their kudai over, and repacking the saddlebags. Elaine had hurried to their chambers to change into suitable riding gear. She returned to the group, shading her eyes against the bright afternoon sun.

They still had the best part of a half-day before the malamajan set in for the night. Enough time to cover most of the distance to the southern foothills of Tubelak'Dun. One positive side-effect of Mad Muir's influence was that Berikatanyan society now had access to the kind of wet-weather gear unheard of before the recent unnatural rains. They planned to ride for as long as possible each day. If they pushed on for the final leg, they could shorten the journey from three full days to little more than two. Starting this early meant they would arrive at the coast after nightfall on the third of the month. He hoped it would be soon enough, but it was the best they could do.

The New Washington crew were already dressed for travel, having only arrived at the Palace earlier that morning. If they were disappointed at having to curtail their stay, or repeat the journey in the opposite direction so soon after completing it, they did not show it. Felice Waters and Jo Granger were all smiles. They appeared to be treating the whole thing as an adventure. If Ahnak's doom laden warning was accurate, they would not be smiling for long. Alvarez, on the other hand, wore a look of concern. Even before seeing hard scientific evidence, she had taken the warning to heart.

He could not say what it was about the young Beragan that led him to believe his story so easily and with such certainty. As the Gatekeeper he was used to looking at things from both sides, but in this case his instinct was strong. Ahnak was telling the truth and they were indeed in great peril. If any doubt remained in his mind it was simply that it may only be the truth from his perspective. A more prosaic explanation was still possible. Only the astronomical equipment at the Earther base could tell them for certain.

Ahnak himself stood with the remainder of their company — Piers Tremaine and the Jester's right-hand man Sebaklan Pwalek. No-one had thought to include Pwalek in their meeting in the Queen's chambers, but clearly he and the whole of the rest of Istania would be affected. Pwalek was familiar with Piers from the Stone Mage's brief time on the Darmejelis. He had elected to travel with them, since there was nothing now to keep him at the Palace. Piers and Ahnak were bringing him up to speed.

'Is everyone ready?' the Queen asked, her staff firmly seated in an adapted saddlebag by her right hand. She turned Pembrang in a full circle and walked her towards the imposing Palace gates. 'I should prefer to do most of our riding today in daylight.'

Words of assent from each of the party echoed across the now empty basilica. The Queen spurred her mount into a gallop. The party of Earthers set off close behind her, followed by Ahnak, Piers, and Pwalek. The two young Elementals rode next, leaving Jann and Elaine to bring up the rear.

As they passed through the gates and out onto the moatside path, Elaine drew alongside him.

'When you visited Tenfir Abarad,' she began, 'how well did you know Penny?'

Chapter 12

road to new washington
1st day of far'utamasa, 967

The company stopped only briefly to water the kudai and take a bite of their bepermaks. They passed to the south of the first ridges of Tubelak'Dun. Now, the sun had dropped behind the imposing mountain range, throwing the deep ridges and troughs of the mountain's flank into shadow. The solid black lines of the rock formations drew an arcane pattern onto the mountain side that appealed to Claire's sense of adventure. As if nature was sending them a message, written in an ancient hand steeped in Earth power and blasted by the other Elements over the centuries. Their route, the most direct to New Washington, involved crossing the Sun Penk and negotiating the low pass between the twin peaks of the Spine of the World.

'This is perfect for us,' Kyle said, breaking her reverie.

'What do you mean?'

'It gives us an excuse to travel to New Washington, together. And once we're there, it will be easier to broach the subject of not returning to the Palace. The Queen is here with us. We don't need to say anything yet. Once she sees the settlement, how it's changed, what it offers us, she'll have no argument.'

'I wouldn't be so sure,' Claire replied. 'You haven't known her very long. She's probably the most resourceful person I've met since I arrived.'

'Even so. She's more Wood mage now than Queen,' Kyle continued. 'And if this weird story is true, we're going to need all the Elements working together — she said as much herself. Surely it will come as no surprise to her if the Elementals want to stick together.'

'I can't see Petani moving to New Washington,' Claire said, 'so there's at least one Elemental your theory doesn't apply to. And Elaine will go wherever Jann is. Neither of them have any affinity with the Earthers. Now they have their memories back, they seem perfectly settled at the Palace. You'll have to come up with a better reason than "Elementals sticking together".'

'Petani isn't with us though,' Kyle said. 'Won't we need him too? He wouldn't like to think he was being left out. Again.'

'Again?'

'Yeah. Last time I saw him he was feeling very sorry for himself. I'm afraid I may have made it worse, banging on about my successes with the sea wall. I was almost done with the story before I even thought of the parallel with his harbour work at the Valley. I tried to recover it by playing down how easy it had been, but by then the damage was done.'

'Oh dear, poor Terry.'

'He always uses Petani now.'

'Yes, I know. Sorry. I still think of him as Terry. He was so good to me when we first worked together in the Forest. You're right. He shouldn't be sidelined. Well, there's an easy solution. One of us should stop off at the Project and tell him what's happened. Our route to New Washington takes us south of the Besakaya, but it wouldn't be much of a diversion to the Project.'

'You know him better than me.'

'That's probably true, but now that we've mentioned a diversion, I've been thinking I might tag along with Pwalek.'

'To Court? Why?'

'Yes, to Court. It's possible the Keeper may have something in his records that would help us.'

'About an asteroid? Don't think that's very likely!'

'Don't scoff. He records absolutely everything, and he's only the last in a long tradition of archivists. You'd be surprised what I've found in those dusty old catacombs. Besides, we've only assumed it's an asteroid. It could just as easily be a comet. And if it has an orbit, it will have passed this way before.'

'If that was true, and it's going to crash down like Ahnak says, why didn't it hit the planet last time?'

the sun penk
1st day of far'utamasa, 967

Having ridden through the nighttime malamajan, the party reached the Sun Penk as the twin moons disappeared below the peaks of Tubelak'Dun. The sudden darkness made it impossible to travel with any speed. Elaine knew they would have great difficulty negotiating a crossing of the river without some light.

If it had been earlier, she would have sent up a fireball to illuminate their path, but they had been riding for long enough.

'We should camp on the riverside for tonight,' she called, reining Jaranyla to a halt. 'It's too late, and too dark, to go further before dawn.'

'Very well Bakara,' the Queen said, 'your counsel is wise. But we must make a start again at first light.'

She was still annoyed at Jann's refusal to discuss his relationship with Penny. She had been unable to shake the image of Ahnak's unusual eyes from her mind the whole day. The enigmatic Beragan had ridden with Claire and Kyle for much of the journey, but his face still hung in the air in front of her, mocking her with a half smile.

She unpacked their bedrolls and looked for a secure place to lay them out. Jann had gone with Piers and Pwalek to hunt for firewood. She joined Ahnak and the girls.

'I'll start a fire as soon as the guys get back with some supplies,' she said. 'It's easier to light wood than try to heat the air with Fire power.'

'I'm still warm enough from the ride,' Claire said. 'Although I don't suppose that will last for long.'

'We were talking about making a diversion to pick up Petani,' Kyle said. 'We might need his help.'

'All three of you?'

'No,' Kyle said, 'just me.'

'I'm going with Pwalek to Court,' Claire said. 'I want to see the Keeper.'

'I go with,' Ahnak said. 'This Keeper sound ironic.'

Elaine was too tired to worry what Ahnak really meant by "ironic." It was good Claire would have company if she too planned a diversion.

'You shouldn't travel alone Kyle,' she said. 'I'll come with you to the Project. It would be good to catch up with Petani again. And it might help persuade him to join us if there's more than one of us presenting the argument.'

'You mean he might not believe me?' Kyle said, jutting out her jaw.

'No, I'm sure you'd find it easy to explain how the whole world is about to be destroyed by an asteroid we had no warning of until a stranger arrived from the North,' Elaine said. 'Just thought it might help if he could see that there were at least two people he trusts who had heard the same story. If you'd rather go alone...'

'No. Forgive me,' Kyle said. 'I let fatigue get the better of me. I would appreciate the company.'

'Nothing to forgive,' Elaine said, as the men walked back through the gloom bearing armfuls of broken branches and bracken.

They made short work of assembling the kindling into a combustible pile, which Elaine duly ignited. Within moments the group had circled the fire. The light of the flames danced across their faces and a thin trail of smoke curled upward until it was lost to the blackness of the night. Across the heap of burning wood Ahnak smiled at her, his expression an uncanny mirror of the mocking look from her thoughts that day.

She took Jann's hand. 'Can we talk about Penny now?'

'What do you want to know?' he said, his voice almost

inaudible above the crackling of the fire.

road to the blood court
2nd day of far'utamasa, 967

Ahnak had begun to wonder if he would ever be warm again.

After the late end to their journey the day before, the morning brought an early start. The group set out while the sky was still only half light. His new travelling companion was called Clayeryamarnee. Her long name could be shortened, like his, to Clayer, although why she did not use Clay as a short form escaped him. She said they only needed enough light to make a safe crossing of something called Sumpenk. All the place names here were strange to his ears, whether settlements, mountains, forests, or rivers. No hot food for breakfast. Not even time to rekindle a fire, though it would have been no trouble at all for the flame-haired woman who wielded its Elemental power.

So, cold and something-just-less-than hungry, he reined his animal to ride beside Clayer.

'Who is this Keeper that you wish to visit?' he asked after they had crossed the river and were passing between the two halves of the great mountain. 'And what will he tell you that I have not already said?'

'He has much learning,' she replied. 'He has read the Court papers many year. I hope he seen paper about other flying rocks. Or he maybe give us time to look at papers ourself.'

'But I've told you what's going to happen. Don't you believe me, Clayer?'

'It's Claire,' she said, laughing.

'That's what I said.'

'Never mind. I not mean we not believe you Ahnak,' she said, 'but we need other proof. And need to know time the rock will hit, if it does.'

'It will!'

Their scepticism was beginning to annoy him. The impact of the doom was a certainty. He knew this beyond any shred of doubt. He was annoyed at himself too, though. His journey to the southern lands, the lands of the Warring Tribes as his people called them, had made him uncertain of the precise timing of the catastrophe. But even if he could not say to the exact day when it would happen, surely they must understand that his knowledge of the impact was beyond question?

The language was a problem, that much was certain. And much more of a problem than his mother, or the village Elders, had revealed. He must try harder to make himself understood. His great hope — that he would find a way to save as many of his own people as possible — still sat heavy in his mind as he rode through the cold dawn.

'We will know for sure once others reach New Washington,' Clayer was saying. 'They have technology — metal magic — that will give exact hit time.'

'So why do we need anything from this Keeper?' he asked. 'His papers can tell only what is past, not what is to come.'

'Truth. But other rocks may have landed before. That something the Keeper's papers could tell us. How many times it happens. How bad it was.'

Their path descended a gentle gradient. The others said something about splitting that Ahnak did not understand. 'What is happening, Clayer?' he asked.

'People going to New Washington take a different path now,' she said. 'Five go north to the Besakaya trees, then you and I will split with Pwalek to Court.'

They bid farewell to the Earth people, and rode in silence for the rest of the morning. Clayer was good company whether or not they spoke. Her smile made the day warm even if the sun was not strong enough to dispel the chill of the season. As they neared the forest, the Fire wielder turned to speak with Clayer.

'We will take our leave here Claire,' she said. 'Have a safe journey. Give my respects to the Keeper, for it is long since I have seen him and I miss his wise counsel. We will catch up with you at New Washington in a few days. Don't delay for too long. We need some answers!'

'Hopefully the Keeper will have some, as well as the long range sensors,' Clayer said. 'I will pass on your regards.'

Before he could ask Clayer what "long rain senses" were, the Fire and Water wielders had left them alone with the grumpy Court man Pwallick, and their journey had continued through the afternoon until darkness came again, and with it the nightly soft rainfall.

the court of the blood king
2nd day of far'utamasa, 967

Sebaklan Pwalek hobbled through the corridors of the Blood Court. It was late, but he was certain Jeruk would still be awake. The only question was where he would be at this time.

The second half of his journey, leaving their first camp almost before the sun had risen, had been even longer than the first, and if anything less enjoyable. His travelling companions — the Air Mage and the strange man with his alarming tale of imminent destruction — had ridden together most of the way. They kept up a conversation the whole day from which he had been excluded, save for the occasional stop for food, toileting, or to ease their sore arses. Two full, long days in the saddle was a lot more than he was used to. Coming so soon after his journey to the Palace, it had rendered him almost unable to walk.

On their arrival at Court, he bid the youngsters farewell. They were intent on visiting the Keeper, and old man for whom Seb had much respect. Though the contents of the dusty parchments he spent his life studying were a mystery to Seb, he could appreciate the diligence of his efforts. Time spent doing something you love was never time wasted, in his opinion.

Dim candlelight shone beneath the door of Jeruk's chambers. He knocked and entered without waiting. The diminutive figure of Jeruk Nipis sat in an armchair by the fire, dressed in a long nightshirt, a half-empty glass of mulled buwangah in one hand.

'You're back then?'

'Obviously.'

'How did the ceremony go? Not as smoothly as expected, by all accounts.'

Seb poured himself a glass of buwangah and took the chair on the other side of the fireplace. 'You're remarkably well informed. I suppose I shouldn't be surprised.'

'You've not long missed our Man at the Palace,' Jeruk said.

'No? He would have been better staying where he was. He should have known I'd be coming back myself to make a report. As it is, I may have missed him, but he was missed himself. Back there. Anyway that's not important. We need to make plans.'

'What for?'

'A way to avoid imminent destruction.'

'Oh Tana — not you too? Don't tell me you believe this story of flying rocks from space?'

'You don't, clearly.'

'Of course not! It's an obvious set-up.'

'Is it? It seemed pretty real to me. The guy staggered in from nowhere looking like he'd been jumped on by a horde of raiders.'

'What better way for that black bitch to gain the upper hand? She can't defeat us in battle so now she's playing mind games. Trying to panic us into running away.'

'To what end?'

'Oh come on! Has a day at the Palace addled your brains? If we abandon Court, the blacks would be able to walk in and take over!'

'Take over what though? What is there here for them that they don't have over there? Water? They have it in abundance. They're next to a river too, in case you had forgotten. Timber? They have their own forest. Okay, we have two, but theirs is bigger than both ours combined. Stone? They're better supplied than us, wedged between Temmok'Dun and Borok Duset. There is literally nothing here that they want.'

'Power!' Jeruk shouted, jumping to his feet. 'There is power here, that they can only gain if we abandon it!'

'For Tana's sake! Listen to yourself Jeruk! There is only one leader in this world who wants power at all costs, and it's not the Black Queen.'

'She really has turned your head, hasn't she?'

'I've hardly spoken to her,' he replied. 'But I have spoken to her steward, and to this Ahnak character. She's not the power-mad harridan you make out Jeruk.'

'So you say. I've seen how easily she goes to war.'

'Only when provoked. By our King. Only we don't have a king any more, do we? We have us. And you're determined to carry on the fights of the past when we have a new threat now. A new enemy.'

'From space.'

'Yes, from space. If the Northerner is right.'

Jeruk laughed, choked on his drink and collapsed back into his chair in a fit of coughing. 'Don't,' he managed, clearing his throat. 'Don't make me laugh. Whoever heard of such a thing? Rocks from space?'

'The Batu'n seemed convinced,' he said. 'They know much more about space than any Istanian. And if he's right — if they're right — then all your plans for taking over the world will crumble to dust. Along with this very castle, once this "asteroid" lands.'

'We're missing a trick here,' Jeruk said, staring at him wide-eyed. 'We can turn this to our advantage!'

'What do you mean?'

'Well if the damned Queen really does believe this story, then she'll be running away somewhere, won't she?'

'I don't know. I suppose so. They've all gone to the Batu'n settlement at the coast to find out for sure whether the Northerner is telling the truth.'

'Well, let's assume he is, and she does. Run away I mean. Then the Black Palace will be empty, won't it? Ripe for the plucking. We can just walk in, just as she was planning to do to us.'

Seb put his head in his hands with a deep sigh. 'You really don't get it, do you? The thing she'll be running from is going to destroy the whole world. At least, our part of it. There won't be a Black Palace to walk into. Or a Blood Court to walk out of, for that matter. It's all going to be gone.'

'I still can't believe you're falling for this,' Jeruk said, refilling his glass and throwing another log onto the fire. You're playing right into her hands, I tell you.'

'Look, if the story is true, and we try to take advantage of her, we're going to be killed. If she makes it to safety, and we're dead, who's the winner?'

'And if the story is false, and we don't take advantage, she still wins! So according to you, there is no way to win at all.'

'Maybe not, but there's a way to survive.'

'Oh yeah? How?'

Seb scratched his head. It was a good question. One that he could not yet answer. But one thing was certain. He was not going to try and turn a natural disaster into a political advantage, and he was rapidly losing patience with anyone who would.

besakaya
2nd day of far'utamasa, 967

For the third time since leaving the others behind at the edge of the forest, Elaine stopped herself from discussing her partner with her riding companion. Kyle Muir was a friend, even though their acquaintance was recent, and a fellow Elemental, but she was not someone with whom Elaine could share her fears.

If only Jann could have answered a straight question with an honest answer. Would it have allayed those worries or only made them real? She had no way of knowing. She suspected the Northern Elders' phrase "sharing her bread" was far closer to "sharing her *bed*" than Jann was prepared to admit.

But if that were true, how could it explain the most obvious connection between the eyes of her lover and those of the Beragan visitor? Jann had left Tenfir Abarad only a few months before, and yet Ahnak was a grown man. A man of twenty-five summers or more. How was that possible? Again, she had her suspicions about that. No hard evidence, but stranger things had happened. If the two men shared an unusual eye colouration it was at least conceivable they shared other traits too.

'How much further is it to the Project?' Kyle asked. 'I've never approached it from this direction before.'

They had entered the relative gloom of Besakaya while the day was still bright. Impossible to tell how late it was now, since the evergreen tree canopy hid the position of the sun from view.

'We will be there while a portion of rebusang still remains uneaten, have no fear,' Elaine laughed.

The Water Wizard coloured under the gentle assault of her mirth. 'Am I that obvious?'

'You are not the only one who is looking forward to a hot meal, believe me,' Elaine said, still laughing.

They rode on for some time in silence, until the trees began to thin, and the sound of voices could be heard. They entered the Project clearing as the men were stacking their tools, having completed work for the day. David Garcia waved at them.

'Hello, and welcome back!' he said.

'We're early,' Elaine said to Kyle. 'The day's stew is not yet even started.'

They tied their kudai at the rail and walked over to the main camp fire, where Nembaka was peeling vegetables.

'Where is Petani?' Kyle asked the little man.

'He is here,' Petani said, walking into the clearing from the direction of the river, 'and very pleased he is to see you both!'

They busied themselves helping with the chores of evening time — cleaning the tools, feeding the animals, and stacking wood for the fire from the plentiful supplies in the woodstore. Elaine lit the pit with a blast of Elemental power.

'Fantastic! I wish we had a Fire mage here permanently,' Garcia said, smiling. 'You wouldn't believe the trouble we have every night getting that damned thing started. Everything is damp at this time of year, or even beginning to rot.'

The evening wore on, every worker returning to camp exchanging pleasantries with the newcomers and whiling away the cooking time with anecdotes and jokes. Some of the Project members recognised Kyle and congratulated her on her inauguration. Elaine gave the girl a warning look, and she took the hint not to mention the abortive ceremony. When the rebusang was ready and everyone had been served, the locals moved a respectful distance away from the fire or even took themselves off indoors despite Elaine's protests that they should stay close for warmth. In a very short time only Petani, Kyle, and herself remained by the fire pit.

'So,' Petani said, blowing on a sunyok-full of rebusang, 'what brings you to Besakaya? More than a chance to exchange insults and jests with my small band of workmates, I have no doubt.'

'We have had... unusual news,' Elaine began.

With an occasional interjection from Kyle, she filled Petani in with the events of the last few days. When the implications of a potential asteroid impact became clear, his eyes filled with tears.

'Damn it all to hell and back!' he said between gritted teeth. He glanced around the clearing. 'Look at all this,' he said, ignoring the fact that night had fallen and nothing of the Project was visible beyond the orange glow of the campfire. 'I have spent almost all my time, since the day I landed back here, helping to create this. An oasis of growth and beauty in the midst of the wilderness that is Besakaya. We provide food to Istania and Kertonia alike, herbs to flavour their meals, vegetables, and flowers to decorate their homes and palaces. And now you're telling me that the whole lot is about to be crushed under—'

He swallowed loudly and dashed the tears from his eyes with the back of his hand.

'— under the boot of a senseless rock, flung out of the void by the hand of some ungrateful God—'

'Gravity,' Elaine said gently. 'In this case, it's just the regular physics of gravity. No God is involved.'

'A God is always involved here,' the old man said, his voice quavering. 'You should know better, Bakara. You're telling me our vaunted Elemental powers are useless against this menace?'

'Well, that we cannot be sure of,' she said. 'At least, not yet. That's why we are all — Elementals and Batu'n alike — congregating at the Earther base. But if their science cannot save us, what is there left but the Elements? We must make the attempt, just as we always have. As we always do.'

'And we have the others now, too,' Kyle added. 'Wood and Stone. And Jann is intending to convince Patrick to help. Perhaps with his power...?'

'I know little of the Juggler's power,' Petani said, 'or Wood or Stone for that matter, though I have at least seen them in action. Yes, perhaps, if we all work together.'

He stared into the fire. Elaine dared not speak. She lifted her hand a fraction, seeing Kyle take the hint not to disturb the Gardener's thoughts. This must be his own decision. Each Elemental brought something to the mix, but each must bring it willingly, without coercion or guilt.

'I have seen beauty crushed before,' Petani said at length. 'And it affected me profoundly. Indeed, it brought me here. Back here, I should say. I have been trying to undo that destruction with my every breath, and for every moment since that day. I may have spent most of my life on Earth, but I am Berikatanyan at heart and to Berikatanya I have returned. How can I now turn my back on it? If there is the slightest chance I can protect the beauty we have created here — and all the other wonders this magical place holds — I must act. I must come with you.'

'Then we should leave immediately,' Elaine said. 'The others will arrive in New Washington ahead of us. By the time we join them, they will know the truth of Ahnak's story.'

'Someone I once knew used to say "third time pays for all",' Petani said, a half-smile playing over his lips. There was no mirth in his expression, and his eyes retained a liquid look despite their tears being gone. 'You are right, Bakara. We must leave at first light. I will tell Garcia.'

He stood, collected their dinner bowls, and walked off towards the main hut.

Chapter 13

the court of the blood king
2nd day of far'utamasa, 967

Ahnak watched the man Pwallick hobble away along the dark, drafty corridor. This Court was cold!. He wished the Fire wielder had come with them. At least she could have warmed the place up a bit. Were they poor, here? And if not, why could they not afford twice the number of fire bowls they had? That would have dispelled some of the gloom, even if it did not provide much additional warmth.

'Where will we find this Keeper?' he asked Clayer.

'His rooms are under,' she replied. 'In the crypt. Close as he can be to his papers unless he sleeps on them.'

She led the way through the confusing maze of corridors, down a flight of stone steps and then a second, rickety wooden stairway. The chill wind blew in from each window they passed. Ahnak shivered. The air became colder with each downward step. At the bottom of the wooden stairs they stepped onto packed earth. The tunnels of the crypt had low ceilings. The cheaper torches lighting this space sparked, and belched a greasy black smoke into the foetid atmosphere.

He followed the Air wielder along more twisting passageways until they came to a set of double doors, standing half open. The sound of a roaring fire came from beyond them, with a blast of heat that made Ahnak whimper.

'Oh, tell me this is where we are going?'

His words echoed along the passageway.

'Who's there?' called a voice from the warm room. 'What are you doing in my catacombs?'

'It's me, Claire,' said Clayer. 'I bring you a visitor.'

'Well don't just stand there young lady! Come in, come in!'

A fire burned in the grate, every bit as fiercely and

brightly as its sound and heat had promised. Ahnak rushed over to warm himself in its beneficence.

'Who's this?' the old man said, getting out of his armchair and setting an ancient scroll carefully on his desk.

'My name is Ahnak, venerable one,' he said, 'and grateful thanks I give for the gift of your fire.'

'Ahnak, this is my dear friend the Keeper of the Keys,' Clayer said. 'Ahnak is from—'

'North of Temmok'Dun,' the Keeper said, speaking perfect Beragan. 'Yes, I recognised his language straight away, though I never thought I should hear it spoken in my lifetime. Welcome to my sanctuary, Ahnak. May I offer you something to eat? A glass of buwangah perhaps?'

'You speak my language very well, Keeper,' Ahnak said. 'I should be honoured to share a glass with you. My thanks once more.'

'Well this all very nice,' Clayer said, 'but if you talk to each other in Beragan, at least slow down so this poor simple Elemental can follow what you say?'

The Keeper smiled gently. 'Hardly simple my dear,' he said. 'I should know, since you have scoured my archives more thoroughly than anyone, myself included!'

He retook his seat after pouring them both a glass. 'And is that why you're here now? I doubt this is a social call.'

'You know me so well,' Clayer said. 'We were wondering, or maybe hoping would be closer to the truth, do the archives hold any information about astronomy? Planetary movements, star charts, that kind of thing?'

The Keeper thought for a moment, sipping his drink.

'Our people do not care much for the sciences,' he said eventually. 'Over the years, some rare individuals have been motivated to study them. So the answer to your question is yes, there are a few — a very few, I should say — works that address such matters.'

Clayer clapped her hands.

'Oh please, my dear Claire,' the Keeper said, 'do not

excite yourself before you've seen what there is. I have stored them all in a single section of shelves, and it is a very small section. Small enough that you will be able to examine the whole thing before retiring for the night.'

the court of the blood king
3rd day of far'utamasa, 967

'Sebaklan!' came a voice from the darkness. 'What news?'

He turned, waiting for the identity of the speaker to become clear. Olek Grissan walked towards him, accompanied by Sadra Penganya.

'News?' he said. 'What have you heard?'

'Rumours, perhaps. Or truth. Or truth wrapped in rumours. Who knows, these days? When the Jester sits alone in his rooms, or at his desk, and attends no meetings, or holds no councils.'

'Best not to let him hear you calling him "Jester",' Seb said, struggling to keep a smile off his face. 'I ask again: what have you heard?'

'That the end of days is upon us,' Penganya said with exaggerated solemnity. 'Out of the darkness our doom comes flying.'

'Doom is a term much used recently,' Seb said. 'Nothing is certain, but in my view we would do well to prepare for the worst, even if we hope for the best.'

'And does... Jeruk Nipis share your view?' asked Grissan.

'We have heard that he does not,' Penganya added. 'And we wonder why he places his trust in rumour rather than fact.'

'Perhaps in the absence of facts, rumour is the more sensible option?' Seb said. 'Of all those at Court, surely we more than most should know that rumour often contains a kernel of truth, whereas a lack of hard facts is only that. A lack.'

'Enough of these word games,' Olek Grissan said with a dismissive wave. 'You sit on the Darmajelis. You rank highly in our... august group. We are happy to take our lead from you Pwalek. All you have to do is provide one.'

'Very well then. I will say this. If the doom is real, there will be no escaping it on this side of the Wall of the World. You should prepare for a journey. You should expect to travel light, and to travel long. There will be no coming back.'

'And why is that?' Penganya asked, leaning towards him.

'Because if the doom is as terrible as the... rumour... predicts, there will be no Court to come back to.'

'So all our careful machinations over the years have come to this,' Grissan said. 'If there is no Court, then there are no courtiers. If there are no courtiers, there is effectively no society. Nothing for us to control, no monarchy, no Elementals. Nothing in any way familiar.'

'Correct,' Seb said. 'You begin to understand my frustration. I am looking for ways to ensure our survival. For us as a group, and for as many of our people as can be saved. The *Jester*,' he emphasised the term he had previously deprecated, 'insists on trying to find ways to turn a disaster into an opportunity. He holds to the old ways of thinking and behaving. He refuses to mobilise or prepare. If we leave it up to him to light our path, then we will all surely die.'

the court of the blood king
3rd day of far'utamasa, 967

'What a pair of sleepyheads!'

The Keeper's exclamation filtered through Ahnak's sleep-befuddled mind, fighting for his attention with the dull ache from his neck. This couch was not designed for spending a night on. He opened one eye. At the desk, Clayer lifted her head from an unrolled scroll. Her pained expression suggested her neck was giving her as much grief as his own. Desks were not designed for sleeping on either.

'I have brought us some breakfast,' the Keeper continued. 'I hope you have not marked that scroll, young lady!'

Clayer reddened and cast a quick glance at the desktop to reassure herself. 'Er, no. It's OK. Sorry.'

'No matter. I am surprised you were able to unroll it intact. The works you uncovered last night have lain undisturbed for several decades. Centuries in some cases. By rights they should have crumbled to dust by now, or at least been so brittle as to be unreadable. It is a testament to the skill of my predecessors that they have been so well preserved.'

They had spent an age in the crypt. Clayer insisted on searching every shelf; every cranny. Since he had no notion what they were looking for, Ahnak's role was one of candleholder and lamp shiner only. He was content. It was enough to spend time with the Air Mage. Who could complain? Close friend and confidante of Jann Argent, an Elemental in her own right, and on top of that, young and beautiful. His companions back home would not believe the story unless he took Clayer back and they could see for themselves.

Though their languages were close enough for simple understanding, conversation had been limited to her requests for him to "shine the light a little closer here" or more often "not so close with that candle! The Keeper will have a heart attack!" Scroll after dusty scroll she had pulled out, inspected, and returned, retaining those whose contents suggested they were useful; discarding most.

When Ahnak was almost asleep on his feet she had finally declared the search done for the night. Between them they carried the small stack of parchments — perhaps twenty in all — back to the Keeper's study. The old man had long since retired to his bed chamber, but the

Air Mage's work was not yet finished. While Ahnak curled up on the couch, she rested the parchments in a neat pile beside the desk and made a start; scan reading the first and moving on to the next.

'How many did you examine, before using one as a pillow?' he asked.

Clayer stopped in the act of filling a plate, her face a mask of concentration. 'Probably half,' she said in the end. 'I lost count when I started reading the one I fell asleep on. I'll have a quick look at the rest, but I think that one is what we were looking for.'

'This one?' the Keeper asked, setting down his plate. 'My word, yes. This is among the oldest of my archives. See, here, at the top. It is dated, but according to the old calendar. The year is 650. More than three hundred years ago.'

'Not long after the Warring Tribes came south, and my people raised the mountain,' Ahnak said.

'It says something about a journeying god,' Claire said. 'Visible in the sky during daylight, and having a host of riders trailing after him. I remember thinking it sounded like a lay-person's description of a comet.'

'Comet?' Ahnak said. 'I don't know that word. I thought you said the doom was an asteroid?'

'Asteroids don't have an orbit,' she said.

He shook his head. 'Your words are strange. I don't understand you.'

'I'm not sure I can explain. If your doom is an asteroid, then it's a one-off. It would not have been seen before. But a comet is another kind of flying rock. Comets are different. The way they fly is predictable. Certain. It's called an eccentric orbit. A path, that brings it close to the sun and then sends it flying out to the farthest reaches of the solar system before circling back. It repeats, even though it can take a long time. Many hundreds of years, some times. But they fly in a circle, so they will always come back to the same place, eventually.'

'So?'

'Well, unless one of the scrolls I've not read yet has another account, it seems this one has a period of around three hundred years. If this rock — your "doom" — has been orbiting — circling — for centuries, why will it hit the planet this time, when it hasn't before? That something the Keeper's papers may tell us.'

'What's that, Claire?' the Keeper said, raking over the ashes of his fireplace and stacking a fresh supply of logs. This far below the Court, the thick stone walls retained their heat overnight, but even so the room was beginning to return to the chill of an Utamasan day. 'What might my papers tell you? Perhaps now that we are all refreshed and ready to begin our day's labours, you can tell me what it is you have been looking for?'

'I was hoping to find evidence of... well... this,' Clayer said, holding up the ancient text. 'Something that would support Ahnak's story.'

The old man regarded him with one clear eye and one milked by a tapuhti. 'And what is your story, young man?'

While the fire caught, and the archivist mixed a warming brew of katuh, Ahnak related his tale. It was a relief to tell it to someone who understood his language and the message of his story. As his account reached its conclusion he was distressed to see the fear and anxiety in the old man's face. A tear rolled down his cheek.

'B...but if that is true, then... my archives! My work! Surely you are mistaken, Ahnak?'

'I am sorry, honoured one. There can be no mistake.'

'How can you be so sure? There is no sign, no indication of impending disaster!' He took the scroll from the desk, held it between them. 'This account, talks only of a flying rock. What did you call it, Claire? A comic? It says nothing about such a catastrophic impact. No death, or destruction, or doom!'

'I cannot explain why it comes,' Ahnak said. 'But I know it will happen. It is as certain as the rising and setting of the sun and moons.'

'Perhaps the equipment at New Washington will give us an answer,' Clayer said. 'I will give the other scrolls the once-over, but this one tells us what we were looking for.'

The Keeper wiped his eyes. 'I cannot allow you to take this work with you,' he said. 'Not even you, Claire. It is too valuable to risk its loss.'

'I understand,' she replied. 'There is nothing here I need to record in any case. The simple fact of the comet's existence, and the date of its last visit, which I can remember. I will tidy everything away before we leave.'

'But what am I to do?' the old man wailed. From the look on Clayer's face it was clear she had never seen him in such distress. Understandable, given he had just discovered his life's work may be destroyed.

'The Court is strong,' Ahnak said, hoping to assuage some of the Keeper's anguish, 'and your archives are deep. It is possible the destruction will not reach this far underground, but I cannot be certain. You should perhaps be more concerned about your own safety. The doom's impact will darken the skies for many years. Most of the people will die, even if they are not taken by the first wave of destruction.'

The Keeper stared at him, his eyes wide and his face paled to ghostly white. 'I must make preparations,' he said. 'These passages have recently been flooded with Muir's rains. Tana alone knows what ill might befall them after this latest disaster.' He ran a wrinkled hand through his thinning hair. 'Though I know not exactly what to prepare for. Forgive me Claire, Ahnak, I will take my leave of you. I must discuss this with my fellow Darmajelis members.'

The old man hurried off.

'I ought to check these others before we leave,' Clayer said, taking a seat at the desk once more, 'if that's OK?'

Ahnak refilled his plate and sat by the fire, content to give his new friend all the time she needed for her studies. At least here, his services were not required for lamp holding. With his breakfast finished, and the log supply in no need of replenishment, there was little to occupy him. The couch had begun to look inviting again but he knew falling asleep on it would be a bad idea.

'Look at this,' Clayer said, holding up two more parchments that had come from the same area of the crypt.

'What have you found?'

'These two scrolls are dated around the time of the other. The one that talks about the comet. They describe "black clouds of swirling destruction". They must be vortices. That description couldn't be anything else.'

'I don't understand.'

'I'm not sure I can explain it for you, but we've seen a lot of these strange twisters recently. We call them vortices. These two documents suggest they are connected in some way with the approach of the comet. It's too much of a coincidence for them both to have happened at the same time twice.'

Many of the Air Mage's words meant nothing to him. He took her plate and stacked it with his own on a side table, where the Keeper had left his. Clayer collected the scrolls and took them back to their home in the catacombs. He moved a fireguard into position in front of the fireplace, which was now roaring and beginning to spit hot embers onto the Keeper's rug. A small white object caught his eye. An offcut of parchment had fallen from the scroll Clayer had read last. It looked nothing like the others, containing no dates or words. Only a few scribbled diagrams. He looked at it from every direction, but its meaning was obscure. Intending to mention it to the Air Mage once she returned, he tucked it into a pocket.

the court of the blood king
3rd day of far'utamasa, 967

'Has she gone? The Yamani girl?'

Sebaklan Pwalek bit back a sharp retort. Until recently he had as little time for Elementals as his hook-nosed companion. They shared as many political and social views as they had shared years together. But his visit to the Black Palace had shown him a different side to those he had always resented and, yes, if he was honest with himself, feared. They had an integrity that he now recognised had been lacking in all his dealings with the Jester and his machinations. An honest approach to the resolution of the problems they faced, and a desire to do the right thing, even in the face of what looked like insurmountable odds. They deserved a shred more respect that this diminutive, narrow-minded fool was ready to give them.

'The Air Mage?' he said, deliberately using her title. 'Yes, she and her companion left as soon as they had broken their fast.'

'Good.'

'The Keeper tells me they found some archival evidence that may support their claim of impending doom.'

The Jester snorted. 'May support.'

'He says they can't explain why it will hit us this time. It's been here before, apparently. But the information they found was enough to throw the old man into a panic.'

Jeruk Nipis' snort turned into a full-blown laugh. 'That old fool always has to have something to panic about! Some reason to move his dusty old scrolls from here to there, or hang his nose over them for another season. Why should it concern us?'

Seb sighed. If he could see it, why was Jeruk blind to the potential for ruin? Once, he had believed him a man of deep thought and understanding. Since the days of mad Muir it seemed Seb had the greater insight into whatever the gods chose to throw at them next.

'What do we have to lose by being prepared?' he asked. 'Fair enough, that Ahnak is a strange one. No argument there. I never did get to the bottom of how he knows what he says he knows, but I couldn't catch him out in a lie. His story held up. He was consistent in every utterance. And now, this archive material, ...'

'A message from the past,' Nipis intoned, with phony gravitas. 'Our ancestors have spoken.'

'Go ahead, mock. Word of this will spread. Rumour will pile on rumour. Unless you have a plan, either to deal with the disaster, or at least to dispel those rumours with facts and evidence, we are going to have civil unrest on our hands like we have never seen.'

'This all started at the Black Palace,' Nipis said, with a conspiratorial smile. 'We'll just blame them. It's perfect! A good reason to see them off once and for all.'

'For Baka's sake man!' Seb could control himself no longer. 'This is not another excuse for war! How are you going to defeat a rock from space with tammok and danpah?'

'I won't need to,' Nipis replied, pushing back his chair. 'Because there won't be one.'

new washington
3rd day of far'utamasa, 967

Silvia Alvarez rode into New Washington at the head of the motley bunch of travellers. Not the most seasoned or experienced rider of their group, she nevertheless had the best reason to be the first. The lack of early warning from their systems was a failure of her leadership. One she felt keenly, and one she intended to address as soon as physically possible. She had spurred the team on through the whole journey, and now approached the border wall late on the second day after leaving the Palace.

'My arse!' Piers said, 'At least we won't have to ride through another malamajan.'

Silvia reined her kudo to a halt at the base of the mooring tower. The Dauntless glowed electric blue in the gathering gloom, spooking the animal. 'Home now,' she whispered in the beast's ear as she dismounted. 'Go on, into the warm and dry.'

Cabrera approached her. 'Welcome back, boss,' he said. 'Why have you stopped out here? Much warmer inside!'

'We need to access the ship,' she said. 'It's a long story. One I don't have time for right now. Trust me, OK?'

If the man had any reservations or objections he kept them to himself. 'Sure,' he said. 'Just you, or...'

The rest of the small group had ridden up behind her. The Queen had never been this close to a Prism ship. Her expression suggested she hoped it would be the last time. Waters and Granger busied themselves with the kudai.

Argent moved to stand beside her. 'All of us,' he said. 'This is too important to leave anyone out. We all need to understand everything, every step of the way.'

'Fine with me,' Cabrera said, 'but don't mess with anything.' He turned back to his boss. 'You need me up there too?'

'No,' she said. 'I can handle it.'

She climbed the gantry without waiting for the others. Before the ship read her chip and released the lock on the main access door, they had joined her at the entry level. They waited while the enormous titanium steel panel slid open.

Inside the massive vessel the cold air smelled stale; a mixture of metal, oil, and neglect. Dauntless had been mothballed since her arrival almost two months earlier. The Utamasan chill had seeped into every bulkhead and compartment. Lights flickered on as they entered. The air systems kicked into life, blowing cold at first but heating up rapidly.

'Follow me,' Silvia said, 'and remember what Cabrera said: don't touch anything.'

She found the nearest teralift and punched a button.

'That's the bridge level,' Tremaine said. 'I visited it on the sim when I went to Armstrong base.'

Silvia looked at him. 'Colony program members don't

usually get to use the sim,' she said. 'What were you doing on it?'

He grinned. 'I'm special,' he said.

The lift let them out onto darkness. Since the bridge was never normally unoccupied, its lights were not automated. Silvia sighed. With the systems on standby she couldn't even use a voice command.

'Wait here,' she said.

The open teralift illuminated a dim path across the bridge. She crossed to the main computer and cancelled its standby mode with a few deft strokes. The lights finally flickered into life.

'Dauntless: recognise Alvarez, comm...' no, she had not been a commander the last time she had been on board her own ship. 'Recognise Alvarez, deputy commander. CP roll number 340037. Authorisation code alpha-alpha-one-nine.'

Across the control surfaces, lights flicked from blue to amber in a rapid wave of activation. The ship responded, its flat, metallic tones sounding bizarrely unnatural after an interval of almost ten years.

'VOICE RECOGNITION COMPLETE. RECOGNIZE ALVAREZ, DEPUTY COMMANDER 340037. PROCEED.'

'OK, come in,' she said, 'and—'

'Don't touch anything,' Argent said.

Resisting the urge to sit in the captain's chair, she moved to the astrogation station. Indicators on the panel glowed with the amber light of operational status, with one exception. With a sense of inevitability, Silvia saw it was the long range scanner.

'Dauntless: diagnose long range scan and report.'

'LONG RANGE SCAN INOPERATIVE. FAILURE OF SECONDARY SENSOR ARRAY.'

She glanced at the nearest smartscreen. 'Display replacement procedure on screen B-3.'

'REPLACEMENT PROCEDURE CANNOT BE EXECUTED. SENSOR ARRAY SPARES ARE DEPLETED FOLLOWING REPLACEMENT ON TWO, FIFTEEN,

TWENTY ONE SEVENTY SEVEN.'

'Dammit!'

'What does it mean?' Tremaine asked.

'It looks like this unit has given the crew problems in the past. The spare LRS has already been fitted and it was the last one.'

'What about the other ships?' Argent said. 'Wouldn't they have had spares?'

'Yes. Endeavour and Intrepid were both cannibalised to build the base, but we stored their tech. Dauntless: access New... er... Pennatanah storage records. Report availability of SSA spares.'

The panel blinked while the system made a connection with the base and synchronised its data.

'SSA 2060-A STOCK LEVELS: FOUR'

'Makes sense,' she said, rubbing her eyes. 'One each from both ships, plus the two spares. Not gonna do us any good though.'

'Why not?' Tremaine said. 'Surely one of the four will be working?'

'I'm sure they're all working. That's not the issue. These ships were redesigned after the Endurance disaster. Rebuilt from the ground up. Virtually all the systems were swapped out for the latest technology. I'd put money on those spares being incompatible. Dauntless: report SSA model number.'

'THE INSTALLED SECONDARY SENSOR ARRAY IS MODEL 2074-C5. THIS UNIT CANNOT BE REPLACED WITH THE AVAILABLE SPARES DETECTED EARLIER.'

'What about my ship?' Argent asked. 'The Valiant. Does she have the right kit?'

'Dauntless: Access build list for Prism ship Valiant. Report SSA model number.'

'THE VALIANT IS EQUIPPED WITH SECONDARY SENSOR ARRAY MODEL 2072-A. THIS MODEL IS COMPATIBLE WITH DAUNTLESS INSTALLATION IF FIELD MODIFICATION PRIS-000155 IS COMPLETED. MODIFICATION DETAILS ARE AVAILABLE ON

REQUEST. REQUIRED EQUIPMENT AND MATERIALS ARE IN STOCK.'

'If I have understood this metal voice,' the Queen said, overcoming her earlier discomfort, 'you will be able to repair your technology with parts of Jann Argent's ship. But I believe that is the vessel lying out there in the Jinsegar.'

'It is,' Tremaine said, 'and they are deep waters.'

'We brought a small selection of SCUBA gear,' Silvia said, 'but the air supplies have long been exhausted.'

'It wouldn't be any use at this time of year,' Tremaine said. 'Those waters are cold enough to kill a man in moments. We're going to need Kyle's help.'

A faint smile creased the Black Queen's face, but she said no more. Silvia had heard tales of her new powers but never seen her use them until she helped the visitor Ahnak recover from his ordeal. She wondered whether the multicoloured staff gave her any influence over the seas.

'She should be here some time tomorrow,' Argent said. 'Elaine won't stay more than a night in Besakaya, whether she manages to convince Petani to come or not. But it's too late to do anything else tonight anyway. It'll be dark before much longer.'

Chapter 14

**new washington
4th day of far'utamasa, 967**

Kyle rode into New Washington behind the Fire Witch and ahead of Petani. The old man had only one speed whether he was riding a kudo, walking, or thinking. Beside the main building a small delegation of her friends and fellow Elementals stood waiting for them in the cold morning.

The base leader, Alvarez, engaged in conversation with her deputy deLange and Felice Waters. The steam of their breath swirled around their heads like a ghostly fourth participant. The Elementals stood apart from the Earthers. Jann waved and smiled, hurrying across the roadway to meet his lover the sooner. Piers Tremaine also waved, but he was not smiling. Beside him the Black Queen stood straight-backed, one white-knuckled hand grasping her multicoloured staff. She stared directly at Kyle, a look that made a nervous tingle run the length of her spine. The woman's expression gave away nothing of her thoughts. If she were pleased to see the arriving party she did not show it.

Elaine jumped from Jaranyla's saddle into Jann's arms and gave herself up to a long, deep kiss of welcome.

'Get a room,' Kyle said. 'Anyone would think you'd been apart for a year!'

'That's the last fun we'll have for now,' Jann said when he surfaced from Elaine's passionate greeting. 'There's serious work to be done.'

'Come inside,' Alvarez called. 'Might as well warm up while we fill you in. We're going to be cold enough for the rest of the day.'

Waters volunteered to stable their kudai. The others moved to the relative warmth of the main hall. Once inside, Argent and Alvarez continued their double act, relating their discovery of the faulty systems aboard Dauntless.

'So the only spare parts of any use to us are out there,' Jann concluded, pointing out towards the bay, 'aboard the Valiant.'

The chill Kyle had felt earlier redoubled, suffusing her scalp with urgent electricity. 'You need access to the ship,' she said, 'and you're expecting me to provide a path.'

'We're out of options, Kyle,' Piers said. 'The waters are too cold to swim in, even if we could reach the hatch.'

'It's quite a leap, as I remember,' Jann added. 'Ask Patrick. And that was on the way out. Pretty sure it's impossible to get back in that way. The hull is like glass, never mind being soaking wet.'

'But Valiant is resting on her dorsal fin,' Alvarez said, 'so the main door should be close to the sea bed. Provided we can walk out to it.'

'That's a long walk,' Kyle said. 'How deep did you say the water is?'

'I didn't,' Alvarez said, 'but soundings show it's around a hundred and eighty metres at the deepest point. There's a shelf about half a kilometre out, so the Valiant is resting in shallower water.'

'Not shallow enough to make a difference,' Kyle said, feeling the weight of expectation almost as heavy as the weight of seawater she was being asked to move.

'Is it so much harder than last time?' Piers asked.

He meant the sea wall, of course. It was an innocent question. She stared at him, his face seeming to watch her from the end of a very long tunnel. Kyle passed a hand through her hair. 'Sorry,' she said, 'but yes. A lot harder.'

'Don't get me wrong,' Piers continued. 'I know it was tiring, but we built an entire wall while you held the waves back. You only had that one slip, right at the end of the first day when you were already exhausted.'

'We were stood on the clifftop,' Kyle said. 'No-one risked death. We only worked one section at once, and you raised the stone in almost no time. You have no idea how heavy all that water is. What we're talking about now, is people. People walking on the exposed seabed, all the way out to the ship. How many people? How long will it take to recover the equipment? This whole idea is... immense.'

She fell silent. The Queen watched her closely. A suggestion of deep, golden light traced the line of her staff. 'There's something else isn't there?' she said, her eyes gentle with concern. 'Something you're not telling us.'

Giveaway tears sprang again in Kyle's eyes. She swallowed down a sob. 'Yes.'

'Bring water, someone,' the Queen said, taking her hand. 'You don't have to hide it from us Kyle. We're all friends here.'

'It sounds so stupid!'

'Nothing is stupid if it's worrying you,' Piers said, sitting beside her. 'Ru'ita is right. Tell us what it is. We may be able to help.'

Jann handed her a glass of water. She took a long drink. 'I can't shut it out of my mind,' she began. 'What happened to Douglas. I know I should be over it by now—'

'It's grief,' Elaine said. 'There's no timescale.'

'Give yourself a break,' Jann added. 'You and your brother were close. Shared the same power.'

'Yes!' Kyle said, 'That's partly it. What he did with Water power was so... dreadful. It scares me that I might turn the same way.'

'You are not your brother,' Claire said. 'I've told you that before. But I guess this isn't something that responds to logic.'

'It's more than that,' Kyle said, taking another sip. 'It's being at the coast — being reminded of the last battle — seeing the waves. It's like I'm fighting the water now, instead of Douglas. And if I get it wrong,' she added, brushing away another tear, 'even more people will die. I don't even know how many we're talking about sending out there.'

'Well let's break it down,' said Jann. 'How many people should be a simple question.'

'It'll only take one to uncouple the LRS array,' Alvarez said. 'I can do that. It should be me. I don't want to put anyone else at risk.'

'Who do you want with you?'

'Well I might need help with the door. Opening it, if it's been damaged, or reaching it if the ship has rolled. It might be a few metres above ground level.'

'So climbing gear, and some brute force,' Jann said.

'We won't need climbing kit if I go,' Piers said. 'I can raise the ground if necessary. I could even make you a staircase,' he grinned. 'Nothing too fancy. But it'll get you up there. I can help with the door too.'

'Plus one for emergencies,' Waters said. 'I'll tag along.'

Alvarez started to protest, but Waters held up her hand. 'I volunteered. Don't try and stop me. I'll get enough of an argument from Jo. When are we doing this?'

'You haven't said how long,' Kyle said. 'I'll tell you now, I can't hold that water up all day.'

'Retrieving the kit won't take more than half an hour,' Alvarez said. 'It's a short run out there. I can cover five hundred metres in less than three minutes. Coming back will be slower, carrying the LRS.'

'Do you have to walk out?' Petani asked. 'Seems to me it would be quicker to ride. How heavy is this LRS thingy? That would be better on the back of a kudo too.'

'You think we can persuade them to step between two swirling walls of water?' Alvarez asked. 'They're nervous animals at the best of times.'

'Patrick has a trick for that,' Jann said. 'I need to speak with him about something else anyway. Give me a moment. Don't start without me.'

He hurried from the hall, pausing at the servery to pick up a slice of pie and eat on the hoof. The first time Kyle had thought about food since that morning. Her stomach growled. There was a conversation she needed to have too, and it would not be an easy one.

'Can we break for a bite of lunch,' she said, 'while Jann's out?'

new washington
4th day of far'utamasa, 967

A knock at his door shattered Patrick Glass's concentration. Before he could react in temper, he recognised the voice of his friend.

'Come on, open up book boy! I need a word!'

'It's open,' he said. 'And since it's you, you can have two.'

'So generous,' said Jann Argent, poking his head around the door. 'Ha! I was right! You were buried in your book. You must know it by heart by now.'

'Most of it,' Patrick agreed. 'Except this last bit. When did you get back?'

'Last night.'

'Good ceremony? Water Wizard all legit?'

'That's what I came to talk to you about. There wasn't a ceremony. Well, it started, but we were interrupted.'

Patrick closed the Tang Jikos, sat back, and listened to his friend's account of the strange events at the Palace and their subsequent journeys.

'And you believe him, this Ahnak?' he asked, once the tale was done.

'I do. We'll know for certain once Alvarez has fixed the long range scanner. But something tells me it will only chime with his tale.'

'Why hasn't it hit before then?'

'Something else we need to work out. I agree it's a mystery, but it doesn't change anything for me. Ahnak has the sound of a man who knows what he's talking about.'

'So what do you need from me?'

'Ah yes. Well. You're not going to like it.'

'I already don't like it. Pretty sure I can guess.'

'It's more than one thing, but I don't want to get ahead of ourselves.'

He outlined the plan to retrieve the replacement equipment from Valiant.

Patrick frowned. 'Still don't see why you need me. Kyle has proved adept at parting the seas!'

'Claire told me you have a trick for calming kudai,' Jann said, a guarded look telegraphing his nervousness. 'I know you're never keen on using these fabulous powers of yours, but I figured—'

'That quieting down a few animals would be fairly harmless.'

Jann shrugged. 'Well, yes.'

'What's the other thing?'

'Will you do the animals? At least let's get that out of the way before we talk about anything else.'

'When?'

'Pretty sure they want to do it today. Before dark if possible.'

'It's almost dark now.'

'Better hurry up then,' Jann grinned.

He never could take anything too seriously. Even the end of the world. 'Tell me what the other thing is first. It's not like you to try and trick me into something.'

'I'm not. The two things aren't connected. Well, not directly. I'm thinking ahead. Assuming the LRS confirms Ahnak's story...'

'Which you think it will.'

'Which I think it will, then we're going to have to figure out what to do about a deadly asteroid that's about to wipe out all life as we know it.'

'I'm getting the feeling that you already have an idea.'

new washington
4th day of far'utamasa, 967

'May I speak with you?'

The gathering had broken into discrete groups to eat. Kyle seized her chance to approach the Queen.

'Of course my dear,' the Queen replied, her expression breaking into a smile. 'I've been wondering when you would.'

'I didn't know how to, at first,' Kyle said, taking a seat at the Queen's table. 'But I can't do this on my own.'

'It is a daunting task, that much is certain.'

'I don't have a lot of experience with the sea. It was Lautan's favourite—'

'He lived in it most of the time,' the Queen said.

'Exactly. I can't begin to reach his level of mastery in any part of Water lore, but especially not with the ocean. I did OK when Piers built his wall, but this? This is something else entirely. The water is deeper, the distance is greater, and I'll have to hold it up for longer.'

'Trust yourself, Kyle,' the Queen said, leaning forward and resting a hand on her arm. 'If I have learnt anything from all my years of association with Elementals, it is that the power is always there. The only thing that can get in the way of it, is you.'

'I know, and I don't have any worries about starting. Well, OK, maybe a small worry. But the main thing is... this is the first time lives will depend on me keeping control over my power. That volume of water will take all my strength to move. I don't think I can sustain it without your help. Your healing energies.'

'Of course, I will be there for you Kyle. I have said I am more mage now than monarch. How can I not offer my services? Whatever I can do to aid you, I will.'

Kyle let out a long breath. 'Thank you! I was so worried. After how we left things back at the Palace.'

The Queen waved a dismissive hand. 'Do not give it

another moment's thought. Your allegiances are your own affair my dear, for you own conscience to inform. It is not my place to try to sway you one way or another. If this coming doom is true, then such petty differences will pale into even less significance. We are Elementals first and foremost. And now,' the Queen continued, taking up her striated staff, 'with Enkaysak's assistance, I may be able to aid you in more ways than you expect.'

new washington
4th day of far'utamasa, 967

Muted conversation filled the main hall as Patrick entered. Jann crossed the room to join Elaine and Piers. The Water Wizard, her face white and drawn, sat at a separate table, in conversation with the Queen. The base Exec stood in the warmth of the servery, with her deputy deLange, and Felice Waters.

'What are we waiting for?' he asked Alvarez. 'Leave it much longer and it'll be dark.'

'I know.' The Exec nodded in the direction of Kyle Muir. 'Can't start without her. From what she said earlier, I'm guessing she's not all that confident she can pull it off.'

'Delaying won't make it any easier,' Patrick said. 'Best to get going if you ask me. Is everything else ready?'

'Kudai are all saddled, yes,' Waters said, 'and we've checked the schematics. The LRS is in the same place on the Valiant as it is on our ships. You never know with those damned engineers.'

Patrick felt his hackles rise on behalf of the engineering fraternity, until he caught Waters' grin. 'OK, leave this to me.'

He walked over to the Queen's table. 'Ladies,' he said, 'welcome back. Are you ready to make a start Kyle? Soonest begun is almost done.'

'God, that's what my Dad always used to say,' the Water Wizard replied. 'If I was waiting for an omen I guess I just found it.'

She pushed back her chair, flashing a weak smile at the Queen. 'If you're ready too, Ru'ita.'

'Indeed,' she said. 'Let us proceed.'

Seeing their movement, the others joined them. Outside, a chill wind stirred the ocean into fluttering whitecaps. Patrick pulled his jerkin closed, and led the way down the gradual slope to the shore. Despite the cold, even those not directly involved in the endeavour followed him. Waters brought up the rear, leading the four kudai she had brought from the stable block. He hoped the presence of so many friends would give Kyle a morale boost even if none of them could offer any practical help with the daunting task that faced her.

'What's the running order, Kyle?' he asked. 'We're totally in your hands here.'

'I have line of sight to the Valiant, so at least direction won't be a problem. I have no idea what the seabed is like, but the easiest thing for me is to create a path straight to it. This close to shore, the ground should be nothing but sand and shingle. If there are any rises and falls, hopefully they'll be nothing you can't handle when riding.'

'I can take care of any rock formations that may stand in our way,' Piers said. 'Don't worry about them. A straight path is our best option, no matter what the ground looks like.'

'Alvarez estimated the round trip at no more than five minutes,' Kyle continued, 'not counting the time to retrieve the LRS. I've asked Ru'ita to support me with healing energies, so I'm hoping that will be enough.'

'Do we have a contingency plan?' Patrick asked. 'Like, what happens if you're exhausted and the path is overwhelmed?'

'I've broken out lifejackets,' Waters said, 'so we won't drown, but we won't last long in the cold water, as Piers pointed out last night. We'll rope ourselves together and Cabrera will pay out the line as we go. If the worst happens, you'll be able to haul us back. Hopefully quick enough that we don't all die of hypothermia.'

'I'll fasten the line to the Valiant once we're there,' Alvarez said. 'We can't move around inside if we're all roped up.' She turned to Kyle. 'That will be the critical bit. Fail before we get there, if you have to, or when we're on our way back. But keep the waters at bay while we're in the ship. If the main door is flooded we'll be trapped inside and either drown, freeze, or starve to death.'

'Wow. I'm glad you persuaded Jo to stay indoors,' deLange said. 'If she heard that litany of cheer she'd have chained you to your chair by now, Felice.'

The deputy's attempt at humour fell as flat as the mood. The more time Patrick spent around the man, the less time he wanted to. 'OK then,' he said. 'Not wanting to push anyone to do something they're not ready for, but it sounds to me like we're as prepared as we can be.'

Alvarez, Waters, and Piers Tremaine mounted up, and held their kudai stationary. The Water Wizard took a step forward, closed her eyes in concentration, and lifted her hands. At the gesture, a ripple appeared in the waves nearest the shore, travelling perpendicular to the natural motion of the sea. Within moments the divergent current had widened and deepened, exposing the shingle in a path broad enough to accommodate twice the number of riders. Its edges resolved into sheer walls of water, the ocean behind the lines of power a deep, glassy blue. Regular waves overtopped the walls, splashing onto exposed rocks at the sides of the path.

Their animals shied at the unexpected sound. Patrick accessed his memory of the Pattern of Peace and waved his left hand, leaving a hint of black smoke in the air as it moved. He murmured a soothing word for the kudai, unnecessary but reassuring for the riders. Their mounts settled. With a grunt, Kyle thrust her arms forward. In response, the burgeoning walls ripped a clear avenue to the Valiant, spray from the displaced water rising and dashing back into the sea. At their highest, the towering walls of water reached a hundred and fifty metres above the ocean floor. Their faces remained as hard and clear as glass. Halfway out, Patrick saw the dark shape of an enormous fish swimming along behind the smooth vertical surface. Kyle, her expression revealing the toll she was paying in moving such an immense volume of seawater, opened her eyes and locked her gaze on the Queen, saying nothing.

Ru'ita raised her staff. A bright ray of cold blue light leapt from the shaft, wreathing Kyle in its glow. The Water Wizard smiled and turned her full concentration back to the ocean.

'Let's go!' cried Piers, spurring his kudo into the middle of the new path.

Fortune smiled on the start of their endeavour. The seabed was sandy beyond the initial line of shingle, and flat. The three riders soon covered the distance to the exposed shining hull of the Valiant. From his position on the shore, Patrick could not make out the exact location of the main access hatch. As they approached the ship, the seabed beneath the riders swelled up to form a mound roughly twice the height of a kudo, shelving gradually down to the seabed on one side. The animals, still under the influence of his earlier Pattern, remained calm as the ground rose under them. The riders dismounted, and congregated around the hatch. Moments later a dark crack appeared, widening as the door slid open. Alvarez entered first, the others following her into the dark interior of the ship.

Patrick glanced at Kyle. Even with the help of the Queen's healing influences, she was visibly tiring. Out in the bay, the right-hand wall of water sagged at its base, ballooning out into the gap.

'Oh, God, no,' she said, her face a mask of fear and horror.

'Can you strengthen her any further, Ru'ita?' Patrick said, stifling a rising sense of panic.

The Queen looked out into the bay. 'No,' she said, 'but there may be another way I can help her.' She grasped her multi-coloured staff in both hands. Aligning the rod with the failing water wall, she stamped its heel onto the rocks. The air in front of the Queen distorted. With a suggestion of shimmering opacity, like a memory of blackness, a line of force shot from the upright wood. It traced the wall of water all the way to its end, and solidified. Through the force the seawater still shone, its blue colour muted as if seen through black glass.

'Concentrate on the left side Kyle,' the Queen said. 'I will ward the right.'

Thus they stood, in rapt concentration on the shore, for what seemed an age. The sun crept ever closer to the horizon and the light of the day began to fail.

'If they do not start back soon,' deLange said, 'they will be traversing the ocean path in darkness.'

'No, they won't,' came a voice from behind them.

Patrick spun on his heel as an incandescent ball of flame flew over his head, coming to rest in the air above the Valiant. It cast a radiant orange glow over the mound Piers had created earlier. The Fire Witch grinned.

'Finally, something practical I can do,' she said, summoning another flaming orb and sending it out to hover over the path at the halfway point.

As the second light came to a halt, Waters emerged from the hatch. Tremaine and Alvarez followed, carrying a large, flat silver box suspended in a tubular framework between them. Alvarez held it by two recessed handles, while Tremaine gripped a row of fins at the back. Slowly they manoeuvred the bulky framework through the opening.

'Looks heavy,' Patrick said. 'Good job they decided on the kudai.'

Cabrera, holding the retrieval line loosely in both hands, nodded. 'It's mostly shielding,' he said. 'Layers of nanosheets inside the device, and then electromagnetic dampeners in the frame.'

Waters held one of the animals motionless while the others attached the LRS to a harness. The kudo appeared, from a distance, to be perfectly happy bearing the weight of the equipment. Once firmly attached, the three rescuers mounted up, and rode down the slope for home, Waters leading the final kudo by its traces.

A ripple of applause passed around the small crowd on the shore. Patrick's attention was taken by a dark movement behind the riders. Barely visible in the orange glow from the Fire Witch's orb, a small vortex had formed in the space beside the mound. To Patrick's horror, it began to twist towards the wall held up by the Queen's black warding force.

He waved frantically at the riders. 'Run!' he shouted. 'Come on! Fast as you can! RUN!'

Their expressions were unreadable at this distance, but they must have heard "run" plain enough. As they kicked their kudai into a gallop the vortex collided with the right-hand wall. Under the light from the floating orb, the surface exploded into a glistening shower of golden rain.

new washington
4th day of far'utamasa, 967

'RUN!'

Patrick Glass's cry from the shore was lost in a sudden roar from behind them. Piers twisted on his saddle. Back at the Valiant the water, which moments ago had stood erect, now flooded back over the pathway in an eerie orange cascade. Under the light from the flaming orb above, it looked more like boiling lava than seawater.

'Come on!' he yelled, digging his heels into his kudo's flank, 'gotta run for it!'

He passed Waters, snatching the reins of the laden animal out of her hands and spurring his own mount on harder. With a muted whinny the heavily loaded beast lurched forward, running hard to ease the tugging on its mouth. His mind raced, calculating how much ground he must cover before invoking his power. Too soon, and he would create an island, too far from shore for them to swim to safety through the icy water. Too late, and they would all be overwhelmed with that water anyway.

He wanted to check on the others but he had no time, or attention, to spare. Both competent women, both leaders. They could take care of themselves. Seconds later, the timing decision was taken out of his hands. The darker wall of water to his left shivered and collapsed in a concertina fashion from its furthest point. Piers summoned his power, lifting the seabed as he had beside the Valiant. He rode up the incline, dragging the huffing and blowing animal behind him.

'Hurry!' he shouted, unsure where either of the others were, or whether they could hear him over the crashing waters. Icy splashes soaked his legs. His kudo shivered under him. But then they were clear of the waves. Riding along the pathway he had raised only moments before. Still several hundred metres from shore Piers kept up the flow of Stone force. He felt his power waning, not knowing how much more seabed he could lift. Almost blacking out from the immense drain on his energies, he became aware of a blue light in the air around him. A feeling of health and strength flowed into him.

He looked ahead. A clean cobalt-blue ray emanated from the Queen, crossing the gulf between them and bathing him in its radiance. With his Elemental strength restored, he could make it! They were going to make it!

But there was a limit even to the help brought by the Queen's healing light. The last fifty metres of ocean bed refused to lift. How deep was the water here? Could he at least raise it a little? He lay down along the length of his kudo's back and sent out the last of his strength. Seawater sprayed into his face, splashed up by flashing hooves. But it was not cold! At least, not the glacial chill he had felt only moments before. This water was nothing worse than an autumn shower. He looked up. The Fire Witch smiled at him from the nearing beach. She had warmed the coastal water. Just enough to be life-saving.

Piers, with Waters and Alvarez following close behind the laden beast, splashed up onto shore and fell from his kudo in a gasping heap.

'Thank you!' he said hoarsely, staggering to his feet. 'Thank you both.'

Elaine took his arm and helped him upright. 'That was well done, Tremaine. All of you. A close call, but well done.'

'We should get this unit fitted,' Alvarez said. 'No time to waste.'

Piers had to admire the woman's energy. All he wanted right now was a warm bed. 'Can you do it when it's wet?' he asked.

'Sealed unit,' Alvarez replied. 'Not a problem.'

'OK,' he said. 'I'm in. Getting our hands on the damn thing nearly killed us. I'm not gonna miss out on seeing it in action.'

Cabrera took the reins and led the animal up the shore towards the Dauntless, floating and shimmering electric blue against the dark sky. He and Waters unfastened the unit and carried it awkwardly aboard.

It took Alvarez no time at all to reverse the removal process. 'OK,' she said, closing the access panel below the astrogation station, 'let's fire it up.'

It felt to Piers as though the whole bridge held its breath until the indicators lit up all green.

'We don't have a science officer at the base any longer,' Alvarez said, 'but I think I can remember enough about this panel for what we need.'

Her hands flicked hesitantly over several buttons. A readout screen illuminated with an orbital trace, shortly joined by a crimson line which clearly intersected the first.

'Is that showing me what I think it's showing me?' Jann

asked.

'I think it's pretty clear,' Alvarez said. 'Our strange visitor was telling the truth.'

'Do we have a date?' Piers asked. 'An impact location?'

'I'll have to zoom in for an exact position,' Alvarez said. 'Gimme a minute.'

She pushed more buttons and twisted a raised silver dial. The image on the screen ballooned until the planet showed as a hatched ball, quickly overlaid by a geolocational grid.

'There you go,' said Alvarez. 'A shade more than five hundred klicks east of here, and a bit south. Looks like an estuary.'

'It is Lembaca Ana,' said the Queen, stepping forward, 'the Valley of the Cataclysm.'

'Couldn't have a more appropriate title,' Elaine said with a snort, 'that place has always had a sense of doom about it. This will be its final chapter.'

'When?' Piers said again. 'When will it hit?'

Alvarez pointed at a date readout. 'April twenty-sixth,' she said. 'Twelve days from now.'

Chapter 15

new washington
5th day of far'utamasa, 967

'It's been a while since I saw the bridge of a Prism ship,' Claire Yamani said, stepping through the doorway. 'I always knew I could make an entrance, but why the stunned silence?'

She beckoned for Ahnak to follow her. He hung back, staying in her shadow. The alien green glow from the unfamiliar technology rendered the dread on his face even plainer. Petani walked around him and joined her on the bridge with a wave to the others.

'You've made good time,' Piers said, crossing the small space to stand beside her, 'I thought I was the only colonist who'd been on the bridge before!'

He frowned. 'Sorry, I shouldn't joke. This is not a good time for humour. Not unless you think several million tonnes of rock landing in your back garden a fortnight from now is funny.'

'Oh! My God. Seriously? Ahnak was right?'

'I tell you,' Ahnak said.

'Slightly less than a fortnight actually,' Jann Argent said, waving a hand at the instrumentation panel. 'It's after midnight. We now have eleven days until impact.'

'Do we have a more accurate estimate of when it will hit?' Patrick asked. 'And how close is Piers' jokey guess to its actual size? Do we know?'

Alvarez fiddled with the controls. A line trace display zoomed and pivoted crazily as her fingers flew across the board. 'Around noon, near as I can say. Berikatanyan calendar sixteenth day of Far'Utamasa, so yes - eleven days from now. Eleven and a half, but I don't see those extra few hours making much difference.'

Waters turned from examining another group of readouts. 'This trajectory would give it something like a three hundred year cycle. It's a comet, not an asteroid.'

A tingle of excitement ran across Claire's scalp at the mention of the orbital period.

'Your people must have some serious astronomical chops Ahnak,' Alvarez continued, 'to predict this.' She looked at the board again, flipping the display to another tab. 'Diameter is something like four kilometres. It's not exactly spherical, but near enough.'

'Jesus!' Piers said. 'That makes it a little over twenty-five cubic kilometres?' He turned to Patrick. 'The answer to your question is "not very close". I was way off.'

'So what's the real answer then?' Patrick asked. 'How much does it weigh?'

'Assuming average rock density, closer to seventy gigatonnes. I can figure a more accurate number if there's a calculator on that panel, and the LRS can give us any idea what it's made of.'

'Don't bother,' Alvarez said, her face drained of colour. 'What's a few billion tonnes in either direction between friends? It will still kill us.'

'I can't even imagine something that big,' Jann said.

'The one that killed the dinosaurs was estimated at thirty-four gigatonnes,' Claire said, 'if it helps. So ours is twice the size.'

A stunned silence fell over the group. She glanced at each of them in turn. Every face mirrored Alvarez' pallid and horrified expression. Ahnak dug an elbow into her side.

'What? Can it wait? This is kinda important. The world's about to end.'

'It not news to me,' Ahnak reminded her. 'But what is news...'

'What?' Claire said again. The young Beragan was staring across the bridge with a strange yearning look on his face. 'Whatever is the matter Ahnak?' she asked, giving him her full attention now that his concern was clear.

'That man,' he said, nodding.

'Which one?'
'The one I not see before. He not at Palace.'
'Patrick you mean? Standing next to Jann?'
'Yes. Him.'
'What about him?'
'He the man who raised me.'

new washington
5th day of far'utamasa, 967

Patrick caught Claire Yamani looking at him with a strange expression, while her Northern friend whispered furtively in her ear. The young man avoided making eye contact with him. Patrick had bigger concerns. 'Do we have any idea why this thing is going to hit us this time, and not on any of its previous three hundred year visits?' he asked.

'We don't have any historical telemetry to compare it with,' Alvarez replied. 'It could be an eccentric orbit, or it may have been thrown off anywhere on its path around the sun, if it encountered another large mass. Solar systems are scary places. We have a comfortable impression of them as safe, quiet, stable structures, but in reality they are often violent and destructive. Ask those dinosaurs.'

'Ours isn't the only data,' Claire said, taking a step towards the console. 'We may not have telemetry, but the Keeper has a record from those earlier times.'

'You've seen this, Claire?' Elaine asked.

'I went looking for it specifically,' she said. 'And what I found is almost certainly an account of the last visit. The Keeper confirmed it was one of his most ancient texts. So old that it was written when they worked with a different calendar. But he said the equivalent date in today's terms would be the year 650. It may even have been written before the original refugees from Ahnak's people travelled south.'

'Warring tribes,' said Ahnak, shaking his head. 'Was

surprised they could write.'

'Did you bring it with you?' Jann asked.

Claire laughed. 'You know the old man better than that. He wouldn't let me take it away. But the message was pretty clear. It described a journeying god crossing the sky. Said it was easily seen in daylight. If that's not a description of a comet I don't know what is.'

'But that just proves my point,' Patrick said. 'It's been this way before, and it didn't hit. What's changed? Something must have happened between then and now to alter its trajectory.'

'Well I can think of something big that happened,' Elaine said. 'Not to the comet, but right here on the planet. Most of us were involved, one way or another.'

'My God,' Jann said, 'of course! The portal ceremony! We opened a vortex.'

The implications crowded in on Patrick. For a moment he was unable to think. But Jann was on a roll. 'And it had a lasting effect,' he went on. 'Until you tore it down, Patrick. That time dilation. Could that have done it? Maybe dragged Berikatanya off its orbit?'

'I'm not familiar with this time dilation,' Alvarez said, 'but it wouldn't take much. I mean, it would take great force to move a planet, sure. But it only needs a small deflection to bring us into the comet's path, over the course of three hundred years.'

'Forgive me,' Petani said, speaking for the first time, 'I may be missing something, but does it really matter why we're in this position? Your sensors have confirmed what Ahnak has told us all along. Surely the question now is — what are we going to do about it?'

new washington
5th day of far'utamasa, 967

Silvia Alvarez turned away from the science panel to face the group. Petani was right, and they did not have time to waste in endless debate. But what could they do? 'We should brainstorm our options,' she said. 'Not that anything comes to mind right now, with the comet almost upon us and nowhere to hide.'

'Can we destroy it?' Tremaine asked. 'Seems the most obvious thing to try?'

Silvia shook her head. 'This is a colony ship. Our last. None of them were fitted with heavy artillery, or even much in the way of defences. Certainly nothing powerful enough to blow apart gigatonnes of rock from a distance.'

'But it is a working ship, right?' the Stone mage continued. 'So could we fly off somewhere? Escape that way?'

'Where do you suggest?' the Fire Witch said with a sneer. 'The rest of the planet is unknown territory. You might only be flying out of the frying pan into the fire.'

'It's a space ship?' Tremaine replied, reddening in response to the Witch's disdain. 'We're not stuck on this planet.'

'Really? The colony program chose this as the first inhabitable world in a hundred light years. Unless you know something about the planetary systems around here they didn't, we're not exactly spoilt for choice.'

Tremaine pointed upwards. 'Out from under the flying rock would be a start,' he said, 'even if it leads us into the unknown.'

'If we're supposed to be brainstorming we should be coming up with options, not shooting them down in flames,' deLange said.

'It does us no good to argue anyway,' Waters added. 'Scoring points off each other isn't helping.'

'Surely Dauntless isn't large enough for an escape plan?' Yamani said. 'There's more at stake here than just us. Hardly an act of an integrated population is it? Flying the Earthers off to safety and leaving the Berikatanyans to die.'

'Well said, Claire,' the Queen said. It was only the second time she had spoken since coming aboard. The newest member of the Elemental fellowship still looked daunted by her surroundings. Blinking lights from the science panel danced along the length of her staff, rendering each wood as a different depth of black. 'Any solution we find has to benefit everyone. We must set aside our recent differences and animosities, and work for the common good.'

'In which case, flying off in the Dauntless is not the answer,' Silvia said. 'Even for a short journey she does not have room for the whole population.'

'Do we even know how many that is?' Argent asked. 'It's not like the Berikatanyans keep much in the way of census information?'

'OK,' Tremaine said, 'if the ship isn't armed, and it's not big enough to carry everyone to safety, can we just fly it into the comet? Knock it off course?'

'You really are clutching at straws now,' Silvia said. She waved a hand to interrupt another protest from Waters. 'Sorry, but some ideas need to be taken off the table as soon as they're put on,' she said. 'I'm surprised at you, Tremaine. For a gifted architect, holder of prestigious awards, you seem to have a woeful lack of understanding about momentum. Or maybe you're simply out of ideas? The Dauntless has nowhere near enough mass to disturb the path of the comet. Not this late in the day, anyway. If we flew it into the rock at top speed it may have been able to deflect it a fraction of a degree. For that to save us we would have had to do it months ago. It's far too late now.'

'There is one other option that the Dauntless can help us with,' Glass said, 'though the risk is hardly smaller than the impact itself.'

The bridge fell silent with expectation at Glass's words. He was never garrulous at the best of times. Always sparing with his comments, but when he did speak he was worth listening to. Silvia had no concept of his power, beyond the knowledge that he had one. Rumours spoke of his perpetual fear of using it. Maybe this crisis would provide the impetus he needed to overcome those fears.

'You have everyone's attention my friend,' Argent said, placing a hand on his shoulder. 'What's the plan?'

Glass paled, looking in turn at each person on the bridge. 'I didn't say I had a plan. Not even much of an idea at this stage, but...'

His voice trailed off into silence. She did not want to be the one to break his concentration. The others waited too, until Glass finally summoned the courage to continue.

'We have everyone here,' he said, his gaze flicking around the bridge for a second time. 'Every Elemental.' He nodded at Argent. 'The Gatekeeper.' He held his hands up, fingers crooked in towards his chest. 'And me. The Pattern Juggler.'

Argent's eyes popped. 'Oh, no. Wait...'

'Are you serious?' the Fire Witch said, thin wisps of smoke rising from her palms.

'What are you talking about?' Yamani asked, her face a mask of puzzlement.

'He wants to create another vortex,' Argent said. 'That's it, isn't it?'

Glass nodded. 'Yes. At least, that's the headline. But this one's different. We need to create it in space. In front of the comet.'

'You did hear the Exec, right?' Argent said, running a hand through his hair. 'This damn thing is four kilometres wide. You think we can open a portal that big?'

Glass laughed. A mirthless, hollow sound that rolled around the space between the men. 'You're the Gatekeeper. You tell me.'

new washington
5th day of far'utamasa, 967

Patrick watched the emotions playing across his friend's face. Eagerness at the suggestion there may be a solution, irritation at his gentle jibe, and finally, fear. But no matter how frightened Jann Argent was at the prospect of opening another vortex, it paled before his own terrors. Jann understood gates. The kind of portal Patrick was talking about would ordinarily be inaccessible to him. Without the power of Void, gates were limited, three-dimensional structures, capable of granting immediate access to other locations on the same surface. Portals had few, if any, such limitations.

'When you say "a portal",' Jann said, 'you mean... one like Elaine and I fell through, right? But "in space"? My memory of that day might still be a little hazy, but I've read the accounts. Four Elements, it took, to create the spinning wheel of magma. How can we do that in a vacuum?'

'That's a good question,' Patrick said. Elaine, Claire, and Petani all watched him closely, obviously keen to learn how their powers would be utilised beyond the atmosphere of Berikatanya. Kyle Muir either missed the reference to four Elements, or did not understand the implications. 'And I can't pretend to have the answer. You're right; it will be difficult to create a magma wheel in a vacuum—'

Elaine snorted. 'Difficult? How do you suppose we can find any rock out there, let alone melt it in the cold of space?'

'Rock is no problem. We can take it with us and eject it at the appropriate point. As for Fire, you're assuming your power is like regular fire. It isn't. My father's book concerns itself with more than my family's inherited power. Fire is Elemental. It comes at your bidding and bends to your will. It is not contingent on the presence of combustible material, or even actual combustion for that matter. In scientific terms I guess it's more like nuclear power, or plasma. You will be able to summon it anywhere.'

He watched the digits of the console clock tick over to 01:00.

'Anywhere, that is,' he continued, 'in the vicinity of this planet, or one like it. As some of us have already discovered, older planets like Earth have long ago buried their Elemental energy potential under a mountain of technology.'

'You got that from your book too?' Claire asked. 'Because Felice and I came to the same conclusion independently. Simply from observation of cause and effect.'

Waters nodded, but said nothing.

'Not always a good indicator,' Patrick said, 'but in this case it has led you to the right conclusion.'

'Water won't be as easy to find in space,' Kyle said. So she had been paying attention after all. 'And if we take it with us it will be a solid frozen lump as soon as we dump it out of the airlock.'

'This isn't getting us anywhere,' he said, taking a seat at the console. 'We don't need a repetition of the overblown portal ceremony in any case. The shockwave necessary to open a crack in spacetime was created by quenching the molten rock as it flew into the air. Deep space is already too cold for that approach, but we have other powers to call on. I only need the Elements to be present. And even then, we have Wood and Stone with us now. Powers the ancients did not have, or didn't know they had.

'How does that help?' Elaine asked.

'In Elemental theory, Void power sits at the top of the pyramid. A third-level power above Wood and Stone just as they sit above Earth, Air, Fire, and Water.'

'Sounds powerful,' Jann said, 'no wonder it scares you.'

'You don't know the half of it, my friend,' Patrick replied, his vision momentarily occluded by dark thoughts. 'Anyway, Void draws on the strengths of all the other powers. As long as they are present, there's — theoretically at least — little I can't do with it. Including opening a portal.'

'So that ceremony? Your Dad could have done it all on

his own?' Claire said, her eyes reddened with emotion.

'You're thinking he could have avoided your parents being lost,' Patrick said gently. 'What a different world we would now be in. You especially. Yes, from what I've learned, most of that ritual was for show. My father could have drawn on the others' powers whether they were using them overtly or not. The whole circus of the wheel of lava lofted into the air and quenched was really only there to entertain the crowd. Who knows whether there was a hidden agenda, underneath it all?'

'Agenda?' the Queen said, drawing herself erect and giving Patrick a look that could shatter diamonds. 'I cannot speak for the Blood King, but for Kertonia there was no agenda. Beyond one of peace, that is. We were told the Elemental forces would usher in a new era of harmony and collaboration. But that is all in the past now, Pattern Juggler. If you have the knowledge to create a new portal, and the wherewithal to do it without similar high cost to us in lost souls, then pray tell us how we should proceed.'

'Flying this ship out to intercept the comet is the first step,' he said, turning to Alvarez. 'I assume she can be flown?'

'Not in her current state,' the Exec replied. 'Normally it would take us at least twenty-four hours. If we start right away and work through the rest of the day she could be warmed up for a flight by this evening.'

'I'll have Cabrera assemble a team immediately,' Waters said, hurrying from the bridge.

'Ow! What's the matter now Ahnak?' Claire said. He had seen the man digging her in the ribs, his face a mask of concern. 'Whatever it is, speak up. You're among friends here.'

The Northerner took a step towards Patrick. 'You not fear the Voiders anymore?'

'What?'

'Beragan know longtime about Voiders. Even before you come.'

'You're not making any sense. You're the first Beragan I've met,' Patrick said. But something about the man's manner telegraphed his meaning, even though Patrick shied away from believing it.

'Tell the story, Ahnak,' Claire said. 'Explain what you mean. Where does Patrick come into it?'

'He in control of the Void. It his power. But our tales tell of past use. Last time flying rock was here. Paper we found when we see the old man. That learning come from my people. They saw rock in sky. And the monsters it brought.'

'Monsters?' Jann said with a nervous laugh. 'As if gigatonnes of comet landing in our garden wasn't bad enough. We get monsters too?'

'Please,' Petani said, rubbing his brow, 'do not speak of it landing in a garden. This is already beyond distressing.'

'Yes, our tales tell of monsters, Gatekeeper,' Ahnak said, ignoring Petani's discomfort. 'Hard to speak their name in the old tongue, but you may simple call them Voiders. Same way Earthers come from Earth. Voiders come from the Void.'

Patrick's scalp exploded in a paroxysm of tingling. Could it be? Those last passages from his father's book he had so far been unable to understand? Some of their first symbols suggested a strange kind of embodiment of the power. 'When did they come?' he asked, hardly daring to hear the answer. 'What did they do?'

'Come with flying rock,' Ahnak said with a shrug. 'Leave when it go. We see first signs before, all around. Black swirls.'

'The vortices? They're connected with the comet?'

'Is all connected,' Ahnak said. 'You must know. It your power. Your learning.'

He did not need another reason to be terrified of his Element.

'They attacked,' Ahnak continued. 'Terrible stories. Actual horror not common known. Simple tales to scare children. Like your — what you tell me Clayer? Boogleman?'

Claire laughed. 'Bogeyman,' she said.

'Yes. That. But this terror real. Beragan people happy it only lasted few days. Rock in sky. Monsters in village. Then all gone.'

'I have to go,' Patrick said. This new-found insight into the lost passages could change the whole picture of what they could do. 'I must study the book, before we take a wrong turn. This could change everything.'

'But we're still going, right?' Piers asked. 'Taking Dauntless to meet the bogeyman?'

'I don't know. Maybe.'

'So Cabrera's team will be working on the ship through the night,' Piers said. 'Don't you think it would be wise to post guards as well? Word of this will spread. Probably has by now. Some of our more militant friends may attempt to flee the planet. Even without a clear idea where they'd go. I know at least a dozen who will find the "anywhere but here" option compelling. If the Dauntless is going to be essential to our plan, we don't want anyone nicking her.'

'It's a good point,' Alvarez said, standing and tugging down the tunic of her uniform. 'I'm on it.'

'Fine. Nothing lost if our plans change, but I must hurry. There are parts of my father's lore still closed to me. From what Ahnak has said, they may be the most important parts. If we don't do this right, I could release a terror on the people of this planet even worse than letting the comet hit.'

new washington
5th day of far'utamasa, 967

'Hold up!'

The voice of Jared deLange carried clearly through the still night air as Patrick made his way back to his quarters.

'Wait!'

He stopped outside a repurposed container. Through a window occluded by dirt and grease, the atmosphere inside looked thick with blue smoke. The tabbuki had finally found somewhere to call their own. 'What?' Patrick said. 'What do you want? Make it quick, it's damned cold.'

DeLange nodded at the door to the tabbuki bar. 'Do you... partake? We'd be warmer in there.'

'No, I don't "partake" thanks. We can talk just as well out here, as long as it's brief.'

The shorter man hopped from foot to foot, rubbing his hands against the cold.

'Come on man! I haven't got all night. I must revisit the book.'

'That's what I wanted to ask. Are you sure about this, Glass? I've seen you many times, watching Tremaine work. All his mighty stone works would have been achieved so much more easily and quickly with your help, yet you never offered it. Why was that?'

Patrick stared at the man, feeling his anger rise in tandem with the old trepidations.

'See?' deLange continued. 'That look. The one you always get on your face whenever anyone dares to mention your power. And yet now you're proposing to take every Elemental on the planet out into space and — do what? Do you even know?'

'You make my case for me. That is exactly why I must consult the Tang Jikos. The lost sections may hold some further knowledge. Some insight into this threat. I must return to this research one last time. The information contained in those passages has eluded me so far. I am unable to decipher them, despite all my efforts.'

'Precisely my worry,' deLange said. 'These Voiders the Northerner spoke of. The bringers of doom. The butt of childhood scare stories. Does anyone really know if they exist, what they are, what they can do? No! But you're prepared to risk unleashing them on all of us for the sake of a vanity project. So you can show us all what the mighty

Pattern Juggler can do?'

'What's it to you anyway?' Patrick asked, taking a step towards the man who stood back nervously, maintaining his distance. 'Do you have a better idea? Do you have some arcane power you have yet to reveal? You heard your boss — this thing, this gargantuan rock, will be here in a few days! We don't have time to waste on what-ifs, buts, or maybes.'

'Those maybes may bring a worse doom than the comet — you said so yourself. Are you ready to be the architect of our destruction?' DeLange's eyes widened. 'That's it, isn't it? That's why you've always been so terrified of your own abilities? My God. We're all doomed, one way or another. Crushed to death by a flying mountain, or torn apart by demons from the dark.'

'This isn't helping,' Patrick said, turning and walking away from the man. 'You're right, they may be alternative fates, but only one of them is certain. If I can fathom the meanings hidden in the Tang Jikos, the other may yet save us.'

new washington
5th day of far'utamasa, 967

The pages of the Tang Jikos which held the rogue sections had become so well-thumbed in recent days, they almost turned themselves. How long had he spent on this? He opened the book at the first elusive page, and rubbed his hands together. These quarters were no warmer than his family home in Duske Pelapan. At least the illumination provided by his globelamp meant he did not have to read by candlelight. It was brighter and without the attendant risk of fire. With the reduced sunlight of the season, and virtually continuous use as he pored over the glyphs and pictograms, even that had begun to yellow and dim.

He was more secure here too. No risk of a random

villager coming to knock down his door, such as had happened to poor Piers. He flipped another page, suppressing a shiver at the thought that this was only a false security. Once the full implications of his plan became clear, the twin dooms laid before them may well lead to some kind of backlash against him. But what choice did he have?

His brief thought of doors being knocked down heralded a real knock. For the second time in as many days, his friend the Gatekeeper had come calling.

'You can't lock yourself away in there again, Patrick!' Jann Argent shouted from the other side of the door. 'We need a plan!'

'It's still open,' he replied. 'Come out of the cold.'

'I could say the same to you,' Jann said, stepping through the door and closing it quickly behind him. 'Ugh! This is no time of night to be out. Or to be reading your damned book! We need some sleep if we're to have our wits about us tomorrow. Later today, I mean.'

'Wits are no use to us without knowledge,' Patrick said, sitting back from the book and steepling his hands on his chest. 'If I don't get this right, we're all doomed.'

'We're all doomed anyway, buddy. Let's not kid ourselves. Since we're talking about a comet and the Void, you could say we're between a rock and a dark place.'

'Always the joker,' Patrick said, unable to suppress a grin.

'But never the Jester!' Jann replied, high-fiving his friend. 'That's more like the old Patrick. You have to work through this mate. Look at the end-game. We've faced big odds before. Uncertainties, nasties. And we've stood together and won. You and I have yet to celebrate our first year together on this planet, and we've beaten the baddies twice already.'

'You're gonna tell me third time pays for all, aren't you?'

'Couldn't have put it better myself.' He pointed at the

Tang Jikos. 'You solved the mystery yet?'

'Not quite. It's becoming clearer, especially with Ahnak's comments about "Voiders from the Void." Pretty sure they're the subject of the passages in this last section. So far I've failed to decode the details of how, why, or what I can do about them.'

'You should bring the book with you. Work on it aboard Dauntless. We don't have time to wait, and we're both gonna need that sleep. You can't comprehend all that squiggle with an exhausted brain.'

Patrick sat forward, resting his head in his hands. 'Deciphering it is only the first of my worries,' he said. 'Even if I can work out what I need to do, the doing of it has its own risks. You know that. We've talked this round and round so many times.'

'Look, I understand your fears. It's not easy. I get it. But however it turns out, whatever happens, any danger from the Voiders — or from whatever you do to try to stop them — is an unknown. The danger from that comet is a known. It's real. It's obvious, imminent, and unstoppable. You can't just choose to do nothing.'

Patrick sighed. He felt the weight of expectation and responsibility so heavily he could hardly sit upright.

'Get some sleep,' Jann repeated, moving to the door. 'Tomorrow we save the planet! See you for breakfast, hero.'

With that, his friend was gone. Taking his jokes and his clarity of thought and his — rightness — with him. *You can't just choose to do nothing.* So there was no choice then. He had to act. He had to find a way to open a portal in the vacuum of space and rid the Berikatanyans of the twin threats from comet and Voiders forever.

Chapter 16

new washington
5th day of far'utamasa, 967

'You going? Even after what Patrick said?'

Claire Yamani mulled Kyle's words over before replying. She munched on a bite of toast and tried to rub away the crawling insects of tiredness from her scalp with her other hand. She had fallen asleep the instant her head touched the pillow, but woken feeling she had hardly blinked. The arguments and discussions from their late night session on the bridge of the Dauntless still echoed around her mind. The others arrived for breakfast in ones and twos, each wrapped in their own thoughts and worries about the day's mission.

'Hello?'

'Sorry! Yes, of course I'm going. I have to. We're all in this together. All the Elementals. Win or lose. Even Ru'ita is onside. She didn't look too comfortable being so close to the tech, but she coped.'

'She's serious about wanting to be treated as an Elemental, instead of a monarch. Have you noticed how she's even stopped referring to herself as "we" now?'

'I wonder if her coping will extend to her joining us for today's jaunt?'

'She'd be more likely to tell you than me,' Kyle said. 'With your special relationship and all. Not sure what use Wood or Water can be in the frigid depths of space. I thought you might feel the same about Air. I mean, there isn't any, right? So...' She shrugged.

'Did you miss what Patrick said? It's not about the physical Elements. He needs all our powers to draw on if he's to bring the full strength of his gift to the job. Everyone has to be there.'

'I guess. Anyway, I can't let you have all the fun.'

'Ha! Fun? Not much of that to go round today. Or any

day from now on. Not if we can't stop that thing. It kind of throws a whole new light on our plans to join the base here. Don't you think?'

'I dunno. I mean, if we lose the comet, then no. Assuming these scary Voiders or whatever they're called go with it. If anything it would legitimise our plan. The Earthers and their wonderful tech will have saved the planet and everyone on it. Should be easy to ride the wave of euphoria. No-one would blame us for picking the winning side.'

'I guess. That's a big if though. "If we lose the comet." I know Jann's never managed a gate of that size before. Even the original portal wasn't four kilometres wide.'

Ahnak joined them at their table. 'Morning, lady. Two lady.' His plate held a single sosij and two pieces of toast.

'That's not much of a breakfast, Ahnak,' Kyle said. 'We could be in for a long day.'

'I not hungry,' he said. 'Worry about flying rock.' He flashed Kyle a puzzled look.

'What's wrong?' Claire asked him. She had enjoyed the young man's company during their diversion to Court. His strange resemblance to Jann — especially his piercing, ice-blue eyes — still sent shivers down her spine. If there was something worrying him, she wanted to get to the bottom of it.

'All days are same length,' he said, taking a bite of sosij. 'Why this one be longer?'

new washington
5th day of far'utamasa, 967

Patrick did not intend to sleep so long. There was much to discuss and little time in which to do it. But Jann had been right: they all had to rest. He had, apparently, needed it more than the others. He was the last to arrive in the main hall.

His friend sat sharing a breakfast with his partner the

Fire Witch, and the erstwhile Queen of Kertonia, now Wood Mage of Berikatanya. With her new striated staff at her side, it seemed the admirable woman had come fully into her power. Perhaps in her own quiet, steadfast way, she had a lesson for him.

Claire and Kyle had the table furthest from the door, deep in conversation with the Northerner. Earth and Stone sat together at the next table, their shoulders shaking in unison at some shared joke.

The base commander and her top team had pushed two tables together near the servery to accommodate six chairs, although only five were occupied. Cabrera, having presumably been working through the night as agreed, looked worried and exhausted in equal measure. He bolted the last of his food as Patrick approached, and hurried off with a silent nod in his direction.

'He looks stressed,' Patrick observed, taking an empty plate from the rack. 'Long night?'

'And a longer day to come,' Alvarez said. 'I've told him the ship has to be fit for an evening launch. Today. I assume you will be ready by then? If your book learning is done?'

'It's never done,' he replied. 'There's always something new. But I know all I need for this. Jann suggested I take it along. I think he looks on it as last minute revision for an exam. I don't even know if there will be time to make it worthwhile. How long will it take to reach the comet?'

'A little under two hours, ball park. I won't plot a course until we launch. The trajectory changes from minute to minute, obviously. How close do you need to be?'

'The only portals we're familiar with were opened in situ. That's not an option here. But to maximise our chances of success we'll need to be as close as possible. Not more than a klick.'

'Scan tells us it's travelling at two kilometres per second. That's not an issue for the Prism drive. We can factor in whatever distance you need and keep pace with the rock as long as necessary.'

'Sorry, no. We can't create a travelling portal. It will be a stationary point in space, directly in front of the comet. We just need to be there long enough to create it.'

'OK, so how long does that take?'

'Good question. I've never done it this way before.'

Jann walked over. 'The accounts I've read suggest the original method was pretty quick. Difficult to calculate an exact time from the writing, but I'd say no more than half an hour.'

He hesitated, wearing the look of someone who had more to say but was not sure how to say it.

'And?' Patrick prompted.

'Oh, nothing really. Only to confirm you need everyone aboard.'

'Well you, obviously. Can't have a gate without the Gatekeeper. The others? Yes. As I said earlier, I'd feel safer having them there. We'd look pretty stupid reaching the comet only to discover we needed them after all.'

'You know you need,' said Ahnak, who had been hovering at the edge of the conversation. 'I tell Clayer and Kyle. Elders tell you too, Gatekeeper. When you visit.'

Jann Argent gazed at the Northerner, his eyes unfocused. 'You mean the Wood and Stone thing?'

'Of course. Pyramid of Elements,' he said, holding his arms out to make the shape of a triangle, fingertips touching at the apex. 'Full Wood power need Air and Water to help. Full Stone power same. Need Earth and Fire. You know this. It why Beragan Elder split these pairings between tribes at time of parting. So all higher powers not there for those travel south. Void power same too. Need all powers for big jobs like this. All Elements work together. Need everyone.'

Patrick turned to Alvarez. 'When will the ship be ready? I don't know about the others, but I need time to prepare myself for this.'

'Last estimate from Cabrera was end of the day. But like I said, I've told him we need it done by sundown.'

'Who's driving?'

'That'll be down to me,' Alvarez said. Her voice had a nervy edge to it, though her expression gave nothing away. 'Captain Espinoza died on the Valiant, and we lost Oduya at the beginning of last Sanamasa. As far as we know Shika Arakawa from the Intrepid is still alive. DeLange would know for certain, but I've not seen him this morning. The man has no stamina. Everyone else is pulling their weight on next to no sleep. I'd put money on him still being tucked up under his covers. In any case it's doubtful Arakawa or Captain Dmitriev could get here in time. So I'm it.'

'Should I be worried?'

Alvarez laughed, though there was little mirth in it. 'I've done my hours.' She held Patrick's gaze for a moment. 'But it was a while ago. Hell, we've been here for more than ten years. Guess I might be a little rusty. But the only tricky part will be pacing the comet.' She glanced out into the bay. 'The landing should be OK. Dauntless has the latest Prism drive and we're not expecting the kind of weather Valiant suffered. So no. Nothing to worry about. Nothing at all.'

the court of the blood king
5th day of far'utamasa, 967

Sebaklan Pwalek waited until the door of Jeruk Nipis' chambers had closed on their informant. 'Do you believe me now? I said all along this Northerner was telling the truth. The Batu'n technologies have confirmed it. Surely you can't still think this is some kind of subterfuge?'

'The Queen is there, isn't she? He said as much. She's been there from the beginning. I wouldn't put anything past that devious bitch.'

'She may have some new-found Elemental powers, but

I don't think they allow her to influence Batu'n systems. They don't rely on magic, in case you hadn't noticed.'

'Who knows what she can do with her new powers?' Nipis insisted. 'Those "systems" of the Batu'n show their information on some kind of special surface, or so I understand from those who have seen them.'

'They call them displays.'

'Whatever they're called, they're read by people. And people *can* be influenced by magic.'

'Are you claiming the Wood mage can control people's minds now?'

'Are you saying she can't? How do we know what their precious systems have or have not detected? They could say anything. And those reading them could be made to think they say something else.'

'This is preposterous! We are already haemorrhaging people to the Earther colony—'

'Earthers returning home,' Nipis interrupted. 'No great loss.'

'— and once news of this "asteroid" gets out, as it certainly will, you seem to have no grasp of the mass panic that will result. We need a plan! It will do us no good for you to sit here at the head of the Darmajelis claiming the whole idea of impending disaster is a fabrication. People talk. They have family or friends at the Palace or at Pennatanah. They will weigh the evidence and make up their own minds.'

'I've told you — there is no evidence! And those who believe there is, have had their minds made up for them, by influences that do not have our interests at heart.'

'You're being ridiculous. What testimony would you trust? Will you still believe it's a hoax when you see the rock approaching over the horizon? When it's too late to do anything about it? You'll have nowhere to run then, Jeruk! And nowhere to hide.'

The diminutive man stood, stretching to the full limit of his small height. 'I shall not be hiding anywhere,' he said, pointing a finger at Seb. 'And Istanians do not run. Not from the Blacks, not from the Batu'n, and not from some fairytale story of flying rocks from space.'

new washington
5th day of far'utamasa, 967

Dawn broke over the mountains that watched in stony silence as Cary Cabrera and his small team busied themselves with their many tasks aboard the Dauntless, diligently waking the behemoth from its two month slumber. The coming journey would be brief. Nav computers estimated a one-point-eight hour trip to intercept the comet, which one of his engineers had christened Nemesis. Mapenzi Okoro's dark humour was tolerated, rather than appreciated, by the others. That short acceleration arc meant the Prism drive would reach less than one percent of its maximum speed. But in astronomical terms the rock was in their backyard. Meeting it was the logical equivalent of stepping through the back door.

Their jaunt would be short, their crew tiny, but still the necessary safety procedures and pre-flight checks needed to be complete. The Wormwood drive, an awesome piece of technology, required lengthy preparations. Careful alignment of the massive crystal prisms which focused the graviton waves, and a three-phase warm up of the wave generator itself.

Hull integrity checks were automated, but any lesions they revealed needed repair. In the cold, hard vacuum of space, they could quickly fracture into larger problems. Life support systems, left ticking over to allow duty inspections to be completed without wearing an environment suit, had to be wound up to full operation. With twelve passengers and crew for this trip, they were only needed for the bridge, its teralift, a single cafeteria, and connecting corridors. No-one expected to be aboard for more than half a day, and they would all have more to worry about than eating. Even so, Cabrera insisted on checking there was one working auto-servery. If the worst happened, and the crew were stranded aboard for an extended period, at least they would have food.

The day wore on, each member of Cabrera's team fully engaged in the job. They exchanged only brief words of banter along with requests to borrow tools or for help with a tricky two- or three-person procedure. With viewports closed and smartscreens disabled to conserve power, the ship's chronometer provided the only measure of the passage of time. Focused on one of his last remaining tasks, the arrival of the two youngest Elementals towards the end of the day caught Cabrera by surprise.

'Not ready for you yet,' he said, as Claire Yamani and Kyle Muir stepped out of the teralift onto the bridge. The ladies, both wearing winter gear, must have expected the ship to be as cold as it had been the night before. They soon discarded their coats. The internal temperature of the ship had reached a comfortable level soon after midday. At one point, Cabrera considered turning down the thermostat. The standard temperature setting was not designed for constant physical activity and he had quickly broken into a sweat.

'No, we didn't think you would be,' Yamani said.

'We wanted to get a feel for the ship now she's woken up,' Muir added.

Cabrera smiled. 'Didn't want her to leave without you, you mean?'

Both women blushed, but returned his smile. 'This is a bit different to the bridge on the Valiant,' Yamani said.

'Oh yes, that's right. You already know your way around a Prism ship better than most, don't you?' Cabrera said. 'I should have asked for you to be on the team. Another pair of hands would have come in useful.'

'It's only book learning,' the Air Mage replied. 'Not practical experience. Do you have much left to do?'

'Everything is green on the board,' he said. 'Only thing left is to fire up the main drive, check that everything is singing, then we're good to go. A bit earlier than I told Alvarez, but that's all part of the traditional space engineer's magic.'

'You can start the engines here on the planet?' Yamani asked. 'I thought it was dangerous to use a Prism drive close to a planetary mass?'

'That was true on your version, on the Valiant. This is the mark four Wormwood. It has some clever occlusion technology. Means the first stage graviton levels can't do anything dangerous, even when the ship is moored.'

'Gravnull is still safer though, yeah?'

'Well, it is, but that won't cut it for this trip. For a ship of this size it's barely powerful enough to reach escape velocity. We'd need to switch to Prism drive anyway beyond the atmosphere, otherwise what will be a two-hour flight would take more like two weeks. Nemesis would be here before we got there!'

'Nemesis?' Muir said, laughing. 'Kinda assumes we'll fail before we start.'

'Blame Okoro,' Cabrera said, laughing along with her. 'She has a weird sense of humour. Anyway you'd better let me get back to it if I'm going to have that pleasant surprise ready for Alvarez.'

Theirs was not the only interruption. As if drawn by some shared Elemental perception, the others drifted onto the bridge in ones and twos from that point on. By the time Alvarez made an appearance there was little to surprise her with.

'Are you and your team coming along for the ride?' the Exec asked him. 'Maybe Okoro would like a closer view of the object she named?'

'Not likely!'

'Well you'd better jump ship then. No point hanging about now you've pulled a rabbit out of your hat.'

She took a seat at the helm controls, checked the

readouts of the comet's latest position, speed and angle of approach, and keyed in a course.

'Get going!' she said, reaching theatrically for the main drive lever. 'And the rest of you, belt up!'

the court of the blood king
6th day of far'utamasa, 967

It was late. So late, the moons had set and the malamajan was done. A thin frost limned the bare branches of distant Alaakaya which sparkled reluctantly under the light of nothing but stars. The few puddles left after the nightly rains had iced over, making walking treacherous. Sebaklan Pwalek beat his arms around his body in an effort to summon some warmth, and continued down the trail away from the dark squat silhouette of the Blood Court.

'Finally,' came a voice from the gloom. 'Freezing my nuts off here.'

A lamp flared into brightness, stinging Seb's eyes. He held up a hand to shield the glare. 'Sorry. Jeruk kept me talking.'

'Yeah? No surprise there. It's all the idiot is good for these days.'

The speaker lowered his lamp. An eerie uplight revealed the craggy features of Olek Grissan but Seb had instantly recognised the man's distinctive throaty growl.

'Am I the last to arrive?' Seb asked. 'Penganya here yet?'

'I am,' said Sadra Penganya, stepping onto the path from behind a tree, 'and Grissan isn't the only one with frosty nuts. Let's get this done.'

Three other faces resolved into the lamplight, all Puppeteers, all displaying various degrees of discomfort. Cotigo, Badabangwan, and the third whose name Seb could not remember. No-one else spoke.

'Happy to,' Seb said, 'if I knew what "this" was.'

'You can surely guess,' Grissan said, 'an intelligent man such as yourself. We all think the current... official... position is less than ideal. We don't agree on much—'

The others laughed. 'We do agree on *that*,' Penganya said.

Cotigo looked askance at Penganya. Grissan continued before he could comment.

'—but we need to do something more than sit around with our thumbs up our arses hoping that the Queen will fuck up enough to hand us the realm.'

'You think it's right? This flying rock story?' Badabangwan asked. 'Sounds incredible.'

'We've had a report from the Batu'n base,' Seb said. Better he should present the facts here, rather than voice his opinions. 'Their technology confirms it.'

'Yeah, but the Jester doesn't believe it, even so,' Cotigo said, finding his voice at last. 'And he's not often wrong. I think he's got a point.'

'So,' Penganya said, 'turns out we don't all agree after all!'

The others laughed again, but it was a nervy, uncertain laughter, and soon died away.

'What do you think we should do, Seb?' Badabangwan asked. 'You're the nearest thing we have to a leader without the Jester.'

'We've still got the Jester,' Cotigo said, taking a step forward. One thing you could say about the guy: it was not hard to work out where his loyalties lay.

'He's in the leader's chair,' Badabangwan said, 'but even you would find it hard to convince anyone he's actually doing any leading, Cotigo.'

'So come on, Seb,' Grissan said, 'before all our nuts turn black and drop off, what do you think we should do?'

Seb scratched his face. How much to say? The group was on the verge of a split, if their comments were any guide. Did it matter? What was the alternative? He could not pretend to line up behind the Jester's approach, and no-one would believe him if he did.

'I'm not sure.' He held his hands up at their protests. 'No, honestly. I believe this disaster is real, and imminent, but I have no more idea of what we can do about it than you do.'

'But you agree we should do something.'

'Of course! But what? Run away? Where shall we run? The impact of this thing will flatten everything in sight. We have nowhere to run to!'

aboard the dauntless
15 apr 2177 23:10

Jann Argent had felt the incredible force of the Wormwood drive pressing him into his seat as soon as Alvarez pulled back the lever. This was his second time aboard a Prism ship but the first occasion on which he had experienced the powerful acceleration the stardrive delivered. On his previous trip, he had been deep in cryogenic suspension when the journey began.

He glanced at the ship's chronometer. After only thirteen months back on Berikatanya the concept of standard dates, hours, and minutes seemed alien. A little over two hours had passed since the Dauntless achieved escape velocity and her passengers could release their belts and walk around the bridge. No-one felt like eating, though Alvarez assured them the nearest servery was functioning should they wish. Jann had never been one for midnight snacks. It seemed the others were of similar mind.

Not long after takeoff, Patrick had set his lore tome on a workstation and began another laborious analysis of its many diagrams.

'What that?' Ahnak said, seeing the book for the first time.

'It is the Tang Jikos — the lore book of the Pattern Juggler,' Patrick replied. 'It belonged to my father. He wrote much of it. Now it passes to me as his heir, though there are still parts of it I cannot decipher.'

'Those patterns? Pictures?' Ahnak said, peering closer. 'No words?'

Patrick chuckled. 'No. No words. The lore of the Juggler is represented only by these pictograms and glyphs. It doesn't lend itself to descriptive text in any language.'

'It look much like what I find in the old man's tunnels,' Ahnak said, reaching into his pocket. He pulled out a scrap of parchment.

Patrick's eyes widened. He snatched the fragment from Ahnak's hand. Clearly torn from a larger document, its edges had yellowed with age. Jann peered over Patrick's shoulder. The piece contained five distinct diagrams. Even to Jann's untrained eye they looked different from anything else he had seen in Patrick's lore book, though their style was similar.

'Where did you say you'd found it?' Patrick asked, though the Northerner had only the moment before told him.

'When Clayer and I were searching the... catacombs,' he said, stumbling over the unfamiliar word. 'This fell from a scroll she find. She take the others back, and it seem to me not fit with them, so I keep.'

His friend held the scrap to the light, examining it from all angles. 'This could be the key!' he said, jumping to his feet. 'The missing piece of the jigsaw!'

He folded the ancient remnant carefully between the pages of the Tang Jikos, closed it, and lifted it from the workstation. 'Excuse me,' he said, 'I must find a quiet spot to work on this. You said the cafeteria was open?' he asked Alvarez.

'Yes. A5, down there. It's not far.'

And with that, he had left the bridge. No-one had seen him since, even when Alvarez reduced power to bring the Dauntless alongside the comet. This was Patrick's show, and he was still trying to work out how to run it.

'You make gate like this before?' Ahnak asked him.

The others eyed him silently. Elaine and Ru'ita, who had been present the last time he created a gate of this type, said nothing. Claire Yamani shivered, probably at the memory of her father, falling with her mother through the vortex to Earth all those years ago. Petani too said nothing. Of all those present, the Gardener fell furthest. Only Patrick's father had travelled further back. The portal extended earlier through time the longer it remained open, a strange feature of large gates that Jann had never fully understood.

'Yes,' he said, conscious of their quiet expectation. 'At least, not quite as big as the one we need this time, but close.'

'Time gate tricky,' Ahnak said.

'Time gate?'

'Large gate like this not behave like normal gate. No matter in space or on ground. Size is what makes difference.'

Jann stared at the young man. 'This isn't the first time you Beragan have taken me by surprise with your grasp of the Elements and other magic. How do you know? And what difference does size make?'

Ahnak hesitated, shuffling his feet. Jann had never seen him look embarrassed but he was certainly doing a good impression of it now.

'I... have a little knowing of gates. Have had doings with them before.'

Not for the first time, Jann felt exasperated at the language limitations. It was not Ahnak's fault, but Jann could never be certain he had understood the man. Did he mean what he said, or did he intend something else but not know how to express it?

'You've seen them?'

'See them, yes.' Ahnak shrugged. 'Little ones. Only talk about big ones. Never see. Until now.' He smiled a disarming smile. 'If Patrick ever come.'

Yes, what was keeping his friend? He had been scratching his head over those last passages for months, and now he had new ones to puzzle over. They must be so much more complicated than the rest of the book. The whole thing looked like so much elementary school scribbling to Jann.

'So what is it about bigger gates that the Beragan think is unusual?' Jann asked.

'Small gate on surface take from one place to other. You do this all time Jann Argent. Same time, different place.'

'Yes. Dipeka Kekusaman was quite right. There are many easy-access gates all around. Opening them gets easier the more you do it.'

'Large gates different. All different, every way.'

'How different?'

'Every way, like I say. Not so many of them. Few places on planet can have them. Maybe different in space, I not know. But where small gates go same time, different place, large gates opposite. Go different times, same place.'

For Jann, the bustle of the bridge, the blinking panel lights, the low hum of the Wormwood drive, all vanished. All he could see were Ahnak's eyes, fixed on him. His words echoed in Jann's mind. *Different times, same place.*

'Wait. So you're saying larger gates — portals, or vortices as we've been calling them — can only be opened to one place?'

'Yes. And while they open, other end move through time. Longer gate open, further back in time.'

The full implication of Ahnak's words rocked Jann back on his seat as the activity of the bridge burst back through his senses. The large gate Jann had traversed — the first portal created at Lembaca Ana — had thrown the Elementals back to Earth.

aboard the dauntless
15 apr 2177 23:20

A mug of coffee sat untouched on the table next to Patrick Glass. He had not enjoyed coffee since first landing on this planet. Now he had the chance, it remained beside him, ignored. The drink had long since stopped steaming. Patrick's attention was locked on his book of Juggler lore and on the scrap of parchment Ahnak had uncovered, hidden in the most ancient of all the texts carefully preserved in the depths of the Blood Court by the Keeper of the Keys. Though small, the fragment held five complex patterns. So convoluted that he wondered how they had even been drawn by the rude tools of the time? He would have struggled to accomplish the same level of detail using the most advanced micro-miniature drawing pens of the twenty-third century. Here, with only quills and pointed sticks, the artist who crafted these pictograms had imbued each pattern with several layers of meaning. Every dash and flick of his instrument gave added depth to the message.

The pictures spoke to Patrick in a language he was as fluent with as any spoken tongue. The dialect of graphics. The patterns of the Pattern Juggler. The drafter of these pictures must have been a powerful Juggler indeed. Maybe even an ancestor of his? The five unlocked the hidden section of the Tang Jikos like a mortice key opening a five-lever lock. The veils of misconception and darkness fell away. A shiver ran through him as he read and understood the final chapter. Its meanings became clear at last. It was not a comfortable knowledge, but it was timely.

The uppermost two graphics revealed the properties of major vortices. Their destinations and the pattern of their passage through time at the remote end. The central image defined the tipping point where what may be thought of as regular gates turned into portals. Surprisingly small but larger than anything his friend Jann Argent would be able to open on his own. The final two glyphs struck an icy lance of terror through Patrick's mind. They described what Ahnak had called "Voiders". The denizens of that parallel dimension where Void power, and indeed all the Elemental energy of the universe, originated. The nameless terrors that sat beneath much of Patrick's fear of what any use of his power may bring. The dark demonic beings that followed in the wake of the comet, caused the outbreak of smaller vortices, and now made his task of dealing with the deadly rock a billion times harder than it already was.

Yet the darkest, most desperate despair came not from these frightful creatures, but from his interpretation of the first of the major vortex glyphs. It revealed that larger portals behaved inversely to small ones. The largest would home in on a single destination. There was no way they could open a vortex large enough to swallow the comet without at the same time delivering Nemesis directly to Earth.

aboard the dauntless
15 apr 2177 23:31

When Patrick returned to the bridge, Jann Argent looked up. He looked as terrified as Patrick felt. The two men spoke at once.

'We have to abandon this plan,' Patrick said.

'We can't open a portal,' Jann said.

'How—'

'It was in the Tang Jikos all along,' Patrick said. 'Ahnak's parchment gave me the key, just as I thought.'

'He knows more about gates and portals than I do!' Jann said. 'Not sure how, but he said if we open one in front of the comet it will—'

'—hit the Earth,' Patrick finished. 'Yes, he's right. It looks like portals are more restricted the larger they are.'

'Except in time.'

'That's right. But even that can't be controlled. The

endpoint moves further back the longer the portal remains open.'

'So maybe this is what destroyed the dinosaurs?' Claire said.

'That's unlikely,' Patrick said. 'I don't know the exact parameters, but for a portal to stretch back sixty-five million years it would have to be held open an awfully long time. Longer than we have before it hits the planet. I'm afraid we would most likely deliver a disaster onto Earth's doorstep equally as bad as the one we are about to suffer here.'

'Worse,' Alvarez said. 'Purely in terms of number of people, orders of magnitude worse. There were almost ten billion souls on Earth when we left. It's unconscionable to save ourselves at the expense of so many, no matter how likely or unlikely it is. Even if we could guarantee sending it back earlier, we would still effectively be killing the same people.'

'By erasing their ancestors, you mean,' Petani said.

'Exactly.' Alvarez turned to the navigation panel. 'I'm taking us back,' she said. 'We have to think again.'

Chapter 17

aboard the dauntless
16 apr 2177 00:43

An uneasy silence fell across the bridge. Patrick watched the approach of the thin blue line separating the Berikatanyan atmosphere from the barren frigidity of space.

Alvarez' peremptory decision to abandon their portal plans had provoked an instant and passionate response from Petani, which initially shocked them all. Having hardly said a word since boarding, the Gardener paced the bridge, gesticulating energetically to emphasise every point of his argument.

'Surely you can't be certain?' he began. 'How many of these portals have been opened? Just because the first took most of us back to Earth, what guarantee can you give that a second would do the same? And what's the alternative? Leave it? Let it land?'

'I understand—' Patrick had held up his hands, trying to placate the old man, but he was in no mood to listen.

'No, I'm sorry Patrick. I respect you, and I'm honoured to call you my friend. But you *don't* understand. You can't. I've spent all my time here — almost all — building something. If this rock hits Berikatanya it will be gone in an instant. All of it. I swore I would never be responsible for that again. Not after the first time.'

Claire laid a gentle hand on the Elemental's arm. 'Perhaps Patrick doesn't get it, Petani, but I do. You've told me the story, many times. But we're all responsible. That's what being Elemental means. We have the power, and also the responsibility. To protect these people and their planet.'

'And how does allowing a gigatonne rock to land on their world protect them?' he asked, eyes brimming with tears. He ran a hand through his thinning hair. 'It doesn't, and you can't argue that it does.'

'I wasn't going to,' Claire replied. 'But surely you can see it's wrong to save Berikatanya at the expense of Earth?'

'Which brings us back to my original point,' he said. 'How certain are you that you would be sending it to Earth.'

'It how portals work, Petani,' Ahnak said quietly. 'Not a matter for certain or not certain. It how it is.'

'Sorry, but how do *you* know? Is there something about yourself you haven't told us? Are you a Gatekeeper? A Pattern Juggler? Exactly what credentials are you bringing to this debate?'

'There is lot I not tell,' Ahnak replied, his cheeks colouring under Petani's onslaught. 'Now not time for that.'

'Calm down, old friend,' Jann said. 'Let's not make this personal. We're all on the same side. Patrick has been trying to decipher the last section of the Tang Jikos since the day he found it. If he says all portals lead to Earth—'

'All portals from here,' Patrick said. 'I'm not saying every portal in the universe ends at Earth, that would be... unusual. But their beginnings and endings are fixed in terms of their spatial co-ordinates.'

Petani sat down heavily beside the long-range sensor panel. He gazed at the readouts unseeing, sighing loudly. 'So what are our options then?' he asked at length. 'If we can't save the planet, how can we save the people?'

His question had hung in the air since the old Gardener uttered it. Patrick kept his vigil at the viewport, watching the shining sapphire globe of Berikatanya swell beneath them. Alvarez returned to her seat at the navigation controls in readiness for re-entry.

'You should all buckle up again,' she said. 'It's been a few years since I did this. Can't guarantee it won't be a bumpy ride.'

The Queen's pallid face turned even whiter. She took a seat and fastened herself in. 'Even your wonderful machines cannot promise a safe arrival?' she asked.

'Automated landings depend on a lot of technology we don't have here,' Alvarez replied. 'Navigation satellites, geospatial telemetry, up to the minute meteorological data—'

The Queen held up her hands and closed her eyes. 'Your words are more complicated than your machines,' she said. 'I will trust in this belt, and in your experience, my dear.'

Patrick glanced at the chronometer. It ticked past 1a.m. as he watched. Exactly a day had passed since they confirmed the comet's trajectory on this very bridge. They were no closer to a solution now than they had been then. Their original plan was in the bin, and they needed urgently to discuss what options remained. He could think of only two. 'We should convene as soon as we land,' he said. 'Sorry, I know we're all tired, but until we have a way forward, none of us will be able to rest.'

'Agreed,' Jann said. 'And I want to hear your story too Ahnak. You say there's a lot you haven't told us, but we have no secrets here. Any more light you can shed on our dilemma may help us work out what to do.'

'I not know what die lemon is, but I will tell story,' the young Northerner said, his ice-blue eyes holding Jann's gaze without flinching.

'A little quiet would be appreciated,' Alvarez said, her fingers flicking over the nav panel. 'I need to concentrate.'

Blue replaced black in the viewport as the ship slipped below the Kármán line. Patrick gripped the arms of his seat and closed his eyes, a vision of a potential solution to their problem crystallising in his mind.

new washington
6th day of far'utamasa, 967

Whether Alvarez had prepared them for the worst while knowing she was perfectly capable of executing a textbook landing, Jann could not tell, but the supposed bumpy ride never materialised. A smooth, rapid descent, and a perceptible but gentle deceleration. The final connection with the mooring mast caused only the smallest tug against his seat belt.

The deep thrum of the Wormwood drive died away, and the intercom crackled into life to transmit Felice Waters' welcome home.

'I'm sick of sitting around in the main hall talking about doom and gloom,' Jann said, 'but I could eat a scabby horse. That's the only place to find a plate of hot food at this time of night. All in?'

'What is scabby horse?' Ahnak asked.

'Ignore him, Ahnak,' Elaine said with a smile. 'He has a strange sense of humour. I suspect he always had it, but eight years in a prison cell did nothing to improve it.'

'You in prison?' Ahnak said, his eyes wide.

'Long story,' Jann said, releasing his belt and levering himself out of the seat. 'Maybe even as long as yours. Perhaps we should trade.'

'I have eaten many things,' the Queen said, 'but I do not believe a scabby horse was one of them. Even so, if such a dish is all that is available, I will take a share. I too am hungry, despite the lateness of the day.'

'Earliness, actually,' Alvarez said, with a wave in the direction of the chronometer. 'It's tomorrow already, but the sun won't be up for a while yet.'

They made their way down the mooring gantry, clutching their clothes tightly around them. The night air seemed even colder than usual after the warmth of the Dauntless bridge. One of the ground team had predicted the travellers would be ready for food on their return. The servery was lit, and a fine selection of hot food steamed under its polycarbonate covers. Wonderful, tempting aromas filled the atmosphere in the hall. Jann's stomach gurgled.

'Let me get on the outside of some of that before we

start talking plans,' he said, grabbing a plate.

'The longer I spend among you Batu'n,' the Queen said, inclining her head at Jann as she spoke, 'even those of you who are not really Batu'n, the less I understand your use of your strange language. I welcome the chance to provide my mind with something to sustain it. It has been a long day and I fear it will be an even longer night.'

One by one they filled plates, then tables, then bellies. When nothing remained but smeared porcelain, Patrick sat back and began the debate.

'It seems to me,' he said, 'the solution — or at least one — is staring us in the face. If a large portal will always terminate on Earth, then surely it provides the ideal escape route? For anyone willing to take it.'

'I am grateful you added the last part, Juggler,' the Queen said, 'for to my mind it is of the essence. No matter the danger here, there are many for whom a leap into the unknown presents even greater fears.'

'Surely that depends on the alternatives?' Kyle asked. 'If the choices are death by comet or travel by portal to a safe place — *safer* place — will there be many who would choose death?'

'Perhaps not,' the Queen nodded, 'but there may be many who refuse to be convinced of the certainty of death if they remain. At least until it is too late to avoid.'

'Do we even know if we could create such a portal?' deLange asked. 'It has only been achieved once before, if my understanding of the history is accurate.'

'We know the mechanics of it, Argent and I,' Patrick said. 'I'd say yes, we can create it, although I am uncertain exactly where.'

'I've been thinking about that,' Jann said. 'My researches in the vicinity of the Black Palace revealed a large number of gates, but none that approached the dimensions we need. I suspect those are far rarer, as Ahnak hinted. We know the previous one was opened at Lembaca Ana, but I don't believe we can repeat the feat there. Pun'Akarnya stands in the way.'

'So we will have to search for an alternative location,' Patrick said, 'and that must be a priority. Anyone electing to leave must have sufficient time to make the journey to it. With luck it will be in a central place, but right now, there's no guarantee.'

'How many people are we talking about?' Claire asked. 'I have no idea of the population here, or what proportion of them would choose to go. It seems like an enormous logistical conundrum to assemble them all in the same place at the same time.'

'We know how many Earthers there are,' Alvarez said, 'at least within rough parameters. We have the crew and passenger complements for all four ships. Some will have died, and in ten years there will also have been births, but roughly speaking it's about eight thousand.'

'Don't assume they'll all be so keen to return to Earth,' Claire said. 'All of them came looking for a new life. A frontier experience. OK they didn't expect a calamity of these proportions, but I'd be surprised if they all vote to run back home given the chance. Especially those who have discovered power here.'

'Are you speaking for yourself?' Elaine asked. 'You fall squarely into that camp.'

'And remember the temporal aspect of the portal,' Patrick added. 'With the exception of the first few, the majority of them will traverse earlier in time. They will still have their frontier life, but on Earth.'

'Given the choice, I would stay, yes,' Claire said. 'But only if we can find some way to stay safe.' She turned to the Queen. 'What about the Berikatanyans, Ru'ita? Do you have any idea whether they would take the opportunity for a life on Earth? If it was the only way to survive?'

'Many of our people are in awe of the Batu'n and their technologies,' the Queen agreed, 'even though our exposure to it has been limited. From what you have said Juggler, I assume there would be less of that as more people step through the portal into your past. But as to how many would go, it depends on the alternative. If it is a straight choice between leaving and dying, then simple logic would suggest a majority would choose to save themselves. They would leave.'

'As long as they don't fall prey to the Jester's lies, and believe this is all a hoax,' Kyle said.

'We must go back to basics here,' Petani said. 'Before we can offer the people salvation, even one as frightening as a jump through the void to another world, we must be certain we can achieve it. Where will this portal be, and can you keep it open long enough for everyone to use it?'

'Every gate has a defined start point and end point,' Jann said. 'I admit I was unaware, until today, that the end would be fixed in the way we've discovered. It makes sense, though, because the openings are. I can't simply create a gate anywhere. Think of them like doors. When you encounter a wall, you don't find a door where you happen to be standing. If there is a door, it's in a certain position. You have to walk to it before you can open it and pass through. Gates are similar. Smaller gates are common, larger gates increasingly rare. I'd be surprised if there are more than two or three places where we can create a portal of the kind we're talking about.'

'We need to start the search immediately. At first light. Can you do that Jann? You haven't slept.'

'We don't have time to go riding across two realms in search of a gate!' Elaine said, throwing her hands in the air. 'The damned comet will be here in ten days! It takes longer than that to travel from coast to coast.'

'Not if we use a flyer,' Felice said. 'We still have one working unit. You can cover the whole of the south in a day. Is that OK Sil? If I pilot it?'

'Of course,' Alvarez replied, 'we're all in this together. Perhaps Argent can catch a few moments' sleep while you're flying from place to place.'

'No,' Jann said, rubbing his eyes, 'that won't work. I

have to be awake to sense the gates. Otherwise we'll be flying around randomly. Don't worry about me, I'll manage.'

Elaine kissed him. 'My hero,' she said.

'We still don't know how many people,' Patrick said. 'Ru'ita?'

'We don't keep detailed records in the way the Batu'n do,' the Queen said. 'I have a rough idea how many villages we have, and how big they are. Half a million is a good guess to work with.'

'And knowing a little about population behaviours from my time on the force,' Felice added, 'I'd say a working figure of something like twenty-five percent will be fooled by the Jester. That leaves around three hundred and seventy five thousand who will use the portal.'

'That's a lot of people,' Jann said. 'Can we hold it open that long, Pat...?'

He glanced at his friend as he spoke, his words dying in his throat. The Pattern Juggler's face was as white as death.

new washington
6th day of far'utamasa, 967

'What's wrong Patrick? You look like you've seen a ghost.'

His friend's words knocked at the door of his consciousness but for a moment the door remained closed. A mental metaphor of the barrier he wanted to keep in place to prevent the ingress of the nameless horrors lurking on the other side.

'Can I fetch you some water, Patrick?'

That was Claire. Always attentive. Always the helper.

'He really does look ill.'

Alvarez. Stating the obvious was a key skill for a leader. Knowing that what was obvious to one was rarely obvious to all.

'Can I offer you some healing energy, Juggler? It has

been a long day, perhaps it would be of benefit for everyone?'

The gentle warmth of the power emanating from the Queen's staff bathed him. The terror abated a little, allowing him to gather his thoughts.

'Thank you,' he said. 'That does feel better. Sorry. Jann is right. It struck me for the first time how long we will have to keep this portal open. Something like half a million people? Even if they can arrive at the portal in due time, they won't move through quickly.'

'I read something about the system they use to keep pilgrims moving during the Hajj,' Claire said. 'We had to study it for a school project. They work on an estimate of two hundred thousand per hour.'

'I have heard Batu'n talk of "hours" many times,' the Queen said, 'but no-one has ever explained how long that is. Your timekeeping is another one of your many mysteries as far as we Berikatanyans are concerned.'

'A complex topic for another occasion,' Alvarez said. 'As a rough guide, if you split a day up into quarters, each of them would be six hours long. So for instance, from dawn to midday: six hours.'

'Thank you,' the Queen inclined her head and smiled. 'At least now I can grasp the magnitude of the problem.'

'But the pilgrims at the Hajj are moving through a relatively large space,' Felice said. 'Surely your portal won't be that big? Like I said, we studied crowd movements in the force. Essential for demonstrations and riot control. Large groups of people move faster towards a visible and well-defined goal. We will have that with a portal, so that should speed things up.'

'Not to mention a comet coming up behind them!' Kyle said.

'Well that might be counterproductive actually,' Felice said. 'We don't want panic, or there will be bunching and crushing. If I can remember the numbers...'

She reached for a notepad. 'Half a million, you said?'

After a few moments scribbling, she held up the result. 'Working on a portal size of five metres, near as I can say it will take sixteen hours to get everyone through.'

Patrick felt the blood drain from his face again.

'What's the matter?' Jann asked. 'Can't we hold it open that long?'

'The duration is one problem, for sure. To sustain the effort over so long a period will be next to impossible. But more worrying is the thing I feared when we first began this discussion.'

'Voiders,' said Ahnak.

'Yes. Exactly. An open portal will attract them. The longer it remains open, the more likely they are to find it. And if they find it, they can pass through it.'

'Can we make the portal larger?' Felice asked. 'Five metres was only a working guess. Double it, maybe? It was only yesterday you were planning to open one four kilometres wide to swallow a comet.'

'But one which would only have been open for a few minutes,' Patrick said. 'Is there a linear correlation between size and rate of traversal? If we double its size will it need to be open half as long?'

Felice nodded. 'Yes, roughly. They might move slightly faster through a larger space. To keep it simple, half as long is a good estimate.'

'That's still eight hours,' Jann said. 'A full working day. We will need help from you, Ru'ita.'

'It's not enough,' Patrick said. 'The Voiders are guaranteed to find a portal that's open for that long. Is there any way we can reduce the number of people?'

'Only if we give them another option,' Jann said. 'A third way. Portal, death, or... what?'

'There is third way,' Ahnak said.

new washington
6th day of far'utamasa, 967

The blond-haired Northerner's statement was so quiet, so restrained, and yet had such an air of certainty about it that for a moment all other conversation stopped. Jann held the man's gaze. Not for the first time he felt as though he were looking in a mirror. Ahnak's eyes had the same icy blue clarity, the same gold flecks as his own.

'You seem very sure about that, Ahnak,' he said at length.

'Yes. I am sure. People may choose to come north. Through the Jur Dapentu.'

'What is that?' Kyle asked. 'I've never heard of it.'

'It is pass through mountain,' Ahnak said. 'For them wish to run away from doom. Live with northern people.'

'I've visited the north,' Jann said. 'And I can tell you you're mistaken Ahnak. There is no "northern pass." The journey is long and difficult, and filled with danger. It is certainly not suitable for thousands, travelling with their families and belongings.'

Ahnak's gaze did not waver, though his cheeks reddened in response to Jann's words. He shrugged. 'I know what I know, Jann Argent.'

'How can you know what is to come?' Patrick asked, a note of exasperation creeping into his voice. 'I was prepared to believe your people had some knowledge of astronomy that was not revealed to Jann during his stay at Tenfir Abarad. Skills that allowed them to detect the approach of the comet and calculate its path. And yes, it's true you were right. No-one can deny what our own sensors have confirmed. But now you're claiming a pass will appear through the mountain? At exactly the right time to save some of us from the same comet you came to warn us about?'

'How does this mountain pass come to be?' the Queen asked. 'Is the Wall of the World blown apart by the terrible impact of the rock from space?'

Ahnak smiled and shook his head. 'No, my lady. Mountain is not destroyed. As for pass... I only know the people used it. It is third way, as I have said.'

Piers laughed, but there was a manic edge to the sound. 'This is preposterous!' he said. 'How can you possibly know these things?'

'If they have telescopes or any other kind of astronomical equipment, I never saw it,' Jann said. 'They were fascinated by Earther technology but there was no evidence of them having their own, or even any science to speak of. The village was a simple, rural affair, with people much as you find here in Istania or Kertonia.'

'My knowledge not come from science,' Ahnak said. 'We do not know "astronomy" or stare at sky with tools. No need for such things when you have lived through catastrophe.'

'Lived through it?' The hairs on the back of Jann's neck bristled. 'What do you mean?'

'What I say. I know rock will land because my mother saw it happen. My earliest memory is sitting out under cloud of dust it threw into air. Day that dust cleared was day of big party in Tenfir Abarad.'

'This doesn't make sense,' Jann said, ignoring the small part of his mind that had acknowledged the truth of it, in the same way he had accepted Ahnak's statements about the comet before they had any kind of proof. 'You must be thirty years old. How can you have lived with the aftermath of something that hasn't happened yet?'

'You already know how, Jann Argent,' the Northerner replied, fixing Jann with his gentle stare. 'I come back in time. From thirty years in your future, to warn you all.'

Chapter 18

**new washington
6th day of far'utamasa, 967**

Ahnak watched the conflicting emotions playing over the face of the man he had come to find. Jann Argent: the original Gatekeeper. Was he ready for the truth?

'I think you had better tell us the whole story, Ahnak,' Jann said.

'I agree,' Patrick Glass said. 'I'm sure we'll all find it fascinating.'

'Sun won't be up for another few hours,' the Alvarez woman said. 'Perfect time for a tale, I'd say. Anyone want more food?'

Having just eaten, Ahnak declined. None of the others moved from their seats. They all regarded him closely. Of the group, as far as he could tell, only Jann Argent looked as though he expected to hear the truth. That was no surprise — the Gatekeeper had been the only one to believe him from the start of this adventure.

'Very well,' Ahnak said. 'Where shall I begin?'

'At the beginning,' Jann and the Air Mage said in unison, raising a brief nervous laugh among the others.

*

My earliest memory is sitting outside our hut, under a shelter mama made to keep the dust away. I must have been two — almost three. That dust was everywhere. I could feel its grit every night when I slid into my bed, taste it in every mouthful of food. Not that we had much to eat. By then, our grain stocks were almost exhausted. Mama had told me the tale of the rock many times. How it came through the air, flaming, leaving a dark trail of fiery smoke through the clear blue midday sky. How the ground shook when it landed, far beyond the mountains.

They saved us, those peaks. Protected the village from

the blast, which would have flattened every building in sight. But the towering spires of snow-covered rock could not save us from the ash cloud. Hitting the ground with such force, our doom threw up a plume of dirt, rock, and dust that rose through the air like an enormous bird. The winds and currents carried the brume far to the north, until it started to drift down on us like some kind of alien snow. Not cold, not clean, but it covered everything. The sky turned as black as night and stayed dark for almost a season.

Mama told how the strangers came soon after, line upon line of them trudging through those long days of twilight. They had travelled from the south, beyond the mountain. When I was a boy, her tales never explained how they had escaped the destruction. Or how they could undertake a journey that had only ever been achieved by one man. Perhaps she believed I would not understand the truth. In the years to come I often tried to persuade her to tell me more about those people. How many of them there had been, who they were, whether she knew anything about their own stories. She would never say much about them, but later, when I was older, she told me about the pass. About the Jur Dapentu. The Stone Canyon. In those days immediately after the doom came, the Elders' main worry was how we could feed them all. Our village was hard pressed to provide enough for our own.

For when the snows should have been receding and the meltwater bringing new life to our land, instead everything remained barren and dry. No new shoots of growth appeared. There was not enough light from the sun breaking through the dust cloud. Without grasses and grain, our animals starved to death. Smaller animals like kinchu that we would have put in our stewpots became scarce. Those we could find were fought over. The people of Tenfir Abarad called themselves the Beragan, which you know as the "Civilised People," but hunger does terrible things to men. Turns them into not much more than beasts. So mama's dreadful tale included stories of murders and even worse horrors. Partly designed to keep us children safe and out of trouble, but as with all such fables there was a nub of truth in them.

After a year, only a thin fog remained in the sky. Sunlight, though much dimmer than normal, broke through enough for some plants to grow again. One of these was a hardy cereal crop. My people had ignored it in the times of plenty. Its yield was poor, the grain had little flavour, and made only the weakest flour, yet now it was all we had. Village Elders decreed that every field should be planted with it. It gave only a few grains per plant, so a huge cultivation effort was necessary to ensure each villager had enough to eat. Even so there was little to go around. I grew up thinking it was normal for a man's bones to be seen through his skin, and for clothes to be made many sizes too big.

And then the day came when the skies cleared. You might think this would be a gradual process, but it was not. We retired to our beds one night when the sun had lit up the dusty evening sky with the intense crimson glow we had grown accustomed to. When we awoke the next day the fug had disappeared and the sun shone brightly for the first time in my life. By the end of that day, I had suffered my first case of sunburn. Mama scalded herself for forgetting the basic lessons of her own childhood, but she had had no cause to remember them for almost three years. As for me, I knew no better than to sit out the whole day. I watched the celebrations for some of the time, but mostly I stared at the blueness of the air, fascinated by the white clouds flying along leaving their muddy shadows on the fields.

It was not long after that memorable bright day that I opened my first gate.

new washington
6th day of far'utamasa, 967

A gasp of astonishment passed around the room at his last statement. He heard someone — he could not tell who — mutter 'What?'

Ignoring the distraction, he pressed on with his tale.

*

That first time was an accident. I had no warning of my ability. Even the Elders, who can sense such power in others, as Jann Argent can tell you, had not seen it growing in me. Or if they had, they did not share their insight with me.

So it was sometime around the date of my fourth birthday. The ash cloud was a rapidly fading memory, not only for me but the whole village. Life had returned almost to normal. Even the population of Tenfir Abarad dropped close to its usual numbers, once most of the strangers left. I cannot tell you where they went, or why. One day they were there, the next they were not. Most of them. A small number stayed. Those who had grown close with other villagers, or even shared their bread. This was another subject mama kept close to her chest. She is the daughter of the senior Elder in Tenfir. She must have known what led to their departure, but she refused to talk about it.

One balmy day in the hottest season of the year I, like any boy of four, had been playing in the fields with my friends. Mama had asked me to be sure and come home for a midday meal. The others brought lunches with them, and I really wanted to stay there and carry on playing, but I had promised. I walked home along the Jur Mayanga where the Ban Rekpupotan has cut a deep ravine over the centuries and the whitewater flows fast and fierce from the northern slopes of the mountains you know as Temmok'Dun. The path follows the river for some distance. It is a regular haunt for the village children. A place of excitement and wonder where we used to watch the waters foaming and spraying up over the opposite shore. Even in the middle of the year the river flowed as swiftly as when the frosts first melted.

Excitement and wonder, yes. But danger too. Parents were always warning us to stay away from the spot, or at least never go there on our own. Safety in numbers, they would say. That way, if one of you gets into trouble, there will be others to help. Or fetch someone from the village. But naturally, we ignored them, and grabbed any excuse to go. It was a small detour on my way home, to be sure, but not so much as to make me late for mama's lunch. I wanted to hear the roaring of the water over the rocks. Even so I was running, wondering what mama might have made for us that day. Hurrying to make sure I would be there when she had it ready. I wasn't watching the path. I tripped over a tree root, and pitched over the edge of the ravine.

The memory of my fall is as clear to me now as it was then. The sudden and surprising chill in the air as I flew through it. The sick feeling in my stomach from my plunge. The sight of the river rushing up to meet me. The glimpse, at the last moment, of the enormous rock lying beneath the surface, on which I was about to crush my skull.

The memory of the *end* of my fall is not so vivid. I closed my eyes. I knew I was going to die, and I knew it was going to hurt. And then I landed in a heap of soft dry bracken. I opened my eyes and discovered to my absolute astonishment that I was on the opposite bank of the river. I was no—

*

He hesitated, unsure for the first time of the word. He caught the Queen's eye.

'What do they call it?' he asked, switching to his native tongue, 'the man who performs physical jumps and tumbles?'

The Queen gabbled something to Clayer, so quickly that he could not understand it. Clayer smiled her sunniest, most heart-melting, smile. 'Gymnast,' she said.

'Yes,' Ahnak continued. 'That's it.'

*

I was no gymnast. I had not flipped or tumbled my way to the far bank. Even if I had been fit enough, and skilled enough, to perform such a stunt, the river was simply too wide for it to have delivered me here. Hearing my story, you will know that I had opened a gate, but I was unaware of such things that day. I only knew something strange had happened. And like any excited four-year-old, not only did I realise how I had done it, I wanted to do it again. Right away. I closed my eyes, remembered the feelings I had in the moment before I expected to hit the rock, and I did it. What I have always referred to since, in my mind, as "doing the thing."

When I opened my eyes, the gate stood before me. Another gate, I should say, on the riverbank. With a young boy's lack of fear I stepped through it, and onto the main street of the village. Only a hundred metres or so from our hut. I could see mama bringing out a small table ready for us to eat in the open air.

I crossed the street and covered the short distance to home, wondering whether or not I should tell her. I should have known she would see something was troubling me.

'What is it, Ahnak?' she said as I approached. 'You're as white as a juberang.'

'I've had a fright,' I said, and burst into tears.

Over lunch and through my hastily dried tears I described what had happened. She did not seem surprised. Did not scald me, or make me promise to stay away from the riverside in future, and — more important to me at the time, because this new-found trick had filled me with excitement — she did not tell me not to open any more gates. So of course, I did. I practised every day from that day forward. I discovered the village was overflowing with gates. I hardly ever had to walk the full distance between any two places after that. It came easy to me. Even at that age I recognised it was a rare ability. Somewhere deep in my mind lurked the expectation that I would eventually have a visit from one of the Elders — probably my grandfather — but no visit came. No-one interrupted me doing the thing. They neither stopped it, nor encouraged it.

And so I went on, playing regular boyhood games most of the time, and practising the thing at other times. The tale of those years is a mundane one, so I will spare you the details. Nothing much of note happened until shortly after I started to grow my beard. I had been on a hunting trip in the foothills with friends. We left our kudai behind for the day. It was easier to find places to hide, or stalk our prey, when on foot. We made a good kill: a juberang in its seasonal white coat that mama had compared me with on First Gate Day. The rest of the group went on ahead of me, carrying the beast between them on two poles. I stayed behind to collect the tammok and panpah that had missed their targets. We were young, and could not easily afford replacements, and we were also lazy and did not want to have to make them.

It took me a long time to gather all the equipment. By the time I finished, I had started to worry that I would miss out on the feast. The others were my friends, for sure, but they were also young men like me. They would not think to wait for my arrival before starting the roast. I would certainly lose the best cuts and if I didn't hurry I could easily be left with nothing but the bones to chew on.

The solution was obvious. With my control of gates I could complete the journey back to the village in the blink of an eye, maybe even beat the other boys back! I concentrated, did the thing, and pitched out of the terminator onto the village green, retching up my guts and crippled with a headache so fierce it temporarily blinded me. Passing through a gate had never had that effect on me before. Even stranger, I was not prepared for the reaction of the first few villagers to see me.

'Ahnak?' the first said, a look of astonishment on her face.

'Fetch Pennamatalayah!' another cried.

Someone ran off in the direction of my hut. The two who had spoken helped me up off the ground. One held my head. The other said 'Where have you been, Ahnak? We thought you were dead!'

Already befuddled by my splitting head, I could not understand what the woman could possibly mean. Within moments mama came running.

'Ahnak! Oh Ahnak, you're safe!' she cried, floods of tears coursing down her face.

'Of course I'm safe,' I said. 'I was only hunting. I was hardly likely to come to any harm. Where are the others? Has the feast started?'

Mama looked at me with a strange expression. 'Started?' she said. 'Ahnak, the beast was cooked and eaten ten days ago. No-one has seen you since Pematan and Pribatom left you at the hunting ground.'

new washington
6th day of far'utamasa, 967

For the second time, the sound of a sharp intake of breath passed around Ahnak's audience. Kyle Muir watched her friend closely. The Air Mage had not taken her eyes off the young Northerner during his entire tale. Another member of the group also stared at their narrator, but while Claire Yamani's expression was one of rapture, the Fire Witch's looked more like mounting horror.

'Well, you have surprised us again Ahnak,' the Witch said. 'I think we should take the opportunity for a short comfort break. We still have some time until the sun is up and we can make a start with our plan. So let's grab a drink, fill your plates anyone who can face more food at this time of night, and carry on. I for one am fascinated to hear where you take us from here.'

A low buzz of conversation sprang up around the room. Kyle turned to Claire. 'You hungry?'

'Not really.'

'Except for him, yeah?' She nodded at Ahnak, who had returned to his seat having refilled his water glass.

Claire blushed. 'Is it that obvious?'

'Only for anyone watching you, I guess. Which I was. You couldn't take your eyes off him!'

'I think everyone else was focused on him too, to be fair. It's a pretty extraordinary story.'

'I should say. Until today I thought there was only one Gatekeeper. I wonder if he's related to Jann in any way?'

'Maybe I shouldn't say anything, so keep this to yourself, but he told me yesterday that Patrick's his father.'

Kyle choked on a mouthful of water, spraying it over her friend.

'Oi!'

'Sorry,' she said, once her fit of coughing had subsided. 'Oh God, you're soaked.'

'It's OK,' Claire said, wiping her shirt and leggings with her hands. 'Hardly soaked. Most of it missed me. And maybe I needed cooling down a bit anyway!' She gave Kyle a wink.

Kyle glanced around the hall. Several of the others had heard the noise and wore concerned expressions. She waved at them. 'It's OK! I'm OK! Forgot how to swallow!'

'Sorry Claire,' she said again. 'Not the best way to keep a secret! But his father? How can that be?'

'The obvious conclusion from what he's just told us is that his gates can take him through time. And he's already mentioned his mother's stories about refugees from the South. Join the dots. I can't wait to hear the rest of his story!'

In curious synchrony with her friend's words, the Fire Witch rapped on her table. 'If we're all ready, and Ahnak is willing, we should continue. It's unlikely any of us could sleep now anyway. There's hardly any of the night left. May as well power on through and catch some rest later, if we can.'

The group retook their seats and an expectant hush fell over the hall as Ahnak cleared his throat.

new washington
6th day of far'utamasa, 967

Though I found it incredible, the others all confirmed what mama had said. Between my friends leaving me at the hunting site, and me emerging from my gate into the heart of our village, ten days had passed. I had created a gate through time.

I have heard the Pattern Juggler's explanation of how the terminator of the largest portals moves through time. Back then, I had no such knowledge. Even if I had, the gates I created were not such grand affairs. As far as I was knew, they were ordinary. If an instant connection between two points in space can be considered ordinary.

I returned home with mama that day and took to my bed after having a bite to eat. The after-effects of my short journey into the near future stayed with me for many days. I was disorientated, almost constantly sick, and the nagging headache didn't leave me for almost a month. Once I felt well enough, I sought out my grandfather. I enquired if the village Elders had ever heard of such a thing happening before.

'A gate through time? No, Ahnak, to my knowledge we have never seen its like. But come with me. I am no expert in these matters, but we both know someone who is.'

We hurried through the village streets to the house of Dipeka Kekusaman. She had recently taken over as

Tamatua, since my grandfather's tenure had ended with the changing of the year. She came to her door in response to our knocking.

'Penjal. How nice to see you. And your grandson! My, how you've grown Ahnak, since last we spoke.'

In the days and months after my powers first developed, I had spent long evenings in the company of this wise woman. We would discuss the principles of gates. I learned much from her immense experience of the lore, which had no other record in our community.

'Come in, come in,' she said. 'To what do I owe the pleasure of your visit today? I think I can probably guess.'

I would have been surprised if she had not already learned of my feat. Not even a full day had passed since I emerged from the time gate, but the story had quickly spread through Tenfir Abarad. Kekusaman smiled at me gently, and offered us a seat at her hearth, wherein the embers of the day's fire still glowed. She lit a lamp and fetched a plate of lokker in the local tradition of never entertaining guests without providing at least some simple sustenance.

'You want to know if I ever heard of a gate that could take its keeper through time,' she said plainly.

'Yes,' I replied. 'My grandfather believes it has never been done before.'

'Well, you are right, Penjal,' she said, inclining her head in the old man's direction, 'strictly speaking. It has never been achieved, but the lore has always suggested such a thing would be possible. And of course,' she continued, poking at the embers of her fire with a long stick, 'we understand the mechanics of the larger gates — the Uterban wherein the demonic Voiders live — in the way they stretch ever further back in time.'

'But my gates do not approach such dimensions,' I protested. 'How can time come into play with small gates like mine?'

'It is not only a factor of size,' Kekusaman said, with

another of her gentle smiles. If ever I try to imagine what pure, distilled wisdom would look like, I think of her. Nothing fazed her, nothing caused any ripples on the serene surface of her life's waters. She was kind, wise, and treated everyone around her with utmost respect. 'The power comes from the family, from your ancestors.'

She nodded again at my grandfather. In that moment, I realised for the first time that he had not changed in the thirteen or so years I had known him. Thinking back to the tales mama told me of how long, and how many times, he had sat in the Tamatua's chair, I began to wonder if this was the source of my burgeoning control over time.

'The lines of inheritance have been split for centuries.' Kekusaman continued. 'Those with the ability to control gates, and those who have the potential to control time, have not joined with each other in all of our history, though we were aware of the likely outcome if they ever did. Nothing overt was done to prevent it, but it was apparent to us adepts that there must be an innate property of the families that normally gives rise to an insurmountable antipathy between them.'

She reached for the last lokker, challenging each of us with her eyes to confirm it was hers. 'It is, of course, something of an overstatement to call it "control" over time. But that conveys enough of the true meaning for our purposes today.'

'It made me ill,' I said. 'Is that what "antipathy" is?'

She laughed. A deep throaty laugh that you might expect to hear in an alehouse rather than the parlour of an Elder. 'No, but I am not surprised,' she said. 'You travelled forward in time. What was it? Ten days? Quite the feat for your first attempt young Ahnak. Most impressive.'

'Does it make a difference, then? The direction?'

'Most certainly. Time is like a river, I'm sure you've heard that said, even at your young age. That is a metaphor, but like all metaphors it contains a kernel of truth. And in the same way that it takes an effort to swim, or row a boat, upstream, travelling forwards in time is harder than going back. Riding into the past is as easy, to an extent, as riding a river downstream.'

'To an extent?'

'Yes. I cannot give you much detail of exactly how easy, or how far, but *any* journey through time will affect you to a greater or lesser degree. Travelling forward has a stronger effect, as you have seen. A journey of only ten days has made you sick for a month. Much further and it could have killed you. You will find it far easier to travel backward. But as you will no doubt have immediately grasped, that itself comes with its own danger.'

I stared at her, puzzled but not wanting to disappoint her. The fact was, my grasp of her meaning had not been as immediate as she assumed. I remained silent for so long, the message made itself clear in the end.

'I see some further explanation is necessary. Suppose for a moment that your first accidental experience with a time gate had been in the opposite direction. Travelling into the past would in some ways have been more traumatic. Seeing events you had already seen, and creating confusion among your contemporaries. Also, having not been "absent," there would be no immediate explanation for what had happened. There is also the chance you would encounter your earlier self, although if that occurred you would of course know about it, from the perspective of that other self. But arriving ten days ago presents two options. You could choose to live through those days again until you arrive back at the time you started. Or, you could "gate" your way back to the future.

'You have already experienced a ten-day journey forwards in time, so you know what effect that would have on you. It would hurt, but bearably so. But since travel into the past does not have such a profound effect on your physiology, you could be tempted to go further. Visit your mother as a child, perhaps, or watch the mountains being raised after the Warring Tribes travelled south.

'I counsel you, Ahnakpenyabangung, not to succumb to such temptation. I know not how many days forward it would take before the adverse effects of the jump became crippling, or even lethal, but I suspect the effect is exponential. Ten days was painful, twenty would likely be devastating, thirty — or even less — would surely kill you. And so having journeyed back anything further than a month, you would be unable to return.'

My grandfather had sat in silence during our lengthy exchange. I knew him. Knew that he was keeping his own counsel so as not to influence my thoughts, or the direction of Kekusaman's explanations. Now, he stood, collecting his walking stick and his bag of herbs from beside his chair, and stretching his old muscles. 'Talking of time,' he said, 'I believe it is time we left the Tamatua to her business.' He left the hut without a further word.

We walked back to my hut. Neither of us spoke. Grandfather allowed me a quiet space in which to think, and I mulled over what the wise Tamatua had told me. Tried to come to terms with the conflicting emotions that her knowledge stirred. The most significant event in my past was obvious. We are living through it now. The impact of the doom. I remembered mama's tales of the strangers. How they came with fear and gratitude, praising the young Beragan who had travelled South to warn them, and as a result saved many thousands of lives.

Who could possibly know of such a disaster in advance? Only someone who had lived through its aftermath and been brought up on tales of doom and destruction, of spirit and salvation. So I knew it had to be me. I must be the one to come back and warn you, and prevent as much of this disaster as was in my power to do.

new washington
6th day of far'utamasa, 967

'You were thirteen when you decided to make the

journey back?' Clayer asked, her eyes misted with tears.

'Yes.'

'And how old are you now?'

'Twenty-six.'

'Continue with your story Ahnak,' Jann Argent said, his expression unreadable. The Fire Witch's gaze flicked between the two Gatekeepers. She looked angry, but in Ahnak's brief experience that was not unusual. 'I sense there is not much left to tell.'

'That is true,' he said. 'I can sum up those thirteen years in one word: practice. I spent every spare moment practising the art of time gates, within the limitations Kekusaman had laid out. I experimented with travel to the future at first. I found I could manage eighteen days. It left me bed-bound for almost an entire season. Fortunately, this time, I had warned mama of my intentions. She tried to dissuade me, as you would expect, but I refused to be swayed. I had to know. That experience marked the end of my experiments. Another day and I could easily have been permanently crippled or worse. I had my parameter and I was content with it.

'I followed this with a lengthy period of familiarity with travels to the past. I engaged in further discussions with both my grandfather and Kekusaman on the subject. And I travelled short distances only. A day or so at first, but slightly longer as I became more expert. I knew I would only have one chance to make my main trip. I believed that if I could gain a "feel" for the use of my power, I would be able to judge how much more effort I needed to arrive back at the right time.

'I had not intended to cut it so close, so forgive me. Ten days is not long to prepare for the end of the world. I wanted to arrive earlier. But it would have been worse to arrive too early. I always knew proving my story would be hard. I had to put my faith in the metal magic of the Batu'n, after the many tales mama told me.

'And of course infinitely worse was the prospect of

arriving too late. All those years of practice, followed by the extraordinary effort of travelling back in time almost thirty years, wasted by arriving after impact.

'So the day eventually dawned when I had to make the jump. Emotions ran high, as you might expect. Mama was distraught, knowing she would never see me again. Worried I would die in the attempt, arrive at the wrong time, or be arrested as a madman and locked in a dungeon, only to be crushed by the very event I was attempting to save everyone from. But I knew she was proud too. Proud of her son, and happy in the knowledge that I would finally meet the man she had told me so much about.

'I had discovered many years before the location of the gate I intended to use. Naturally I had been unable to include it in any of my practices. Even a day into the past is too far when the physical end of your practice gate is almost three hundred kilometres away, on the other side of the largest mountain range in the land. But I knew where it was, and I knew what I needed to do. I also knew that the effect of such a long journey to the past would be profound. I did not expect it to kill me — that would have been pointless to say the least — but I did think it likely I would be unable to move for some days. I filled a backpack with provisions, water, bepermaks, and some bandages and salves in case of accident. I bid farewell to my friends, mama, grandfather, Kekusaman and the other Elders. Putting my fears aside, I set off alone for the gate.

'In the end the traversal went more easily than I expected. On arrival in your time, I was surprisingly fit, though I had another blinding headache. The stomach-churning dizziness that came with it did not pass until I had covered quite some distance.'

new washington
6th day of far'utamasa, 967

Jann regarded the young Northerner closely. Ahnak's

story had always struck a chord with him, and of course now it was clear why. But more than that, the man himself was someone who — unusually for Jann — he had warmed to from their first meeting. Something about his forthright demeanour and the bravery and good humour with which he met every question, every dissent, and every disbelief. The reason he was so convinced of the truth of his story, now revealed, no doubt lay at the heart of this, but for Jann there was more. Something he could not quite get a handle on.

'So you fetched up some distance from the Black Palace?' he asked.

'Fetched up?' Ahnak said, puzzlement clouding his expression momentarily. 'Ah, yes. The gate terminated in a ravine west of the forest. Naturally I had no ride, so I faced a full morning's walk before interrupting your ceremony. My apologies, Kema'satu.'

He bowed to Kyle, snatching a surreptitious look at Claire.

'No apology necessary,' Kyle said, smiling. 'If anything I was happy to be interrupted. I've never been one for much pomp.'

'I'm glad to hear the Elders are still providing such good counsel,' Jann said, 'especially Kekusaman. She was a great help to me at a time when I needed it most.'

'And to me,' Ahnak said. 'I never expected to find anyone who knew anything about time gates. She gave me the confidence to begin my experiments, so in a way you could say she is responsible for my being here.'

'Along with your parents, of course,' Jann added, only half in jest. 'You said Penny... er... Pennamatalya, was your mother? And your abilities with time come from her?'

'Yes. Of course the long lives of my family are well known in Tenfir, but the reasons for it are understood by only a few.'

Ahnak regarded him with a strange expression, as if there was more he wanted to say but was waiting for permission. Jann too had more to say, but his throat closed on the words. Unexpected tears started in his eyes. He focused on the table in front of him for a moment.

'So presumably your gatekeeper powers come from your father. You never said who he is?'

'Patrick, right?' Kyle said, grinning. Her gaze flicked between Claire, Patrick, and Ahnak, her wide grin fading into a worried look as their reactions unfolded.

Claire's expression telegraphed anger. It was clear that this "knowledge" had come from her and she had intended it to be kept private.

Patrick sat bolt upright, eyes wide. 'Me?'

Ahnak stared at Kyle, astonishment plain on his face. 'Patrick? No! Where does this idea come from?'

'Claire told me that's what you said?'

'My apologies again, Water Wizard, and to you Juggler, but that is not what I meant. Perhaps the fault of my language. Subtle differences in our words can lead to misunderstandings. No, what I should have said is that Patrick Glass is the man who raised me. But he is not my natural father. That is the man I have long wanted to meet. My second, and perhaps in many ways my main, reason for risking the journey back in time.'

A cold shiver of nervous electricity ran down Jann's spine as the Northerner turned back to stare into his eyes. 'It is you Jann Argent. You are my father.'

new washington
6th day of far'utamasa, 967

Her worst fear landed squarely on her lap as Ahnak's voice died away. The others' stunned expressions, and her lover's astonished and guilt-ridden glance in her direction did nothing to quell the rising sickness in her stomach, the shame, and the sudden volcano of rage that erupted in her mind.

Days of torment. Since the Northerner's first

appearance she had suspected the truth. His eyes — so like Jann's: clear, ice-blue, rimmed with dark cerulean — his manner, even his gait gave away his heritage. But at first, it was a suspicion only. In quiet moments, when alone, she had cast her mind back to Jann's tale of his sojourn over the peaks of the Wall of the World. His time spent in Ahnak's village of Tenfir Abarad. And principally the days during which he had been tended by the woman Penny. Pennamatalya; Ahnak's mother. No more than a girl, really, from Jann's description. She had cared for him so diligently and tenderly, dressed his wounds, emptied his night soil, dripped water onto his parched lips at the height of his fever, and shared his bread. The revelation that this woman was mother to the stranger had seemed too strange a coincidence. At the time of his arrival she had not suspected that this fact was only the first piece in the jigsaw of her suspicions.

She had focused for a time on that bread thing. Sifting through the memories of exactly what Jann had said about the woman in the next hut, Penny's reaction to her, and Penny's father's mention of the incident during Jann's meeting with the village Elders. It was all loaded with double meaning. Although she had not wanted to believe the other interpretation, it had been there all along. Another piece in the jigsaw, and one that began to reveal the whole picture.

But he had never said anything more! *"I shared her bread."* Even after Ahnak's arrival, and his immediate warming to the man, still he kept silent about the truth of their relationship. As long as she had known him, Jann Argent had been a loner. Reticent when asked about his power. Having few friends and — as far as she knew — no other lovers before her, though he came to her as a man well versed in the arts of love. Other memories crowded in, displacing the lava flow of her anger with a more gentle, liquid heat. She shook her head. No. This was not a time for her gentle side. The side that he had insisted was there and that she should give free rein. The side that had blossomed beneath his slow touch and the murmur of his kind words. Was it a lie? Their relationship? Did he still harbour feelings for his northern girl? The doubts and jealousy had ebbed and flowed through the days since Ahnak's arrival. They drove a wedge between the lovers even as she tried to quell the images that crowded in during her most passionate moments.

And now this. *"It is you Jann Argent. You are my father."* The final piece of the jigsaw; its picture clear and undeniable. Her anger boiled over once more, gouts of flame flaring up from the palms of her hands. She flung her arms aloft in a gesture of futile denial.

'No!'

Her mental image of that fateful puzzle burst into its scattered pieces, flying over her head before raining down on her, their sharp edges stinging as they delivered a myriad tiny cuts. Tears blurred her vision. The Fire Witch ran from the room, singeing the door frame with wild flame as she left.

Chapter 19

new washington
6th day of far'utamasa, 967

Jann leapt to his feet as Elaine ran from the group. Blood pounded in his ears. The dining hall door slammed shut behind her, the odour of charred wood reaching him. Desperate to follow, to explain, to reassure, still Ahnak's revelation gripped him. The young man held his gaze, his expression yearning for some reaction from his — Jann's stomach flipped again — from his father.

The others said nothing. Were they stunned? Shocked? Waiting for Jann to react? He needed to say something, but the words would not come. Words? He could hardly form the thoughts!

'I...er...' he began, collapsing back into his chair and running both hands through his hair. 'Wow, that's... unexpected. She — Penny I mean, your mother — she never told me.'

'She didn't know,' Ahnak said. 'When she discovered she was pregnant, you were gone.'

'Of course.' Jann breathed. At least one level of guilt fell away. One layer of skin from a very large onion. 'Yes. After that first meeting with the Elders, I only stayed a few more days.'

'And nights,' Piers said, grinning.

'I'm sorry, Ahnak,' Jann said, giving Piers a hard stare. 'Sorry I wasn't there for you.'

'Don't be,' his new-found son said. 'You couldn't know. And you were there for me. In a way. Mama always talked about you. Though you only had short time together, she relived it over and over in her tales of those days. It always clear she had strong feelings for you. And,' he added with an embarrassed smile, 'without you: no me.'

'Has she...' Jann started. 'I mean, has there been anyone else since? Does she have someone?'

Jann caught Ahnak's gaze flick momentarily in Patrick's direction. So quickly that no-one else could have seen it, but the message was clear. He had already revealed who brought him up. No surprise that Penny would grow close to a man who provided for her only son.

'When I left,' Ahnak said, maintaining eye contact with Jann, 'I made sure she would be looked after. Yes. She has someone.'

'I'm glad,' Jann said. It was the truth. Penny had taken good care of him. She deserved to be happy. 'She saved my life.'

'And now, will you return the favour, Jann Argent?' Ahnak asked, leaning forward. 'Will you save my people, father?'

A tingle crept across Jann's scalp at Ahnak's use of "father". What was his son asking? How could he save a distant village full of people from the coming doom?

'I... save them? From the comet? But you said they live through it.'

'They do. But that does not mean they have to.'

Patrick held up his hands, a look of utter horror distorting his features. 'Woah!' he said. 'Hold on. You're talking about changing the future. If that's what you mean?'

'I mean you have decided to open a gate, and save all the people of the south,' Ahnak said. 'Why then can you not save the people of the North? Do they not deserve to have their years of starvation and darkness taken away? Can they not step through your portal to this "Earth" you have all seen?'

Jann shook his head. A gesture of resignation rather than denial. 'I don't think we're saying they don't deserve it,' he said. 'But it's dangerous. First, there's Patrick's point about a possible temporal anomaly.'

He stopped; Ahnak's confused expression reminding him of the differences in language.

'Temporary what?' his son said.

'Sorry. I mean any change you make here, in this time, will affect everything to come. You are here now, but pretty soon you'll also be alive as a young boy in Tenfir Abarad. A boy who lived through the aftermath of the impact, watched the refugees travel to his village, and determined to become the one who saved them all.'

'I don't understand,' Ahnak said. 'What is problem?'

'If we find a way to save your people,' Jann said, 'by bringing them south and sending them through this portal—'

'Assuming we can create it,' Patrick said.

'—if we fetch them,' Jann continued, 'and send them away, you would be one of them. And if you're "saved" in the here-and-now, then your entire childhood will change. You will not be there to experience the hardships you endured. You will not return to warn us, as you have. You may not even be on this planet at all.

'That's a big enough problem in its own right, but there's another. Time. We simply don't have time to travel north and bring your people back here before we have to open the gate.'

Ahnak brightened. 'We could gate to the North,' he said. 'It need not take any time at all.'

'Perhaps we could,' Jann agreed, 'and that would reduce the travelling time, assuming a gate exists near to where we'll be creating the portal. But we don't know where that is yet, and even if we did, the travelling is only one part of it. How do you think your mother will react to a man she doesn't recognise walking up and saying "Hi, I'm your grown-up son. You need to come with me through the mountains so I can save you from a flying rock"? Remember how worried you were that we wouldn't believe you. Same applies in reverse. Worse — they don't have our Long Range Scanner. They can't prove the truth of what you're saying. You'll be like a mad man to them.'

Tears started in Ahnak's eyes as the truth of Jann's words became clear. Had he said enough? He needed to find Elaine, and repair the damage Ahnak's tale had wrought.

'There is a third problem,' Patrick said quietly.

Jann and Ahnak turned as one to stare at the Pattern Juggler.

'This tale of refugees from the south trekking to Tenfir Abarad,' he said. 'We still don't know how they'll make their way over Temmok'Dun?'

new washington
6th day of far'utamasa, 967

The Pattern Juggler's words sent an icy shiver along the length of Ahnak's spine. He had known the man as his step-father his whole life, yet this younger version was a complete stranger. Ahnak found his bald statement antagonistic at best. Had he not told them all of the journey the southerners made to escape their doom? Was this merely another of his stories these people found hard to believe?

His anger at the question that hung between them vied with the ice in his veins. The chilling realisation that despite long familiarity with the story of the strangers' arrival, in all his years he had never asked his mother, his grandfather, or any of the village Elders how this feat had been achieved.

'You told us how difficult the adventure was for you, Jann,' Patrick Glass continued. 'The days of hard climbing, the dangers you confronted, the lack of supplies. At the last, you only made it into the northern lands by a stroke of the most unusual luck. Had you fallen onto rock instead of into deep snow, you would have been killed outright.'

His father nodded at each point the Juggler made. 'All true,' he said, 'it was a perilous journey. One I was fortunate to survive.'

'You were but one man,' Glass added. 'How can we expect hundreds, or even thousands, of men, women, and children of all ages, to undertake the same trek? Many of them will be unfit, or have a fear of heights. They won't make it.'

Ahnak could remain silent no longer. 'And yet they did,' he said. 'Even in the face of all these dangers and problems, many hundreds came north in the days after the doom. I never heard of anyone coming to harm, or dying, on the trip.'

'But you don't know how they achieved it?' Glass asked him, his gaze unwavering.

Ahnak felt the colour rise in his cheeks. 'No,' he said.

'I think I might,' Piers said, taking a step forward.

All eyes turned to the young Stone Mage, whose face also displayed the badge of his heightened emotion.

'Ahnak has called this pass "The Stone Canyon." But Jur Dapentu is more accurately translated as the Canyon of the Stone Mage.' He looked at Jann Argent. 'You've told us how the Beragan Stone Mage raised the Wall of the World all those centuries ago, to keep the Warring Tribes from returning to their homeland. Perhaps now is the time, when they must flee back north to save their lives, when the mountain must be flattened again?'

A gasp passed from person to person around the room as the implications of Piers' words became clear.

Ahnak felt a thrill of excitement. Could it be true? 'Is it possible?' he asked. 'Is it something you can really do?'

The Stone Mage grinned. 'I won't know until I try,' he said, 'but it's the same power. If it can be done, then it can be undone.'

'I think I may be able to help,' Jann Argent said.

Piers snorted. 'You have Stone power to go along with your Gatekeeper abilities?'

His father laughed, but his eyes looked stony enough to hold the gift of which Tremaine spoke. 'No. But I can show you where to use yours.'

'Of course!' Clayer gasped. 'The caldera!'

'Exactly,' his father said. 'The ancient volcano and the

centuries of erosion by the source of Sun Besaraya have done a lot of your work for you. Probably half the breadth of the mountain range — possibly more — is already at ground level, or close enough. If we approach at the right point, you will only need to remove a fraction of the rock that bars our way along the rest of Temmok'Dun.'

'It must be the answer!' Ahnak said, his voice rising with excitement. 'Mama always said the people came from that direction. From the same place she had found you!'

'Then it all fits,' Piers Tremaine said. 'I must flatten Temmok'Dun and create a passage from south to north.'

'If I may help you in any way, Stone Mage, you have only to ask,' the Queen said, gripping her staff.

'We must time this to coincide with the portal,' Alvarez said, 'it will take careful planning.'

'I've always wanted to see the caldera,' Clayer added, 'ever since Jann first told us about it.'

'This is all very well,' his step-father said, his expression still troubled, 'but I don't think it can work.'

A stunned silence fell once more across the room.

'Well?' his father said, rising to his feet, 'come on. You can't leave us hanging. Why won't it work? You think Piers isn't up to it?'

'Oh, I don't doubt his abilities,' Glass said. 'I've seen him raising sea walls and land walls. OK the mountain is an order of magnitude or two larger, but it's still only more of the same.'

'What then?' Jann Argent pressed.

Ahnak felt a glow of pride in his father. He had only known the man a few days, yet it was clear that he had inherited more than the power of the Gatekeeper from him. A measure of his determination and grit had been passed on too.

'Don't you see?' Glass said, raising his hands in an empty gesture of resignation. 'Ahnak tells us his people were protected from the after-effects of the impact — the blast wave and its accompanying destruction — by the very mountain you're talking of flattening. The more I think of it... opening a pass could be the worst possible option. The entire force of the blast will be channelled through that small gap. It will hit Tenfir Abarad with many times the destructive power it would have if it had been spread over a larger area. No-one will survive.'

The rising and falling emotions of the conversation made Ahnak feel dizzy. First his people were doomed, then saved, now doomed again. 'This is terrible!' he said, dropping to his seat and holding his head in his hands. When he looked up moments later, his father was gone.

new washington
6th day of far'utamasa, 967

A knock came on the door. Elaine Chandler pulled the covers closer to her chin and shuddered. Tracks of dried tears on her face itched, and without a fire the room was cold even under the bedclothes. Piers Tremaine had provided fireplaces for the apartments in each of his newly built homes, but she could not summon enough power to warm herself, let alone set flame to the grate. Better insulation may have been preferable.

'Go away,' she said, hardly loud enough to be heard on the other side of the wood.

'Can we talk?'

It was Jann. Of course it was him. Who else would dare? Claire maybe, but that was unlikely. They shared an uneasy friendship at the best of times, and this was definitely not the best.

'What is there to talk about?'

'I want to explain.'

'Bit late for that, isn't it? It's been almost two months since the last time you knocked on my door. When you returned from keeping her bed warm. Plenty of time to "explain" before now.'

'Except now it's "our" room. I'm not with her. I don't

want to be with her. I'm with you.'

'You think?'

'We both know. Come on, Elaine, don't make this any harder.'

'Why should I make it easy for you? You fucked her. You could at least be honest about it.'

'OK yes. Obviously. You and I weren't together then. Can you at least open the door? I don't want the whole of New Washington to hear our most intimate details.'

'Your intimate details you mean. I wasn't there, remember?'

He did not answer, but she did not hear him leave. Damn him! Fresh tears started in her eyes, overflowed along the same itchy tracks. How had he done this to her? Slipped past all her guards and barriers, and found his way into her heart? She threw back the covers, crossed the room, and opened the door.

'Thank you,' he said, stepping inside. He shivered. 'No fire?'

Her reaction to his ingenuous remark kindled her power in an instant. She sent a firebolt into the grate, where the kindling ignited with a loud "whoosh." An angry tongue of flame leapt up the narrow chimney.

'Woah!' Jann exclaimed, staggering backwards. 'OK!'

'Be thankful I sent it into the fireplace,' Elaine said, rubbing at her face to quell the itching and remove the obvious tear tracks. 'Say what you came to say, and go.'

'I hoped—'

'You're not sleeping here tonight, if that's what you were thinking.'

'Then where—?'

'I don't care where. Come on, get it over with.'

'Don't be like this, Elaine.'

'Like what? I just found out my lover has a child by another woman! What the fuck am I supposed to be like? You want me to just smile, nod, and open my legs for you? I'm angry Jann! I'm hurt! This is not something that will just go away. He's right there. Right *here*. Your son. *Your* son, not ours. We never even talked of children. Never once! And you already had one.'

'Hey look! I just found out myself, OK? She didn't even know she was pregnant, not 'til after I'd left!'

Elaine closed her throat on the angry retort she had been about to deliver. That was new. 'Really?'

'Yes, really. He just told me. I'd been gone a few days before Penny realised.'

She sat back on the bed, letting the revelation sink in. OK, he did not know about the child, but...

'You should still have told me. Even if you didn't know about the kid, you can't pretend you didn't know you'd had a relationship with his mother.'

'Hardly a relationship!'

'Oh, right. You're gonna tell me it was just the one time?'

He coloured up. Guilty as charged. Elaine kept quiet. He was not going to get off the hook so quickly. After a lengthy and careful examination of his fingernails, he summoned the courage to look at her. 'Twice, actually.'

'Right.'

'Honestly! The first time took me by surprise. The day she took off my bandages. She was washing me—'

'Spare me the details.'

'OK so first I should have told you, and now I'm telling you and you don't want to hear it?'

She stared at him, feeling the anger swelling in her chest. Smoke curled up from between her fingers. A panicked look flashed across Jann's face. No. She was not going to burn him. Damn him, she loved him. Still loved him. But he could be such a prick. She rubbed her hands together, quelling the smoke.

'Took me by surprise, that's all I meant,' he went on. 'I'd been gone for more than a month. Suffered through all that fever, broken bones, attacked by birds with razor sharp bills. Here I was — saved, fed, warm, and dry, and being tended to by—'

'A beautiful young woman. Yeah, I get the picture. So that excuses the first time—'

'I didn't know I needed an "excuse". Like I said, we—'

'Weren't together. You said.'

He shrugged.

'So what about the second time?' she asked. 'You enjoyed it so much you went back for more?'

'You wanted me to spare you the details. She made all the moves.'

'And you were still too weak to resist.'

'Hey — for once could you look at it from my point of view? When it happened, she was still the only person from Tenfir that I'd met. And she was feeding me every day. I relied on her for everything. Food, water, toileting—'

Elaine held up her hands.

'OK, sorry. Too much information. But you see what I mean? What was I to do? Say no? I don't want you. Thanks for all the help and everything, and the meals, but don't get fresh? Come on!'

Despite herself, Elaine had to admit he had a point. 'Just two times?' she repeated. 'Can't have been *that* good.'

'Wasn't about how good it was,' he said, giving her a stern glance that made her stomach flip over. 'I knew I wasn't going to stay. But by then it was too late. It wasn't long after that we had the bread incident with the neighbour. I began to understand that the social protocols there were quite a way removed from what I'd been used to. I worried I was in too deep already. Didn't want to make it worse.'

'By carrying on?'

'Yes, exactly.'

'So it wasn't guilt that made you stop then? You weren't thinking about me?'

'Oh, come on! I mean sure, you and I had danced around each other a bit. Flirted. Some loaded comments.

But it was hardly serious. Back then I mean.'

'Maybe not for you.'

'Ah, right. So you were biding your time. Sounding me out. Even then? Not sure I believe that.'

'So I'm a liar?'

'I'm not saying—'

'I think you'd better go.'

'But—'

'I'm not joking! Go! Get out! I need to think.'

She lay back on the bed and pulled the covers over herself, staring at the man she would have died for, but right now would also have killed. Maybe. He hesitated. She turned over in the bed and showed him her back. A few moments later, the door closed behind him.

new washington
6th day of far'utamasa, 967

For a small group of people, they sure made a lot of noise. Piers could hardly think. In the moments since Patrick's bald statement that leaving a passage through the mountain would result in the destruction of Tenfir Abarad, everyone had jumped in with opinions and suggestions.

Everyone except Jann Argent, that is, who had jumped instead at the chance to leave. If Piers was any judge, the Gatekeeper had a hard task ahead of him. To salvage his relationship from foundering on the rocks of revelation about his newly-discovered son.

The hubbub showed no signs of abating, fresh arguments springing up as older ones were abandoned, and still the obvious solution remained unstated.

'You cannot save your own people at the expense of mine!' Ahnak was saying. 'And your ideas would not save them any ways! Death will come through the pass and kill all, northerner and southerner alike.'

Piers rose to his feet and held up his hands. 'Stop!' he said. 'The solution is staring us in the face. If I can lower the mountain, then I can raise it again. Close the gap behind us, once everyone has reached the northern boundary.'

Patrick smiled. 'Sometimes the most obvious answers are not so plain until someone spells them out,' he said. 'Brilliant.'

'You have saved the day!' Ahnak said, crossing the room and embracing Piers, who stood in rigid embarrassment for a moment before disentangling himself from the younger Gatekeeper.

'Steady on,' Piers said as he stepped back. 'I'm not even sure I can do the first part yet.'

'There is another question you need to answer even before that, Stone Mage,' the Queen said, her expression clouded. 'If you are to achieve the closure of the gap then it is likely there will not be enough time remaining for you to make the journey to the portal.'

'Our esteemed guest is right,' deLange said. 'It is virtually certain you will not be able to do both Tremaine.'

'Where's Jann?' Claire asked. 'Right now, we don't know where the portal will be. It may be close enough to the mountain pass that Piers can do both.'

'That would be a fortunate happenstance indeed,' the Queen said, 'but we may not know for a day or two. We have not debated how the Gatekeeper will find the best candidate for a portal. I do not believe the Stone Mage should base his decision on it.' She turned to face him. 'You must confront the probability that you will have to remain here on Berikatanya, young man, rather than returning to the planet of your birth.'

Piers needed no time to ponder the question. From the moment he had offered to take on the task, he had been certain it was the right thing. Both for the people of this world, and for himself.

'I have confronted it, Ru'ita,' he said, 'and embraced it. In a way, I made my decision when I boarded the Dauntless the first time. There was nothing to keep me on

Earth back then, and there is nothing now that would tempt me to return.'

'Even the threat of death by comet?' Kyle asked.

Piers laughed. 'Well, we hope it won't come to that, don't we? Ahnak survived, as did those who travelled north, so from his perspective I've already succeeded. Kinda gives me the confidence to try, if you know what I mean. But there's more to it. With this power I can make a difference here. More than I could ever make back home.' He stopped. That was wrong. 'No. Not back home. Back there. I am home. Berikatanya is home. And I have to help save it. I will open the pass. And I will close it again — with me on the other side.'

He staggered backwards as Ahnak threw his arms around him once more.

new washington
6th day of far'utamasa, 967

Jared deLange left the main hall in such a hurry he almost knocked Jann Argent over. The Gatekeeper was returning from wherever he had been, and he did not look happy. Being barged into by the deputy Exec did nothing to improve his mood.

'What the fuck? Watch where you're going, can't you?'

'Sorry,' Jared said, 'didn't see you.'

'Is the meeting still on?'

'Yes, yes, they're all still there. They could use your input, as it happens. Starting to debate where the portal might be.'

'Did they resolve the mountain problem?'

'Yes. Piers is the man. He'll tell you. I have to go.'

'Where are you going at this time of night? In such a rush?'

'Official business,' Jared said, leading his kudo out of the makeshift stable block and checking the tightness of the saddle he had strapped on earlier. He swung onto the beast and took the reins in both hands.

'It's pitch dark, man!' Argent exclaimed. 'You'll break the poor beast's legs.'

'Don't worry about me,' Jared said, 'or him. He knows the way.'

He steered his mount past Argent, its breath steaming in the light spilling out from the doorway, and kicked it into a gallop.

'Official business?' Argent shouted after him. 'All the official business is in here!'

Jared ignored him. There was more business afoot than the rest of the Earthers could possibly imagine.

new washington
6th day of far'utamasa, 967

Claire Yamani heard the clattering and banging sounds of the breakfast service starting up behind the servery. In Earth terms that meant it must be six a.m., though the numbers would mean nothing to Ahnak or Ru'ita. Earthers had had little success transferring their concepts of timekeeping to the Berikatanyans.

Jann Argent reappeared through the main hall door, his face set in a hard grimace. The chill of the Utamasan early morning came in with him. Clearly his attempts to win Elaine over had been unsuccessful. They could do without the distraction of a fractured relationship when they faced the terrifying prospect of a cometary impact, but it was not always possible to dictate timing in matters of the heart. She stole a glance across the table at Ahnak, who caught her look and smiled. Fracturing or establishing; perhaps the timing was wrong for both? Or maybe not.

Other members of the group had spent the night debating their options in respect of comets, portals, and the flattening of mountains. Now, they stretched, yawned, and sniffed the air to catch the first tenuous scents of breakfast drifting over from the servery. Claire ignored the hunger gnawing at her stomach, and dismissed a niggling worry at the scale of the issues they had discussed. There was a time when her only concern had been which pizza joint to choose for a meeting with friends. Now she was helping to save an entire population.

'You OK?' she asked as Jann joined her and Ahnak at their table.

'I'll live,' he said, 'assuming we're successful. DeLange told me you'd sorted out the mountain question?'

'Yes!' Ahnak said, his voice hoarse with fatigue and excitement. He recapped their solution while Claire excused herself and went to fill plates for them both. When she returned, father and son were sitting in comfortable silence. The sudden thought that Jann Argent may end up as her father-in-law caught her by surprise. She choked on the first swallow of juice.

'Careful now,' Jann said, thumping her back in exactly the same way her father used to. The irony clanged in her mind.

'Hey!' Ahnak dropped the fork he had loaded with sosij and grasped Jann's hand. 'You careful! Why you hit Clayer?'

'It's OK,' she said. 'He wasn't hurting me. I'll explain later.'

'Yeah, calm down and eat your breakfast lad. I would no more hurt Claire than I would you.'

Ahnak looked unconvinced, but retrieved his fork and examined the meat before taking a mouthful. 'I still want to save my people from the doom,' he said. 'Not sure I understand why that is problem. Explain temporary family to me again?'

Having spent her childhood reading science fiction and studying the principles of time travel, Claire was well versed in the ideas of temporal anomalies. She also knew how hard they were to explain to someone not so clued up.

'Start with the basics,' she said. 'Remember what

Kekusaman told you about time being like a river? It flows in one direction. Anything that happens upstream affects what happens downstream. If you throw a log in at one point, it will be seen by anyone further down the river as it drifts past.'

'Yes, I can see that.'

'Now imagine what happens if you dam the river, or divert it close to its source. Downstream the water dries up in one place, and flows in another place where before there was no river. After a while, the original riverbed will become overgrown and no-one could tell there had ever been a river there.'

Ahnak nodded, and reached for a slice of toast. 'This is all make sense,' he said.

'So now think of changing something in the here-and-now, that would affect the future. Which is pretty much anything,' she added. 'Even something really small.'

'Like what?'

'Well, we have a massive example hurtling towards us. The damned comet. What if we had sent it through a portal in space, and it hit my home planet many thousands of years ago, killing everyone.'

Ahnak paled. The parallel between that scenario and what was about to happen here was obvious. 'If your parents were killed, before you were born...'

'Not wanting to complicate things, but my parents were actually from here, so it doesn't apply to me, but it does to — say — Piers. His distant ancestors would be dead, so he would never be born. The Batu'n would never have come to this world. Even if they weren't *all* killed by the comet. It would only take the death of the great-great-grandfather of Silas Wormwood, and the Earthers may never have developed Prism ships. They wouldn't be able to travel vast distances through space. That would affect you too.'

'Me? How?'

'If the comet disappeared, it would never hit this planet. You would have had no refugees travelling from the South. Never meet Patrick Glass. You would have been brought up by someone else entirely. Maybe only your mother, or maybe someone else she met instead of Patrick. You would have had no incentive to learn how to make a gate through time. But there's another complication. If Earthers did not have the Wormwood drive, then Jann Argent, the Fire Witch, my parents, and all the other Berikatanyans who fell through the original portal would have been stuck on Earth. With no way to return, Jann could never have met your mother, and you would not have been born at all.'

Ahnak raised his hands to his head. 'Argh! It feels like it will explode!'

Claire smiled, and took both his hands in hers. 'I know. It's scary stuff. But that's what could have happened if the comet had been sent away. We're not doing that now.'

'So we can save my people?'

'Think about it, Ahnak. Think about what I just said, and then about other changes we are going to make in a few days. How will it change the baby Ahnak who will soon be born in Tenfir Abarad.'

He fell silent, nibbling thoughtfully on his sosij and sipping his juice. Claire took the chance to eat some of her own breakfast, which had grown cold while they had been talking.

Jann looked as if he was chewing through a plateful of wasps. He did not seem to be listening to the conversation at all.

'I would bring mama south,' Ahnak said at length. 'Maybe with baby me, or she may still be pregnant.'

Mention of Ahnak's mother grabbed Jann's attention. 'And she would leave through the portal we are going to create,' he said. 'So where would you grow up in that new future?'

'On Earth?' Ahnak said, his eyes wide.

'Exactly. And if young Ahnak is on Earth,' Jann continued, 'who will travel back in time from the future of

Berikatanya to save us?'

Claire smiled. 'In that particular example, no-one needs to. Our Ahnak would already have saved everyone, and created a divergent timeline. In the alternate future, things play out differently for everybody. It's impossible to predict all those differences.'

'Can we talk?'

Every head at their table turned towards the new speaker. Unnoticed while they had been engaged in the conversation about all things timely, the Fire Witch had entered the hall. She regarded Jann with liquid amber eyes.

new washington
6th day of far'utamasa, 967

Elaine watched the colour rise in the young Air Mage's cheeks. 'Come on, Ahnak,' Claire said, rising to her feet, 'let's clear these plates.'

'But—' the Northerner began.

'Now!' Claire said, picking up Jann's plate along with her own and moving away towards the servery.

Jann looked at her. The anguish on his face tore at her heart. 'Yes,' he said, 'of course we can talk.'

She pulled out a chair and sat beside him, reaching for his hand. 'Sorry,' she said.

The tension left his hunched shoulders. A weak smile crept across his face. 'No. You had every right to be angry. I should have said something sooner.'

An uneasy silence fell over the table. Elaine looked around the hall, which had mysteriously emptied since she entered. She snorted. They were all being very diplomatic.

'No,' Jann said quickly, 'I should.'

'Oh! I didn't mean... I just noticed we're alone.'

'So what changed your mind?'

'I had time to think. Realised it's not only you who owes your life to Penny. I owe her too. Without her, I wouldn't have you, so I think it's only fair to accept that I shared you with her.'

'Briefly.'

'Yes. Briefly.' She sighed. 'Let's not go over old ground. We've— I've— wasted enough time on that, and Baka knows we have more important things to worry about. Do we have a plan yet? How to handle this doom, as Ahnak calls it?'

Jann had begun to explain their plan for a portal, when Patrick and Piers came bursting back into the main hall. The double doors crashed back against the wall with an ear-splitting clang.

'Jann! Elaine!' Patrick cried, panic distorting his features. 'Quick! They're attacking the Dauntless!'

Elaine leapt to her feet, with Jann not far behind. 'Who...?' she said.

'Doesn't matter who!' Jann yelled, running for the door. 'Come on!'

new washington
6th day of far'utamasa, 967

Jann ran outside. A narrow hint of dawn outlined the crest of Tubelak'Dun behind the canteen block, but the light that attracted his eye came from the opposite direction. From the blazing mooring gantry. Four masked raiders stood on the stairs, adding wood to the fire. A larger group, armed with swords and pitchforks, maintained a perimeter around the bottom step. Cabrera and his team, who had not long completed the systems shut-down, were trying without success to reach the flames.

'Fetch water!' someone shouted.

'It is already here,' replied Kyle Muir, emerging from a doorway to Jann's right. A shining ball of water materialised in the air above the flaming metal framework, its slowly rotating surface turned an even deeper blue by the reflection of Dauntless' gravnull field. A moment later, the orb collapsed over the stairs, dousing the fire and soaking those who had set it. One of the four lost his footing on the slippery staircase and pitched over the edge. He landed inside the circle of his fellows several metres below with a sickening crunch.

A bolt of white fire flew over Jann's shoulder, striking a second firestarter squarely in the chest. It passed through the man without pause, leaving a smoking hole. An expression of surprise registered on his face before he too fell soundlessly from the steps. The other two started downward, their faces contorted with dread, their eyes fixed on the Witch.

'Get back!' one of those guarding the gantry cried. 'Your magic don't frighten us!'

The look on his face gave the lie to that, but despite their fear and the swift, gory death of their two companions, none of the others moved.

'If this Doom is real,' another man added, 'you won't escape it this way!'

Piers appeared between two buildings on the opposite side of the mooring mast. He closed his eyes and stamped his foot. A shockwave of power rumbled through the rock of the promontory, shaking the earth as if a quake had struck. Two of the raiders stumbled. From Jann's left, a miniature tornado resolved out of the darkness, catching the outermost raider and spinning him to the ground. Claire had joined the fray, standing to Kyle's side with Ahnak close behind her. A faint smile played over her face as she gestured with her right hand. The twister flew toward the next raider in line.

Elaine moved to stand behind Jann. She sent up a fireball to illuminate the scene with a bright orange glow.

'Still not frightened?' she yelled. 'There's more where that came from! You want some?'

The raiding party broke into a run, several of the burlier base dwellers chasing after them, shouting and swearing. Alvarez rode out from behind the canteen, her kudo's eyes flashing in the amber light.

'Oh,' she said. 'I thought I might need to chase them off, but...'

Jann laughed, taking Elaine's hand. 'I think they've had a big enough fright for now.'

A beam of white flickered over the hull of the Dauntless. Cary Cabrera stood at the foot of the charred gantry with a flashlight.

'Well,' he called across the luminous space between them, 'you solved the most urgent problem, so thanks for that. Unfortunately, you also created another.'

Jann looked up at the section of hull illuminated by Cabrera's torch. It was the Dauntless' main hatch. Distorted by the blowback from Elaine's first firebolt, its edges had melted and fused together, welding it shut.

Chapter 20

the court of the blood king
6th day of far'utamasa, 967

Jared deLange barrelled into the basilica of the Blood Court as the sun reached its pale, low, Utamasan zenith. His kudo's breath panted plumes of odorous steam into the chill air. Thick, creamy foam decorated its coat, a testament to the morning's hard ride. The old Court ostler hastened across the square to take the animal's reins.

'Bless me you've almost killed him sir! What were you thinking? He's fit to drop!'

'Take him then,' Jared snarled, dropping from the saddle into a run, 'and less of your lip, or your master will hear of it.'

'I have no master here, young Batu'n', the old man said under his breath, 'save Tana himself.'

Jared was out of earshot by the time he had conjured a retort. Trust the fool to choose the Earth god to invoke. Slow and dull, a fitting choice for a stable hand. He hurried through the winding corridors of the Court to the Darmejelis chamber, and threw open the doors.

The long blackwood table was sparsely occupied. The Jester, his lieutenant Pwalek, and three others Jared did not recognise. Jeruk Nipis leapt to his feet at the sudden interruption.

'By Utan's beard!' he shouted. 'Are you mad? It's broad daylight! How many saw you arrive?'

'No time for subterfuge or hiding in the shadows now Jeruk,' he said, crossing the room and pouring a glass of buwangah. He took the drink in one swallow, wiping his lips with the back of his hand. 'I've been riding since before first light to bring you news. News that cannot wait on the cover of another night.'

Nipis glanced at the others. 'Leave us,' he said.

'If these are your leaders,' Jared said, pulling out a chair, 'better they remain and hear what I have to say. There must be no room for misunderstanding.'

'What—' Nipis began.

'Spare me your protestations!' Jared held up his hands to stem the little man's outrage. 'I'm well aware my report will not be what you want to hear, but it is the truth even so.'

'You're talking of the Northerner's tale?' Pwalek said. 'This "doom" he came to tell us of? Have the Batu'n discovered the truth of it?'

'They have,' Jared said, 'and it is worse than we imagined. The doom is exactly what he foretold — a flying rock from space. The Batu'n word for it is "comet". It is vast indeed, and it is almost upon us. It will hit in ten days, somewhere near Lembaca Ana.'

Pwalek rocked back in his chair, his face grey. The remaining members of the Darmajelis all began talking at once.

'What madness is this?'

'Looks like you were wrong after all, Jeruk!'

'Baka save us! What are we to do?'

'Please!' Jared said, holding up his hands once again. 'If you will let me finish! The Elementals have cobbled together a plan of sorts. Honestly, I think the two strands of their plan together provide the best options open to us, but we need to move quickly.'

'And what are these "options" that are all we have?' Nipis said, suppressed anger still clear on his face.

'Argent and the Northerner Ahnak are planning to open a gate — similar in size and effect to the original vortex. Anyone wanting to escape the doom will be able to step through it.'

'To where?' Pwalek asked.

'They say it will take them to the same destination as that first one,' Jared said. 'To Earth.'

Nipis barked a disdainful laugh. 'Ha! And who would want to take a one-way trip to Ketiga Batu? The Batu'n came here to escape that life! Will they all now return? Pathetic! And if they choose to stay? What is the second strand you spoke of?'

'The Stone Mage Tremaine intends to open a pass through Temmok'Dun. A route to the lands of the North.'

'Ahnak's homeland?' Nipis scoffed, his shoulders shaking with renewed mirth. 'Well this is a pretty arrangement, isn't it? The Earthers return to Earth, the Northerner returns to the North. And the rest of us die.' He took a swig from the foaming ale tankard on the table in front of him. 'You expect us to believe this rubbish?'

'Believe it or not,' Jared replied, 'it makes little difference to me. I am only reporting what I have learned. What you do with the knowledge is up to you.'

'She's turned you hasn't she?' Nipis said, leaning forward and staring at Jared. A hard frown creased his face. His eyes betrayed no fear. Indeed nothing in his demeanour suggested he had even understood the message let alone saw any need to run from the coming disaster.

'Who?'

'The Black bitch Queen. I know she went with them to the Batu'n base. Long have been the days you have spent in her company. What did she offer you? A seat of power in exchange for a rout of the Blood Court? Send us all scampering northwards, or jumping through some fell gateway to Tana-knows-where? I have played the fool in the past,' he continued, 'but it is you who are the fool if you think I will believe this story.'

'But the Batu'n technology—' Pwalek began.

'Technology be damned! Whoever heard of a rock coming from space? Has it ever happened before? It is the stuff of childhood fairy stories. Something to frighten babes with so they will do as they're told! Well here sits one grown man who is not about to pay heed to such an obvious confection! Does she really expect us all to run away and hand Istania to her on a plate?'

'Are you serious?' Jared asked. He had suspected there

was more of the fool to this man than his costume. Now the truth of that suspicion was out. He was no more than a conspiracy theorist, and a paranoid one at that. 'There will soon be nothing left of Istania to hand over to her. Or Kertonia either. The Queen will not be staying behind to oversee the shattered remnants of any realm.'

'Oh, really? So which of these delightful options has she chosen? And where is this gate to be opened? Like as not they're hoping most of us will die on the journey to it.'

'They don't know where it's going to be,' Jared admitted. 'At least, not yet. I did not stay long enough to learn which option the Queen plans to take. You can be sure she has more sense than to remain here.'

'Ho ho!' Nipis said, standing and pushing back his chair with a loud scrape. 'So I have no sense, is that what you're saying? Have a care, traitor. For traitor you were when you set off — to your own people — and traitor you remain, whether to me or to them. One way or another, you are a turncoat. I may not have what you consider good sense, but I have wits enough to see through your schemes! No, Jeruk Nipis will not flee like a frightened tiklik. He will endure. Let the flying rock — this "comet" — let it come. And then we will all see the truth, and Istania will be safe from incursion by the cursed Blacks!'

'And what of those who believe the tale?' asked the man sitting to Pwalek's left. He wore the uniform of the Blood Watch but without any visible insignia. 'Forgive me Jeruk, but not all of us are so... certain... of your interpretation of these matters. It seems to me if a journey North is to be possible, then we may at least stay on familiar ground while this apocalypse takes its course. Even if that ground is not Istanian.'

'If you believe any part of this tale,' said the older man on the other side of the table, 'then I for one do not find that journey to be an attractive prospect.' He wrung his wrinkled hands together like an old washerwoman. 'The years following such an incredible impact are likely to be...

difficult... at best. The destruction may be even more extensive than any of us can predict. As you rightly say, Jeruk, nothing like this has occurred before. It is impossible to know the outcome, but I expect the disruption may last for a long time. No, I do not believe I will be taking the Northern option.'

'Good!' said Nipis. 'At least you agree with me, Kilpemigang!'

'I'm sorry,' Kilpemigang said, 'if I have given you the wrong impression. I do not agree with you. I believe deLange, and I trust the Batu'n technology. It is most impressive. Though it is beyond my understanding, I would not ignore its message. If there is to be a way to escape this doom — whether that be to Ketiga Batu or anywhere else — then I will take it, and be glad to do so. In my experience the Batu'n have been a force for good on Berikatanya. The opportunity to visit their world appeals to me.'

Nipis moved away from the table, a black look rendering his face even uglier than normal. 'You're all mad,' he said. 'All fools. You will see.'

He left the room, still muttering.

new washington
6th day of far'utamasa, 967

Conscious that another long day lay ahead, Patrick forced down a few mouthfuls of unwanted late breakfast. Alvarez joined them, setting down her plate and sliding over another table to butt up next to theirs. 'I guess that solves the problem of whether we can use the Dauntless for any aspect of this mission,' she said.

He wrinkled his nose. Her clothes still carried the smell of the fire. 'So it's out of commission for certain?'

'Oh I'm sure if we had time we could cobble together an arc welder or something and get her hatch open. Or ask the Fire Witch to undo her handiwork. But the ship is unlikely ever to be spaceworthy again. Even flying in an atmosphere would be tricky.'

'We don't have the time for a lengthy repair,' Waters said.

'Quite right,' Jann said, wiping up the last of his breakfast. 'And talking of time, we should get going with the first part of the plan. We can't tell anyone who is intending to use the portal where to go until we know where it's gonna be.'

'Do you have any idea?' Patrick asked his friend. Deep lines of exhaustion criss-crossed the Gatekeeper's face, but they both knew they would have no time for sleep today.

'I have a question for you first,' Jann said. 'Whenever our combined talents have created an Uterban in the past, it's been in mid-air. Above ground. That's not a lot of use if we're expecting people to walk through it. I mean, all the surface-level gates I've been using are fine, but this is a different beast.'

Patrick nodded. 'This is part of the lore I'm most familiar with. The section I decoded first. The size and shape of the Uterban won't present any problems, as long as we can find the right location.'

'Uterban can only be opened in a few places,' Jann said. 'The most obvious would have been Lembaca Ana, but we've rendered that unusable. The mass of Pun'Akarnya will stop any kind of gate being opened there.'

'Any clue where the next best place is?'

'Well that's the problem. Once I'm within a few klicks of the place I'll get a sense of it, but I have no idea where to start.'

'I can work out a flight plan that takes us within two or three kilometres of everywhere on the peninsula in the most efficient way,' Waters said. 'They may be small, but those flyers have a pretty hot nav computer.'

'Once you know where this Uterban is going to be,' Claire said, 'it'll be best to use the flyer to send the word out. I could use Air Mail, but it's still a bit flaky. I wouldn't trust it for such a crucial message.'

'Sounds like we have a plan,' Jann said. 'We should make a start now, if our pilot is ready?'

'She is,' Waters said.

'Splendid,' Patrick said. 'I'm coming along too. I can't detect the gates, but I can help you decide on suitable candidates, if there's any doubt. Wouldn't want you discounting a good location on the assumption it won't support a big enough gate.'

'Good call, my friend,' Jann agreed. 'I know what I'm looking for, but I've only experienced Uterban once before, and I can't claim the memory is reliable.'

'Is that automated flight plan idea the best way to begin,' Waters asked, 'or is there somewhere you want to try first?'

'Yeah I've been wondering about that. We'll only have a few days for everyone to reach it. It has to be somewhere central if possible.'

'Per Tantaran is the most central location,' the Queen said. 'That's why it has been our main battlefield over the years. It would be gratifying to use it for the purpose of saving lives, rather than taking them.'

'A good place to start,' Jann agreed. He pushed back his chair and looked at Waters. 'Maybe set up that flight plan to take us on a spiral path after we've checked Per Tantaran? Expand the search outwards in all directions until we find something close to that mid-point?'

Waters stood, pulling her tunic straight and brushing herself off. 'Sure, I can do that. We can override it any time you sense something worth stopping for.'

'OK,' Patrick said. 'Let's go.'

new washington
6th day of far'utamasa, 967

Silvia Alvarez watched the three leave, happy for once that someone else had volunteered to take the pilot's seat.

Ordinarily she would have been first in line for the excitement of a hunt for hidden treasure. The prize of a gateway from destruction was compelling. Her manager's head insisted she was needed here, to organise their imminent evacuation to places unknown.

Beyond that, she had a more personal decision to make: go, or stay? Along with the majority of the colonists, she considered herself a frontiers girl. She craved the simple life, where security and comfort were attained through honest hard work. Living in a megalopolis had its benefits, but they were conferred by some anonymous government. That life also had danger, but city dwellers were shielded from it through being a single, small target among the many millions in Earth's sprawling cities.

Whatever challenges they had sought by travelling all those light-years, no-one expected to have to live through the aftermath of a comet strike. So was her frontier spirit strong enough to survive years of scraping a living under an ash-cloud? Half starved and blinded by the dust, cold and dispirited and longing for the sunlight to return?

For her, now, staying also meant leading. More naturally a second-in-command, she had been forced to step up after Oduya's untimely death. Fine, while life had been chugging on as normal. "Exec" was more of an administrative title than anything else. But what faced them now was anything but normal. She would not have admitted it to her closest friends and colleagues, but she did not relish the idea of leading the refugees through the difficult days ahead. Argent, Glass, and their talk of a magic door back to Earth loomed large in her mind — an escape from the doom and from the burden of responsibility. If what they said was right, about the Earth end moving through time, then she may well end up in a frontier of sorts anyway. A frontier from recent history, and one more familiar than anything on offer here on Berikatanya.

'Are you still with us?' The Yamani girl watched her, a

half-smile playing across her mouth. 'Your body is here, but you sure weren't.'

Kyle Muir smiled too, but said nothing.

Silvia returned their smiles. 'Sorry. Weighing my options. We all have big decisions to make in the next few days. But,' she added, slapping her hands on the table and levering herself to her feet, 'I have no more time for pondering right now. There's organising to do!'

new washington
6th day of far'utamasa, 967

Claire watched Alvarez walk away, considering her own options.

'Big decisions,' Kyle repeated. 'Made yours yet?'

'I thought I had,' she replied, staring across the room. Ahnak stood at the servery, filling his plate with a third helping.

A mischievous grin crept across her friend's face. Claire waited for the inevitable jibe.

'A healthy appetite in a healthy body,' the Water Wizard said. 'I can see why he whets your appetites.'

'Stop it!' Claire said, feeling the heat of colour in her face. 'I would have stayed. There are still a bunch of reasons to stay.'

'Like what? Duty? Honour? Access to power?'

'All of the above, I suppose' she agreed. 'Duty to the Queen, although now she's comfortable with her own powers she won't have as much need of "her Air Mage" in future. Honour? Well, there's the Guild. And helping those who remain with the aftermath of the impact. Maybe Air power could dispel the ash clouds more quickly?' She shrugged. 'Who knows. So yeah, I guess my power was the biggest reason to stay.'

'Competing with the biggest of reasons to go?'

Claire was silent for a moment, waiting for the stinging behind her eyes to stop. Hoping it would, before tears fell.

She was not embarrassed about showing her emotions in front of her friend, but Ahnak was making his way back to their table. He balanced a plate piled with a haphazard selection of third breakfast.

'Yes,' she said, hardly trusting her voice with more.

'So you'll be visiting Earth, Ahnak,' Kyle said, smiling broadly at him as he took his seat. 'The most widely travelled man in time, soon to become the — one of the — most widely travelled men in space.'

'And even more well-travelled in time, if Juggler is right,' Ahnak said. 'Unless we step through early, we'll be going back. Perhaps long way.'

'We,' Kyle repeated, with another smirk.

Claire glared at her friend.

Ahnak glanced quickly between the two of them, his face a mask of consternation. He clutched at Claire's hand. 'We go together, yes? I thought you had decided.'

Claire covered his hand with her own and smiled. 'I have,' she said. 'We are.'

Kyle clapped. 'Hooray! That makes three of us!'

'Friend carefully avoids letting her own decision slip while asking about others,' Claire said in a headline tone. 'How long have you known? And what made you decide to leave?'

Kyle stole a pancake from Ahnak's plate. 'I've never been what you'd call "comfortable" with the idea of power,' she said, taking a small mouthful. 'My brother jumped in with both feet like he always did, and look where that got him.'

'You are not your brother.'

'No, that's right. I'm almost exactly his opposite. Instead of jumping in with both feet I prefer no feet. Not jumping at all. As long as I stay here, I'll be the Water Wizard. I never asked for it, I never sought it out. It landed on me, like a cold bucket of water on a midwinter morning.'

'You never said.'

'What good would it have done? There was no way to escape it. Until now. The comet, and the prospect of living through its aftermath, is really nothing more than a convenient excuse. I was a leaver even before I had the chance to leave.'

Claire noticed the Queen, sitting two tables away. Their newest Mage said nothing. She did not even look in their direction. Yet from the set of her jaw and the tension in her shoulders, it was clear she had heard every word.

'No Air Mage, no Water Wizard,' Claire said, 'this will be a strange place indeed for the next few years. How will they cope?'

Ahnak had ploughed through more than half the food on his plate, with occasional help from Kyle. 'Beragan manage with no magic,' he said after emptying his mouth. 'No Elementals. No Mages. Still manage.'

'What you've never had, you never miss,' Kyle said. 'Or at least, not had for three centuries. Comes to the same thing.'

'Come on, Ahnak,' Claire said. 'Finish your breakfast. If we assume Patrick and Jann will be successful in their search for an Uterban, we have a long day's work ahead.'

'May I have a word with Ahnak before you go?' the Queen's voice carried clearly across the now deserted hall from the direction of her table.

new washington
6th day of far'utamasa, 967

Ru'ita listened with mounting horror as the woman she still thought of as "her" Air Mage discussed abandoning Berikatanya with her friend the new Water Wizard, and the enigmatic Ahnak of the North.

Yet how could she blame them, when she had considered joining them? For the young women, it was no more than going home. Though it would most likely be a part of that home — and a time — they had only read about in history books. For Ahnak the journey was more of a step into the unknown, but he had his own reasons for undertaking it. The strange effects of travelling through time tied her mind in knots. She was not certain she understood what Claire had meant, but the emotion of her message came across even if the meaning did not. Ahnak had not known himself while growing up, so he could not. There had, if his account was accurate, been no mysterious adult figure in his life who could have been the older version of himself. All his relationships had been straightforward. She suppressed a chuckle. If being brought up by the Pattern Juggler could be considered mundane.

Thousands of her contemporaries, including those who until recently she had considered subjects, would also make their transitions to Earth. She already spoke the language passably well, unless the portal would strip that from her along with her other memories? So what was keeping her here, on her home world? In the face of imminent destruction? Should she remain, suffer the years of dark, cold, and starvation but use her new-found powers for the good of those left? Or should she leave, desert the only home she had ever known, lose those powers when she had only begun to explore their potential, but be safe from the damage this "comet" was about to inflict?

Her years in the seat of power, and her experience of government and diplomacy, told her it was a decision impossible to make without more detailed information. She stood, and walked towards the table from which the young people were about to leave.

'May I have a word with Ahnak before you go?' she asked.

The Northerner gave her a half bow, his gaze flicking between her and Claire. 'I... er...'

The Air Mage put a proprietorial hand on his shoulder. 'Of course, Ru'ita.' She smiled at Ahnak. 'We'll wait for you. By the door. It's too cold to stand around outside.'

'How can I help, Kayshirin,' the man said, surprising her with the ancient term for Wood Mage.

'Tell me more of your early life. I am keen to learn how the Beragan coped with those years after the doom came.'

Ahnak retook his seat, wiping up the last of his sauce with a crust. 'You must understand, I was not yet born when it happened. All I know of those first years is from mama's tales. I have no first-hand experience. My earliest memory is the dust being everywhere. But by then the air was clearer and our food crops beginning to recover.'

'But how hard was the life?' she pressed him. 'Did your mother tell you how many died? How long the starvation lasted?'

'I can't tell you how many, Ru'ita. The people of Tenfir Abarad are... stoic. They never talk of their hardships. Mama told me nothing of numbers of deaths. And of the hunger, only a handful of stories. It was hard, certainly. Everyone lived with empty bellies for almost two years. The Elders rationed supplies with great care. Anyone found stealing food would have been dealt with harshly. I saw in my youth how less serious crimes were handled. But mama never related any tales of thieving and I have always assumed there was none. We are a law-abiding people.' He shrugged and offered a mischievous smile. 'All the Binagan — the Wild People — came south.'

The Queen laughed. This ingenuous young man hid nothing. But if, in his past, she had decided on the journey North rather than the Earth-bound portal, would there not have been some mention of the Wood Mage in his story?

'You have said the Pattern Juggler raised you,' she said. 'Do you have no memory of me? Did your mother have no stories of a Wood Mage and her powers of healing during those harsh times?'

He sat still for a moment, gazing towards the door without reply. Had she embarrassed him? Kept him away from her Air Mage for too long? 'I cannot remember any such tale, Kayshirin,' he said, holding up his hands. 'As you know my grandfather often sat in the chair of the Tamatua. Even if mama had not mentioned it, he would have. If there was anything to tell. And now,' he said, standing and picking up his empty plate, 'if there is no more help I can offer, I should catch up with Clayer.'

She smiled at his idiosyncratic pronunciation of Claire's name. 'Of course. I'm sorry to have kept you from her.'

'No ma'am, it is I who am sorry. That I was unable to be of more help. We all have hard decisions to make, although my own has almost been made for me. The prospect of stepping through such a powerful gate is daunting, believe me, even for one who is also a Gatekeeper. I think if I had the chance, I would choose to stay, but of course you must make up your own mind.'

With that, the young Northerner left her, now alone in the hall and no closer to a resolution than she had been before.

Chapter 21

plain of per tantaran
6th day of far'utamasa, 967

Felice rested her hands lightly on the flyer's controls. These birds could be alarmingly responsive, something which caught young pilots out time after time. She was many years removed from novice status. Under her sure touch, the flyer leapt across the sharp shadow which the pale, mid-afternoon winter sun cast at the edge of the vast Besakaya forest. Beneath them lay the plain of Per Tantaran, their first stop.

'Feel anything?' Patrick Glass asked.

'No,' Jann Argent replied. 'Not a thing.'

According to the chronometer, they had been travelling for more than three hours. If Argent had not sensed a gate in all that time, it did not bode well for this quest. Or their survival, for that matter.

'Nothing at all?' she said, failing to keep an edge of panic from her voice.

Argent flashed a faint grin. 'OK, sorry, not "nothing". We've passed dozens of potential gates. All of them have been regular ones. The kind we could use to move about the southern realms. One or two have led North. But none that are any use. Trust me, if I'd spotted one of those, you'd know about it!'

'We're overflying Per Tantaran now,' she said. 'Where did you want to stop? In the middle?'

'As good as anywhere,' Glass said, staring out at the landscape unfolding swiftly beneath them. 'And better than most,' he added, 'since it's virtually equidistant from both Court and Palace. Statistically we should have similar numbers from each choosing transition.'

'A sensible assumption,' Argent agreed. 'What about you, Felice? Are you leaving, or remaining here with Patrick?'

Felice glanced at the Juggler. 'I didn't know you'd decided to stay?'

He shrugged. 'In a way the decision has been made for me,' he said. 'Since Ahnak says it's me that brought him up. It seems I have a destiny to fulfil.'

'Sounds a bit grand for you, that does my friend,' Argent said, his trademark grin creasing his face.

They fell silent, only the low hum of the gravnull field filling the cabin. Felice was glad Jann Argent had not pressed for an answer to his question. The question that stared them all in the face and to which she currently had no answer. They left New Washington before she had chance to speak with Jo. On the one hand, Felice was sure she would want to take whichever option Jo chose. But if Jo had the same idea, as she often did, they would be left in a decision vacuum. One which the comet would fill for them in the next few days. Leave or stay, they had to decide in time to make whichever journey they chose. North, through the mountains, or... in an unknown direction to a presently unknown destination.

After ten years on this world, it felt like an admission of failure to run away back to Earth. But even her redoubtable frontier spirit baulked at the idea of two years of starving under an ash cloud. For a twenty-second century girl, any earlier period was a kind of frontier. Even more so if their jaunt took them before the turn of the millennium. As a same-sex couple they would face cultural adversity every bit as harsh as the physical. Any earlier and they may even suffer accusations of witchcraft or worse.

'Will you be able to predict how far back in time we'll go?' she asked. 'I remember you saying the end of the Uterban will shift back the longer it stays open.'

'"We"?' Argent grinned again. 'Sounds like you have decided.'

'Not entirely. But knowing what year — or at least what century — we're likely to end up in would help.'

'I can only tell you what we know from the first portal,'

Glass said. 'The Fire Witch was the first to fall, and she "landed" four years before the Valiant departed. So in absolute terms roughly forty years into the past. We don't have a clear idea how long the portal had been open at that point, but what we do know is that our friend here traversed four years further back. Jann can only have been minutes behind Elaine at the opening. Claire Yamani's parents were next. She was born on Earth but her mother was already pregnant, and she was — what? — fifteen when Valiant started out. Then Petani. He was a young man when he arrived on Earth and almost sixty when he boarded our ship. And my own father lived his whole life on Earth, had me, and I was fifty-five when I left.

'So as a rule of thumb I'd say it's something like a decade further back for every minute the Uterban remains open. That help?'

Felice nodded, her mind awhirl with the maths. They had calculated it would take eight hours for half a million people to walk through the portal. Even if half of them chose to go North instead, the Uterban would need to be held open for four hours. The travellers would be spread through Earth's history over almost two and a half thousand years.

It took the plucky little ship another thirty minutes to cross the battle plain. Drifts of snow flew out from under the flyer as it descended, impelled by the massive static charge that built up around the hull from the gravnull engines. Felice brought them to a stop with an almost imperceptible bump.

'Nice landing,' Glass said. 'You're really good at this.'

'Got my triple-A pilot's badge three years before I left Earth,' she said. She would never normally brag about it, but in the company of the Gatekeeper and the Pattern Juggler a little extra status couldn't hurt. 'And I chased many a criminal down with a police flyer in my time.'

She flipped the door toggle. The three companions picked up coats, fastened them tightly against the freezing air of the late Utamasan afternoon, and climbed down the short flight of steps to the hard, rocky surface. In this season, little vegetation survived; the plain barren, and deserted.

With hands thrust deep into the pockets of his overcoat, Argent faced in one compass direction after another, staring out across the landscape. The others kept silent. Felice was unsure whether speaking would diminish his chances of discovering the Uterban they sought, but did not want to risk it. With no time to retrace their steps, they only had one chance in each place.

Looking at last to the south, Argent took a step forward. Was this it? Felice held her breath. Their earlier discussions had concluded the battle plain was the best location in terms of travelling logistics, but that would mean nothing if there was no gate here.

'Fuck,' Argent said, coming to a halt and stamping his feet against the cold.

'Nothing?' Glass asked.

A pointless question. It was clear from the look on the Gatekeeper's face. What they were seeking would not be found here. His reply surprised Felice.

'Not nothing, exactly,' Argent said. 'But...'

'It's not big enough.' Glass peered in the same direction, as if he could discern what they sought just as well as the Gatekeeper himself.

'I'm not sure. It's bigger than I've seen before. By some margin. It's close. The best I've found so far. Even so... you're right. Too small. I doubt we could keep it open long enough, even with Ahnak's help.'

'Keep looking, then?' Glass suggested.

'Nothing else we can do. If we don't find anything better, we'll have to try and make it work here. Dangerous, but if there's no other option?'

'Come on then,' Felice said. 'Time's a-wasting. Let's try somewhere else.'

new washington
6th day of far'utamasa, 967

She should have gone with him. Jetting around the region in a warm flyer with the man she loved had to be better than mooching around the base, reluctantly helping out with preparations for leaving. Even if he could be the most annoying man she had ever known.

No-one yet knew how far the journey to the Uterban would be, so most were preparing for the worst. Travel during the months of Utamasa was never easy, but the comet would not wait politely for warmer weather. They had to make the best of it. Elaine travelled light. She had finished packing her few belongings almost before Felice Waters completed her pre-flight checks. When the flyer took off and flew past their window, disappearing rapidly from view in the direction of Besakaya, she had packed most of Jann's too. She suppressed another pang that clenched its fist around her heart.

Leaving did not bother her. This had never been home. Nowhere had felt comfortable since her return to Berikatanya. The memory of being welcome at the Blood Court, in the days before the first portal, seemed to belong to someone else. Even after finding some solace in the arms of Jann Argent, wherever they lived together had not provided enough of a sanctuary for her. The more simple-minded Earthers often parroted something about "home being where the heart is." If she allowed herself to believe her heart lay with Jann, she still did not feel settled in any of the lodgings they shared.

Part of her problem arose from her quick irritation with her companions. Friends had never played a large part in Elaine's life, but at least among Elementals she believed she had found people she could relate to. Recent events showed her how wrong she'd been. Her mounting temper brought the power to her hands, wisps of pale blue smoke curling up from her palms. She needed air!

Outside the base, the weak sun had begun its daily journey downward. Elaine headed for the wall, intending to perform a cursory security check as an excuse for abandoning the travel prep. The cold air felt crisp and clean, even if it did make her nose ache. She summoned a weak pulse of Fire, suffusing herself with a deep orange glow and melting the snow underfoot.

Being outside felt better, but it could not stop her thoughts returning to the thorny subject of her relationships with the others. First up for opprobrium: Claire Yamani. Elaine had been... incensed was too strong. Disappointed not strong enough. Anyway the Air Mage's loyalty to Earthers had been a source of irritation, even if it was easy to understand. She had the genetic inheritance of a Berikatanyan, but the upbringing of an Earth girl. One of her old ringmaster's stock phrases came to mind. "Give me a child until he's seven, and I will show you the man." The lecherous rogue never mentioned women, which was unusual for him, but the principle remained. Even after attaining her power, the girl's first thought would always be an Earther thought.

A similar, but perhaps more robust, argument could be made for Kyle Muir. Leaving aside the traditional antipathy between Fire and Water, the girl would always have an Earther-bias. She did not even have the excuse of genetics. As far as anyone knew her powers arose entirely from an accident of birth, unconnected in any way with Berikatanya.

With two of the most powerful women at the Black Palace siding with the Batu'n, it may have been natural for Elaine to favour the Queen's company. But even after the discovery of her Wood powers, she was a cold fish, not given to spending time with anyone. Her snubs led inexorably to a similar feeling of antipathy. No, of all the potential companions at the Palace, only Jann had lit a fire in her belly. She had found the dark corridors of the Palace increasingly uncomfortable in their final few days there, a situation which had not improved since moving to New Washington. With the Court denied to her for obvious and historical reasons, she had been left with no real home. The consequent unwonted feelings of vulnerability had fired her temper. She was the Fire Witch! Such weakness was for lesser mortals! Her mounting levels of exasperation — at both herself and everyone else — manifested as random expressions of anger and, inevitably, Fire power.

Jann had done his best to calm her down and remind her of previous successes with controlled expression of power and gentleness. Her initial scepticism waned, only to be rekindled by the revelation of his relationship with Penny. The pain of that knowledge kept returning, crashing over her like waves on the beach that now came into view below the clifftops. Jann's insistence it was never a "relationship," and he had left Penny to come back to her, was a poor barrier to those incessant floods of emotion.

She stood watching the waves for a time before turning back inland. They held a lesson for her too. Their constant pounding would eventually wear rock down to sand. Her partner's equally abiding attention would chip away at her resolve the same way. No-one had ever — could ever — get under her skin the way he had. Though she feared the loss of memory another portal traversal would cause, she had to admit she would rather be with Jann and lose her powers than keep them and lose him. He would have to remain until the last, holding open the great Uterban, which meant if she went with him they would be cast into prehistory. Perhaps that terrifying prospect had a silver lining? If they traversed far enough back in time, some of Earth's Elemental strength may still be there for her to tap into.

As she neared the opening in Piers' wall, a rider came through, thrashing his kudo with a thin stick even though the poor animal was already running at a gallop. His face wrapped in a thick blue scarf, Elaine did not recognise him until he shouted an angry admonishment at his mount.

'Come on, damn you! Faster!'

It was Alvarez' slimy deputy, Jared deLange. Where in Baka's name had he been that demanded such a pace? The animal was foaming with sweat. Its laboured breath plumed like the miniature steam train that had taken groups of children around Miles Miller's Marvellous Manifestations back on Earth. She shrank back against the stone to avoid being seen, but deLange's concentration was fixed on the road ahead and his speed such that he passed her in moments.

In the cold, dry air the kudo's wake dragged clouds of powdery snow from the ground. For a moment, the white swirls hid a darker current. At first, it appeared to be dirt, thrown up from underneath the snow by the animal's passage. When the black twister ate a chunk out of the wall a few metres from her, Elaine realised it was another vortex.

flyer, heading south
6th day of far'utamasa, 967

Patrick Glass watched the plain of Per Tantaran fall away below them as Felice Waters piloted the flyer to a safe cruising altitude.

'Where to now, then?' she asked, setting the controls to a holding pattern and checking her readouts.

Patrick looked at Jann. 'Any ideas? Or should we start that spiral flight plan?'

Jann stared out of the window at the shrinking hills and snow-covered tussocks of the battlefield. Several moments passed before he replied. 'It'll be dark soon,' he said at length. 'I hoped to find somewhere today. With so little time before impact, we can't afford to waste time flying here and there.'

He fixed Patrick with a stare. His face shone pale white

in the light from the viewport, his brow furrowed with worry. 'I think we have to try the Valley. It seems to be at the heart of everything.'

Patrick nodded. 'No doubt about that. Maybe the problem of Pun'Akarnya won't be as bad as we've assumed.'

'Won't know until we look,' Jann said.

'Lembaca Ana it is then, Felice, thank you,' Patrick said.

Their pilot's hands flew over the controls. The flyer straightened out from its circling, and headed south. Felice consulted the panel overhead.

'We're just under two hours away at maximum speed,' she said. 'Make yourselves comfortable.'

Patrick appreciated the irony. Flyers were not equipped for comfort. He shifted on his seat, resting on the other buttock so at least he was only aching on one side.

'I never properly answered your question about me remaining here on Berikatanya,' he said. He finally felt comfortable airing his deepest fears now, in this relatively safe company. Jann was probably his best friend in this world. Felice Waters was a trusted member of the burgeoning government of New Washington. She had been a decorated police officer before that. Someone who knew when to keep her mouth shut.

'I was telling the truth about Ahnak. He says I brought him up, and I cannot confirm or deny his story since the events have not yet happened. There's no reason for me to shy away from the duty. He's an honest and decent young man. If I have a hand in that, even in a small way, then I shall be proud and happy to undertake the role of stepfather. But even without the imperative of future duties, there would be another compelling reason to remain.

'I know I can trust you both not to take this conversation outside this cabin,' he continued. His phrasing was entirely accurate. He did know that. Even so, it bore saying for certainty's sake. 'I have often said Void power is a frightening tool. The things I could achieve with it have — literally — no boundaries. And in a way that is exactly why I do not use it, unless forced. But if the power itself were the only thing to worry about, I would perhaps trust myself to wield it more frequently.'

'It's not the only thing?' Jann prompted.

'No. The approaching comet drags in its wake inhabitants of the world between. The place where Void power originates. The realm that your gates traverse.'

'Is that where I sent the kuclar, that time in Tenfir Abarad?'

'Yes. And, if it survived the ordeal, it may be there still, though I know not what it would find to eat or drink. The main dwellers of the Void world — Ahnak has called them Voiders, and that is an accurate epithet as both the Tang Jikos and the Keeper's records confirm — the Voiders are following the comet. No, not following. They have no choice in the matter. It is dragging them. For such powerful beings, to be unable to resist the pull of the rock, and be forced to travel wherever it goes, would be... annoying.'

'Great!' Jann said, barking a mirthless laugh. 'A megaton rock isn't enough of problem. Now we have to deal with angry titans too.'

'I don't understand,' Felice said. 'How does the presence of these beings influence whether you stay or go?'

Patrick fell silent again, staring back out at the ice-covered land over which they flew. The battle plain was now far behind them. The towering eastern peak of Tubelak'Dun approached rapidly, painted with the startling crystal whites and pale blues of the season.

'In two ways,' he said. 'There are only a few of us whose power is sufficient to withstand an onslaught by Voiders. At most a few. It may be that only I can resist them. Once the Uterban opens, they will be attracted to it. From their perspective it will present an opening onto a world ripe for devouring. Our best estimate is that we shall have to hold the Uterban open for four hours. Even that requires my help, but once the Voiders come — and come they will — then I shall have to both maintain the vortex and protect those traversing it from the monsters.'

Felice looked to be on the verge of fainting. Jann's face had taken on an even whiter pallor than before, glistening with a sheen of sweat. Neither of his companions made any comment.

'So that alone means I must stay until the last of our refugees has traversed the portal,' he continued. 'But at that moment, I might have expected to follow them, closing the vortex behind me.'

'I hardly dare imagine the reason you can't,' Jann said, wiping the oily sweat from his brow. 'I know you're going to tell us anyway.'

Patrick forced a smile. 'Yes. By that time the Uterban will have been open for so long, the presence of Voiders is a virtual certainty. They will sense — smell, if you like — the Void power in me. I imagine I will resemble a tasty morsel. If I jump to Earth, they will follow me. The Uterban will provide a path for a few of them to slip the bonds of the comet. I have to hope the route to Earth will initially appear no more attractive to them than Berikatanya. This planet is certainly closer. They may not even be able to discern Earth, at the far end of the Uterban. But were I to jump, that would be an irresistible incentive to follow.'

'So we would be inflicting on Earth exactly the kind of destruction we thought we were avoiding, by not sending the comet through.' Felice said.

'Exactly,' Patrick agreed. 'But it's worse than that. Once on Earth, I would lose all access to Void power. I would be impotent. Incapable of defending myself, or anyone else, against the wrath of the Voiders. No,' he added, though the emphasis was surely redundant, 'I have to stay.'

He shivered. The chill of the Utamasan day had

somehow found its way from the air outside into the cabin, and into his very bones.

lembaca ana
6th day of far'utamasa, 967

Patrick's revelation put a dampener on conversation for the rest of their trip to Lembaca Ana. Jann sat by the viewport, watching first Tubelak'Dun and then the winding blue strip of Sun Penk slip below the flyer. The sun was nearing the ridge of the western peak of the Tubelak mountains when the Valley came into view. The strange place that had been the site of so many powerful events in the history of Berikatanya and now seemed certain to play host to one last cataclysm. Though they were still twenty minutes away according to the glowing blue digits of the flight timer, he had the beginnings of a tingle in his head. The first hint that maybe their assumptions had been correct, and the Valley held what they sought.

'Where do you want to set down?' Felice Waters asked, breaking the lengthy silence.

'At the foot of Pun'Akarnya probably best,' Jann said, before realising that the Earther woman had never journeyed this far. 'Sorry. You can't miss it. Enormous rock tower in the middle of the Valley. A few hundred metres from the coast.'

'I can see it now,' Felice said.

She banked the flyer and lost height. Jann's stomach flipped. He reached for a handhold at the same time as Patrick.

'Sorry!' she said with a laugh. 'I forget you guys aren't used to flying anything as small as this.'

Jann swallowed a gush of saliva. 'It's fine. Once per trip is enough though, thanks.'

The flyer levelled off and sank to a perfect landing in the shadow of the new mountain. The whine of the gravnull died away as Felice cut power and moved to open the doors. Jann retrieved his coat, but not before an icy blast sliced through the cabin.

Standing on what remained of the granite quadrangle, he immediately sensed this place offered their best chance of success. He watched Patrick navigate the flyer's steps.

'We're gonna have to work out what to do about that,' he said, pointing at the dark rock face. 'It's in the way.'

Felice looked puzzled. 'In the way?'

'It's blocking the Uterban. The site of the original portal. We could reopen it here, at ground level, if…'

'If we lost the mountain,' Patrick said, joining them to stare at the imposing edifice. 'That's going to be a problem.'

'I know.'

'Why's it a problem?' Felice asked.

'You have a habit of asking questions with two answers,' Patrick said, smiling his mirthless smile. 'I don't think we can tear Pun'Akarnya down without Piers' help, and we need him to create the pass through Temmok'Dun. He's a powerful mage, but he can't be in two places at once.'

'I think we'll be okay on that score,' Jann said. 'This place is an incredible nexus of power. There's a gate over there.'

He pointed inland, along the line of the Sun Besaraya towards the Pilgrim's hut, where he and Patrick had shared a bowl of rabbit stew. On that fateful evening, the old man had revealed the truth of the memory images that had plagued Jann since returning to this planet.

'I can send Piers right to the foot of Temmok'Dun. Provided knocking down the mountain doesn't exhaust him, he should be able to open his pass in time.'

'And the second reason?' Felice asked.

Jann gaze remained fixed on the mountain, remembering their battle with the Blood King. 'We locked the Rohantu up in that tower,' he said. 'It's quite likely they're still alive in there.'

new washington
6th day of far'utamasa, 967

'They're back!'

DeLange's shout broke Elaine's reverie. She had been nursing a cup of katuh since sundown, replaying over and over her last conversation with Jann. Often at the mercy of her temper, this time her own thoughts had raised her temperature. She flipped between wondering whether she could ever truly forgive him, and the more logical viewpoint. That there was nothing to forgive. They were not together when he bedded Penny, as he had pointed out several times. She had little room for logic in her thoughts, especially where Jann was concerned. And since he flew off, she had a third prong to her triumvirate of tribulation: worrying where he was and what had happened with his quest.

That at least was no longer a source of anxiety. He was back. She leapt to her feet and ran out into the dark, remembering at the last moment to snatch a coat from the rack against the chill of the night. The twin beams from the flyer's headlights pierced the gloom, illuminating Tremaine's wall as it overflew the structure. The small vessel dropped smoothly to the ground in a flurry of snow beside the ruined Dauntless.

A small group of Earthers gathered to welcome back the three travellers, eager for news of their search. Piers Tremaine and Silvia Alvarez joined her beside the door.

'Fingers crossed,' he said.

'Mine have been crossed since they left,' Elaine replied.

'I never expected them to be gone this long,' Alvarez said.

The flyer hatch cracked open. Jann and Patrick emerged, wrapping their coats tight around them. An icy wind blew across the landing area, lifting dancing snow devils that glittered in the brilliance of the lights until Waters killed the beams. She followed the two men down the steps.

Elaine elbowed her way to the front of the crowd and threw her arms around her lover. 'Welcome home,' she said, nibbling his ear. 'Did you find it?'

'Come inside, out of this damned weather,' he said, taking her hand. 'Malamajan is due, it's bloody cold out here, and I'm starving.'

'We all are,' Patrick added. 'We shared our last bepermak before we reached the Valley.'

Elaine shivered, memories of their previous visit to Lembaca Ana still fresh. Still frightening. 'The Uterban is in the Valley?' she asked.

'Inside,' Jann repeated. 'This is news for everyone, and I've seen enough snow for one day.'

They entered the main hall, the crowd following close behind. The Queen, Petani, Claire, and Kyle sat together at a table beside the wall. News of the flyer's return spread quickly through the base. Others hurried to join the group, crushing into the space until there was standing room only.

Patrick stood at the servery, thanking Elaine for her foresight in persuading the cook to keep some hot food on the go. Jann took his piled plate to find a seat at the table next to the other Elementals. From this position they could see the whole room while Jann related the tale of their search.

'Well?' deLange said, once the last person had squeezed in and closed the door. 'Did you find it?'

Elaine stole a morsel from Jann's plate and eyed the annoying deputy. 'Give him chance, will you?' she said, flashing him an angry look. 'They've been out since dawn.'

'And we've been waiting for news since then.' Elaine did not recognise the woman who spoke, but she melted back into the crowd after suffering another of Elaine's thousand-metre stares.

'We found it,' Patrick said, setting his plate on their

table and pulling out a chair. 'It's in the Valley of Lembaca Ana. Not exactly the most convenient location, but we can't help that. It is where it is.'

'So what happens now?' another disembodied voice asked.

'We get some sleep!' Jann laughed. 'If we can. And then we must take word to everyone as soon as possible. We'll need to work out how they can converge on the Valley so the Uterban is open for the shortest time.'

The room erupted into a cacophony of questions and worries.

'How long is the journey?' a red-faced man asked.

'I don't even know where the Valley is,' said another.

'Can't you just open it and leave it?' asked a third.

'Do we have enough time to reach it?' a blonde-haired woman shouted, her expression telegraphing concern that they may not.

Elaine scanned the crowd, looking for Alvarez. The base leader stood at the front, close to the corridor that led to her office. 'We could use some help with the logistics,' she called to the woman.

'Of course,' Alvarez replied. 'The Valley is something like five hundred klicks from here,' she continued, raising her voice over the clamour in the room, 'So that's a five-day journey for a large group carrying winter gear and provisions. It lies almost directly east, on the other side of Tubelak'Dun.'

'Yes,' Elaine said, 'anyone intending to traverse the Uterban to Earth and leaving from here can take the direct route south of the mountains. But we need to take word to Court—'

'And to the Forest,' Petani said.

'—of course. So whoever does that will have to go the long way round, north of the mountain.'

'I must somehow send word to the Palace,' the Queen said, 'and the more far-flung villages of Kertonia. The furthest is Duske Raj'pupu, on the east coast. We cannot leave anyone behind.'

'Duske Raj'pupu? I've never heard of it,' Alvarez said.

Cabrera, who had been standing at his boss's side, disappeared along the corridor in the direction of the office.

'They are an isolated settlement, it is true,' the Queen said. 'Nevertheless, they are Kertonians. Until recently I was their Queen. I will not abandon them, though it is eight days away on kudoback.'

'That's almost a thousand kilometres. We don't have time to ride there and still reach the Gate before impact,' Alvarez said, frowning.

'Is there a gate we can use, Gatekeeper?' Petani asked. Elaine smiled. The oldest Elemental never said very much, but when he did it was worth listening to. Except when he interrupted her to moan about his beloved Forest project.

Jann pushed the remains of his meal away. 'There may be, but I can't risk it. Even if only half the people we estimated traverse the Uterban, we'll have to keep it open for something like four hours. I daren't expend any energy on gates before that. We'll have to rely on everyday ways to send the news to those who need it, wherever they are.'

Cabrera returned, bearing a large sheet of fan-folded paper. He pushed through the crowd, with Alvarez following in his wake, and spread it out on the next table, in front of the Queen. Elaine pulled her chair closer, the better to see what it held.

'This is an image of the peninsula,' Cabrera said. 'Closest thing we have to a map. We cobbled it together soon after the arrival of the first ship. It's an amalgam of aerial photographs Commodore Oduya requested when the Endeavour made its final approach.'

'I miss him,' Alvarez said. 'Such foresight. Such a clear thinker. We could use his help right now.'

The Elementals all stared at the image in silence for a moment. The detail was impressive. Settlements, even the smaller villages, were easily visible.

'Is this Duskraj... that village?' Cabrera asked, pointing to the only likely candidate on the east coast.

'Yes,' the Queen replied, 'though I have never seen it so clearly, or visited, I am familiar with its location.'

'It's around five hours flying time,' Waters said, looking over Cabrera's shoulder. 'We can take the flyer.' She passed a hand over her face.

'What's wrong?' Elaine asked.

'Well, for one thing, it only seats six, so we'll need to decide who must go, besides Ru'ita and whoever pilots it. But more importantly, it's the only one still working, and it's almost out of fuel. We probably have enough to reach that village, but it'll be a one-way trip. We can't bring anyone back. Whoever goes will have to make their way to the Valley from the coast by road.'

The Queen gave a small bow towards Felice. 'Thank you. But we cannot assume everyone in the area will wish to — what did you call it — traverse? Many will no doubt prefer the known to the unknown. They will opt to take the passage north. We shall have to ride there via the Palace, if we cannot use your flying machine for a second trip.'

Alvarez faced the crowd. 'We don't need an audience while we grapple with these logistics,' she said. 'You have the headlines. The portal back to Earth will be opened at the Valley as soon as we can arrange for everyone to meet there. We'll organise into two parties. I imagine most of you will be taking the "leave" option, but you have a few days to decide. Anyone who chooses to remain must travel with the northern party to the mountain pass via the Blood Court and the forest of Besakaya. For now, I suggest you all try and grab some sleep, and think about what you want to take with you.'

A murmur of assent passed through the crowd. They filed out into the night. Elaine's attention returned to the map. 'I think we should work back from the time of impact,' she said. 'And hope we still have enough time left for everything that needs to be done.'

new washington
6th day of far'utamasa, 967

For the second time that day, Ru'ita sat alone in the main hall.

Planning the enormous task of evacuating so many people in such a short space of time had, to everyone's surprise, not taken very long. Once their audience dispersed and they could focus on the job, the necessary steps were obvious. They relied heavily on the populace doing what they were told, and doing it quickly. An assumption that sat uncomfortably for her, knowing her own people well, and having an age-old jaded view of the Istanians. Still, what choice did they have? Doom was coming, and would wait for no woman.

So it had been agreed that Felice Waters and her partner would pilot the flyer to Duske Raj'pupu with her aboard. Its final flight. She suppressed a shiver at the thought that Waters had not been certain the small vessel had enough fuel for the trip. To be flying would be bad enough. To fly with the chance of crashing...

Anyway, once at the coast, they would begin the task of informing the people of their doom. The Batu'n, and the other Elementals had assumed anyone hearing the tale would opt for one of their two alternatives: gate to Earth or passage to the North. There would almost certainly be a third contingent. Those who did not believe the story of impending disaster and would refuse to abandon their homes and familiar lives. No-one would admit to sharing her view. They had no time to wait until the truth made itself plain to the doubters. Doom was coming, and would wait for no woman. Those people would have to be left behind when she and the two Batu'n women set off on their long trek to the Black Palace.

Waters and her partner intended to traverse, so they

would break their journey in the last village before the Valley. Almost too small to see on the Batu'n map, it straddled the Sun Lum to the south of Borok Duset. There, the Queen would turn north, passing to the west of the small peak in a straight line for home. Waters would remain behind with the other leavers until the day the Uterban was opened.

On arrival at the Palace, she intended to appoint her steward as leader of the Palace Remainers, tasked with taking that group north to Temmok'Dun.

The largest group of Elementals faced the monumental task of preparing for, and opening the Uterban. The two Gatekeepers, Jann Argent and Ahnak, would ride directly to the Valley by the southern route. They would be accompanied by — she suppressed an inadvertent sob — her Air Mage, the Fire Witch, the Water Wizard, the Pattern Juggler, and the Stone Mage. The timing of that journey was critical to the success of their plan. They had assumed the destruction of Pun'Akarnya may release the trapped Rohantu. A frightening prospect, and one that would take all of their strength to overcome. But it was essential to clear the space for the Uterban.

They had spent most of their planning time on this aspect. The whole proposal hinged on Piers Tremaine. They needed his Stone power to deal with Pun'Akarnya, but he was also essential to the creation of the passage north. Jann Argent had assured everyone that Lembaca Ana was a — what was the word he used? — a "nexus." That there would certainly be a gate close by, which would deliver Tremaine to the foot of Temmok'Dun in time. If the Gatekeeper was wrong, their plans would all come to nought. The northern contingent would die under the doom on the cold bones of the Wall of the World.

Alone of the Elementals, the Gardener, Petani, was to journey north from New Washington to the Blood Court. After presenting their options to the Istanians, he would — she smiled at the memory of his words — stop at the

Forest Clearance Project in Besakaya to pick up his companions. This group would then split into two. One leaving the forest following the course of the Sun Penk directly to the Valley. The other crossing the plain of Per Tantaran, to meet up with the Kertonian remainers and await the arrival of Piers Tremaine to open the passage.

Finally, the majority of the Batu'n here in New Washington, under the leadership of Silvia Alvarez, would follow the Elementals on the southern route to the Valley. Their journey had to be timed so they arrived as the Uterban was opened.

It was an audacious and complex plan, but no more than they needed to face the threat of imminent extinction. May the four Gods protect them, and give them the strength to see it through!

When the meeting ended, she had once again tried to persuade Ahnak to reveal an answer for her. Did she go, or did she stay? For a second time, his words said he did not have one, but his contorted facial expressions and nervous body language told a different story. He knew something. For reasons of his own, he refused to impart that knowledge. Perhaps that was an answer in itself? If there was something to know, what else could it be but that she had been there? He must have seen her himself, or heard stories.

She sighed. In the end, did it matter? Their plans had placed an implicit burden on her Wood powers. She was unable to leave, whether she desired to or not. She had one further compelling reason to stay. Ahnak had mentioned several times how carefully the Beragan eked out their supplies of grain. How quickly the crops had regrown once the air had cleared. Petani had yet to declare a decision one way or the other. If he elected to remain, his Earth power would have aided in the crops' recovery. But so far that was only a possibility, and two years was a long time to survive with almost nothing to eat. It was obvious to Ru'ita that the healing powers of Wood must also have been present to ensure the Beragans' survival.

She had her answer. She must stay.

new washington
6th day of far'utamasa, 967

'So she asked you outright?' Clayer asked.

Ahnak felt the blood rush to his face. 'What does it mean? "Outright"?'

They stood at the entrance to the fourth building of the fourth block of dwellings that Piers Tremaine had created less than a month before. In common with all the new housing, the interior was bare. No-one had had time to decorate, or furnish, or improve their new homes, and now, no-one ever would. In a few days they would be crushed back into the rocks from which they had been raised. This corridor contained four doors, one of which led to Ahnak's room, one to Clayer's.

'She just came out with it,' Clayer replied. 'Said something like "was I there, or not?"'

'That's pretty much exactly what she said, yes.' He shivered. It was almost as cold inside as out. Decoration wasn't the only thing missing. The blocks had no heating yet, either.

'And what did you tell her?'

'I remembered what you said. About the temporary... about changing the future. I didn't tell her anything. I said I remembered no stories, and no-one had ever mentioned her.'

'Is that true?'

Ahnak gazed at her face, wanting to reach out and stroke it. Kiss it. He moved a strand of hair away from her eyes. She smiled, her sky-blue irises reduced to thin circles surrounding widening pupils. More blood rushed to his cheeks. Some also rushed to other places. He stopped that thought in its tracks.

'Well, is it?' Clayer prompted.

'No,' he admitted. 'Mama was always talking of her. Though no-one ever called her "the Queen." I guess because she no longer was Queen. But she was still the Wood Mage. The Kayshirin. Oh!' His hand flew to his mouth.

Clayer touched his arm. 'What is it, Ahnak?'

'I think I called her "Kayshirin"! The first time she asked me about life after the doom. She looked surprised. How would I know that word, if not...?'

Clayer shrugged. 'It's an ancient term. Maybe it wouldn't be unusual, if its origins are Beragan? She might assume that. The words, and the knowledge of Wood and Stone, came to us from your people, when they spoke with your father.' She squeezed his arm, her hand warm and comforting. 'I wouldn't worry.'

'I hope you're right Clayer,' he said. 'If I have corrupted the future at the final moment, after all I have gone through to protect it...'

She yawned, holding a hand in front of her mouth. 'Sorry. I'm sure it'll be alright,' she said. 'We should get to bed. It's late. Long day tomorrow.'

'They will all be long days,' he said, nodding. 'From now until doomsday.'

'I doubt I'll be able to sleep,' Clayer said, opening her door. 'It's so cold in here.'

She turned back towards him, staring into his eyes. Her normally pale face was flushed, despite the chill in the air. 'Would you come in and keep me warm?'

Chapter 22

the court of the blood king
7th day of far'utamasa, 967

The first flakes of snow from the cold-weather version of the nightly malamajan brushed Sebaklan Pwalek's window. Above the treeline of the darkened Alaakaya, a third moon competed with Pera-Bul and Kedu-Bul. A brilliant white orb that had appeared for the first time the night before. It was not really a moon, Seb knew. It was Ahnak's Doom.

A knock came on his door.

'Who is it?'

An unexpected face peered around the edge of the door as it cracked open. It was Petani, the Earth Elemental, his shaggy brown hair displaying many more streaks of grey than the last time they had met.

Seb leapt to his feet. 'Good evening, kemasatu,' he said with a respectful bow. 'This is indeed a surprise.'

'Forgive the intrusion,' Petani replied. 'I had wished to meet with Jeruk Nipis, but he has refused to see me.'

'Come in, please. Sit.' He moved a stack of Court paperwork from a chair, and swept it clean of crumbs with the palm of his hand. 'Is this about the doom?'

'The comet, yes,' Petani said. 'How did you know?'

'An educated guess. Can I offer you a glass of buwangah? It's not long been mulled.'

'That would be most welcome, thank you,' the old Elemental said, settling into the chair. 'Your manners and your hospitality are infinitely better than your leader's.'

'That is hardly saying much, these days,' Seb smiled, handing over a filled mug and pouring one for himself.

'I won't enquire on your sources, Pwalek,' Petani said, 'but what do you know about the comet?'

'I was present at the ceremony, when the northerner made his appearance. I heard his tale, indirectly. Beyond that, word has... reached us that the Batu'n have confirmed the story. Date, and point of impact. I believe there is a plan to evacuate.'

'Your intelligence is accurate and almost entirely up-to-date,' Petani said, exhibiting no surprise. He blew on his mug and took a careful sip. Seb's window rattled with a sudden gust of wind, startling them both. The Gardener set down his drink on a side table. 'So all that remains is to give you the details of that evacuation plan.'

Seb sat back in his chair and nursed his drink while the Elemental laid out the plans. To his uneducated ear, the timing sounded tight, but achievable if the population could be persuaded to move quickly.

'It all sounds reasonable,' he said, 'with one major drawback.'

'Oh? Anything to do with the Jester?'

'Only obliquely. You have made provision for two options — leave or remain — but the remain half only allows for evacuation to the north. Forgive me, but it would be an unattractive proposition to many people in the best of weathers. In the depths of Utamasa, few will be persuaded to undertake a trek lasting many days, over a frozen mountain.'

'*Through* a mountain,' Petani corrected, with a faint smile.

'Even so, the pass will be at some elevation. Colder than sea level. And from what the northerner said, his village, the first habitation, is yet some distance beyond the range on the other side.'

'A more attractive option than being flattened.'

'Indeed, if you are one of those who believe the tale.'

'I have seen the proof.'

'And I believe you, though I have not seen it with my own eyes. And yet there are others—'

'Nipis.'

'—not only him, but certainly taking their lead from him. Those others do not believe. Will not believe. Cannot believe. And with Jeruk bending their ears with his stories of corruption and subterfuge on the part of Kertonia, even some of those who may have been persuaded will no longer be inclined to listen.'

'Then they will die,' Petani said, draining his mug.

'Another?'

'If there is one, though it feels a little strange to be supping mulled wine while debating the end of the world.'

'Indeed,' Seb repeated, moving to the door. 'Excuse me for a moment. I should start things moving here without delay. I'll arrange for the Blood Watch to post notices everywhere before dawn. We won't even lose a day of preparation.'

'Excellent.'

The corridors in this wing of the Court enjoyed regular patrols. He stopped one of the Watch guards. 'Take word to Tepak Alempin,' he said. 'Ask him to meet me here in my quarters as soon as he can. A matter of the utmost urgency.'

'At once, sire,' the guard said, disappearing with military haste along the passage.

'So, leaving aside those who will pay with their lives for their trust in our good Jester,' Seb said, closing the door, 'we must organise into two parties. When is all this happening again? Sorry, I was listening. I want to be certain I have it right.'

'Of course. The Uterban will be opened at dawn on the sixteenth of Far'Utamasa, and the northern path as close to the same time as we can.'

'What of yourself, Petani? Which of these options do you find the most attractive?'

The old man stared into his wine and did not respond for some time. 'As you can tell,' he said, taking another sip, 'I have not made up my mind as yet. I spent most of my life on Earth. The prospect of returning there holds no fear for me. Though the traversing would once again wipe my memories of this place, and my power. On the other hand, if I were to remain and arrive at Temmok'Dun in due time, I would be able to offer such help as I can with the mountaineering.'

Seb smiled. The Elemental had not lost his sense of humour even in these dark times. Mountain engineering — mountaineering.

'Though I'm sure Tremaine will have little need of my assistance,' Petani added.

'He will be grateful for moral support, at least,' Seb suggested. 'I liked him, for the few days he was here. Better than the Muir boy, at any rate.'

Petani nodded, and emptied his mug for the second time. 'Very nice, thank you. Well, you seem to have things under control. The northern contingent from New Washington, such as it is, came with me. Everyone we left behind will be travelling south eventually. There are only six of us. If you can find us a bed for the night...?'

'Of course.' He pulled on a bell rope to summon a houseman.

'Thank you. Then we will leave at first light for Besakaya. I know they have enough accommodation for us there to wait out the few days before setting off for the north. Or the south. I shall have to come to a decision by then, but at least the Project is on the direct route from here. We will await you there, and we can all travel on together.'

'A good plan. If anyone wishes to pass through the void to Ketiga Batu, still they will have to take the path through most of Besakaya. We will split the two parties up near the eastern border, where the Sun Penk emerges from the woodland.' A knock came at the door.

'Come!' he said.

Tepak Alempin entered. 'You wished to see me, sir.'

'I'll wait on your man in the refectory if you don't mind,' Petani said, vacating his seat. 'The wine has given me an appetite.'

the court of the blood king
7th day of far'utamasa, 967

A single candle relieved the gloom of the throne room. Jeruk Nipis sat in his usual place behind the ruined throne, staring at the flickering flame and pondering his fate. Footfalls echoed through the cold, dark space, approaching from the direction of the main door.

'What are you doing, sitting in the dark?'

'Thinking.' Jeruk replied. 'An activity you would do well to engage in, Seb, instead of believing every fairytale you are told.'

'The fairies are in the sky right now,' Pwalek said, 'if only you would care to look. This refusal to believe the truth is getting old, Jeruk, even for you.'

'Why did you come here? If only to trade insults then I will bid you goodnight.'

'Petani has been to see me.'

'Ah. I wondered if he would seek you out after I refused to entertain him.'

'He said. He brought news of the Elementals' plan.'

Jeruk barked a mirthless laugh. 'Another bunch of losers we would be better off without.'

'A few more days and your wish will be granted,' Pwalek said, 'one way or another.'

'Good. Long have we planned and schemed for such a day. It should be a time to celebrate!'

'Are you mad? Open your eyes Jeruk! Point them at the sky! What do you think that bright light is, if not this doom the northerner came to warn us of? You will be celebrating from beneath the ground, if you wait long enough. From the fiery orb of Baka's realm, or the choking dust of Tana's eternal mountain.'

'Listen to yourself quoting the gods at me! Who are you? I no longer know you.'

'I am the one who has been beside you since we first shared our plans and dreams. Years beyond counting. And

I'm begging you to see the light the rest of us have seen. Make a choice. Choose to live!'

'And what is your choice, Sebaklan Pwalek of all those years? To sell out our land and run away to the north?'

The flickering candlelight played over his lieutenant, revealing a surprising truth.

'No! You are going to make the jump? Step across the void to Ketiga Batu? Don't bother to deny it! It is written in your features. In your eyes. Clear to see even by the light of a single flame.'

Pwalek leant against his desk, running a hand across his face and through his hair as if to wipe the evidence of his thoughts away. Jeruk stood and picked up his candle.

'I have heard enough. Take yourself off to Lembaca Ana, and—'

'How do you—?'

'The rat deLange has already been to see me. He travelled with Petani on some pretext. Said something about it being his last act of service to the Court. The man is more of a fool than I ever was. I'm right, aren't I? You're going with the Batu'n?'

'Yes. As Kilpemigang said when deLange first informed us of the truth about the doom, their technology is most impressive. I can only imagine what life will be like, surrounded by it. Using it every day. And now, I no longer need to imagine. I shall see it for myself.'

'Begone then. Another fool, on another fool's errand.'

Jeruk turned on his heel and strode from the throne room, leaving Pwalek in the dark. He walked so quickly, the candle guttered. He cupped the flame in his hand until he entered the hallway, where the torches burned bright and hot.

In his rooms, the chamberman had set his fire for the evening. It had not been burning long. The room still had a chill in the air. The glowing wood and leaping flames relieved the blackness in his mind a little. A simple meal of tepsak and a leg of dingas sat on his table beside a flagon of buwangah. He ignored the food and filled a glass, walking with it to the window to stare out at the night sky. Three lights. How had they conjured the third? Was it some trick of that Batu'n technology Pwalek was so enamoured of? Or some Elemental illusion? That damned Witch. Her fall through the original vortex had changed her, and not for the better. He would not put it past her to have switched her allegiance completely. Working with the Blacks to undermine him and his plans for a royalty-free, Elemental-free future.

He drained his glass in a single draught, turned his back on the hoax and returned to the table for a refill. And what if it were true, this tale of doom? What then? He shivered, despite the heat from the grate. Let it come.

the court of the blood king
7th day of far'utamasa, 967

Jared was holding court in the refectory, enjoying a late dinner, when Sebaklan Pwalek caught up with him. He amused himself with the idea of "holding court at Court", but that was his sole source of entertainment. The council members and Puppeteers who shared his table were a dour bunch. The news he brought on his most recent two visits had done nothing to improve their mood. Pwalek did not look happy either, as he marched into the hall.

'So this is where you're hiding, you little worm!'

Jared opened his arms in an expansive gesture. 'Hardly hiding,' he said, forcing a smile. 'Unless you mean hiding in plain sight?'

'Do you always talk in clichés? I mean, what possessed you to bring your news to the Jester without consulting me first? I had to wait and hear it from the Gardener!'

'I wasn't aware I was expected to "consult" with you, Pwalek. I was engaged by Jeruk Nipis and to Jeruk Nipis I shall report, until he tells me otherwise.'

'I imagine he gave you short shrift,' Pwalek said. 'He

doesn't take well to news he neither wants to hear, nor believes when he does hear it.'

Jared stared at his empty plate. 'You are right about that, at least,' he said, avoiding the man's gaze.

'Never mind the damned Jester,' Kilpemigang said, pointing a finger at Jared. 'DeLange has told us of the Batu'n plans. Now we have a definite date and a location, we need to make arrangements of our own. It won't be an easy journey at this time of year, but it can't be helped.'

'I've asked Alempin here to post the news,' Pwalek said, swinging a leg over the bench and perching at the end of the table. The Puppeteer nearest him slid a bowl of fruit in his direction. 'No, thank you,' he said, pushing it away. 'I've eaten. Though I have no appetite.'

'I'm not going anywhere,' the old man sitting opposite Jared said. Though indoors, he wore an overcoat, hat and gloves against the cold and had loaded his plate almost to the point of toppling over. Jared recognised him from his previous visit, but he had never been good with names. He could not remember this one, even though the man had re-introduced himself on Jared's arrival. Half his food remained, congealing in an unappealing pile before him. 'I've been around long enough to have seen the Blacks' plots many times. Jeruk is right: this is only more of the same. We'll be fine here. Just need to wait it out, and not fall for their lies.'

He reached out and plucked a cut of blue meat from his stack, chewing on it with an open mouth. Jared turned away in disgust, both at the man's eating habits and his attitude. Some people refused to acknowledge the truth even when it stared them in the face. Or landed on their heads.

Tepak Alempin stared fixedly at Pwalek. 'It'll come as no surprise to you that I plan to go North. Kilpemigang is right, we need to organise ourselves. When do we leave?'

'We're not expecting anyone else from the Batugan camp,' Pwalek said. 'The handful of Batu'n who are staying here came with Petani. They will depart in the morning for the Gardener's works in Besakaya. We will follow them and join up to proceed to the north or south in time to arrive when the two escape routes are opened.'

'Precisely my point,' Alempin said. 'When will that be? I have an entire house to pack up, and my two boys and their families the same. How long do we have?'

Pwalek shook his head. 'You will not be able to take everything. The doom will be here in only nine days. In any case, those intending to traverse this "Uterban" to Ketiga Batu can take no more than they can carry. Items of sentimental value will have no meaning by the time they arrive on that world. These "vortexes" erase the memories of anyone who ventures through, according to what I've heard.'

'How convenient!' the old man said, spitting a morsel of the blue meat onto Jared's arm. '"Come with us! You won't remember why you did, but it's the only way!"' He stood with a grunt, and snatched a greasy leg from his plate before stepping over the bench. 'You're all mad, and I won't sit here listening to it any longer. When all this is done and there are only a few of us left, Jeruk will reward my loyalty, you can be certain of that!'

Alempin took up his thread again. 'But I am not "traversing",' he said. 'I am travelling north, as I have said. So presumably, now that there will be a pass through the mountain, it will be safe enough with a wagon?'

Pwalek thought for moment before replying. 'I expect so,' he said, 'but you have reminded me that I must speak with the Keeper. He will certainly need more than one wagon for his records, and that must take priority over more mundane belongings.'

Alempin began to protest, but Pwalek walked off without another word.

Jared smiled. 'I'm sure there will be a wagon left for you, my dear Tepak,' he said, 'though perhaps only one per family.'

'You haven't told us of your intentions, deLange,' Kilpemigang said. 'I suspect a man of your intellect has reached the same conclusion as I. You will be returning home, yes?'

the court of the blood king
7th day of far'utamasa, 967

The air in the Court catacombs was surprisingly warmer than on the upper floors, but Sebaklan Pwalek appreciated the silence more than the temperature. Especially after the clamour of the refectory and the sharp words he had exchanged with Jeruk. No-one got under his skin as quickly, or easily — or as often — as that damned man. The man who had been his friend, and comrade-at-arms, since the days when Seb had worked the Court kitchens. A memory so distant it was almost beyond recall.

As they all soon would be, he thought ruefully, once he stepped through Jann Argent's Uterban. But he had tasks to perform before that fateful day. People who needed his help. And the gentle, learned old soul who lived in these dank spaces was one of them. He approached the Keeper's rooms, and knocked.

'Yes, yes, come in, come in,' came a voice from inside. 'Can't you see the door stands open?'

'I didn't want to intrude,' Seb said, stepping over the threshold. The heat from the Keeper's grate hit him full in the face like a blast from the Fire Witch herself. 'I'm surprised your scrolls survive in this heat without crumbling to dust,' he said, smiling.

The Keeper regarded him from his one good eye, the other clouded and sightless. His forlorn expression brought a pang of instant regret, redoubled by the archivist's reply. 'You jest, Sebaklan Pwalek, but that is exactly the problem with which I am grappling! One of the many problems, I should say, since they are legion.'

'How can I help?'

'How long do you have? I am not yet finished clearing even the first of my chambers.'

Scrolls littered the floor of the Keeper's rooms. A shocking sight. Even as a rare visitor to the Court archives, Seb was well aware of the rules. Unroll slowly, only ever on a table or desk, never the floor, put them back where you found them, no candles! There were almost as many rules as there were scrolls, and an equal number of ready admonishments in the old man's keen mind, should any be transgressed. All along the longest wall, where the Keys of the Keeper's title hung in their serried ranks, the parchments had been opened and stacked in neat piles of various heights.

'I don't believe I have ever seen so many unfurled,' Seb said.

'They occupy less space. But that is a problem in itself. Some of these are so old, they do not survive the unrolling. Normally I would treat them. It gives me chance to copy out their contents before they fall apart. But I have no time for such niceties now. I would still be here at the turn of the century!' The Keeper shook his head. 'Or should I say, I would not, for I would be long dead under the boot of Ahnak's Doom.'

He rested for a moment against the edge of his desk, running a wrinkled, blue-veined hand through his long, white hair. 'Even so, I do not have sufficient boxes for the ones that remain intact. I am having to make some distressing decisions regarding which records I can take, and which must be consigned to the dustbin of history.'

'So, how can I help?' Seb repeated.

A faint smile played over the Keeper's lips, his eyes reddening. 'You are a good man, Sebaklan. But I'm afraid I cannot trust even you with those decisions.'

'I would not presume—'

'So if you can begin packing this pile,' the Keeper waved a hand at the largest of the stacks, 'then I shall be free to continue with my hard choices.'

They toiled at their allotted tasks as the old man's candles burned, guttered, and were replaced with fresh. The Keeper added to his stacks at an astonishing rate, while Seb subtracted from them, stowing the papers as carefully as he could in crates fashioned from thin sheets of kaytam. And so the piles grew and diminished, grew and diminished, as the night turned past its middle. The Keeper disappeared into his tunnels at intervals, returning with more armfuls of archives.

When the candles were reduced to puddles of wax for a third time, the Keeper finally spoke. 'We should stop for now, Sebaklan. I don't know about you, young man, but I can do no more tonight. Thank you, for your assistance and your company, but it is late. In any case I have only sufficient wicks remaining to illuminate my breakfast on the morrow.'

Seb nodded. 'Of course. I was glad to help. I shall come again. I have one more duty to perform, though, before I can rest easy. I bid you goodnight Pelaran. Sleep well.'

'And you, my friend,' the Keeper's whisper followed him out into the relative cool of the main passage. 'And you.'

the court of the blood king
8th day of far'utamasa, 967

He hurried up the creaking wooden stairs to the main level. The corridors and passageways of the Blood Court were deserted, save for the occasional glimpse of a member of the Blood Watch going about his or her guard duties. Those who caught sight of him waved or nodded, passing no remark on seeing him out of bed in the middle of the night. As Jeruk's deputy, Sebaklan Pwalek had the run of the place. He answered to no-one.

Though the malamajan had ended, and the twin moons were long set, he had no doubt the Jester would still be awake. His time with the Keeper had allowed his anger and irritation to subside. More than that, the archivist's diligent attention to his beloved records had somehow stimulated Seb's own sense of duty. He was reminded of his long association with Jeruk Nipis. The things they had shared; good and bad. And there had been bad. Plenty of it. He would not have plunged full-bodied into a lake of stinking ichor for anyone else. His stomach roiled again at the memory, threatening to pitch its contents steaming to the red flagstone floor.

He took the stone stairs to the upper level two at a time, strode quickly past his own door, and came to a halt outside Jeruk's chambers. He owed it to his friend to make one final effort. Convince him of the truth of Ahnak's Doom, and offer him one of the two salvations available to everyone. A shiver ran along Seb's spine. There was a distinct possibility he would still be angry. May not even allow him in. If the man's annoyance at their words had been half as strong as Seb's, and he had been stewing on it alone ever since, he would not be abed. Still, no sounds came from beyond the heavy, panelled door.

He knocked, and waited. There was no response. He pressed his head against the wood. He could hear nothing. No movement, no musical strains from the old celapi Jeruk played to calm his temper, not even any crackling from his fire. The room stood in total silence.

He rapped again, to be sure of his propriety and avoid causing further offence. When moments passed without word, Seb cracked the door and peered inside.

'Jeruk?' he said quietly. 'Are you awake?'

Dim yellow light from a single candle illuminated the bedchamber. This could not be the same candle with which the Jester had left the throne room. The Keeper had burned through three full-length wicks since then.

He scanned the room, opening the door wider. The hinges moaned. Their dull metallic complaint matched the creak of the rope from which Jeruk Nipis dangled. Slung over the beams above his bed, he hung a metre from the floor, still swaying slightly. His head bent at an unnatural angle, his blackened tongue protruded from between his lips. The sour stench of a dying man's last shit filled Seb's nostrils as he backed out into the corridor and closed the door.

Chapter 23

the court of the blood king
8th day of far'utamasa, 967

'I brought you some breakfast, old friend.'

Petani stopped at the door to the Keeper's rooms, staring at the chaos within. The old archivist sat slumped in a chair beside his fireplace, his head in his hands, staring at the scant embers that remained. Their dim glow did nothing to relieve the gloom of the windowless chamber. They emitted no heat.

'Whatever has happened? It looks like one of young Claire's jamtera has taken on a mind of its own and blown your archives apart!'

Paper, parchment, and scrolls lay in every corner of the room, as far as Petani could see. A fine dust covered everything, lending an aspect of dereliction to the scene. He held up his lantern, revealing more haphazard piles stretching through to the bedchamber on the left. Against the far wall, wooden crates had been stacked almost to the ceiling. Empty ones of similar construction had been lined up in front of the stacks, their lids propped beside them at jaunty angles.

'I'm packing,' the Keeper murmured between his fingers. 'Did you say breakfast?' he added, sitting up straighter and pulling on a pair of slippers. 'That's most thoughtful, Petani. You would be welcome indeed at any time, but I have found no time for a bite since yesterday morning. Move that pile and take a seat. I don't suppose the doom will come before I have had chance to break my fast with you.'

'We have some days yet, my friend,' Petani said, moving into the room. He set down the tray on the Keeper's large desk, and cleared a chair of its burden of ancient scrolls.

'Where shall I— ?'

'Oh, those are staying,' the Keeper said. 'Dump them on the floor.'

Petani stepped back in surprise, but said nothing. He placed the scrolls carefully beside the chair, and sat.

'I wanted to see you,' he said, 'before I left.'

'You're leaving already? You only just got here.'

'I've been here since yesterday, but caught up in matters of state. At least, trying to be. In the end I had to make do with speaking to Pwalek.'

'A more productive conversation than you would have enjoyed had you met with the Jester, I'm sure,' the Keeper said. 'He came to see me yesterday too. Pwalek, I mean. He was a great help, to be honest.' He waved at the archives littering the room. 'As you can tell.'

The old man crossed to his desk and took a chunk of tepsak and some kacajunus. 'Most thoughtful,' he repeated, with his mouth full. 'What did you want to see me about?'

'I think I have my answer,' Petani said, looking around the room. 'I had thought we shared a problem. That the coming disaster threatened both of our lives' work. I hoped you might have some insight into an alternative solution. Some way to avoid the wholesale destruction of my gardens and earthworks. But I see more clearly now. Although Ahnak's Doom impacts us both, your work is at least mobile.'

The Keeper regarded him in silence for a time, chewing on his kacajunus and filling two glasses from the jug of sabah juice on the tray. 'Barely,' he said at last. 'Three hundred years of archives on my shelves. It is tearing out my soul deciding which to take and which to abandon.'

Petani accepted one of the glasses, swallowing half its contents in one draught to still his initial reaction to his friend's words. At least the Keeper had the decision to make. He could save something. Everything Petani had toiled to create would be gone in an instant without hope of deliverance.

'I can see what you're thinking,' the Keeper said. 'And

I'm sorry if my words seem harsh. I know how you love your gardens.' He shrugged. 'All of Istania knows. But you see, Petani,' he waved his hand around the room again, 'all this is irreplaceable. From the last stroke of a quill on the youngest, most pliable parchment, to the fading lines on the most fragile ancient artefact, almost none of it remains in living memories. When it is lost, it is gone forever. Though your plantings are indeed things of great beauty, once the doom is past, you can recreate them. You can rebuild, wherever you find yourself. The Garden will bloom again. The archives can only pass into obscurity, never to be recalled.'

An uneasy silence fell. He could not argue with the old man. His words were true and full of wisdom. It was an insight he had needed to hear, though it did not dispel the pain of loss he felt. At least he would have the chance to see the Forest one last time.

'So where will you go, Petani?' the Keeper asked. 'Surely not back to Ketiga Batu?'

'My heart is not really there, even though I lived most of my life under its single moon.'

'We will need you here, you know, once the doom comes. Your powers and skills will be sorely pressed in the aftermath. Have you not thought of it? Though we have not experienced such a thing before, it is easy to predict what such an impact will do. Even without Ahnak's account to guide us. Years of dark; wholesale death of plants and animals; long-term hardship for all the survivors.'

'You paint an attractive picture,' Petani laughed. 'It is hard not to jump at the chance to live through such times.'

'You being among us will make life so much better for so many. If anyone can stimulate the crops to bear fruit and give grain in the near-dark, it is you my friend. And, since you have said your heart lies here, it sounds to me as though you have made your decision.'

'I am leaving for Besakaya shortly,' Petani said, standing

and setting his empty glass back on the tray. 'I would stay and help you with your final packing, but my friends at the Project will also need time to stow their belongings for the journey. There are few days remaining to us.'

'I will meet you there, then. Have a safe trip.'

the court of the blood king
8th day of far'utamasa, 967

Jared deLange stared out across the dark silhouette of Besakaya. The twin moons rode low in the sky and the snowfall from the malamajan had begun to slow. It lay like a shroud over the land. Bright white and sparkling in the lights from the Court windows, fading to grey and then black before the thin silver line of the Sun Hutang traced the edge of the forest. It was cold atop the battlements, but Jared hardly felt it. The difference between the temperature of the air and that of his mood was so small as to be imperceptible. He had climbed to the top of the eastern turret in search of — what? An answer to his problem? No. He did not expect to find that, if indeed one existed. With the death of the Jester his future was now even more uncertain than the impending "doom" had made it.

He snorted at the thought. Doom. The simple word had become an accessible shorthand for the simple fools who did not — could not — understand what was about to happen to them. Or did not even believe it. Like their newly-dead leader, they supposed it to be some elaborate plot to steal their land, or homes, or lives. The imagined Kertonian bogeymen, always behind every Jester-inspired terror. Only a mechanism to keep the population under control, but no-one ever saw through the Jester. Except perhaps Pwalek.

'What are you doing up here,' came a voice through the dim moonlight. As if summoned by Jared's thought, Sebaklan Pwalek approached from the stone staircase. 'My guards told me you had climbed the tower, but I didn't believe it.'

'Why not? You think me incapable of a few stairs?'

'Always believed you were more of a social climber,' the man replied with a vacuous grin. Was this what they had to deal with now, in the place of leadership? The Jester had not been dead a day and already Jared felt his loss keenly.

'I needed some air,' he said, turning back to the battlements. The red stone took on the colour of dark blood under the waning moons. It rose and fell in traditional crenellations around the circumference of the turret, alternating between merlons as high as his chest, and wide crenels through which missiles could be fired or dropped onto attackers. Had the Blood Court ever been subjected to an attack? He had no idea. The smaller of the two moons disappeared behind the forest as he watched. 'This place is stifling.'

A gust of wind blew through the nearest crenel, cutting an icy path around his legs like the Scythe of Sana. Fuck! He had been in this forsaken place too long. He was beginning to curse with the local gods.

'Not surprised you feel uncomfortable,' Pwalek observed. 'What are you going to do, now your man is dead and Ahnak's Doom is almost upon us? Surely you don't believe his paranoid delusions? You've seen the evidence for yourself!'

'Of course I don't believe it! Ten years in the company of fools does not make me one of them. One of you.'

'No? No, certainly not one of us. Never that. You trod a dangerous path between worlds, deLange, and now it has crumbled away from beneath you. The Jester may have protected you, had he lived. May have found you a position in his company. Briefly, of course, since he did not intend to leave and there will soon be nothing left here. This "comet" may more properly be called Jeruk's Doom. At least Ahnak has the sense to save himself.'

'Going home, is he? Back North?'

'No. Petani tells me he intends to take the portal. He is coming to Earth.'

'*Coming* to Earth? So that is your choice too?'

'I have made no secret of it. I have long been fascinated by tales of your world. Fascinated by it and, yes, thirsting for it. For an end to subterfuge. Plot and counter plot, over and over without end. I am done with it.'

Jared laughed, his raucous snort echoing down the Court walls and into the night. 'Good luck with that, Pwalek! You'll find no end to subterfuge among the people of Earth, trust me. If anything they are even worse than the Berikatanyans. Be careful what you wish for!'

Pwalek shrugged, rubbing his hands together against the biting wind. 'With you as an example, it is not hard to believe. Even so, I am happy with my decision. And speaking of Petani, you have missed him, if it was your intention to travel on with him to the forest. He left this morning. So what will you do now, deLange? Will you turn tail and run back to the homeland? You don't strike me as the type to suffer the years of deprivation that will follow the impact? Not long to decide, whichever path you take. We leave at daybreak.'

'You will need to rest then,' Jared said, his gaze fixed on the second moon. 'Why are you wasting time up here? Important man like you will have to be fresh for what's ahead. No need to babysit me.'

'I don't trust you.'

Jared laughed again. 'I am no threat to you.'

'A man with nothing to lose is always a threat.'

'Perhaps. But I also have nothing to gain. As you were happy to point out, there is nothing here for me now. Unfortunately, there is nothing there either. Back on Earth. I made my decision on that score. Why else would I be here?'

'I don't know. Perhaps you could tell me? But it's too cold up here for stories,' Pwalek said, beckoning. 'Come, let us share a bite before bed at least. In the warm.'

'You don't want to hear my story. And there is no warmth to be found, though I should stand in the very flames themselves. The chill I endure has no connection with the weather. Go, find a fire for yourself if you like. Leave me alone.'

Only a thin segment of Pera-Bul remained over the treeline now. Stars had begun to appear above the opposite horizon. Unfamiliar, unnamed patterns. The Berikatanyans had no interest in astronomy or astrology; no mythical heroes strode their night sky. Pwalek left without another word. After a moment the last sliver of moon disappeared, and with it the last of the light. Jared stared down through the crenel at which he stood. It was impossible to see the ground below. One step over the edge and it would rush rapidly and invisibly up to greet him and welcome him to the Jester's new Court. They did not have a god of Death, either, these people. A gust of chill night air whipped around his aching cheeks, bringing tears to his eyes. The dark stone of the building sent needles of icy pain through his hands. He blew on them, and rubbed them together, but the cold had seeped into the bones of his fingers, robbing them of all feeling. Pwalek had spoken the truth: there were few paths open to him now. And the easiest lay before him.

new washington
9th day of far'utamasa, 967

Kyle Muir stared out along the massive sea wall that stretched into the bay. Steely waves rolled and peaked under the grey sky, white caps whipped by the wind scattering sprays of foam over the glistening hull of the downed Valiant. No-one had thought to rename the ship's last resting place when the settlement was newly christened. It should more properly be Washington Bay now, with or without the "New", but in the end it no longer mattered. All their work would soon be gone. The comet would impact inland, far to the east, but even so the subterranean shock-waves may raise a tsunami to rival the terrifying spectre that still haunted her dreams. The wall of water created by her brother as his final desperate act in this strange world.

She shivered against the bone-deep cold of the evening. Her preparations for leaving long since complete, there was nothing now to do except wait, and her empty room had begun to suffocate. Their plans demanded that the Elementals arrive a day early at the Valley, but there was no value in setting off yet. They would all leave the base together, in two days' time when the main group could travel at a sensible pace and still reach the site in time to traverse.

Kyle struggled to grasp the immensity of the task. She had heard talk of "the Valley" many times since the Dauntless docked. It took on almost mythical proportions in her mind. The site of the original vortex that cast Jann, Elaine, Petani, and the parents of both Claire and Patrick, through time and space back to Earth. It had huge significance from that single event alone, but other incidents littered its history. Centuries of conflict between the two realms as they attempted to seize and hold it for themselves, their long-cherished dreams of seaborne exploration held in abeyance as the battles raged. Decades of desolation under the strange glamour of the time-dilation effect, tales of which both Jann and Patrick had related on various occasions. Petani's struggle to build a harbour. Piers Tremaine's eventual success, which had risked rekindling the conflict.

But the strangest tale of all — the Battle of the Blood Clones — may yet have another chapter. The fearsome Rohantu created by the Blood King may, Patrick Glass had suggested, still be alive under the rock of Pun'Akarnya. If they could ever have been said to live in the first place. She shook her head. If they were not alive, then surely they could never die?

Kyle thrust her hands deep into the pockets of her coat and began the short walk back to the squat grey buildings of the base. The clifftop path had been cleared of snow by the weak sunlight. Ice was now forming in the puddles that gathered in the many depressions. The day was late and sundown was coming. Memories of childhood sunsets seen from the cliffs of her youth begged her to stay and watch one last glorious display of evening colour. Her sensible adult self shivered again at the deepening chill of the air, and longed for a warm fireplace and a mug of hot panklat. Perhaps she could share one with Claire. And Ahnak, of course. The two had become inseparable.

'Have you decided yet?' Claire had asked her over breakfast.

The question plagued her throughout the day. She had yet to answer it, and time was running out. Though she had achieved some phenomenal success with Water power since her first faltering steps, there remained vast, unexplored potential. To have this new-found ability torn from her — even the memory of it! — by traversing the Uterban and returning to Earth was... distressing. Yet this new life, that she had looked forward to so ardently, had not turned out how she imagined. The loss of her brother, no matter how warped he had become, still hurt. If she must face life alone, would it not be better to do that somewhere familiar? Avoid having to face yet more unknowns in the aftermath of what everyone was calling Ahnak's Doom?

Their plans included an escape route to the north for those who had to wait until the final moments before impact. She clung on to that possibility. It provided an excuse to put off a decision for few more days. The door would close on both of those options, eventually. She stared up at the bright speck of the approaching comet, now plainly visible in the evening sky. The first faint hints of red painted the air, like a planet-wide warning light.

Doom is coming, you must decide. Remain a mage or take a ride.

Even the hottest mug of panklat would not be enough to dispel the cold of this night.

new washington
11th day of far'utamasa, 967

The grey light of the winter dawn crept over the distant peaks of Tubelak'Dun, sparking frost diamonds in the thick snow that had fallen overnight. It was still, and would always be, "winter" to Silvia Alvarez. Even after ten years in a world that called it Utamasa. Ten years now rapidly drawing to a close. She took one last look around her office, and closed the door. She reached instinctively for the key in her pocket, before letting it fall out of her hand with a grunt. Who was left to lock out?

In the crisp, cold morning air, the largest herd of kudai ever seen in New Washington stood quietly. Their plumes of steamy breath combined into a thin fog that curled and swirled in a slow dance to the frozen ground. The placid animals made no sound beyond the occasional snort. Their limpid eyes watched the humans closely, betraying the keen intelligence anyone who had ever ridden one knew all too well. She had called in years of favours from local villages to assemble this many animals, but even so most of them would be riding double.

Jann Argent and Elaine Chandler emerged from the main hall. Of all the Elementals, the Fire Witch had been the most irritable in recent days. Once their plan had taken shape, she wanted to crack on with it. Sitting around waiting to leave made everyone testy. In the Witch's case that petulance had overflowed into regular and frequent bursts of Fire power, to which the scorch marks on the outside of several buildings gave mute testimony.

'At last,' she said, approaching Silvia. 'Another day shut away in this forsaken tomb and I would've burned the place to the ground.'

'You already made a start in several places,' Silvia replied, nodding at the nearest wall. A particularly violent reaction had occurred here after nightfall two days before. The leading edge of the roofing sheets had melted and sagged.

The Witch blushed. 'Yes, sorry. No harm done though, eh? We're leaving now anyway.' She hurried away.

'She's worried someone's gonna steal her favourite kudo,' Argent said with a grin. 'I doubt anyone would be so foolish.'

He followed his partner towards the herd. Silvia looked for Felice Waters' face in the crowd, before remembering she was several hundred kilometres away, helping the Black Queen spread the word and lead her people to their salvation. With her gone, and her "deputy" deLange having disappeared, Cary Cabrera had stepped up as her second. The guy was a workhorse. He had been up for two hours by the time she emerged from her bed. Fed and watered the kudai for the first leg of their journey, mustered the kitchen staff to put the final touches to their travelling supplies, and made a last check of the Long Range Scanner in case — for whatever reason — Nemesis had undergone a late change of heart and decided to execute a flypast of the planet instead.

'No such luck,' he had said to her as they shared a hurried breakfast. 'No change in trajectory or timings.'

She belched, holding a hand to her mouth. The meal sat uncomfortably above her belt. She never liked to eat much before lunch. Or ride, but there was no avoiding it, today of all days. She stepped off the boarded walkway and strode over to the kudai, frost crunching under her boots. Piers Tremaine approached from the direction of his new accommodation blocks. Having not seen the Stone Mage since their planning meeting, she assumed he had travelled to Court with his close friend and earth-working rival Petani.

'Good morning,' she said. 'I thought you had left for the north?'

He checked the tightness of his kudo's girth and swung into the saddle with a grunt. 'No. Jann and Ahnak are convinced there's a gate to the North. I hope they're right, or several hundred thousand people will perish at the foot of Temmok'Dun. But they can't take down the mountain without me, so I'm caught...'

He grinned.

'Between a rock and hard place?' Silvia finished for him, laughing.

'Kind of. Only they're both rocks and they're both hard places, so I dunno. Either way, it scares the shit out of me. If I can't demolish Pun'Akarnya, the others won't be able to open the Uterban. All the leavers will die. If I can't make it to the mountain, or if I arrive and can't lower the pass, all the remainers will die. I can hardly think about it.'

'I don't know what to say,' Silvia said. 'Except that Oduya always used to tell me, "a diamond is just a lump of coal that did well under pressure." He had a pithy phrase for every occasion, but he was usually right.'

'Ha! Well, I sure feel more like a lump of coal than a diamond. Maybe pressure is all I need?' He spurred his mount. 'Thanks Alvarez! Truth is there's pressure ahead whether I need it or not!'

Led by Cabrera, and with the rest of the Elementals close behind him, the residents of New Washington rode out into the increasingly bright day. She dismissed a thought about checking the accommodation blocks for stragglers. Too much worrying! No-one had missed the briefings. Everyone knew what they needed to do. There would be nothing left here but empty rooms and discarded tech. All their hopes of a fulfilling new future — in making the journey here in the first place, and the more recent dreams of a thriving Earther community to rival the two great houses — all gone. But Silvia Alvarez was not big on regret. She had no tears for this place, or its sudden end.

Her future lay on a different path. The path which the long train of riders in front of her were now taking. She mounted her kudo and steered the animal out of the base behind the last of those riders without a backward glance.

besakaya
12th day of far'utamasa, 967

Sebaklan Pwalek stood on the bank of the Sun Hutang, watching the fast-flowing river carry dead branches and small chunks of ice through the clearing. This part of the mighty Besakaya had been tamed by the diligent work of the Project members, and the application of almost constant Earth power by the master Gardener, Petani. He could understand the old Elemental's pain at leaving the great work behind. Something he had brought up again the night before as they sat around the Project's fire pit.

Normally home to only a small number, the camp had swelled during the day until it held countless thousands of refugees from the Blood Court. Numerous other, smaller, fires had sprung up to surround the main camp area. They dotted both the clearing and the uncleared forest with cheerful blazes in a wide circumference. While the crackling logs warmed the travellers and cooked them a sparse meal, they had brought no cheer to the Gardener.

'Have a care there!' he called, pacing around the clearance. 'Watch that dumwheat! Your fire is scorching the grain!'

The camp leader, Garcia, who Seb had met and grown to like during their return journey from Kyle Muir's aborted inauguration, trotted after the old Elemental, pleading with him to return and sit in the warm.

'The project is done, Petani,' he said. 'Please. These people mean no harm. Any damage they cause will be as nothing once the comet hits. Surely you realise that?'

And so, with much huffing and puffing, Petani had been persuaded. He had sat beside the fire, chewing slowly on a leg of kinchu and staring into the flames. Seb thought perhaps he saw the track of a tear down the old man's cheek. A clean white line through the soot that smeared his face. When he looked again a moment later, it was gone.

The Keeper of the Keys sat beside the Gardener, resting a hand on his knee in friendly reassurance. 'If it helps you, my friend, I am every bit as restless. My cart is too close to these many conflagrations. A single spark is all that's needed to destroy centuries of records. Yet, what choice is there? As I have said to you before, you can rebuild this place north of the mountains. The wonders of flower and grain, leaf and tuber, will return under your careful hand. Worry not. Nothing of yours will be gone forever.'

'I am sorry, my dear Pelaran,' Petani had replied with a wry smile, 'you're right, of course. Is there anything I can do to protect your treasured archives? Perhaps...'

To Seb's astonishment, the Earth Elemental had stared out towards the cart, standing at the edge of the clearing and brightly lit by a myriad flickering flames. As he watched, a pile of earth grew from the ground, banking itself up in front of the loaded wagon until the topmost crate of parchments disappeared from view.

The ancient archivist clapped his hands. 'Oh, marvellous! Thank you Petani! Tana bless you my friend. You are a wonder!'

Seb stepped closer to the river, cupped the ice-cold water and splashed his head and neck several times, dashing away the last of the morning's grogginess along with the previous evening's memories. No time for reminiscing today! Back at camp, Garcia and the other Project members were putting the final touches to their saddle bags, making sure all the fires were out, and checking axles, wheels, and straps on the carts which would be heading north.

It made sense for the two groups to separate here. The proposed pass through Temmok'Dun lay slightly east of due north-east from their camp, while Lembaca Ana was a little east of due south. Leavers and remainers would bid their farewells before taking different paths out of Besakaya. He knew of no families that were divided in their decisions. All those he had spoken to were either journeying together to the northern lands, or together had decided to risk the same jump into the unknown which Seb himself would undertake.

But if this crisis had brought families closer, it had certainly divided friendships. Arguments on the relative merits of each option had continued late into the night. Seb sent silent thanks to the four gods that, here at least, only two options were debated. Anyone who sided with the late Jester had not set out in the first place. They remained, physically shuttered and psychologically blinkered, in their Court chambers, shacks, and houses, awaiting whatever fate their closed minds imagined. He had long ago abandoned attempts to persuade them otherwise.

'Seb!' called Temaperlan as he strode back into the camp. 'Shall we ride together? If I'm to step into obscurity I would at least like to do it at the side of a friend.'

Seb smiled. This man, a Puppeteer of many years' standing, had hardly registered with him while Seb had been at the Jester's right-hand. What else had those years kept him from? How many good people had been frightened off by the fool? Today was a new start. If he had the chance to make that start with new friends, he could avoid repeating those mistakes. 'Yes indeed, Tem,' he said, slapping him on the shoulder, 'some good company would be most welcome in these strange times!'

'You're both mad,' came a cracked voice from the shadows beside Petani's mound of earth.

Seb shielded his eyes from the slanting morning sun. 'Who is calling my sanity into question?' he called.

The bent and bony figure of the Pilgrim stepped out around the embankment. 'I survived one near-death experience,' the old man said. 'And spent far too long under the influence of a portal. You two can go jumping through time and space if you must, but I am less than keen to repeat the ordeal.'

Seb and Temaperlan laughed. 'Well I suppose I can understand that,' Seb said, 'from your point of view.'

'You do know your jaunt will cost you your memories?' the Pilgrim continued. 'Mine are fading anyway, they need no help from unnatural sources. No, you can keep your portals. I shall travel with Petani and Pelaran.

'Three old men together,' Temaperlan said. 'Sounds like a lot of fun.'

'For myself,' Seb added, 'there are few memories of this place I shall be sorry to lose.' An image of a corpse floating up to the surface of a bloody lake came unbidden to his mind. He swallowed down the spit that swarmed into his mouth. 'Always new memories to make, old man.'

'And always a new pilgrimage for the Pilgrim,' the Pilgrim said, smiling broadly at the irony. 'Though the journey will be arduous, and the life it leads to full of hardship and toil, still those things are familiar to me. I take some comfort from that.'

'We must take our comforts where we may,' Seb said, nodding. 'Good luck to you my friend. To you and all those who travel north.'

'And to you Sebaklan Pwalek,' the Pilgrim said. 'And to those who jump with you into the unknown. Tana keep you safe.'

the palace of the black queen
12th day of far'utamasa, 967

The sweet, pungent smell of decaying leaves and old bracken filled her nostrils. Ru'ita tightened her grip on her multicoloured staff and breathed deep, closing her eyes against the sudden sting of tears. The screech of a lone ghantu echoed through the bare branches of Timakaya, swiftly followed by the rattle of its wings as it took off in search of lunch. She had wanted to return one last time to Huramapon. To absorb its restful energies and inhale its strong, peaceful scents. To bid farewell to the place she had hardly begun to call home. Who was she saying goodbye to, really? In her absence the impressive structure had stood silent, a sanctuary for only crawling insects, burrowing beetles, and the occasional brave hoofed animal that might venture up the walkway to sniff out a tasty morsel of loose bark.

When engaged in the creation of Enkaysak, she had believed she could hear the trees. Followed their calls to uncover the bounty they offered: the woods that now intertwined into the powerful staff which accompanied her everywhere, and had allowed her finally to unlock the immense power of the Kayshirin. She had tried again to still her mind during this last visit. Tried to hear, or sense, the intent of the forest. To offer one last word of gratitude for its gifts. A weapon; a channel; a home. She held Enkaysak in both hands, lifted it up in homage to the mighty trees from which it came.

'Thank you,' she whispered. 'Thank you all. And farewell!'

Nothing happened. This mighty wood, the second largest in all Berikatanya, stood astride the Sun Besaraya as it wound its way down to Lembaca Ana. Her destination, and where the coming doom would play out. But with the river carving a channel through the land between here and there, nothing stood to protect the forest. The force of the impact when Ahnak's Doom finally hit would be directed north, to strike at the heart of Timakaya. The ancient trees and groves, the nests and burrows, the entire structure of Huramapon, all would be blasted to nothing in moments. Fresh tears started in her eyes at the thought. They could save themselves, Berikatanyans and Batu'n alike, but they could do nothing for the other lives this place had nurtured.

A light breeze blew up, shaking the few remaining tenacious leaves that had held on to their twigs and branches during the whole of Utamasa. A thrill of surprise tingled through her as she began to perceive a message. A whisper of an idea, borne from the depths of the woodland.

'*Fear not, Kayshirin. We will grow again.*'

She shivered. At the cold, the wind, and the sepulchral utterance. But it was a thrill of hope, not a tremble of fear. A smile creased her face. She raised a hand in acknowledgement.

'*And you will rebuild,*' the last zephyr said. A single golden leaf fell from the kaykaste growing beside Huramapon. It tumbled gracefully downward in front of her and landed in the palm of her outstretched hand.

*

'You're sure you understand, Seteh?'

'Yes, Majesty. Your instructions are perfectly clear.'

The bleached white Utamasan sun had climbed to its noonday height. Time to leave. Ru'ita's stomach churned. She would be glad to put this dark, cold edifice behind her. Even a morning spent here was too much. She could feel it leeching away the beneficent energies of Timakaya in which she had earlier walked.

In the great basilica of the Black Palace, roughly half the populace were assembled. Those who had decided to take the Uterban into the unknown. Many more than she expected. Some had long associations with Batu'n settlers in Kertonia. Hearing their tales over the last decade had inspired dreams of a life in their world. Dreams that now had a path into reality. Some of their close friends, who had been uncertain which of the momentous decisions was the right one, had been persuaded. All of these now sat astride their kudai, filling the basilica with a shuffling mass of pungent animal bodies and a thick blanket of steaming breath. The throng spilled out of the basilica onto the moatside path and the field beyond, patiently awaiting Ru'ita's command to depart.

The other half stood at doors and windows ready to bid their friends, comrades, and family goodbye. They had chosen to endure the coming hardships in the security of a known world, even though the northern territories were less familiar than their homeland. Ru'ita took heart that, one way or another, her subjects faced up to their challenges. None of them had been stupid enough to believe Ahnak's Doom a hoax. Within days these black towers would be deserted, even emptier than her beloved Timakaya. Their granite would withstand the force of the Doom no better than trunk or branch.

'You must arrive at the foot of Temmok'Dun no later than dawn on the morning of the sixteenth, you understand?'

'As I have said, Majesty, your instructions were clear. The journey is a simple one, and preparations are almost complete. We shall leave at first light on the morrow. The only hardship will be an early start on the last day, but it is nothing. Everyone going to the mountain understands what is required.'

'Good. I can think of no-one better to lead them, Seteh. I am so very lucky with my deputies. I know you will take care of those going north. And I have Penagliman Lendan to ensure continued progress for this group, once I leave them to ride ahead to the Valley.'

'Your people are good because you give us the best guidance and support, my Queen,' the skeletal man said with a bow. 'Luck plays no part in it. Although I cannot deny hoping that fortune will indeed smile on our endeavours. Your task is far more dangerous and arduous than mine, majesty. May Utan guide you to your goal, and Sana always protect your back.'

The man's choice of gods was cleverly done. Since their path followed the line of the Sun Besaraya, the Water god would indeed be guiding them, from one viewpoint.

Having the wind behind them also meant journeying away from a blast wave. Something she would soon be doing, provided the Elementals could achieve their audacious plan.

'Thank you Seteh. I hope your gods are equally diligent with your protection. Very well, we must leave. If all goes to plan, we shall meet again in the shadow of Temmok'Dun four days from now.'

She mounted Pembrang, reaching forward to stroke the black kudo's neck and tickle his ear. He snickered and tossed his head. 'You are just as eager as I to be off on our journey,' she said with a laugh.

'Lendan!' she called to her commander. 'Let us begin!'

Chapter 24

Iembaca ana
15th day of far'utamasa, 967

'Never thought I would spend another night in this place,' Jann said, poking at the embers of the previous night's fire. 'Kinda missed the old man's stew. It was almost as good as rebusang!'

Patrick stared out over the muddy brown waves of the Lum Segar and took another bite of bepermak. 'I know what you mean. A hot meal would've been welcome, for sure. Not convinced I could've kept it down though.'

'Nervous?'

'Aren't you?'

A bolt of incandescent orange shot past Jann and exploded in the pit. The blackened logs leapt into life, hot bright flames flickering up almost to his face. 'Oi!' he shouted, staggering backward.

'Why waste time with traditional methods when you live with the Fire Witch,' Elaine said, a broad smile curling the edges of her mouth.

'Fair point, but there's no need to set *me* on fire,' Jann said, rubbing his scorched eyebrows. 'At least not with... you know... actual fire.'

'How are we going to do this?' Piers Tremaine asked as he emerged from the Pilgrim's hut.

It had been a squeeze, all seven of them spending the night in the old man's single-roomed dwelling, but at least they had no trouble keeping warm. As far as Jann knew, his lover had not called on her powers to maintain a comfortable temperature even in the dead of night. Body heat had been enough.

'If you don't know, we're all doomed,' Kyle laughed, following him out into the cold, grey day.

'Has anyone felt anything of the Rohantu?' Claire asked. 'I haven't, but we're quite a distance from the mountain up here. Perhaps we should start down?'

Jann retrieved three more bepermak from his saddlebag and handed them out. 'I told Ru'ita to meet us here,' he said. 'I don't want to leave before she arrives. Sit. Have your breakfast, such as it is. And no, I've had no sign.'

'What do you mean, "felt anything"?' Kyle asked, taking a seat on a large rock beside the fire pit. 'I've heard you talk of these golems before but I'm not sure I understood the story.'

Jann left it to Claire to explain the strange mental double-vision that occurred in the presence of the Blood Clones. He stood with Piers and Patrick, gazing towards the setting of the tale she told. After a moment, Ahnak joined them.

'Where is this Punkana?' the young northerner asked.

'Pun'Akarnya. It's down there,' Jann said, pointing along the rocky valley path to the mouth of the Sun Besaraya, 'in the centre of the granite quadrangle.'

'How far?'

'Only a short ride, once the Queen joins us.'

'And you're sure this is the only place?' Piers said. 'There are no other locations where an Uterban can be made?'

A memory of Petani's words, spoken during the battle that had created the mountain, came back to Jann. '...*the rocks of the Valley have spoken to me. This is not merely the best place for the portal ceremony. It is the only place. If we can stop it here, today, we will have stopped it for all time.*' He opened his mouth to reply, but Ahnak beat him to it.

'It not case of "can be made",' his son said. 'Gate is gate. It is where it is. Only need to be opened.'

'He's right,' Jann nodded. 'And the larger the gate, the more distant its end-point, the fewer of them there are. I can't be certain, but this may well be the only gate that can be called an Uterban.'

'We've told everyone it's here now anyway,' Patrick said. 'Too late for a change of heart.'

'This very powerful place,' Ahnak continued. 'Many gates here. Hundreds.'

'So you'll definitely be able to get me back to Temmok'Dun?' Piers asked. 'To be honest I'm more worried about that than I am about taking down your mountain.'

'Gate to Temmok'Dun over there,' Ahnak said, pointing.

'There's another one, down near the beach,' Jann said. 'I noticed it when we were here with Felice. We won't need to use it, unless you're in a hurry to leave. Won't be anyone at the Wall of the World until tomorrow. You may as well spend another pleasant evening with us, and gate northwards in the morning.'

'Felice should be pretty close by now,' Patrick said. 'Somewhere over there,' he waved a hand in the direction of Borok Duset, its small peak visible above the hills to the east. 'I expect they'll be the first to arrive.'

'Let's hope we have something for them,' Piers said.

At the sound of kudo hooves on gravel behind them, the four men turned as one. The sight of the Queen, dressed all in black, galloping down the hill on her black mount, her ebony hair streaming out behind her, sent an electric thrill along Jann's spine. She moved like a memory of midnight, a stark contrast to the gleaming white of the snow-covered ground and the pale grey of the early morning sky.

'Ru'ita!' Claire called, standing and waving. 'Over here!'

The Queen raised her staff in acknowledgement, and spurred her galloping steed to even greater haste.

Pembrang looked unaffected by their hard ride, but since the Queen was a master of healing, perhaps it was only to be expected. Jann held the animal's reins as she dismounted.

'Well met, my fellow Elementals,' she said, smiling. 'When do we start?'

'Do you not want to rest a while, Ru'ita?' Kyle asked,

'after such an arduous journey?'

A faint flash of blue light ran the length of the Queen's staff from heel to tip in response. 'I am rested enough, thank you my dear,' she said. 'Well begun is half done. And if this task is to be anything like as macabre as these gentlemen have suggested, we may all need our rest *after* the fact. We must face tomorrow's tests with fresh hearts and minds. I am ready to begin now, if you are?'

A murmur of assent passed around the fire pit. Elaine and Kyle stood and joined the rest of the group. Claire and Ahnak led their kudai from the makeshift corral beside the Pilgrim's hut.

They completed the short ride to the base of Pun'Akarnya in silence. Jann's thoughts were occupied with the enormity of tomorrow's task. The mountain was Stone work. If the Rohantu were indeed still alive, in the face of all logic, he would deal with that problem when it arose. Elaine rode close beside him, glancing at him from time to time but saying nothing.

The path ended at the edge of the granite quadrangle. It still bore the scars of the battle that had taken place here only eleven months before. Pun'Akarnya towered over them, its glassy black surfaces reflecting the pale day in distorted lines.

'How many Rohantu were there?' Piers asked, dismounting without taking his eyes off the mountain.

'Five,' Jann said. 'One for each of the Elements — sorry, *first-tier* Elements — and one for him.' He jerked a thumb in Patrick's direction, grinning.

'No Gatekeeper clone?'

'No. We all wondered why, and commented how dangerous a gate would be without a keeper, but we never uncovered a reason. Maybe the old King only had enough Bloodpower for five?'

'Too late to ask him now,' the Queen said.

'Thank Baka!' Elaine said, with a shudder.

Piers walked over to the base of the mountain. It had

been created from towers of rock, summoned from the earth by Petani, heated into soft magma by the power of the Witch, and rehardened under the influence of Wind and Water. The face rose sheer from the quadrangle. Its vertical lines twisted into a spiral where the powerful cyclone called up by the Air Mage had taken hold. Fully one hundred metres high, the top thirty metres or so curved inward before lancing through a perfect annular ring of crystalline rock. The circumference of what would have been a new vortex if the Blood King's plans had been realised.

The Stone Mage lay a hand on the surface of the rock and closed his eyes. The group remained hushed, allowing him to focus his attention on whatever message the rock would convey. Only the crashing of the Lum Segar, its muddy brown waves flowing in and out of the river mouth, disturbed the silence.

Piers opened his eyes. 'This rock is very brittle,' he said, 'quite common for igneous material. I could shatter it. Bring it down in one go. But that would scatter boulders over the whole Valley. We'd have to retreat back up the hill a way. And if those Blood Clones *are* still alive, we would have to clamber over a pile of debris to reach them.'

'You can't tell if they're in there or not?' Kyle asked.

'I'm a Stone Mage,' Piers said, frowning. 'I can tell there's a chamber in there. The rock solidified where it stood, it didn't collapse in. But I can't sense Bloodpower. I doubt I'd recognise it if I tripped over it.'

'No, you would know,' Elaine said, her face set into a grimace of disgust. 'Especially if you were the one who'd been cloned.'

'So what's the plan?' Jann said. Noon was rapidly approaching. If they did not make a start soon they could well be fighting the Rohantu as night fell.

'We're all here,' Piers replied, 'except Petani, but that's not a problem. We don't need more Earth, we need to get rid of what we have. I think the safest way to take it down is the same way you put it up.'

'Melt it, you mean?' Elaine said. 'How is having hundreds of tons of flowing lava less dangerous than a valley full of flying boulders?'

'I can direct the flow. Soon as it starts to sag I can send it down the valley, away from us. Start at the top, with that ring. No danger of opening up the chamber at that point. Work down from there. By the time any Rohantu can emerge we'll have most of it down and can concentrate on dealing with them.'

'And how do we do that?' Claire asked. 'If they are alive then four of us will be next to useless. We'll be feeling like zombies as soon as the clones appear.'

Piers shrugged. 'If you can't open the Uterban here while the mountain stands, then it needs bringing down. Once I've done my bit, the rest is up to you guys.'

'The Stone Mage is correct,' the Queen said, stamping the heel of her staff against the granite floor, 'and we should make a start. I will assist where I may.' She held out her staff. 'There is more to this rod than you have seen me wield up to now. The healing, and the warding I employed during the expedition to the Batu'n ship. Take heart, my friends. We will meet this menace and defeat it, have no fear.'

'Very well then,' said Elaine, stepping forward. Jann felt a backwash of Fire power as his lover summoned it. The first soft glow of warmth escalated rapidly until he could no longer stand near her. He backed away, his eyes never leaving her. A stream of flaming power leapt from her hands to the top of Pun'Akarnya, suffusing the granite ring with fiery orange light.

For a moment, nothing happened. The ring remained, sitting rigidly at attention atop the mountain. It began to glow, darkly ruddy at first but soon turning a brighter red. Slowly, it relaxed in the wash of heat, melting into the mountain side and dripping in large gobs of crimson magma down the eastern face.

'Perfect!' Piers said. 'Now the summit.'

'I know, give me chance!' the Witch replied lifting her hands from her sides and directing her power in twin beams which struck the peak from left and right.

Jann took hold of Piers' arm and pulled him away from Elaine's side. He stepped closer to speak into the Stone Mage's ear. 'Her temper rises with her power,' he said. 'I'd advise against any further "help". She knows what she's doing.'

Piers stared at Elaine, standing rapt with power and continuing the flow of sparking energies. 'Yes,' he said, looking back at Jann. 'perhaps you're right. I need to focus on my own gift in any case.'

He moved away, taking up a position behind Elaine but further uphill. Her efforts had reduced the height of Pun'Akarnya by almost ten metres. Under Piers' influence the lambent rock streamed to the far side, funnelling safely down in a red-hot torrent. It flowed rapidly to the water's edge, where it sent up a plume of spitting steam.

'We should all move back,' Jann said, standing behind Piers and noticing for the first time that the Queen was sending pale streams of healing energy to the two working Elementals. She nodded, and stepped away from the mountain. Patrick and Kyle complied. Claire and Ahnak remained where they were, staring up at the glowing peak.

'Come away, you two,' Jann said. 'Ahnak? Claire?'

Claire gave a strangled cry. Her hands flew to her head and she collapsed onto one knee. 'Aaaah! They are alive. I...' She glanced around, holding out her hands in front of her. '...I can't see.'

Ahnak rushed to her side, taking hold of her shoulders to save her from toppling forward. 'What is it Clayer?'

'The Rohantu. My clone is...'

The mirrored streams of Fire power from Elaine faltered and died. She put one hand to her eyes. 'Mine too,' she said. 'I can't access—'

A bolt of pure white Fire emerged from the top of the

mountain, shooting straight upwards and blasting away what remained of the lava. Smoking blobs of molten rock the size of kudai rained down on the Valley, striking the ground and splashing in fiery cascades. The thin trails of blue light from the Queen's staff ceased as she stepped in front of Jann and held the wood aloft, swinging it in a wide arc.

A pane of smoky black energy followed the path of the staff, above the Elementals. A dome of protective warding force similar to the dark wall Jann had seen at the coast. As the dome flexed into position, a ball of molten rock struck it, bursting into a myriad teardrops of fire which fell harmlessly to the ground all around them.

From inside the mountain, a tornado of dark, red air arose, twisting out of the Rohantu's prison.

'Aaaah!' Claire cried again, her eyes rolling up to reveal bloodshot whites as Ahnak cradled her head.

The gust of contorted crimson air doubled in size. When the first drafts carried over to the Elementals, it brought smells of old blood and rotting flesh.

'Ugh!' Kyle said, grimacing. 'Are these things alive or not?'

The remaining stump of Pun'Arkanya glowed dully. The force of the swirling red wind peeled it back like a grisly alien fungus, releasing its spores. The Rohantu emerged, climbing over the hot rocks as if they were taking a morning stroll. Three of them appeared as Jann remembered - blood-red mannequins without distinguishing features. The remaining two, leaving the pit together, had lost their colour and now appeared to be completely translucent without any discernible hue.

'What's happened to those two?' Patrick asked, holding his hands to his head. 'I can tell my double is still active, though its influence feels diminished compared with our last encounter.'

'Perhaps it is you who are enhanced, Juggler,' the Queen said, keeping her eyes on her protective shield, 'rather than the golem which is lesser?'

'Lautan is no longer with us,' Jann said, staring at the approaching figures. 'And Petani travelled north. Could they be the Water and Earth clones? Kyle, do you feel OK?'

'I'm scared shitless if that's what you mean,' the new Water Wizard replied, 'but I don't feel any of that doubling you've all talked about.'

'Will that help us stand against them?' Ahnak said, helping Claire to her feet. 'If half cannot access any Elemental power?'

'I feel a little better now,' Claire said, wiping a hand over her face. 'It's passing off.'

'You're right,' Elaine agreed. 'I'm feeling stronger too.'

'Lucky you!' Patrick said, holding his stomach. 'I feel sicker than ever.'

Jann had not taken his eyes from the Rohantu. They negotiated the rocks with dogged determination and would soon attain the Valley floor. They could not be more than two hundred metres away. The two pale clones walked in lockstep, side by side. To his horror, their arms touched, and coalesced, flowing together to form a single limb. The one on the left turned to move closer to the other and then seemed to step into its companion. Within moments they had become one figure, roughly twice the size of the originals. The new giant took on a blue hue.

'Oh God!' Jann exclaimed. 'Look!'

Once the amalgamation of the two non-aligned clones was complete, the remaining pair, initially imitating Air and Fire, also coalesced. As the last distinguishing feature of the absorbed clone — a hand — disappeared, the lurching figure glowed a dull orange.

'No wonder you feel better Claire. Elaine. They are no longer tapping your powers.'

'Then who—?' Claire said, glancing around in terror. Beside her the Queen stood motionless, staff held limply in her right hand. Her pale face was locked in a vacant expression as she stared at the marching golems. 'I...' she said.

The shield of black warding force blew apart, dissipating into the afternoon air as mysteriously as it had appeared. With a shock of understanding, Jann glanced at Piers. He too stared sightlessly at the place where the mountain had stood. A thin trail of drool ran down his chin.

'They've abandoned the first-tier Elements!' Jann said. 'Wood and Stone are more powerful, and they are here! The golems have templates they can copy!'

'We must retreat,' Patrick said. 'They are almost upon us!'

'Elaine!' Jann took her arm. 'Can you hold them off?'

The Fire Witch stepped in front of him and sent a bolt of white Fire at the nearest Rohantu — the Wood clone. A black smudge of warding power appeared in front of it, absorbing the flame. The clone continued its advance.

Claire dragged Piers away while Ahnak tugged at the Queen's arm. 'Come, Rooter!' he shouted. 'You must move up the path!'

In response to his words, the Queen's staff began to emit a thrumming sound. A lance of cardinal red energy flew from the wood, over Ahnak's shoulder, and struck a durmak tree growing beside the path. The trunk exploded in a shower of splinters.

'Ach!' Ahnak cried, falling backwards and clutching his neck. The beam had burned a track across his shirt. Blood welled into the scorched material, soaking out in a dark red oval.

'Ahnak!' Claire screamed as another red bolt passed over his head, narrowly missing him.

'It is attack force,' the Queen mumbled. 'I can't...' She dropped her staff and fell to the ground in a faint. A third jet of bright attacking energy fired upwards, dissipating harmlessly in the air. Kyle flicked a hand toward the wood. A torrent of water appeared above it, crashing down and dousing its power. The staff steamed.

'It can access the power, but not with any control,' Jann said. 'Not even with the staff.'

'We can't rely on that,' Kyle said. 'And my Water won't stop the staff for long.'

A memory of a kuclar and a group of children came clearly into Jann's mind. Would it work? Did they have any other options? 'Elaine! Claire! And you Kyle! Do anything you can to keep them together. And keep them coming.'

'Coming?' Elaine said, flashing him a horrified look. 'We want to stop these bastards, not give them the come-on!'

'This will stop them, if I can time it right,' he said, moving around behind the Queen. 'Just persuade them in this direction.'

The Witch fired off a volley of fireballs which landed in a line behind the Rohantu. They continued their measured approach, not speeding up or slowing down, and not deviating from their course.

'Good!' Jann said. 'More of that!'

Elaine shrugged. 'Sure. It had zero effect, but if it makes you happy.' Her hands flew back and forth, calling up Fire from all directions. Small, swiftly moving fireballs rained down, each closer to the clones than the last. A stiff breeze blew from the south, pushing their adversaries forward. Finally, Kyle summoned a truncated stream of water which dogged the blood clones' footsteps, discouraging any retreat.

'Why have they not—' Jann began. The rock in front of him erupted, rising swiftly into a small hillock and knocking him off his feet.

'Used Stone power?' Patrick said, grimacing. 'Perhaps it feels new to them. They haven't got the hang of it yet? More worrying is if — or when — they will use Void power.'

'I think I can stop them before then,' Jann said. 'With your help Claire?'

'What do you need?'

'The strongest pulse you've ever conjured, from the same direction as your wind. Imagine knocking them onto their faces.'

'Just tell me when,' the young Air Mage replied. 'It'll be a pleasure.'

The Patrick clone, the only remaining Rohantu of original size, veered off to Jann's left.

'Dammit!' he yelled. 'Ahnak?'

'I understand your plan, father,' Ahnak called. 'I am ready. We will require another Air pulse Clayer.'

Claire shot him a questioning glance.

'Do these two first. On my command. You'll understand in a moment. Follow that with the same for Ahnak. You OK with two in quick succession?'

She smiled. 'No problem.'

Jann held his breath as the Rohantu marched towards him. At the point where they would have crossed the gravel path, he gave his signal. 'Now Claire!'

The Air Mage clenched her fists and brought both arms to her chest in a hugging gesture. 'Nej!' she yelled.

With a loud soughing sound a powerful blast of air hit the largest two Rohantu in the back. They pitched forward. In front of them, at ground level, the grass rippled as a gate opened, swallowing the clones and closing with a pop.

'Perfect!' shouted Jann.

'Again Clayer!' shouted Ahnak, who now stood directly in front of the Juggler clone, almost close enough to reach out and touch it.

Another pulse ripped through the air. The Rohantu turned at the sound but it was too late to avoid. The current knocked the figure backwards into Ahnak's gate.

The Queen sat up, blinking. 'Where did they go?'

'I can't honestly tell you, Ru'ita,' Jann said, helping her to her feet. 'But they won't be back.'

lembaca ana
16th day of far'utamasa, 967

Dawn approached, painting the distant horizon with a pale, thin stroke. The day Patrick had long feared, and which had haunted his dreams since news of the Doom first broke, was here at last. For once, he had avoided those nightmares: he had not slept. His thoughts flipped between replaying their encounter with the Rohantu and imagining the terrors to come, once the Uterban was open.

'Did you sleep at all?'

Jann Argent emerged from the Pilgrim's hut, rubbing his eyes and squinting at the distant rays of dawn. He stopped at the woodpile, collected an armful of logs, and dumped them into the firepit, sending up a spray of dull red ash devils.

'No. I gave up in the end. Your snoring didn't help.'

'I don't snore,' Jann said, taking a seat beside him. 'You must be thinking of Elaine.'

'You cheeky beggar!' the Fire Witch said, taking a third perch. 'Fine, well-rested bunch we are,' she added. 'The future of everyone on the planet depends on a handful of mages who can't even conjure a night's sleep for themselves. At least I can do something about this!'

She pointed at the struggling fire, which immediately erupted with long, snaking tongues of flame.

Patrick held out his hands to the warmth. 'We were lucky with the clones,' he said.

Jann snorted. 'Lucky? That was pure skill.'

'A few centimetres lower with that bolt of red from the Queen's staff, and Ahnak would be dead. And without him, that last golem — my golem — would have reached me, and maybe even...'

His throat closed on the words. He hardly dared imagine the horrors a Juggler-clone could create, let alone give voice to them.

'How is Ahnak, anyway? That was a nasty wound.'

'Ru'ita dealt with it,' Elaine said. 'Not much more than a red welt there now. He's fine.'

'Deny it all you like.' Patrick continued. 'We came through the encounter by pure chance. And compared with what we might be up against today, they were like children's dolls. We need a plan. It's too dangerous to wing it.'

'A plan for what?' asked Claire as she, Ahnak, and Kyle joined the others by the fire. 'Breakfast? I'm all for that kind of plan.'

'I have no appetite this morning,' Patrick said, 'for food or sleep. I'll be glad when this day is done, whatever the outcome.'

'Do not be so melancholy, Pattern Juggler,' the Queen's voice echoed from inside the hut. Her face appeared in the doorway. 'I have confidence in all of us, you especially. You must trust yourself. Your studies have been long and deep. You know your father's work inside out and back to front. Everything will play out as it is meant to be.'

'Thank, majesty, for gift of healing,' Ahnak said, rubbing his shoulder. 'Pain all gone.'

'You are most welcome, young Ahnak,' the Queen said. 'And please, as I have requested many times, I am not "your Majesty", especially in this company. Ru'ita, Kayshirin if you must — or Wood Mage — but I no longer consider myself royal. This day marks the end of the great houses in any case. The line of the Blood King is ended, I shall be the last Queen, and the realms will soon be nothing but rubble and dust. Your people do not have royalty, do they?'

'They do not, Ru'ita.'

'Well then. It makes no sense for me to cling on to airs and graces, bowing and scraping. I am one of you, and you are all my equals. Now. What of this plan you speak of Juggler? And what part is there in it for me?'

The morning wore on as they discussed the options. The feeble sun crawled reluctantly clear of the mountains and slowly dispelled the early morning mists from the valley below them. They made a simple breakfast with what provisions remained from their meagre stores. Their last meal together and, for some, the last they would eat on this planet. Jann had selected another log for the dwindling fire when a voice echoed down the valley from the path above the hut.

'Whose friendly fire is this that offers warmth and comfort to the weary traveller?'

Felice Waters, riding beside her partner Jo and heading a long line of refugees from the eastern villages, made her way down the incline towards them.

Patrick caught Jann's eye. 'I guess that means we'd better make a start,' he said.

'As must I,' Piers said.

The last to emerge from his bed, he at least had managed a decent sleep. Patrick suspected the Queen had been sending healing energy his way throughout the night. Even after his Elemental exertions of the previous day he looked fresh and renewed.

'If you would oblige, Gatekeeper?' the Stone Mage added, bowing in his direction.

'Give me a moment, Jann Argent,' Ru'ita said, 'if you will. I must ensure you are at your best for the task ahead, Banshirin. I shall not be there to aid you in your endeavours.'

She reached out with her staff, touching Piers on the forehead. No spark or bolt of healing energy left the wood. Instead its entire length was suffused with deep cerulean, the soft glow increasing until blue light illuminated the sides of the Pilgrim's hut. The faces of the surrounding Elementals took on an alien hue, their eyes reflecting the power back towards its wielder. With a soft susurration, the blue energy flowed from the staff until it covered Piers from head to toe. It radiated from his outline as though — a flash of a memory from one of Patrick's advertising campaigns came to his mind — as though he had become radioactive.

'Wow!' Piers said, smiling broadly. He turned his hands over in front of him, watching the lines of blue energy flux and swirl. 'I feel like I could split the comet from here, never mind take down a mountain.'

'Then my work is done,' Ru'ita said, returning his smile. 'Your turn, Gatekeeper.'

'What? Oh, yes. Of course. It's up here.'

He turned and walked past the hut, past the log store, and across the rock-strewn surface of the western valley slope. Piers followed.

'We'll just wait here then, shall we?' Felice shouted from the path. 'Not like we've been riding since midnight or anything.'

Patrick laughed. 'Sorry! Give us a moment. No point dismounting. You can follow us to the quad once Jann taken care of Piers.'

The pop of a closing gate resounded from behind the hut. Jann returned, hands in his pockets. 'OK, that's done,' he said. 'Let's go.'

The Elementals led the way along the rocky path to the valley floor, followed by Felice and her contingent of leavers. Elaine dropped back to explain what would be expected of them. Part of their overnight discussions had involved the kudai. The animals had never existed on Earth, so none could ride through the Uterban. There was more than one reason for this decision. Kudai were easily spooked at the best of times. Their rough calculations had made no allowance for any interruption to the flow of people through the portal.

Patrick's stomach flipped at the sight of the ruins of Pun'Akarnya. That was yesterday's battle. Today's lay before him, imagined horrors pulling at his resolve, tearing his confidence, and shredding his concentration.

Though they believed the three of them — himself, Jann, and Ahnak — could create the Uterban on their own, they must keep something in reserve. Their final escape also required a gate. The plan was tight, with no room for error or delay. When the last of the leavers traversed the portal, the comet would be almost upon them. If they had nothing left for that last gate, they would die alone in this barren and fateful place.

Claire, Elaine, and Kyle took up their traditional positions at the corners of the quadrangle. Since the Uterban would open at ground level there would be no ring of flying magma. Instead they would supplement Patrick's Void power with streams of Elemental energy. In Piers' absence, Ru'ita stood at the Earth corner, completing the square. Though Wood power was not associated with Earth, it was the best they could do in the circumstances.

'Come on,' Jann said. 'Let's do this.'

'Well begun is half done!' called the Wood Mage from her corner.

'I swear I'm gonna kill someone the next time I hear that,' Patrick said through gritted teeth.

Jann laughed. 'You're only annoyed because she's right.'

Patrick reached inside his tunic. He had been wearing his father's amulet for so long, he no longer noticed its weight, or the way it swayed under his clothes. It was warm from his skin. Its familiar pattern of interlocking circles soothed his irritation, nestling in his mind like a key in a lock, or an enzyme operating on a substrate. He could feel the power building. Though the flat, barren landscape lay undisturbed, he already held an image of the Uterban in his mind. He closed his eyes to concentrate on it more fully. The familiar black smoke of Void power swirled behind his eyes, waiting.

'Whenever you're ready guys,' he murmured.

Jann and his son had never worked together to open a gate before. But this was no ordinary gate. The original had involved components no longer available to them. Music being the main one. No records existed to explain exactly what it brought to the mix. Only the Pilgrim exhibited any understanding of that aspect of magic, and he was not here. Its absence was another worry. He hoped having two Gatekeepers acting in harmony might restore the balance of energies, but nothing was certain.

With his eyes closed he could not watch what father and son were doing, but he could feel its result. A small ripple in space, a few metres above the ground. Too high!

'Lower Jann,' he said, but his friend was already on the case. The ripple he had felt was only the top of the Uterban. It opened a few degrees from the vertical, so the uppermost edge appeared first. He took the amulet in his right hand, gathered his power, and sent it streaming towards the emerging portal. A murmur of surprise passed along the ranks of evacuees waiting patiently in the cold morning. A few kudai snickered their alarm at the unnatural sight. Patrick renewed his concentration and his line of energy. The amulet trembled in his palm, the first time it had been used since his father fell through the original portal. The heat of his body was supplemented by the artefact's own heat as the power passed through it and out into the centre of the quadrangle.

'It's done,' Jann said.

Patrick opened his eyes. At the intersection between the four corners, an opaque grey oval stood. Fully twelve metres across and perhaps six high, its circumference delimited by a thick cloud of roiling Void power, the almost-vertical surface of the Uterban surged and swelled like an uneasy ocean. Unlike the original vortex, and the more recent one that had started to open before being shattered by the spear of Pun'Akarnya, nothing could be seen beyond it. No stars, no tunnel, not even blackness. Only the faint grey swirls, an unnerving combination of pellucid pool and obscured glass.

'Let's go!' Patrick said, waving at Felice while maintaining his concentration on the massive gate.

Felice and Jo Granger stood ready. He remembered

them saying something about wanting a frontier life but worrying about being treated like witches. They had been determined to go first. Hand in hand, the two women ran across the valley floor and up onto the raised quadrangle. They covered the short distance to the Uterban in no time, waved to the Elementals, and hit the portal without hesitation. The grey mist absorbed them soundlessly. Nothing marked their passage. One moment they were there, the next, gone.

'Come on, all of you,' Jann shouted. 'You've seen how it's done!'

The next small group of leavers, who appeared to be part of the same family, joined hands and hurried to the Uterban's surface. After a short pause, they stepped through. No sound. No sign. The absence of any reaction bolstered the confidence of the long queue. Those at the front who were on their feet moved as one towards the grey. Those behind began swiftly and quietly to dismount. No-one spoke. Whether they did not trust their voices with words of encouragement, or had said everything that needed saying, Patrick could not tell.

'Let's hope your lot get here as quickly, Ru'ita,' Jann said.

'Indeed, Gatekeeper,' she replied, 'and the Reds. So far, so good.'

A shiver ran along Patrick's spine. There was time enough yet for trouble.

foothills of temmok'dun
16th day of far'utamasa, 967

Piers Tremaine stepped from the gate feeling like he had been twisted inside out. His first journey through a gate, and he hoped it would be his last. He ran his hands carefully over himself. Other than nausea and a nagging headache, he could find no physical damage.

'Stone Mage!' called a familiar voice from behind him.

'At last!'

He spun around. Petani approached from the direction of the mountain, together with two other grey-bearded men, all shielding their eyes from the low morning sun. The Gardener's comment, and the brightness of the light compared with the Valley, gave him a tingle of concern.

'Am I late?'

'Tana bless you boy, no,' Petani laughed. 'We are early. We have been camped here since last night. The sun has not long been up.'

'And all this morning mist is softening my scrolls,' said the man on his left. Recognition dawned on Piers. It was the Keeper of the Keys. The other old soul was a stranger. He said nothing, but gazed into the distance with rheumy eyes.

'Indeed,' Petani continued. 'As I understand the plan, we should make a start as soon as you feel up to it. You look a little pale.'

Piers smiled. 'Only minor after-effects of one of Jann Argent's gates,' he said. 'I'm sure it will pass. Where is the point of entry?'

'We have surveyed the area, and all is as the Gatekeeper related,' the Keeper said. 'The origin of the Sun Besaraya is over here.'

He walked off towards a gentle slope, the earliest beginnings of the imposing wall of rock that stood before them. Temmok'Dun. Shadows thrown by the slanting sun cut deep black lines on its face. Before long, Piers heard the roar of falling water. As they rounded an outcrop of rock the cascade came into view. 'This is close enough,' he said. 'Where is the rest of your party? Once I begin to lower the mountain, whatever lies behind that fall will be released. I have no control over it. They must keep their distance.'

'Yes, yes, we have thought of that,' the Keeper said with a shake of his head. 'Our camp is over there, the river is over here. The flood will still follow its course, no matter how rapidly you release it, Stone Mage. At least, I hope fervently that is the case. Any overflow will—'

'Soften your scrolls,' Piers finished for him, smiling. 'Yes, I get the picture.'

He waited, watching the sunlight moving over the rocks, looking for any hint of a natural fault line or eroded crevice that might provide a starting point. In the end, with many millions of tons of mountain to move, it mattered little where he made a start. The caldera Jann Argent had spoken of lay several hundred metres behind the waterfall. It was a vast bowl, impossible to miss when moving directly north from this point. He looked around. The three old men regarded him with unreadable expressions, holding their silence. The weight of expectation settled on Piers' shoulders. Almost as heavy as the mountain. With a silent prayer of thanks to the Wood Mage for her parting gift of healing strength, he summoned his Stone power and bent to his task.

The old men switched their attention to the rockface. At first, nothing happened. Piers closed his eyes, the better to concentrate. The intense feeling as the energies began to flow — stronger than he had ever known — made him gasp.

'Stone—' Petani said, silenced instantly by Piers' upraised hand. He reached out towards Temmok'Dun and redoubled his efforts, opening himself totally to the source of Stone power and channelling it towards Sun Besaraya's spring. The rock groaned. He opened his eyes to see what was happening. Below the waterfall, the face of the mountain shivered. For a moment, it seemed the water had turned black. But it was not water. The stone itself was flowing. Not molten — it showed no sign of heat — it softened and ran in a dozen streams down the rockface, like rivulets of wax on the side of a pillar candle. With a redoubled roar, the reservoir atop the waterfall gave way. A solid curtain of silver dropped behind the rock, hitting the ground at the base of the mountain and flying up in a glittering shower of droplets, turning to liquid mercurial fire as they caught the morning sun and fell back into the river.

Behind the flood, the rock continued to subside, like a dark, deflated balloon. Before the final full wave of the lake had flowed away, a passage fully fifteen metres wide had opened in the mountainside, its depths hidden by the hard shadows of the early morning. A fine spray of mist lit the opening in rainbow colours, lending another air of magic to an already otherworldly scene.

With his arms still raised, Piers glanced at Petani. 'Tell everyone to prepare,' he said, 'and follow along behind me. I must move closer now to maintain the flow of power to the right place. We have to start moving the people through the pass if the last of them are to cover enough ground for me to raise the mountain behind us.'

'At once, Stone Mage,' Petani said with a curt nod. He shepherded his fellow ancients off in the direction of their camp.

Piers returned his attention to the pass. He stepped forward, down the slight incline. Drops of spray misted his face, chilling his skin and hinting at the beginnings of another headache. He ignored it. The depths of Stone power he had called upon brooked no interruptions; no distractions. He entered the mouth of the pass he had created, singing a song of Stone that the ancient mass of Temmok'Dun could not ignore.

Iembaca ana
16th day of far'utamasa, 967

They had been lucky so far.

From the position of the lambent sun in the pale winter sky, Patrick judged it to be mid-morning. Soon after the liquid grey surface of the Gate had crystallised, it became clear to the other Elementals that their energies were not required to maintain it. They had taken on supervisory duties, ushering the crowd into position, murmuring words of encouragement and instruction, and releasing their kudai. The animals, freed of their human burdens, took no persuading to run away from the rippling Uterban, their eyes flashing white with fright.

Led by Sebaklan Pwalek, those travelling from Court had joined the throng of leavers from the east shortly after the Elementals had brought the Uterban into existence. Pwalek did not take his turn at the portal when he came to the head of the queue. Instead, like a true leader, he hung back to allow his people to take their step into the unknown. His gentle words of encouragement reached Patrick across the still air of the morning. The man also lent a hand with the kudai, treating the animals with the same respect as he had the people. The more Patrick saw of this man the more impressed he became. If only it had been him at the Blood King's right hand in place of the crooked Jester. How different things might have been. A brief glance at the approaching comet set him straight on that score. The course of history in the interim years may have changed, but they would still have brought everyone to this point.

He had yet to feel any ill-effects of such prolonged use of Void power. As far as he could tell Jann and Ahnak also fared well. Their expressions showed signs of weariness, perhaps, but so far they had voiced no complaints, and the stream of refugees continued unabated and unabashed. No-one shied away from stepping through the grey curtain. Indeed many had appeared joyful and relieved at the prospect of their escape from the Doom.

And — Patrick suppressed a shiver — there had also, so far, been no sign of the creatures of the nether world through which the Uterban passed.

The Wood Mage stood on one side of the quadrangle, her staff planted on the granite in front of her. Three thin streams of brilliant blue healing energy snaked out from the staff towards the three who held the Uterban open.

Where the power touched him, Patrick felt a warm glow, but otherwise its impact was unnoticeable. Except, of course, that it made him feel he could keep going for the rest of the day and probably all of tomorrow. His fears regarding use of his power almost forgotten, he nevertheless kept a watchful eye on the greyness. They would come, he was certain. It was a question of when, not if.

'Here,' said a voice, catching him by surprise. Claire Yamani stood beside him, holding out a waterskin. 'You must be thirsty.'

'Thank you,' he said, accepting the heavy skin and taking a deep draught. The water was cold and clean. He felt it all the way down. He waited for the brain freeze to pass before taking another drink.

'How's it going?' Claire asked.

'So far, so good,' he said. 'How are the others doing?'

'Everyone seems in high spirits. It helps that there's a constant stream of people leaving. Boosts the confidence to know others have preceded you. I was impressed with Felice and Jo. Not sure I would've gone first!'

'Don't you trust me? Or Jann?' He winked at her. 'Surely you trust Ahnak?'

She laughed. 'I guess. I trust him enough to go with him, when it's his turn, so there's that.'

'He can't leave until the last. You knew that, right?'

'I know. I've not thought about much else. Especially what you said about the time element. Who knows how far back the terminus will have stretched when it comes to us. We'll be traversing all the way into prehistory, knowing my luck.'

An uneasy silence fell. Patrick had no words of encouragement. The girl was right, and there was no avoiding the fact.

'I should go,' she said at length. 'Other thirsty customers.'

'Thanks.'

Above them, dominating the sky, the comet approached, now appearing twice the size of Pera-Bul. No-one had yet panicked, but nobody in the queue was hesitating either. Patrick looked up the hill. He recognised a few faces from Court. In the distance, starting down the path beyond the Pilgrim's hut, he thought he made out the figure of Seteh Seruganteh. The Palace contingent had arrived.

Across the quadrangle Claire was busy quenching Ahnak's thirst. From the corner of his eye Patrick spotted a strange ballooning at the Uterban's rim. Leavers continued to step through in the centre, but its edges began to stretch, giving the portal the appearance of an enormous donut. His heart hammered in his chest. His worst fears had been realised. They were here.

As he watched, black smoke billowed from the distended edge of the portal. It punctured the grey surface in several places, pouring out onto the ground where it roiled and swarmed.

'Heads up!' he shouted, catching the attention of the Elementals at the head of the queue. 'We've got company!'

The dark cloud gathered itself together, taking on a frightening form that resembled a demon from gothic horror. The refugee closest to the Uterban — a dark-haired woman Patrick recognised as one of the musicians from the Blood Court — screamed, her face twisted into a rictus of utter terror. She scrambled from the quadrangle, crashing into two others in the queue behind her who followed her example without a backward glance. The rest of the line backed away nervously. Two kudai reared, snickering in fright and unseating their riders. The ebony smoke beast stretched up on its half-formed hind legs, in an arcane mirror of the terrified animal. It raised black arms, rippling with dark sinews and terminating in enormous black-taloned claws. The monster stared directly at Patrick, sniffing the air. It opened its cavernous mouth and roared at him. Hot, foetid breath smothered him, stinking of death and decay. Beside it, to left and right, two further plumes of smoke issued from the sides of the gate and began to coalesce.

Behind the three Voiders, the centre of the flat grey surface of the Uterban started to spin, drawing its pearlescent face into a faint spiral pattern.

Chapter 25

Iembaca ana
16th day of far'utamasa, 967

A piercing beam of red energy flew across Patrick's line of sight. Ru'ita had called on the attack force of her staff, which the Wood-clone accessed the day before. The real Kayshirin had a far greater degree of control over her powers. The well-aimed bolt crossed the quadrangle, striking the first Voider on the shoulder. It passed through the beast, emerging on the other side and leaving a gaping hole around which the black smoke of Void power swirled. The monster roared at the impact, swivelling around to face its attacker. It grasped the line of force with both clawed hands and broke it into pieces like a rod of glass.

A feedback pulse of crackling red fire shot back towards the Wood Mage, knocking the staff from her hands and forcing her to stagger backward, arms flailing for balance.

'Ru'ita!' Claire called from the front of the queue. She sent a pulse of her own Air power in an attempt to unbalance the black beast. The shot missed its target and passed harmlessly through the second Voider, a small plume of dark smoke issuing from the monster's hip in its wake.

'Your powers are no use against these denizens of the Void!' Patrick called. 'Best you can do is distract them.'

The lead Voider remained focused on Ru'ita. It took a step towards her, venting another blood-chilling cry. A thick tendril of dark power issued from its chest, curling through the air in her direction.

'Save the Queen!' came a voice from Patrick's right. A mounted figure rode onto the quadrangle, its kudo's eyes milked with fright. It was Seteh Seruganteh, the steward from the Black Palace. 'Protect the Queeeen!' he shouted again, leaping from the saddle and throwing himself between Ru'ita and the vile black smoke. It hit him squarely between the shoulders. His battle cry faltered, reduced to a fearful, hollow gurgle. Where the Void power struck, his body dissolved into grey mist that fell to the ground and spread across the surface of the quad. Seteh's kudo screamed; a ear-piercing noise Patrick had never before heard. The terrified beast galloped white-eyed from the granite, barrelling into Kyle and knocking her over.

'Where do they come from?' Jann shouted, not taking his eyes from the nearest. 'What do they want?'

'I know not where they come from,' Patrick replied, 'only that they live in the void between worlds. The void your gates pass through. As to what they want, the answer is the same. Trapped in the void, they envy those who live in the real world and wield power here. They are hungry for that power. It feeds them. It promises freedom.'

The Voider Jann had been watching moved towards him. 'It senses your power. It is similar to its own,' Patrick said. 'It's unlikely you can trick it as you did with the Rohantu.'

'Well,' said his friend, 'it's the only trick I've got so...'

He stared hard at the approaching Voider. A shimmering silver gate opened immediately in front of it, too close for the beast to avoid stepping into it. Patrick held his breath in a silent prayer to whatever God was listening. For a moment, he believed Jann's ploy had worked. The Voider continued to move towards him until almost half its body had been consumed by the gate. A heartbeat later, the rear face of the gate glimmered in mirrored counterpoint to the front and the beast's leg reappeared. With a bizarre, momentary pause, as though the gate were several metres thick but compressed into a thin, sparkling oval, the Voider stepped through and back into their world, apparently unaffected.

'Best I can do,' Jann shouted. 'It only delays them a few seconds.'

'Argh! Death to the fell beasts from the netherworld!' came a cry from the crowd.

Patrick turned. Another rider sped out from the head of the queue. Sebaklan Pwalek, a drawn sword in his hand and a fire in his eyes. He reined his kudo to a skidding halt at the end of the quadrangle and jumped from the saddle, hitting the granite at a run.

'Pwalek! Stop!' Patrick cried. 'Your blade is no use against these creatures!'

But it was too late. The man reached the third Voider and took a swing at it. The Fire Witch ran after him, whether to stop him or help him, Patrick could not tell. Kyle Muir too picked herself up and followed the Witch. Perhaps they intended to attempt the power combination that had felled the girl's brother?

Pwalek's blade passed through the beast's arm. Against all logic, it appeared to sever the limb. But the cut did no more damage than a broom handle passing through smoke. The arm reformed behind the weapon almost as soon as it emerged. A ball of Fire from the Witch hit the Voider square in the chest. The beast appeared to inhale the glowing sphere. Its light dissipated in glowing lines across the monster's body before melting to black. As the veins of power faded, the beast grew taller, and broader. It roared again, its companions echoing the cry, which resounded along the Valley sending a chill through Patrick.

'You're feeding it, Bakara!' Patrick yelled. 'Don't use your powers against them directly.'

She did not need to be told twice. Redirecting her attention, she sent a bolt of Fire onto the rocks behind the monster. Granite exploded as the surface liquefied instantly. Chunks of rock passed through the smoky figure, puncturing small holes that filled as quickly as the cut in its arm. Undisturbed by the passage of the fragments, the beast turned its scrutiny back to Pwalek, who was still lunging and swinging with his sword.

To Patrick's horror, the enormous beast — now almost

twice the size of the others — took hold of Pwalek's sword arm with one claw, and swung him around. His blade flew through the air and buried itself point first in the soft earth beyond the granite quad. With its other claw the Voider grasped the man's leg, lofting him above its head with a guttural roar. Stretching its arms, the demon tore Pwalek's body in two, spraying the dark stone with his lifeblood. The grisly act was over before the Jester's right-hand man could make a sound. A stunned silence fell across the Valley, replaced almost instantly by a myriad screams and shouts from the line of refugees. They scrabbled and scrambled to escape back up the hill.

'We don't have time for this!' the Witch cried. 'Unless we stop them soon, the comet will be upon us before half these people are through the Uterban! Patrick! Do something!'

He glanced up, though no reminder of the impending Doom was necessary. The comet now filled fully a third of the sky. Heating up in the higher atmosphere, it left a smoky trail; a frightening reflection of the Void power below.

Elaine directed another bolt of Fire power at the Voider. Whether distracted by the closing threat from above or simply in frustration at their inability to stop the attack at ground level, Patrick did not know or care. If she continued, the three dwellers from the deep would soon become too powerful for anything to stop them.

'Elaine—' he began, the cry dying in his throat. The third Voider had taken hold of the flying Fire power in the same way the first had grasped Ru'ita's red beam. With an effortless flick of its enormous claw the beast reversed the Fire. The bolt of incandescence flew back towards the Fire Witch, striking her in the face. At the last instant, her hands flew up, too late to save her from the impact.

Her scream added to those from the crowd. She fell to the ground, holding her head. A huge gout of water appeared in the air above her, cascading down to douse the flames in a roiling cloud of steam. Kyle Muir knelt over her, murmuring something Patrick could not catch.

'Elaine!' Jann cried. Still trying to delay the first Voider by opening one gate after another, he could not reach his partner. Across the quadrangle, Ahnak opened a third gate, directly between the two his father had created. The Voider was forced to pass through all three to make any progress. Ru'ita stepped from the granite slab to retrieve her staff.

'Will there be any more?' Jann said, his face telegraphing his agony at being unable to help his lover.

His friend's question rolled around Patrick's mind before swivelling and clicking into place like the last piece of a jigsaw. All his many months of study had led to this moment. All his observations, all his long, lonely nights of vigil sat staring out across the bay. He had examined the knowledge from every angle, and puzzled over the last page of his father's lore book which had clung steadfastly to a secret it refused to reveal. Now, at last, in a surge of sudden, unexpected, and crystal clarity, that secret was uncovered.

'No,' he said. 'There will be no more. Not while these are here. They travel in threes.'

As the last word left his lips, Patrick knew what he had to do. He reached once again inside his tunic, where his father's amulet nestled. It was hot to the touch.

Another roar came, this time from the second Voider. The first was still delayed by the two Gatekeepers' maze of gates. The third had been temporarily distracted by Bakara's bolts. But during Patrick's brief moment of introspection, the Voider which emerged from the furthest edge of the Uterban had crept close behind Kyle Muir. Now, it took hold of the Water Wizard, an arm in each claw. She screamed, twisting and struggling in a vain attempt to free herself.

'Help!' she cried, 'Elaine! Claire!'

At her cry, the Fire Witch's hands fell from her face,

revealing a mass of blisters and deep, angry red burns. She stared sightlessly after Kyle, her eyes swollen shut. 'Kyle?' she cried, an edge of panic in her voice. 'What's happening to her, Claire?'

Where the monster's claws gripped Kyle, her skin turned black. Dark lines of Void snaked up her arms and disappeared under her sleeves, to reappear seconds later at her neck. The beast dragged her backwards, towards the Uterban, still kicking hopelessly. Her fearful screams took on an unearthly hollowness, as if her voice had already left this world and occupied the Void before her body joined it.

'Patrick!' Claire shouted. 'Do something! Stop them!'

There was nothing he could do. The Voider disappeared back beyond the Gate, dragging Kyle Muir soundlessly behind it.

lembaca ana
16th day of far'utamasa, 967

The last few metres of mountain melted away in front of Piers. The warm air of the caldera blew gently into his face, dispelling the chill of Utamasa that had followed them along the pass all the way from the southern face of Temmok'Dun. The volcanic bowl looked every bit as beautiful as Jann Argent had said, but he had no time to enjoy the view. There was yet more work to do this day, and it must be done while he still had strength.

'Can you not take a moment's rest?' Petani asked. 'At least have a drink, now that we are certain of our water supply.'

'Fill me a skin then,' he replied, 'and I'll take it with me. But I must start back. Look.'

He pointed upwards. Petani and his two ancient shadows needed no reminding. The comet, with its smoking tail, dominated the morning sky.

'If that hits before I close the pass, or before I can

raised enough mass of rock, this whole journey will have been in vain. All this beauty, which we have only this moment laid our eyes on, will be blasted to dust.'

'I know, I know,' the Gardener said. 'Should I come back with you? Perhaps I can—'

Piers held up a hand. 'Thank you, Petani. I know your offer comes from a good place. But I can travel more swiftly alone. Help the others. We may have to stay here for some days. I doubt I will have strength left for more mountaineering after today. Without Ru'ita we cannot restore my health with any haste. We are fortunate this oasis is so well stocked. I'm sure these good people will be happy for the rest and recuperation a stay here will afford.'

He gripped the old man's hand, shaking it firmly. 'I will be back soon, have no fear.'

He took the newly-filled water skin from the Keeper of the Keys. 'Good luck Stone Mage,' the wrinkled archivist said, smiling. 'May Baka and Tana guard your steps and lend their strength to your own.'

'Thank you, Pelaran,' he said, returning the old man's smile. Trust the Keeper to quote the names of the two gods whose Elements combined in the power of Stone. His learning was legendary and unparalleled. 'From your lips to their exalted ears.'

He bowed, and turned back to the pass. A stream of remainers issued from the rock mouth, gratitude and relief spreading smiles across all their faces as the warmth of the caldera met them. Several called their thanks and greetings to him as he passed. If only their good wishes could convey renewed strength. He was at the limit of his powers, but he could not delay. His architect's mind busied itself calculating exactly how many metres of rock would be required to stop the blast wave from Ahnak's Doom. The result was not good news, but it was correct, and unavoidable.

While he ran back to the southern end of the pass, dodging the oncoming carts and kudai, his thoughts turned to running of another kind. Running away. Something he had been doing almost since he had been old enough to think. And something that had led him, in one way or another, to this place and this time. He had believed Perse, as it had naively been called before his arrival, would be his last escape. The furthest he could run from his past. Fate had other ideas. He had run to this planet, run from the Earther community to his village, and run from the superstitious, and eventually violent, villagers. Even then, he was not done. Before long, he had to run away from the Jester and the influence of Mad Muir. Finally, after a few wonderful days when he believed he had found somewhere he no longer needed to run from, came the news of the Doom, and the need for one more escape.

If there was a bright side to the impending disaster, it was that he had at last concluded he was done with running. The chance to run back to Earth had been offered, and he had declined. He was happy to be a Remainer, and to offer his Elemental services to those who needed him. What the future held, no-one could tell. There was no Elemental power for prescience. But whatever it was, he would face it head-on, not looking over his shoulder as he ran away from it.

The last cart in the long line of remainers passed him, leaving him alone in the pass. A hundred metres or so in front of him, the rockfaces met at the opening. He stopped, and readied himself. There was time. He could do this. As he summoned his power, a movement caught his attention. A lone rider came swiftly towards him, following the bank of the Sun Besaraya and splashing through the puddles that had yet to drain back into its engorged waters. The rider reined his kudo to a stop and threw back his hood. It was Jared deLange.

'Another moment and you would have been too late,' Piers said. 'I was about to close the pass.'

'Don't let me stop you,' deLange replied, digging his heels into the animal's flank. The kudo whinnied, lurching forward and forcing Piers to jump out of its way.

Putting a surge of irritation at the latecomer's ignorance from his mind, Piers bent once more to his task. He accessed his core, and began to raise the mountain.

Iembaca ana
16th day of far'utamasa, 967

'Kyle! Oh my God!'

Claire's face contorted into a mask of horror. She stretched out her arms towards the swirling surface of the Uterban, through which Kyle had been pulled moments before. The Fire Witch clung to her, blinded by her swollen face and unable to use her power. Patrick's heightened Void senses felt the intensity of her impotent rage.

He took out his charm. In the presence of so much raw Void energy it was almost too hot to hold, but he had an answer for that. He did not need to touch it. It floated above his hand, turning gently in an inexplicable parallel to the spinning of the Uterban. Its complex pattern of interlocking circles sparked with every colour, hinting at the solution Patrick had imagined only moments before.

All around him, a thousand other things clamoured for his attention. The first Voider stalked Ahnak, lumbering towards the young Gatekeeper and repeating its earlier sniffing motion, sensing the northerner's power. Elaine stood at the edge of the quad, her damaged face turning this way and that. Claire, her whole body still wracked with sobs at the loss of Kyle, held on to Elaine's arm with one hand, the other resting on her shoulder for reassurance. She watched the Voider closely. When it made its move on Ahnak she straightened up and screamed at him to run. He stood his ground, steadfast in his efforts to maintain the Uterban.

Jann's body language screamed his desperate need to rush to Elaine's side, offer her some kind of comfort, yet he too refused to abandon his task. Above them, in the clear blue sky of the Utamasan morning, the Doom approached ever closer. They were running out of time.

Claire shouted a few words of Istanian. A jamtera! The force of her words struck deep into Patrick's mind like a blow from a cold steel hammer. The urgency of the situation, the augmentation of the surrounding Void power, and the threat to Ahnak's life combined to create the most powerful manifestation of Air Patrick had ever seen from the young woman. A tornado sprang into existence in the centre of the quad and crossed rapidly towards the Voider. Sensing the twister, the dark demon side-stepped, moving away from Ahnak and lurching from the granite onto the soft earth of the Valley floor.

Ru'ita, who had retrieved her staff scant moments earlier, stepped in front of the Voider, her expression a combination of suppressed fear and deadly focus. She planted the heel of the staff in the earth and took hold of it with both hands. A bright green light, the colour of new spring growth, burned along the length of the wood. It reflected against the Wood Mage's skin, lending it an alien quality. Her eyes glowed with the same viridian colour as she stared fixedly at the Voider. It turned to face her with a low, guttural roar. Black smoke leaked from between its fangs as it took a step in her direction.

From the earth beneath the monster's feet, a thin white seedling sprouted, swiftly followed by three others. The growths stretched skyward, wrapping themselves around the Voider's legs and thickening to the size of saplings. The Voider stepped out of the entwining young trees with one leg, only to be caught immediately by four more erupting from the ground where its hoof landed. Enkaysak thrummed with power, turning a brighter shade of green and casting its light across the space between them. A dozen more trees sprang up around the Voider, each with four or five branches that spiralled skywards to encircle the monster's waist and wrap themselves around its arms. The growths could not hold the beast for long. Each new cord, and coil, and braid was defeated when the creature smoked its way free, only to be caught by new growths, and new branches sprouting from each trunk. Within moments the Voider was surrounded by a small forest, thwarting its movements at every turn.

On the hillside, Alvarez worked with a small team from New Washington. Never shrinking from her leadership role even in the face of such horrors, she shepherded the refugees back into line, barking orders and calming the most panicked. The rush of people from the Valley floor had been halted, but they were still too terrified to approach the Gate. A little less than half the leavers were still to traverse. He glanced at the sky. There was still time. Maybe. But none to spare.

He returned his attention to the amulet, still slowly spinning above his palm. The third Voider had seen it too. The beast approached, leaving a dark, smoking trail in its wake. The lines of pattern on the spinning orb now had a predominantly green tinge, confirming Patrick's notion. He concentrated outward on his charm, and inward to his core. The sphere began to glow, and to spin faster. It flashed now with many other colours. Red, blue, black and white, all the colours of Ru'ita's Wood powers, interspersed with dark orange, brown, and yellow, glinting with the flinty opalescence of Stone power. The beast, possibly sensing the danger, increased its pace. Patrick smiled. It was too late. He lifted the revolving orb and sent forth all his strength in a single, tightly focused beam.

The shaft of coruscating Void power hit the last Voider in the face. It screamed, a gut-wrenching cry that echoed as though from the deepest pit of Hell. The monster's head exploded in a shower of black droplets that evaporated into the air as they flew. Below the space where the creature's head had been, the rest of its body unravelled into a swirling cloud of sooty vapour. The brume hung in the air for a heartbeat before being sucked backwards and disappearing into the rim of the Gate.

'Ru'ita!' Patrick called. 'Ward the rim! More may follow, now two of the three are gone!'

Could she use more than one aspect of her power at once? His brief concern proved unfounded. Perhaps the still-sprouting forest no longer required any further supply of her green energy? Ru'ita turned to the Gate and held her staff in front of her, spinning it in both hands to match its rate of rotation. A glossy black ribbon of warding power, similar to that she had used at Pennatanah Bay, spiralled out from the staff. Where it touched the Uterban, it stuck to the rim, forming an annular ring. Inside the circle, the swirling grey spiral of the Gate began to spin faster.

An electric thrill shot down Patrick's spine. He slowed the amulet, reattached it to its lanyard and slipped it beneath his tunic. 'Hold on to something, my friends,' he shouted. 'It's going to get rough!'

He beckoned to the small group at the front of the queue, now some distance up on the hillside. 'Alvarez!' he shouted. 'It's safe now. Start them down!'

She nodded, spoke to those standing beside her, and began to usher the others down. Hesitantly at first, but with increasing confidence, the line started up again. The lead group glanced nervously around, many of them keeping an eye on the only remaining Voider. The dark creature still fought to escape its woody prison. It soon became clear the beast no longer posed a threat.

Claire left Elaine's side and approached him. 'Can't you send that one to the same place as the other?' she asked.

Patrick favoured her with a weary smile. 'I have almost nothing left,' he admitted. 'Jann and Ahnak opened this Gate, but they could not have done it without my help. I must keep up a constant flow of Void power or the Uterban will collapse. Dispatching the third Voider took every last bit of strength I had. As it is, I can barely stay awake.'

'I'm so sorry,' the Air Mage said, laying a hand on his arm. 'Is there anything I can do? Maybe Ru'ita—?'

'No!' Patrick said, taking hold of Claire by the shoulders. 'Say nothing! Her growing power is keeping the first beast imprisoned, and her warding is preventing others from entering this dimension. I doubt she has any reserves left either. Any further distraction may prove disastrous.'

Claire nodded. 'OK. What did you mean when you told us to hold on to something?'

He nodded towards the Gate, now spiralling so rapidly that its face no longer showed any pattern. It had taken on a concave aspect and attracted a thin trail of dust, kicked up by the line of leavers stepping through. 'My action in ridding us of that Voider has a corresponding reaction,' he said, 'which I believe is about to make things a little... uncomfortable.'

Claire returned to Elaine's side without another word. She helped the Fire Witch to her feet and led her from the quad to the nearest large boulder — a remnant of Pun'Akarnya that had fallen clear of the granite slab the day before. Elaine whispered something. Claire nodded again and hurried over to speak with Jann.

Patrick moved to stand next to Ahnak behind the vortex as it picked up speed. On the opposite side, Jann would suffer the full effect of the coming maelstrom. Having wedged his feet into the fractures on the surface of the granite slab, he clearly knew what to expect. Once Claire had passed her message on to Ru'ita she returned at last to stand with Elaine. Perhaps she could protect them both with some counteracting Air currents. Around Ru'ita's feet, tendrils of new wood rose from the soil, wrapping themselves around her ankles and anchoring her to the spot.

Moments later, the increasing suction from the vortex lifted the nearest refugees from the slab. Three of them floated clear of the ground and flew in a graceful arc, disappearing through the Gate, their expressions a comical mix of astonishment and delight.

Iembaca ana
16th day of far'utamasa, 967

Claire watched the line of leavers abandon their footings and fly through the mouth of the Gate. The scene reminded her of a horror story her father had read to her as a young girl. Whether he intended it as a lesson, or a thought experiment, she had never worked out. A man awoke to find himself alone on a high circular ledge. As the story continued it became clear that he stood on the rim of an enormous tubular structure, like a chimney. The man could see the ground below the outer wall, and knew that a fall in that direction would result in certain death. The inner wall fell away into blackness, its base unknown and his fate, should he jump that way, correspondingly unfathomable. The man spent most of the story considering his options, and trying to guess the intent of whoever had brought him to this place. In the end, he was forced to make a choice. A thin steel blade rose from the rim, leaving him with insufficient room on which to balance either side. If he continued to hesitate, the razor-sharp edge would eventually slice him in half. After waiting until the last possible moment, the hapless victim chose to leap inward, into the dark. The smallest chance of salvation may lie in that direction, compared with the certainty of doom on the outside of the tower.

And here, years after she had first heard the story, the Doom was above them instead of below, and this long line of people had come to the same conclusion as the man in her father's story. Preferring a leap into the swirling grey unknown to the certainty of being crushed to death by the comet which now filled the sky.

Scant minutes remained. The roar of the comet as it burned through the atmosphere filled her ears. The few leavers still on the hillside now ran for the Gate, jumping into the air as they felt the influence of the vortex take them. Alvarez hung back to the last, encouraging Earthers and Berikatanyans alike towards their new lives, and away from their Doom. Claire felt a pang of regret that none of those traversing the Gate would remember the woman's steadfast execution of her duty, and neither would she. The best of humanity was on display here, and none of those who benefited from it would ever know.

She maintained a constant countercurrent of Air, protecting herself and poor blinded Elaine from the worst of the buffeting winds. Across the Valley floor, the gale bent Ru'ita forward. Her long ebony hair flew out in front of her like a black flag of Hell, whipping around her face and neck. Her staff, still gripped in both hands, emitted sparking bolts of green and black. The energies kept the last Voider imprisoned in its wooden cage, while maintaining the warding sheath over the edges of the Uterban. At least those who were left behind would remember the skill and bravery they had seen here today, in the strange nexus of power that was Lembaca Ana: the Valley of the Cataclysm.

Finally, it was done. The last refugee from the Black Palace flew through the Gate, waving farewell to her monarch in her final moments on this world. Ru'ita, her head encased in whirling eddies of her wind-whipped hair, did not see the gesture.

'Ahnak!' Claire called. 'It is time!'

She dropped onto her knees and hugged the ground as she crawled across the granite slab to the young man with whom she wanted to spend the rest of her life. Where would they end up? They had no way to know. Not where, and not when. The Gate had been open since dawn and the sun, though now hidden behind the mass of Ahnak's Doom, must certainly have attained its zenith. They may even travel back into prehistory. At least they would be together, and their passage through the strange spinning portal would erase her painful memories of loss. Douglas, Lautan, and now Kyle: all gone.

Once behind the Gate and out of the full force of the vortex, Claire rose to her feet and walked the last few metres to her lover's side. Ahnak hugged her briefly, just as aware as she of the little time that remained. He glanced at his father, and the two men nodded. Jann Argent raised his hand, waving farewell to the son he had only known for a few days, and the woman who might have been his daughter-in-law in a more normal life. Claire swallowed past a sudden lump in her throat, and took Ahnak's hand. Together, they walked around the rim of the Gate and into the maelstrom.

Iembaca ana
16th day of far'utamasa, 967

Jann watched the Air Mage and his son hugging each other, their time here almost done. His son! His eyes stung with sudden tears and a sob rose in his chest. They never had the chance to know each other, and now he was leaving. His scalp tingled at the thought that in a few moments — this same day — he would have to meet Penny again. What would he tell her? She must be carrying Ahnak right now. He was going to have to introduce her to Elaine, and she to Penny. It was too much. He dashed the tears from his eyes with a shake of his head.

Ahnak waved, and a fresh burst of emotion threatened to overwhelm him. He had to get a grip! Without Ahnak's strength he was keeping the Uterban open alone. A few more seconds! Hurry, son! And daughter! His stomach flipped at the thought. The lovely, strong, vibrant young woman he had met only eleven months and a hundred years ago at the end of one life and the beginning of another he could not have imagined. One he had grown to love as a daughter without ever conceiving of the possibility that she could end up as exactly that.

He nodded to his son and raised his own hand in farewell. The couple joined hands and walked in front of the vortex, caught immediately in its pull and lifted from the Valley floor. They embraced in mid-air, the spiral motion of the Gate starting to spin them around. They turned faster and faster as they approached the barrier, until they were revolving so fast it was impossible to tell who was who. In the final moment before they disappeared, the force of the wind ripped their clothes from their bodies, and they passed, naked and alone, through the raging vortex and back to the dawn of time.

Jann closed his eyes and let the tears finally fall as the Gate winked out of existence with a dull pop. The gale ceased, the buffeting in his ears replaced by the deafening rumble from the comet overhead.

'Jann!' Patrick's voice rose above the roar 'The last gate! Quickly! We're almost out of time!'

Ru'ita had released herself from her woody ankle restraints and was helping Elaine find her way towards him. Patrick hurried across the quadrangle. The last Voider, no doubt sensing danger from above, redoubled its efforts to free itself from the trees. It was no use. Though the supply of growing energy from the Wood Mage had ceased, enough remained in the ground to keep the monster trapped while they made their escape.

He was exhausted. Patrick's face too was lined with fatigue, his eyes red and his hands shaking. He could barely walk. And Elaine. Oh dear Elaine, with her swollen, ruined face. He had no time to dwell on her injuries or how she could ever recover. Only Ru'ita seemed to have any strength remaining. A side-effect of her healing powers, no doubt.

'Jann!' Patrick said again, but he was already on it. A shimmering silver gate appeared before them, much smaller than the one he had held open all morning, but large enough for the four to pass through together. The noise of the comet reached a crescendo and Jann felt, momentarily, the heat from its burning surface, before the familiar and unmistakable feeling of *twisting* gripped him and he fell to his knees in the cold, clean air north of Temmok'Dun.

somewhere north of temmok'dun
16th day of far'utamasa, 967

Patrick Glass staggered from the gate, the ground on this side a few centimetres lower than at the Valley entrance. He could forgive his friend this small slip — creating a gate with moments to spare before they were crushed to death could well have landed them in the middle of a lake. He would happily take the slight misstep.

He reached out and helped Jann to his feet as the ground shook, threatening his footing for a second time. Ru'ita and the Fire Witch gasped, the sound subsumed by the low booming noise rolling over the mountain behind them.

Patrick gazed back over the rise of Temmok'Dun, towards the south, and the only home he had known since first setting foot on this world. As he stared, a cloud of dust and ash billowed above the crest of the rocks. An empurpled, mushroom-shaped pillar that reminded him of atomic bomb pictures he had seen as a boy. Around its base a tendril of thick, black smoke spiralled up, encircling the cloud as if it were gripped by a dark fist. He held his breath, but the vapour dissipated without spinning into a vortex. There remained no vestige of Void power at Lembaca Ana, and the last occupant of that fell dimension must surely now be crushed under the weight of Ahnak's Doom.

'You OK?' Jann asked, laying a hand on his shoulder.

'I am now,' he replied.

'Let's go then. We should make Tenfir Abarad before nightfall.'

Thank you for reading Juggler. If you enjoyed it, you can make a big difference

Reviews are very valuable to indie authors. Most readers rely on quality reviews when they're deciding whether to take a chance on an author they've not read before.

So having recent, honest reviews of my books really helps to bring them to the attention of new readers. If you've enjoyed Juggler, please consider taking a couple of minutes to leave a review (doesn't have to be an essay, but a few words more than just a rating) on the book's Amazon page.

Thank you very much!

Glossary

Abbaleh
Small, web-building creature similar to a spider

Ahmek
Large, portable dwellings similar to tents. Ahmeks are made from heavy material that doesn't lend itself to being carried by individuals or even small groups, so their use is restricted to the military, or semi-permanent camps like the Forest Clearance Project

Air Mage
The Elemental who controls Air

Alaakaya
Forest behind the Court ("Medium wood")

Albert Yamani
Claire's father. Previous Air Mage of Berikatanya

Alempin
A Tepak of the Blood Watch who has a seat on the Darmajelis

Amegola
Gold

Baka
The god of the Fire Element

Bakamasa
"Fire season"—the Berikatanyan equivalent of Summer

Bakara
Elemental name for the Fire Witch

Baleng
Farm animal grown for its meat. Similar to a pig.

Ban Rekpupotan
Northern river beside which the young Ahnak played

Banshiru (banshirin)
Stone magic (or one who wields it)

Barajan
The term Lautan coined for the "new rains" that began during Water Wizard

Barawa fish
A blue fish, considered a delicacy

Batarian
The language of the people who live north of Temmok'Dun

Batugan
Of, or pertaining to, the Batu'n

Batu'n
Berikatanyan term for Earth people (both languages)

Bepermak
Food suitable for consuming when travelling. The contents vary, but are tightly wrapped in edible leaves (similar to dolmades) for both preservation and portability

Beragan
The name for the people who live north of Temmok'Dun ("civilised people")

Berjengo
An Elder of the Beragan, with a particular interest in, and knowledge of, their history

Berikatanya
Local name for the colonised planet, home to the Elementals & Princips

Besakaya
Berikatanyan forest, part of which is undergoing the Forest Clearance Project ("Great wood")

Binagan
The Beragan word for the people living south of the mountains. Translates as "wild people"

Bin-segar
Wild Sea

Birbab
Type of blue rock, used for the sculpted waterfall at the Water Wizard's inauguration

Black Queen
Unofficial title of the ruler of Kertonia

Blembil
The noise made by a farm animal

Blood King
Unofficial title of the ruler of Istania

Blood Watch
The honour guard of the Blood King

Bogdan Dmitriev
The captain of the Dauntless

Bolabisaman
Berikatanyan vegetable. Closest equivalent to an onion

Borok Duset
Eastern Mountain ("Devil's Boil")

Bubayem
Dark purple Berikatanyan fruit grown in the southern regions

Bumerang
A Berikatanyan fruit, red in colour and similar to an apple

Butam
A type of black fruit that grows in the forests. (Offered by the Queen at breakfast)

Buwan
Cloud fruit – pressed to make buwangah

Buwangah
Cloud fruit wine

Car'Alam
Berikatanyan term for the Ceremony that led to the opening of the vortex

Cary Cabrera
A member of Felice Waters' team at the Pennatanah landing base

Celapi
Berikatanyan musical instrument similar to a guitar

Claire Yamani
Daughter of Albert and Nyna Yamani who makes the journey to Perse aboard the Valiant

Clone rout
Alternative name for the Battle of Lembaca Ana

Cok-segar
The sea at Patrick's village. ("Brown sea")

Court
Home of the King of Istania

Dak-jamtera
See jamtera

Danpah
Istanian weapon – bow (see also Panpah)

Dauntless
Prism ship—intended to be the last ship to make the journey to Perse—completes its journey during Book 2 Water Wizard

Darmajelis
The governing body of Istania, led by Jeruk Nipis, constituted in the absence of a monarch following the death of the Blood King

David Garcia
Team leader of the forest clearance project

Dingas
Berikatanyan animal prized for its tender meat

Dipeka Kekusaman
An Elder of the Beragan, she is sensitive to the presence of Elemental power

Douglas Muir
A passenger on the Dauntless, which completes its journey during Water Wizard. Brother to Kyle

Dumwheat
An experimental cereal crop created by crossing wheat brought from Earth with the local Berikatanyan grain used to make tepsak

Dunela
Berikatanyan vegetable

Duntang
Berikatanyan equivalent of a potato

Duska Batsirang
The village where Piers Tremaine lives and works (Duska is the term for an inland village)

Duske Pelapan
The village to which Patrick Glass travels in search of the lore of his father (Duske is the term for a coastal village)

Duske Raj'Pupu
The village where Sepuke Maliktakta lives

Eladok
A bird of prey native to the Temmok'Duk mountains. Its beak is laced with highly poisonous saliva

Elaine Chandler
Fire poi artiste with Miles Miller's Marvellous Manifestations travelling circus who later makes the journey to Perse aboard the Valiant

Elemental
A supreme mage who can control a single Element. Leader of the corresponding Guild

Endeavour
Prism ship—the first to make the journey to Perse

Endurance
Prism ship—intended to be the third to make the journey to Perse, but destroyed by a failure of its Prism drive

Enkaysak
The name of the remade Staff of Power used by the Wood Mage

Eradewan
The governing body of Kertonia, led by the Black Queen

Etrumus Kepalawan
A villager from Duske Raj'Pupu who leads the rebellion against Sepuke Maliktakta

Felice Waters
Senior officer at the Earther planetary immigration station at Pennatanah Bay

Fire Witch
The Elemental who controls Fire

Ghantu
Berikatanyan bird that lives in woodlands. Known for its screeching call

Gravnull
A technology that nullifies gravity, allowing vessels equipped with it to hover. Used in planetary flight, not for space travel

Guild
An assembly of Mages

Haande
A suhir of the Earth Element who works with Petani at the Valley harbour project

Hampanay
Derogatory term for a non-native who displays ability with Elemental powers

Harimeladan
The Keeper of the Queen's Purse and member of the Eradewan

Hodak
A rank in the Queen's forces

Huramapon
The name of the Wood Mage's "home tree"

Intrepid
Prism ship—the second to make the journey to Perse

Istania
Local name for the Blood King's realm

Istri
Wife of Penka

Jambala
Berikatanyan fruit, often juiced to make a refreshing drink

Jamtera (and dak-jamtera)
An expression of Elemental power. Equivalent to a "spell" in traditional magic. Dak-jamtera is the corresponding defence or counter-spell.

Jann Argent
A colonist who journeys to Perse aboard the Valiant. Later revealed to be the Gatekeeper

Jantah
Cloak, or overcoat

Jaranyla
The name of Elaine's kudo—chestnut mare ("Horse of the Flame")

Jarapera
The name of Patrick Glass's kudo ("Horse of the Artisan")

Jeruk Nipis
Full name of the Yellow Jester, who installs himself as head of the Darmajelis

Jester
Principal advisor to the Blood King

Jin-segar
The sea at Pennatanah/New Washington. ("Gentle sea")

Jo Granger
Plant geneticist who helps Felice Waters with her DNA analysis project

Jojo grass
Tall Berikatanyan grass often dried and fed to animals

Juberang
Large predatory animal that lives on the northern slopes of Temmok'Dun, above the snow line (literally: "snow bear")

Juggler
See Pattern Juggler

Jur Dapentu
The Beragan name for the pass through Temmok'Dun created by Piers Tremaine

Jur Mayanga
Place where Ahnak creates his first gate

Jurip
Head of the Kertonian military, occasional attendee at the Eradewan

Kacajunus
A savoury food made from fermented tree-nuts. Eaten cold, usually with tepsak

Kamesa
Beragan word for town

Katuh
A hot beverage

Kayketral
One of the largest species of tree on Berikatanya, one of which becomes Huramapon

Kayshiru (kayshirin)
Wood magic (or one who wields it)

Kaytam
Black wood native to Berikatanya

Kedewada
The Beragan maturity ritual

Kedu-Bul
Smaller of the two moons of Berikatanya

Keeper of the Keys
Custodian of the Court keys, archives, and ceremonial costumes

Kema'katan
The "power pulse" air spell

Kemasara
A generic honorific title conferred out of respect (in Istania). Literally "eminence"

Kema'satu
An honorific title conferred on Elementals out of respect (in Kertonia), literally translated as "force of nature"

Kepka Lemda
An ostler at the Black Palace

Kepka Tuala
Head ostler at the Blood Court and friend of the Keeper of Keys

Kepta
Honorific title for a village leader. Equivalent to a mayor

Kepul Seri
A fire mage. Leader of the Fire Guild until the Fire Witch resumes the guild leadership role

Kertonia
Local name for the Black Queen's realm

Ketakaya
Forest between Pennatanah and the King's Court ("Small wood")

Ketiga Batu
Berikatanyan term for Earth (both languages)

Keti Caraga
Beragan word for the people relocated south of Temmok'Dun ("the warring tribes")

Kilpemigang
Keeper of the Coin at the Blood Court, has a seat on the Darmajelis

Kinchu
Small Berikatanyan herbivore similar to a rabbit

Klikeran
Decorative material made from the shells of marine creatures found in shallow coastal waters. Used for all manner of trinkets in Berikatanyan culture, notably for fret markers on celapi

Krupang
Beragan word for crutch

Kuan-Yin Ning
Earther who returns to Pennatanah seeking sanctuary from the political turmoil and flooding at the Blood Court

Kuclar
Big cat, native to Berikatanya, that lives in forested areas

Kudo (pl: kudai)
Berikatanyan word for horse (in both Istanian and Kertonian)

Kyle Muir
A passenger on the Dauntless, which completes its journey during this Water Wizard. Sister to Douglas

Lautan
Elemental name for the Water Wizard

Lem Tantaran
Valley Plain

Lembaca Ana
Berikatanyan name for the Valley of the Cataclysm. Location of the original Car'Alam ceremony which opened the vortex.

Lendan
A Pena-gliman in the Queen's forces who accompanies her to the Valley for an inspection of the harbour works

Lokker
A small sweetmeat served as a treat. Like a cross between a biscuit (cookie) and a cake

Luki
Beragan word for tree bark

Lum-segar
The ocean at the mouth of the Valley ("Mud Sea")

Luum
Beragan word for moss

Mahok Ginkadaya
Historical name for the obsidian tiara worn by the Black Queen. Although its derivation has been lost to history, the name comes from an ancient tongue and means "the crown that cools the power"

Malamajan
The rain that falls on Berikatanya once the sun has fully set ("Night rain"). Instigated centuries ago as a result of a powerful Water spell

Martuk
A stonemason of Duska Batsirang who attempts to take over one of Piers Tremaine's building projects

Memhomak
The species of tree that confers carrying power

Mizar
One of the major rivers of Berikatanya. It rises in the foothills of Tubelak'Dun and flows through the forest of Besakaya before reaching the western coast.

Mungo Pearman
The full name of the Purple Piper

Nembaka
One of the Berikatanyan natives working on the forest clearance project

Nerka jugu
Berikatanyan expletive (literally "hell's teeth")

Nyirumi
A suhir of the Earth Element who works with Petani at the Valley harbour project

Olek Grissan
One of the more verbose Puppeteers

Palace
Home of the Queen of Kertonia

Panklat
A creamy sweet hot beverage flavoured with local spices

Panpah
Istanian weapon – arrow (see also Danpah)

Parapekotik
Court musicians' town

Pashbala
Army

Patrick Glass
Graphic designer who makes the journey to Perse aboard the Valiant and befriends Jann Argent. Later revealed to be the Pattern Juggler

Pattana
One of the Berikatanyan natives working on the forest clearance project, now retired

Pattern Juggler
Controller of Elemental forces during the Car'Alam ceremony. Capable of directing forces to achieve particular aims, but not of generating those forces in the first place

Pembrang
The name of Black Queen's kudo—black stallion ("Black Rider")

Pembwana
The name of Claire's kudo—black mare ("Bearer of the Wind")

Pena-gliman
A rank in the Queen's honour guard

Pena-lipan
A rank in the Blood King's forces (equivalent to pena-gliman above)

Penjal Mpah
The senior Elder of the Beragan people

Penka
An elder from the village of Duske Pelapan who comes to the Black Palace in search of Patrick Glass

Pennamatalaya
A young woman of the Beragan people who finds Jann Argent's unconscious body during her kedewada, rescues him, and subsequently nurses him back to health

Pennatanah
Earther Landing point (Land of the newcomer)

Pennatanah Bay
Landing site for the colony program

Per Tantaran
The battle plain on the border of Kertonia and Istania

Pera-Bul
Larger of the two moons of Berikatanya

Perak
The name of Jann Argent's kudo—silver stallion

Permajelis
The ill-fated "peace council" which the Black Queen attempts to set up in the wake of the Battle of Lembaca Ana

Perse
The colony planet first targeted by humanity

Petani
Elemental name for the controller of Earth power

Piers Tremaine
An Earther stonemason who arrived on the Intrepid and took up residence in Duska Batsirang

Pilgrim
Character who inhabited the Valley of the Cataclysm

Pilattik
Combat blade, dagger, stiletto

Piper / Purple Piper
Principal advisor to the Black Queen

Pipit
Small water fowl similar to a duck

Pondok Pemmunak
Villager of Duska Batsirang who commissions Piers Tremaine to build a house

Ponektu
A species of Berikatanyan tree

Princips
Generic term for senior courtiers / landowners / Blood King & Black Queen

Prism drive
See Wormwood star drive

Prism ship
Colony ships powered by the Wormwood "Prism" drive

Pun'Akarnya
The new mountain created as a result of the final battle in Book 1 of this trilogy

Puppeteers
A shady group of dissidents led by Jeruk Nipis who plot and scheme to overthrow the monarchy in favour of a more egalitarian form of government

Ra-mek
A larger and more opulent version of an ahmek for the exclusive use of royalty

Racun
a poison secreted by the glands of several Berikatanyan animals

Rampiri
Ancient term for combining Elemental powers to create more powerful effects

Rascang
Backpack/rucksack

Rebusang
The meat stew eaten at the forest clearance project

Repgola
Silver

Rektan Malikputran
Best friend, and right-hand man, of Sepuke Maliktakta

Remalan
Months

Rohantu
The blood clones. Literally "soul phantom"

Sabah
Fruit juice

Sakti Udara
Elemental name for Air Mage

Sana
The god of the Air Element

Sanamasa
"Air season"—the Berikatanyan equivalent of Winter

Sangella
Claire's maidservant

Saptak skin
The cleaned, dried, and stitched skin of a Berikatanyan ruminant, used to carry water

Seba-tepak
A rank in the Blood King's forces

Sebaklan Pwalek
Long-time confident of Jeruk Nipis and a fellow conspirator/Puppeteer

Sepuke Maliktakta
Distant cousin of the Blood King and leader of the village of Duske Raj'Pupu

Sickmoss
A variety of Berikatanyan moss that induces violent and immediate nausea on contact

Suhir Haande
See Haande

Suhir Nyirumi
See Nyirumi

Suhiri
The Berikatanyans name for mages who are not Elementals

Su'matra
Berikatanyan name for the people

Sun Besaraya
The river that runs from Temmok'Dun to the coast at Lembaca Ana ("big river")

Sun Hitaraya
The river that has its origins on Borok Duset and joins with the Besaraya southwest of the Black Palace ("black river")

Sun Hutang
The river that winds from Tubelak'Dun, through the Forest Clearance Project to the coast south of Duska Batsirang ("forest river")

Sun Lum
The river that runs from Borok Duset to the southernmost coast ("mud river")

Sun Penk
The river that runs from the centre of Tubelak'Dun to join the Sun Besaraya northeast of Lembaca Ana ("short river")

Sunyok
A Berikatanyan eating tool

Tabukka
A Berikatanyan narcotic leaf

Tabukki
Those who are addicted to tabukka

Tamatua
Principal, or head, Elder (in Tenfir Abarad)

Tammok
Istanian weapon – spear

Tana
The god of the Earth Element

Tanamasa
"Earth season"—the Berikatanyan equivalent of Autumn

Tanaratana
Berikatanyan native who replaces Pattana on the team working with Petani at the harbour project

Tang Jikos
The Book of Void Lore

Tapuhti
Beragan word for a cataract, or milking of the eye

Te'banga
The agreement between Elementals whereby they divide their loyalties and efforts evenly between the ruling houses

Telebi Ana
The bay at the harbour project site

Tema'gana
Istanian equivalent of Kema'satu

Temmok'Dun
Northern Mountains ("Wall of the World")

Tenfir Abarad
The town north of Temmok'Dun where Jann Argent recuperates after his journey

Tepak
A rank in the King's honour guard. Equivalent to an army captain.

Tepsak
A Berikatanyan bread

Terry Spate
Horticulturalist and gardener who makes the journey to Perse aboard the Valiant and befriends Claire Yamani. Later revealed to be the Earth Elemental

Tiklik
A Berikatanyan rodent, similar to a mouse

Timakaya
The forest close to the Black Palace, where the Queen finds her staff ("Eastern wood"), and later builds her home

Trapweed
A rapidly growing form of plant life, similar to bindweed but much stronger and faster growing. It reacts to any movement by wrapping itself around the unwary intruder.

Tuakara
Fire Witch at the time the Te'banga was first agreed. Distant ancestor of the current Fire Witch

Tubelak'Dun
Western Mountains ("Spine of the World")

Ukba
Glow beetles. They sit on railings and other horizontal surfaces of Huramapon to light the Wood Mage's path

Umtanesh
One of the Berikatanyan natives working on the forest clearance project

Uta Tantaran
The Northern Plain—land between the Black Palace and the foothills of Temmok'Dun

Utamasa
"Water season"—the Berikatanyan equivalent of Spring

Utan
The god of the Water Element

Uterban
Beragan word for vortex, or portal

Utperi'Tuk
Coastal region close to the Red Court ("Sea Nymph's Cove")

Valiant
Prism ship—the third to make the journey to Perse

Valley of the Cataclysm
see Lembaca Ana

Water Wizard
The Elemental who controls Water

Wormwood star drive
Propulsion system for the colony ships which reaches near-light speed. Known colloquially as the "Prism" drive since it focuses energy through a series of extremely dense prisms.

Yumbal
Writing implement. Shaped like a quill but made from wrapped charcoal

Berikatanyan Calendar

Although the day length on Berikatanya is virtually the same as on Earth, the planet orbits farther out, making the year much longer. Seasons are named for the four main Elemental gods:

God	Season name	Earth equivalent
Water	Utamasa	Spring
Fire	Bakamasa	Summer
Earth	Tanamasa	Autumn
Air	Sanamasa	Winter

Each season is divided into four periods of thirty days, which may be thought of as equivalent to Earth months. Indeed the concept of month has, over the time since the first Prism ship, transferred into Berikatanyan culture especially in the centres of civilisation.

The periods are named for their position in the season:

Period	Name	Derivation
1	Far	The "dawn" of the season
2	Ter	The "rising" of the season
3	Run	The "falling" of the season
4	Sen	The "dusk" of the season

So the first month of Spring would be Far'Utamasa and the third month of Autumn would be Run'Tanamasa. Here's a handy look-up table:

Season / Period:	Far	Ter	Run	Sen
Utamasa	1	2	3	4
Bakamasa	5	6	7	8
Tanamasa	9	10	11	12
Sanamasa	13	14	15	16

ABOUT THE AUTHOR

Since the first time a story of his made the rest of the English class screw up their faces in horror and disgust, John Beresford wanted nothing more than to write. He was 12. Later that year he came second in a sponsored writing competition with a short story about how the Sphinx is really a quiescent guardian against alien invaders. He won £10. That was big bucks in 1968.

For more than three decades, real life stepped in between him and his writing. During a 38-year career in computing he wrote dozens of design documents, created and delivered presentations to audiences from 1,000 technical experts to a handful of board members, interviewed innumerable technical candidates and taught core skills and development subjects to many younger colleagues through both formal courses and ad-hoc coaching. But all that was really just a way to hone skills that might be useful as a writer. And, of course, to pay the bills and support the family. A man's gotta do...

In 2001 John woke up to the passage of time and decided to get serious about writing before it was too late. His first novel – War of Nutrition – took 7 years of spare time to write and was published for Kindle in 2012.

Since beginning that first novel, John has also created work as a songwriter, screenwriter, freelance TV reviewer and playwright.

Juggler is John's fourth novel and completes the Berikatanyan Chronicles trilogy. Now retired from the computing industry, he is working on a new series of sci-fi thrillers.

Connect with John online:

Facebook: https://www.facebook.com/garretguy
Twitter: https://twitter.com/#!/garretguy
Web site: http://www.johnberesford.com/

Printed in Great Britain
by Amazon